CHALGATHI

CHALGATHI

ELYSIUM'S MULTIVERSE | BOOK 1

Ranyhin1

Podium

I'd like to dedicate this book to my parents and two brothers, who supported me throughout the process and encouraged me when times were rough. I love you all.

Cover design by Daniel Kamarudin

ISBN: 978-1-0394-4728-8

Published in 2023 by Podium Publishing, ULC
www.podiumaudio.com

Podium

CHALGATHI

CHAPTER 1

The wall cracked underneath the weight of the creature, sending splintered wood and paint flying in all directions as a shock wave caused Riven to stumble and fall. His heart pounded, and the screams around him only urged him onward even more as he picked himself off the hardwood floor of the old house to scramble ahead.

His brown hair was matted down with blood, and a jagged gash across his left shoulder screamed at him with pulsing blasts of pain. His ruined jeans briefly caught on the edge of a piece of furniture when he rushed past, and the words that'd first appeared to every person on Earth half a day ago were still burned into his mind:

[Elysium initializing.]
[Elysium initializing.]
[Elysium initializing.]

[Apocalypse has commenced. Earth to be merged with worlds Zazir and Elhisterii to form the new world of Panu at the end of seventy-two hours.]

[Worldwide Quest: Escape the First Wave. Your world has been inducted into Elysium's multiverse. Millions of monsters with a variety of tiers have been unleashed into your realm. All planetary citizens and wildlife must survive the next seventy-two hours or make it to an Elysium portal to escape the incoming horde. All Elysium portals have been highlighted with pillars of light across the world. Reward for surviving: Brief introduction to the multiverse and Elysium's administrator.]

Within seconds of those words being displayed on little teal-colored holographic screens to every man, woman, and child on the planet, all hell had broken loose. Creatures from Riven's very nightmares had materialized right in front of his eyes in the middle of the street and started ripping people apart by the dozens. They were all sorts of sizes, shapes, and species—but they all had the same bloodlust about them as they wreaked havoc on humanity.

So here he was.

"Allie, run!"

Riven pushed his little sister ahead, nearly throwing her thin body over the couch and toward the back door. The young woman wore a hoodie and skinny jeans and had the same chestnut-colored hair that he did—though hers was much longer—and she glanced over her shoulder with frightened hazel eyes before Riven's best friend, Jose, pulled her to her feet and dragged her out the back.

Riven vaulted over the couch a second later and kicked the swinging wooden door to fling it open again, feeling the hot breath of the abomination behind him snapping just inches from his neck.

He landed down the set of stone steps running, ignoring the screams for help from nearby houses and flinching at the sound of gunshots to his right. Whirling around in the dim light of the setting sun, he drew his own pistol out and checked to make sure it was loaded. Then he pointed and aimed at the doorway.

There, struggling to get its large frame out of the back door, was a large black brute of a creature. It had six insectoid legs that were clawing at the wood of the Victorian-style house and armorlike chitin plating its body with a bulbous back end and the general frame of a spider. Though it certainly wasn't a spider, not only because of the missing set of legs but also because its head was more wolflike—extending out from its hairless body by a couple feet on a plated, serpentine neck. Its yellow eyes blazed furiously at him, and its rows of teeth snapped repeatedly in his direction.

His hands shook just slightly due to the adrenaline, but he didn't hesitate and fired rapidly three times at the opened maw of the creature as it tore off another chunk of wall through brute force. He felt the gun recoil with every shot and was relieved to see his aim was on point.

Blood sprayed from open wounds in its neck as the bullets cut into the softer parts of the monster's body, causing it to screech and reel itself back inside the house.

Turning back around and sprinting ahead, he caught up to Allie and Jose in no time. They were waiting for him around the corner of the suburban fence amid the backdrop of a neighborhood gone to hell, and each was panting heavily after their strenuous run toward their distant destination. Fire blazed along many of the roadways, and there was even a large, plumed griffon flying over the embattled streets.

Sweat trickled down Jose's bald head. The young Latino man was Riven's oldest friend and somewhat of a partner in crime; they had similar backgrounds in many ways. He was twenty-six—the same age as Riven. He wore a flannel shirt, brown shorts, and tennis shoes. He wasn't used to this kind of workout, and he held up his hand for just another moment of rest. "Give me a sec…"

"We can't wait long," Riven said between huffs as he took another look over the fence, finding solace in the fact that the creature was still rampaging inside the house. However, upon seeing the battle in the nearby street between three shotgun-wielding rednecks and another, even larger squid-like alien creature—his heart began to sink again. Their screams echoed long after the last of their shotgun blasts penetrated the surrounding area as they were eaten alive, and soon Riven decided the break had been long enough. He pointed to the pillar of light towering overhead into the heavens—a bastion of promised sanctuary far out beyond Dallas's suburbs. This was what they needed to reach before they ended up dead like so many others.

"Let's go."

Allie walked with a limp, supporting her weight on her older brother, Riven, shakily looking out into the dark forest and finally having a chance to catch their breath. The moon and stars were overhead, and fires still blazed on the eastern Dallas skyline with occasional explosions visible even from here. There was also the large pillar of light that they were closing in on, making the surrounding forest at least seeable during their trek despite it being the dead of night.

"Are you okay?" Riven gave her a soft, gentle smile. "You look worn-out."

She glared at him incredulously between huffs, but then caught the slightly teasing smile. She let out a groan and a barking cough that shook her entire body. "That would be the understatement of the century."

"Well, buck up. We're going to make it." He gave her an encouraging nudge, then bent down to encourage her onto his back without another word when her ragged breathing became heavier.

She smiled graciously, then hopped on—and they were off again. "Thanks, Riven."

Stepping over a half-eaten human body, they came along the corpse of another one of those squid creatures that'd been torn apart by a hail of bullets. Long, thick tentacles with serrated spines along its suckers and smooth, brown skin were testimonies to how deadly this thing was. It was also far larger than any of the three of them—probably weighing as much as a rhinoceros or maybe even an elephant. Its ugly green eyes lay dilated in death, and the trio took a moment to stare at it before they kept on going.

Leaves crunched underfoot, and the hoot of an owl sounded out from above. Their nerves were on edge, and Riven palmed the cold steel of the single gun they had in their group. He only had one magazine left, and they were only nine-millimeter bullets…not nearly enough to kill any of the bigger creatures they'd seen thus far—but maybe enough to kill the smaller ones. A couple of the monsters they'd seen were as small as household pets, but they were still very dangerous, as some of them spit acid or shot fireballs out of their little clawed hands.

"What the hell is going on?" Jose muttered under his breath, grimacing as he clutched at a wound he'd sustained while running earlier that day. "The apocalypse? This is un-fucking-believable."

Riven snorted, still carrying Allie and comfortingly squeezing the hand that latched onto his shirt. Straightening to his full height of around six feet while adjusting his posture, and readjusting Allie's weight, he felt his back crack with the stretch and sighed. "I've never been the religious type...but this certainly does seem like the apocalypse to me."

"It said something about an administrator and a multiverse..." Allie mumbled from behind, her skinny legs wrapped around his waist while she still nervously looked around. "I don't know what that means, but I'm scared. This is scary, Riven."

Riven gave her another squeeze of reassurance. She was so frail...and she was the one person in the world Riven would do anything for. The one remaining family member he had, and he loved her more than anything. He'd be damned if he let anything happen to her. "I'll make sure you're safe. We'll be fine."

Her voice was on the verge of tears. "Promise?"

He smiled and tried not to chuckle at how childish the question was, but now was not the time to tease her about something like that. "I promise."

Putting the gun in its holster and brushing his hands through his hair with an exasperated sigh, Riven trudged onward with Jose just slightly ahead.

He pulled out his phone. It only had 6 percent battery left. The major news sites were all down, but social media was still ablaze with chatter. This event was worldwide.

Riven called Jose over to watch, and their jaws dropped in unison. The White House had been overrun with giant, carnivorous beetles that shrugged off most small arms fire, and the president's corpse was being dragged across the lawn on what had been a live recording, shot earlier that day via helicopter.

The news reporter in the recording was in a state of shock; her voice sounded like it was on the verge of tears as she screamed over the winding blades just overhead and into the mic. "THE PRESIDENT HAS BEEN KILLED! OH MY GOD! THE PRESIDENT HAS BEEN KILLED! WHAT THE HELL IS GOING ON?! WHY ARE THEY ATTACKING US?! THE ARMY IS STILL TRYING TO SAVE OTHER VIPS FROM THE CAPITAL, BUT THESE ALIENS ARE LITERALLY EVERYWHERE. THE SITUATION IS LOOKING BLEAK!"

From there her words were lost in static, and Riven moved on to the next video. And then the next, and the next. Carnage, burning buildings, mass death, and an exodus of people from the cities toward the randomly scattered beacons of light that numbered in the tens of thousands or even more across all the countries of the world—this is what they saw until Riven's phone died with a beep.

Neither Allie nor Jose had their phones on them in the mad scramble they'd taken out of the apartment they all shared earlier that day, but none of them wanted to look any more after that, anyways. It was depressing, realizing that everything around them was being destroyed. All of civilization's accomplishments and creations, just being obliterated almost overnight by a wave of alien creatures that came in all shapes and sizes.

The pillar of light in the distance pulsed with a warm, white light, radiating power that the trio all felt across their skin as a pleasant embrace. It was a promise of safety, one that they could only take on the word of the strange notifications that'd appeared as holograms in front of them right before everything had gone to hell.

"It seems to be expanding," Riven stated calmly, turning to the other two and nodding his head in the direction of the pillar of light. He gave a comforting smile to both of them. "Come on, then. We probably have another hour to go… Hopefully it really is safe there, like the message said."

Jose snorted in dissatisfaction but trudged onward after looking back at the corpse of the monster nearby. "Let's just hope we aren't eaten along the way. I really don't want to become octopus food anytime soon."

Riven gave Allie a wink and pulled her along. "I think we can all agree with that notion."

[Worldwide Quest: Escape the First Wave—Complete.]

CHAPTER 2

[Worldwide Quest: Escape the First Wave—Complete. Welcome to Elysium. Welcome to the multiverse. I am the Elysium administrator, caretaker of this new universe. Riven, Allie, and Jose, you and hundreds of millions of others from Earth are being uploaded into Elysium at this very moment. Laws of physics have been altered. Spells have been introduced. Miracles have been introduced. Martial arts have been introduced. Multiverse initiated. Cultivation and the Dao have been introduced. Earth is now being incorporated. Common language for Elysium's multiverse has been instilled in all participants for equal communication opportunities.]

[Please review your status page by thinking or saying the words *status page* with intent.]

[ERROR—REROUTING PARTICIPANT. UNIQUE OPPORTUNITY ACQUIRED. SYSTEM NOW CONSIDERING ALTERNATE PATHWAY.]

Riven blinked as he found himself in a large void of white light. Hadn't he just touched that pillar of light? Was he inside the pillar now? He was no longer wearing his previous outfit, and as he looked around into the vast nothingness, he found that even his body was missing. His brown hair, slim, athletic body, and green eyes were entirely gone. The twenty-six-year-old man was completely missing his physical self.

Where had his best friend and sister gone?

[System Analysis Complete: Riven Thane is registered as a match for Chalgathi's Lineage Starter Quest. Criteria met: Extremely high magical affinity detected for the Unholy Pillar and all related subpillars. Unnaturally high affinity detected for the Blood subpillar related to unique bloodline.]

[Initializing loading sequence. Starting location acquired. If you successfully complete the starter quest and tutorials afterward, you will be reunited with Allie and Jose as long as they, too, succeed in their own independent trials.]

[Upload finishing in 5... 4... 3... 2... 1...]

[Welcome to Elysium's Multiverse.]

Riven came to his senses with a gasp and shot up from his position on the cold stone ground. Water pelted his skin as a torrent of rain launched into him from the stormy heavens amid heavy claps of thunder and flashes of lightning.

He gagged, his muscles spasming as he hurled and dry heaved—twisting around onto his front and trying to clear his head of the nausea as black ichor trickled from his mouth onto the ground.

Wait...black ichor?

[***Chalgathi's Lineage Starter Quest: Special, One-Time Event*** Your first step into Elysium has not been an easy one, and you have been given a test to complete prior to your tutorial. Your past haunts you, and your future is uncertain. You have fallen from the grace of your peers and have been forgotten, a lone man in a sea of those who care little about you or your circumstances... Yet, you find that you don't need them. You can do this on your own. All on your own... Let the world be damned in your wake as you tread the path few dare to take.

***Notice: All 1,672 participants on Earth having Unholy-related bloodlines have been rerouted into Chalgathi's Lineage Starter Quest.

***Notice: You have been afflicted with the Curse of Anthus, and your body begins to painfully rot from the inside out. Be within the first two hundred participants to reach the top of the pyramid—or die.]

Another crack of lightning lit up the sky, and despite the immense amount of nausea and pain his body was riddled with, Riven couldn't help but gape at his surroundings now that his vision was beginning to clear.

In front of him was a massive, looming pyramid of almost Aztec design. It had at least two hundred large steps before the top and, simply put, it was huge. Stone statues of gargoyles, hooded skeletons bearing scythes, gigantic skulls, and black knights were placed at intervals around the pyramid all the way up to the halfway point along the side. At the top of the pyramid, a pillar of green fire rose skyward into the dark heavens amid the downpour.

Despite the pillar of eerie green flames reaching to the sky at the top of the pyramid, the structure seemed to soak up light around it, and the flaming pillar did little to illuminate the pyramid given its size.

The pyramid sat as a monolith amid a barren wasteland of dead trees in a sprawling forest that spread out into the horizon. Cold winds blew through their dead branches and rattled their old, withered bark with a sound that could only be described as that of sandpaper rubbing against sandpaper, though even this was somewhat dampened by the continued booming of thunder and torrent of water falling from the heavens.

Lastly, and to Riven's growing confusion, he saw hundreds of other people just like him crawling to their feet and orienting themselves to their surroundings. Men and women of many ages glanced over at one another in shock, surprised to be here, by all accounts; a few of them tried yelling to one another over the blasting sound of the storm.

Why had Allie been taken from him?! This damnable alien god-figure could go straight to hell!

Riven felt a lurching sensation in his gut again, and he doubled over with an intense coughing fit that left his insides reeling with pain. Looking down in astonishment as more black ichor shot out of his mouth and splattered along the stone ground at the pyramid's base, he went wide-eyed. Panic set in when he noticed there were growing clumps of blackened, necrosing veins slowly spreading across his abdomen and chest.

Many of the others around him were in similar states of shock and denial. Some looked to one another as if to ask whether or not this was real; others keeled over in pain, and even more of them stood staring up at the pyramid like deer caught in headlights. But when one of the other young men nearby began to get up and sprinted headlong toward the pyramid's steps, then started ascending despite his own body showing signs of the same rot that afflicted Riven—that's when the horror truly hit home.

If that prompt that'd appeared had been true, he needed to get moving, and he wasn't about to bet his life on all this being some kind of nightmare. He could find the answers to the plethora of other questions he had later.

Adrenaline flooded his body, and Riven's muscles nearly spasmed as he shot forward across the short gap between himself and the steps leading up the dark pyramid. He could only curse and bound up the large carved steps—each at least three feet high—as a swarm of other people quickly began to follow, a mixture of horror and frantic need setting in across the scattered crowd.

The sky rumbled, and the wind and rain continued to crash down upon him. His bare feet pushed against the cold stone, slipping more than once as he drove himself—step by step—up the dark pyramid's face. A looming statue of a knight came into his field of view while Riven tried in vain to wipe rainwater from his face amid the downpour. Riven paused, briefly looking up and into the dull, set eyes, when he heard a sharp crack of noise, and the figure quickly started to crumble along its joints.

"Ah… Fuck you."

Heart picking up its pace as the knight began to move, with chips of stone breaking off its body as it whirled on him, he shouted out in panic and lurched to the left to narrowly dodge a slow-coming sword strike that shattered part of the step he'd been on not even a moment before.

He felt like his chest was going to explode. The rolling pauldrons of the creature shifted; the statue that was easily twice his size looked his way…and it silently turned to meet him once more. All around the pyramid, as people began encountering their own monstrosities made from the bedrock of the pyramid's body that they'd thought were just statues, screams began to erupt amid the clash of thundering clouds. The torrent of water falling from the skies did little to drown out the horrified wails.

The statue let out a creaking, guttural groan and lifted its weapon again— but Riven didn't wait around to let the slow-moving attack bash him. He dodged left—slipping and skinning his arm in the process as a stinging pain shot up the length of his left limb when another blow crashed into the stone steps nearby. Grunting in exasperation and disbelief at his current situation while he made a mad dash to regain the lost ground, he set his sights higher. He only gave the statue that'd swung at him a very brief look over the shoulder, then powered ahead with renewed determination.

He shoved ahead, barely passing two others on his left before the next attack from a new opponent missed him by inches. A fire-breathing skull of stone turned and washed away a woman frantically climbing next to him, and he could feel the burning heat of flames that he'd barely scraped by. She screamed and writhed, falling from her perch to bounce down the now dozens of stone steps like a burning beacon in the night. An old man to his right and a little farther above him made the unfortunate mistake of getting a little too close to a stone gargoyle, which pounced on him and devoured him, to the horrid sounds of begging, screaming, and snapping bones.

The pained or horrified looks the people around him gave, black ichor mixing with their own blood that dribbled along the pyramid steps before being slowly washed away by the storm, only did more to make him nauseous. On top of that—his body wasn't responding the way he was used to. He wasn't out of shape by any means, or at least he hadn't been…but now he found himself getting winded by doing half of what he could have done prior to arriving here. He had no idea why, but he felt significantly weaker and slower. Perhaps it was just the "curse" he'd been afflicted with?

He had no real answers for what he was doing here other than those god-damned text-box holograms that would have seemed utterly ridiculous to him if he wasn't here at the moment. Had some angry god come down from the heavens to smite his world? Had aliens abducted him? Had he been slammed into some kind of ridiculous fantasy world without even having fulfilled his sexy Latin maid fantasies?

He really…really didn't want to fail, or die. He was too young for that shit.

His muscles started to give out on him as he got up to the halfway mark, and he found himself panting—all the while continuing to retch up that disgusting black gunk that seemed to coat his insides like coal in a chimney. The screams had dwindled down now as most of the statues had been passed by this point—with only the stragglers at the very back still keeping up with the monsters. The glistening stone gargoyles, reapers, skulls, and knights all seemed hesitant to follow them up, so the only problem now would be the other people.

Of which there were still hundreds.

About half of the men and women who'd started here were dead, having met their untimely ends one way or another by now.

Riven heard a curt scream from up above, and he narrowly avoided another man about his age tumbling down the pyramid slope to bounce unceremoni-ously with audible cracks and crunches on every hit. The screaming stopped a couple steps down from where Riven gawked back at the man, the poor guy's head oozing out blood as he remained wide-eyed on the steps, a large gash along his skull and his neck twisted at an abnormal, sickening angle.

The storm continued to roar overhead, and he stared at the corpse while taking in deep inhales between coughing fits.

"Don't stop!"

He turned. The call was from a middle-aged Asian woman to his right. She, too, was heaving, trying to catch her breath as her slick black hair was coated to her face and the signs of necrosis were evident along her bare stomach and breasts.

It was just like his own body, where the black signs of rot were beginning to creep into his pectoralis muscles and even his right thigh.

"Keep moving!" She puked, throwing a hand back down to the trailing people behind them and to the few men and women who were climbing ahead. "We are in the forefront! Don't let yourself die because you get a weak stomach!"

"Yeah… Yeah, you're right…" Riven gulped shakily, nodding to her and trying to smile in appreciation at her words of encouragement. But he failed this attempt when another wave of nausea overcame him. Instead, he pushed himself up onto his hands and knees, willing himself to move forward despite the sickness and pain that afflicted his body.

Only halfway to go… Only halfway…to go…

The second half of the pyramid's climb was far, far harder than the first half—despite the lack of enemies. Instead of abrupt and violent ends to meet them, the participants found themselves huddled over and clutching at their stomachs or bleeding from their eyes as they desperately tried to finish the quest prompt for the promise of relief.

Riven, fortunately, appeared to have more willpower than the others. Even some of those who'd gotten head starts on him began to sag behind. He crawled, struggled, and breathed heavily while closing his eyes to shut out the pain—trying to concentrate on the steady stream of roaring water that berated him as if to deny him his goal. His muscles pumped and spasmed, moving despite the heavy amount of damage his body had accrued, and his mind internally roiled with a torture unlike anything he'd ever experienced before…as it became his new, all-encompassing reality.

"Out of my way!" A desperate snarl from ahead caused Riven's face to lift, and he saw someone he could barely distinguish through the storm shove the Asian woman Riven had briefly spoken with.

She was obviously dizzy and weak, far too weak to catch herself, and she began to stumble backward past Riven's own spot just behind her.

He blinked rapidly, and with a Herculean effort managed to catch the woman with violent vertigo setting in upon the effort. He fell forward, collapsing with the stranger who'd encouraged him earlier onto the stone steps and saving her from a brutal backward fall.

They locked eyes through the downpour, both panting on the steps with ichor leaking out of their eyes, noses, and mouths.

"Keep moving…" Riven managed to say with a pained grunt. "Don't let yourself die now!"

She stared at him, remaining where they'd fallen face-first onto the steps, and winced as new patches of rot began spreading across her right cheek. "I owe you one…"

He gave the woman an encouraging nod and glared up the pyramid toward the climbing man who'd nearly killed her. "Come on."

Riven hoisted himself up through blinding pain and tears, his body screaming at him and trying to get him to stop. He looked over his shoulder when the woman faltered in her own attempts to move. He reached down to help her but was overtaken by a dizzy spell, nearly falling over as he stumbled onto the forward step. His body tried to deny his efforts to help, to keep going, but through sheer force of will and a defiant sneer on his face, he reached down and hoisted the woman up.

Silently, they powered on.

They struggled, leaning on one another when the other was weak. They muttered encouragement to each other as they trudged ahead, and despite their failing organs and the immense amount of pain they felt, they persevered. Riven's mind was set on only one thing—survival. It was a base instinct he could not ignore, a driving force that far outweighed any motivator that'd been present in his life prior to this moment. He just focused on putting one foot in front of the other, one crawling hand in front of the other, until he finally found himself at the top of the pyramid.

The top was devoid of any structures, but it had a large circular pit in the center where rippling green flames of the skyward pillar still erupted at the center. His body immediately rid itself of the rot when they passed through a thin, shimmering veil of gray mist—and a system notification appeared in front of his face.

[You have completed part one of three in the Chalgathi's Lineage Starter Quest.]

He gasped and spasmed, finding simultaneous delight in his sudden lack of pain and despair after having gone through such a strenuous ordeal. Tears leaked down his face to mix with the rainwater, and he lifted his shaking hands into the air with a primal scream of defiance toward the heavens.

Beside him, the panting Asian woman who'd been encouraging him earlier gave him a sideways glance of relief before puking onto the pyramid's stone rooftop. Dozens of others around them who'd also reached the top were in similar states: emotionally discharging with sobs, wails, and hysterical laughing fits befitting madmen.

They'd survived.

CHAPTER 3

[Two hundred participants have reached the pyramid's summit; 1,472 people have been disqualified and are now set to be executed if they have not died already. Part one of three in the Chalgathi's Lineage Quest line is now over.]

Screams of agony and terror rippled across all four sides of the pyramid, and rays of white light began illuminating the corpses of the fallen. The still-living, still-climbing participants outside the gray sheen of the veil begged and pleaded, clawing at a translucent veil in front of Riven that now seemed impenetrable to them. He even tried to reach through, to pull them in, but found that it was as if a force field had been erected there...

So he could only sit and watch, dumbstruck and horrified, as the men and women in front of him and down the pyramid's face began to wither and rot. Then the rot accelerated amid more flashes of white light that burned them from the inside out.

And in only a minute more of that torturous, evil display of power, they were simply gone...evaporating into the air as wisps of blackened ash that set upon the wind to be carried away into the great expanse of the dead forest about them.

"Holy shit..." He shook his head, not sure what to make of all this. What was the purpose? Why had he been one of the people selected to undertake this "quest line"? Where was he?

His answers would have to wait for another time, because in a great burst of green flame, the pillar exploded in all directions and enveloped everyone atop the pyramid in a searing, heat-filled rush. As his body burned away, he felt his soul twist and roil until he, too, had disappeared from the pyramid's top as if he'd never been there to begin with.

* * *

Fortunately, he hadn't died after all. He found himself in an odd, dome-shaped room along with many of the others who'd reached the top, materializing right in front of his eyes with puffs of sickly green mana until their flames all died out simultaneously.

He began to look around.

The ceiling was a mosaic, picturing various skeletal warriors praying to a robed figure that held a green-tinted lantern in one hand and a great scythe in the other. With more scrutinizing detail of the mosaic, he saw a crooked jaw that made the skeleton look like he was grinning out at the vast crowd while perched upon a throne of bones, and behind him a city burned. And all around the room, along the walls, were a series of torches in racks that flickered ominously, casting shadows about the center where the crowd of people now stood.

[Part two of three in the Chalgathi's Lineage Quest now commencing. Your willpower has been tested and found not wanting... Congratulations on your ascent. Unfortunately, the trial is not yet over, and you must still pass two more tests in order to acquire the power Chalgathi is offering. This time, you will be tested on your wit... Failure follows those who charge headlong with reckless abandon... Success follows a sharpened mind.

Notice: Navigate the labyrinth by completing puzzles that test one's ability to think critically. The first one hundred people to reach the end of the labyrinth will survive this test. The rest will perish.]

Who or what the hell was Chalgathi?

A grating sound quickly accompanied this new message as twenty large doors previously hidden within the stone walls surrounding them began to sink into the stone floors—causing Riven to snap out of his confusion and whip his head around to take in the sight on reflex.

A larger, bald man probably a good six inches taller than he was, nearly knocked Riven over with a disgusted scoff as he made his way toward the door. "Move it."

Riven stared blankly at the back of the guy who'd pushed past him, seriously considering breaking the man right there and then. But he quelled his irritation, deciding there were more important things to do than pick fights right now. His life was on the line, and he needed to get moving.

Others had the same idea and started for the doorways. Unfortunately he was centered amid the crowd of suddenly shoving, kicking, and yelling people as they tried to dash toward the doors—which were only large enough to let a couple people in at a time. There was fighting, brawling, and screaming that picked up in the choke points as fortunate others ran through at breakneck speed while trying to be in the leading group to complete the trial.

Riven watched in displeasure as he saw one man completely beat in the head of a smaller teenager before whipping around and marching through the doors. It occurred to him there and then, as that young man bled out on the floor with a caved-in skull: If he wasn't careful, he could just as easily end up in the "deceased" category before reaching the end of the labyrinth. No doubt many of the others wouldn't balk at killing in order to whittle down the numbers for a greater chance at survival and making it to the top one hundred spots. Not after what they'd seen on the pyramid just over the last hour.

He probably shouldn't have been so surprised about their behavior. He was a dog in a cage filled with other rabid animals, and they were all out for their own survival.

Wishing he had a set of clothes and really disliking the way things were going, Riven pushed both hands up through his short brown hair with a snort— his defined musculature now dried after being vaporized by the green fire a minute earlier.

He had so many questions…but at least things were getting interesting. His heart was pounding like it hadn't in years, and for the first time in a long, long time…he felt alive.

The crowd thinned over time, and eventually it slowed to a trickle with only four other people aside from himself still remaining in the chamber with the ceiling mural. Three trampled bodies remained limp and dead on the floor, but they did not garner Riven's attention. Instead, he remained to study the artwork overhead.

"This time, you will be tested on your wit… Failure follows those who charge headlong with reckless abandon… Success follows a sharpened mind." He repeated the words aloud. To him it was an obvious clue for what *not* to do, and another balding man nearby glanced his way with a wry smile.

"You caught that, too, did ya?" the man stated while clapping his hands onto his outstretched belly. "It told us not to rush headlong, literally, and then they all did it. Absurd."

Two of the others, an elderly woman with thinning hair and another younger man in his late teen years, both nodded their agreement. The last of them, a middle-aged Chinese man with dragon tattoos, plucked at his neatly trimmed beard with a concerned expression.

Riven, meanwhile, turned his gaze back to the artwork, looking for something that could provide any further clues as to what that phrase had meant. "There's got to be something here, some other clue that we can home in on… and the only things I see are—"

He stopped short as the torches along the perimeter began to flare, and the previously blank stone walls holding them now began to change. The mural from the domed roof spread and began to morph, with the skeletal robed figure growing new arms. The robed figure now had four in total, and all four arms pointed beyond the depictions of skeletal warriors and burning city toward symbols along four of the twenty corridors leading out. They were positioned over each of the four doors and gleamed in brilliant neon-green. One corridor depicted a skull with a long, serpentine tongue snaking out of it. Another depicted twin daggers crossed over one another dripping blood. The next depicted a burning flame. The last was a picture of a bird in flight.

After that the walls filled in more with additional murals until the entire room was encompassed, and very quickly Riven found it to be telling a story. The others no doubt had figured this out themselves, but to what extent each of them understood it relative to each other was up in the air.

The story started with a crow that soared across the heavens, observing people far below as they worked their farms and lived simple lives. Then a stranger appeared in their village, a hooded man with a skull face and serpentine tongue. The pictures showed him bargaining with them, or attempting to, but they cast him out of the village. It showed the man leaving, but after having tied up and kidnapped one of the villagers to bring him away. The skull-faced man was depicted sacrificing the prisoner with two bloody daggers, and still the crow watched from overhead. The villagers scoured the landscape, looking for their lost comrade, but they could not find the skull-faced man or their lost kin until the crow showed them the way. With makeshift weapons and a stampede of men, the villagers were taken to the spot where the skull-faced man was feasting upon the corpse of his sacrifice, but when he looked up, they all fell into a trap and were burned alive with scorching flames.

All except the crow.

The villagers had been led into an ambush, and the skull-faced man thanked the crow with a blessing. Red sparks erupted from the crow's wings, and it found itself flying faster and higher than it ever could before. The crow left the village to contend with the skull-faced man alone, and they soon succumbed to his two daggers and balls of fire until he'd raised an army of the dead—skeletal minions forming from the remnants of the villagers while he sat atop a throne of bones.

Riven's eyes rested on the end of the mural, only for his eyes to drift up again toward the robed, four-armed skeleton pointing toward the four passages adorned with symbols.

"Interesting," Riven stated slowly, coming up closer to the nearest of the passageways. This one was adorned with that of the bird in flight, likely the crow that'd been depicted along the murals. And as he inspected the archway and took a step forward, the hallway leading out began to change. Space warped in front of him, sucking him into a completely different passageway with a *WHOOSH*.

He staggered to a stop, then looked over his shoulder to stare blankly back at a stone wall—the room he'd been in was now gone. It was a dead end; the people that'd been there with him were now all gone, and he slowly turned his head forward again to see a stone statue depicting an old woman with a crow perched on her shoulder and a small hole in the stone at her feet. Four stone walls encompassed a moderately sized room with a single lantern emitting a dull green light from overhead. In front of the statue was a pool of softly sizzling acid a couple yards in diameter; a pair of odd-looking tongs as large as his right arm were chained to the near side, and a small rowboat floated in the middle of the pool.

Riven hesitantly took a step forward, unsure what to make of this odd scenario. He walked over to the edge of the pool, then looked across at the statue. Curiously he circled the pool and inspected the statue more thoroughly, though there wasn't any clue of what he was supposed to do here—until he saw words inscribed onto the back of the old stone woman.

He read the words aloud. "Let the acid gently pour between my feet, and thou shalt receive my blessing."

Huh.

He circled back around again. There was indeed a small pathway carved into the stone leading into the statue's base from the pool of acid, however, the sizzling acid was at a level where it wouldn't be high enough to glide across the carved pathway.

Riven was very hesitant to try and push any of that acid, either. He plucked some hairs off his head just to make sure it actually was acid and let them fall. The hairs hit the sizzling liquid with instantaneous eradication, and Riven quickly backed up so he wasn't so close to the vile stuff.

He thought about it, looking over to where the metal tongs were chained to the far side of the pool across from the statue. Then he looked to the wooden boat that was mysteriously not taking any acidic damage. Curiously enough, he also noted another set of chains from that same position next to the tongs—only he hadn't seen these chains before, because they were attached to the boat and scaling along the bottom of the pool. There was also an odd black ball at the bottom of the pool, and it looked to be made of metal.

If the chains weren't being eaten, perhaps he could break off the tongs and use them to scoop acid into the small, elevated pathway leading toward the statue of the crow and the old woman?

He circled around again, coming to where the tongs were placed, and gave the chains three sturdy yanks. They held firm, and he tried dipping the binding chains in acid for a while before trying again to no avail. In fact, the acid seemed to slip off the metal without any problem.

"Hmm."

He pulled on the chain connected to the rowboat, yanking the wooden construct over to him. It drifted silently back, coming to nuzzle against the edge of the stone pool but completely evading his grasp when his fingers slipped right through it.

He tried grasping the boat again, only to see his hand pass right through the boat like it was some kind of ghost ship.

Puzzled, he began to think of other ways to try and get acid into the pathway on the opposite side leading toward the statue's base. He tried splashing some of it across the pool with his tongs but only cursed when a small droplet of it got on his skin and ate a small, shallow hole into his forearm. He tried pushing the boat across the pool to make waves, but that didn't work out very well, either. Grabbing the tongs and grasping the metal ball at the bottom of the pool with them was somewhat of a struggle because of the weight of the object; he took the black ball out and rested it against the stone floor.

Immediately the level of the pool dropped by nearly an inch.

"Well, that's the opposite of what I want..."

Riven rubbed his chin thoughtfully. He lowered the ball back into the acidic pool and watched the level rise again, repeating this action a couple times to see if he could create waves that way.

He couldn't. Was there anything else to put into the pool to displace more of the acid, causing the level to rise so it could move into the carved path between the statue's feet?

A sinking feeling overcame him. There was his body, or parts of his body, but nothing else.

Frowning and shaking his head in adamant refusal, he tried a few more times, but it was only when he accidentally nudged the boat when taking out the black ball that he considered another idea.

He'd originally thought the boat to be some kind of ethereal construct, only to be touched by the chains and acid—but the ball also made contact and was able to push the boat away with a slight nudge.

"That's it." A relieved and victorious smile overcame Riven's features. Though taking the ball out of the pool actually lowered the fluid level, metal was far denser than wood. It was a pretty neat physics concept and reminded him of a riddle his old physics teacher had once described. Due to the density, the ball should theoretically displace less water—or in this case, acid—than it would if it were in a container like the boat. It would be heavier, pushing the boat down and causing the level to rise far more than if the ball had just been sitting down there at the bottom.

And it sure as hell beat sacrificing an arm or leg.

Quickly he grasped the metal ball with his tongs again, and then he dropped the object into the boat with an audible *thunk*.

Immediately the boat lowered, and the fluid level of the pool rose. Acid began to flow into the carved divot on the opposite end where the statue remained and flowed through the shallow passage toward a hole at the bottom of the statue's feet.

A pulse of energy radiated outward from the statue, and the eyes of the crow and the old woman both turned a vibrant red—changing the tone of the sickly green to a more sinister hue across the room in an instant. In the back of the room, a hidden door swung open—revealing a passageway that led off into the dark.

[You are one of the few to heed this trial's warning. Take this boon as a reward, and let your path be graced with the flight of the crow to guide you.]

Riven was frozen in place, and his eyes went wide when he felt his body go cold. Black and gray miasma began to billow out in front of the statue before being interlaced with crimson, and an electrical current pulsed out about a baseball-size globe of energy while Riven failed to react despite his body screaming at him to run.

In a blinding flash, the power erupted and tore into Riven's body. He felt currents of cold and hot fluctuations course through his muscles, over his skin, and through his veins, but it wasn't painful. It surprised him enough to cause him to yell out in alarm and stumble back...but the energy felt good. Really good...and it was as if his body was...was on fire? He felt pumped!

[You have acquired an ability: Blessing of the Crow (Unholy).
Blessing of the Crow: Activate this ability up to once per day for an hour's worth of increased Stamina regeneration with a significant boost to Agility.

This ability is a blessing and does not require learning, as it draws power from a pillar or deity. This blessing is currently temporary, but you may choose to acquire the blessing permanently if you wish. You have an extremely high affinity toward the Unholy Pillar, and it will accept your body as a conduit if you wish to utilize its power. Warning: Choosing this blessing will permanently orient you toward the Unholy Foundation Pillar. Doing this will allow you to specialize in various Unholy-related magics and its subpillars but will close off many other avenues of power in turn.

Affinities affect how fast you learn, how powerful your abilities are, and what you will be able to perform under a chosen foundation. Your current affinities for the Foundational Pillars are generalized as follows:

Unholy Foundational Pillar: Extremely High
Holy Foundational Pillar: Extremely Low
Fae Foundational Pillar: Low
Archaic Foundational Pillar: Low
Harmony Foundational Pillar: Very Low
Machine Foundational Pillar: Low

Do you wish to acquire this Unholy ability permanently and bind
to the Unholy Foundational Pillar? Yes? No?]

He blinked. He could assume that pillars were categories of magic? If what this notification said about affinities was true, it was a no-brainer. This wasn't the first time the trial had informed him of his extremely high affinity toward Unholy magics, either. Without much further ado, he selected yes.

CHAPTER 4

[You have opted to keep Blessing of the Crow, Tier 1, as a permanent ability.]

BOOM

The shock wave that radiated throughout his body was like a thunderstrike to his soul, and he fell to the ground gasping for air with incomprehension while his innards felt like they were violently rearranging themselves. His eyes went wide and bloodshot as green, black, and crimson lights illuminated across his skin in strange patterns before shimmering away to present elsewhere—causing burning sensations wherever they went.

His eyes rolled back into his head, and everything went black as his body spasmed, but from somewhere deep inside him…his consciousness began to emerge again.

Only it wasn't…it wasn't aware of his surroundings. Rather, it was aware of who he was as a person…of his desires and the reasons for having them. It was almost as if he was in a meditative state, and all the pain from his body rapidly disappeared as his senses dulled to make way for this new wave of inner sensation.

Then, from somewhere within the jumbled thoughts and chaotic disorder of the rampaging energies running through his body…a glowing sensation of warmth began to emerge.

He saw them now—the green, crimson, and black lights. They were digging through his thoughts, tearing at them only to piece the thoughts back together one by one until the lights sensed this core.

It was the core of his soul.

The lights began swimming through the jumbled chaos to get to it. He watched as they surged forward, clinging to one another and then accumulating their energy into one mix and match of a swirling vortex as it came face-to-face with the inner ball of energy Riven's body contained.

Gently, ever so gently, the vortex reached out…and touched the essence of who and what Riven was as a being.

Instantly the connection became solid as tendrils of that bright orb stitched themselves to the vortex of darker power until it was able to stabilize the vortex—calming it into a slower-moving pool of light that exchanged energies with the core over time.

[You are now permanently oriented toward the Unholy Pillar. You may not bind to any other Foundation Pillar, but you may now specialize in subpillars related to the Unholy Foundation Pillar.]

[System Message: Congratulations on your acquisition of a Foundation Pillar and the first step on the path toward greatness. As a newly acquainted citizen to Elysium's multiverse, it is pressing that you understand the basics. There are six Foundation Pillars of power with which you may choose to align yourself in striving for the top, each with their own major subpillars. In turn, each of these major subpillars has its own innumerable expansions that lead down pathways to power through insight to the Dao. The foundational pillars and their major subpillars are as follows:

- The Unholy Foundation Pillar, with the major subpillars of Blood, Shadow, Death, Infernal, Depravity, and Chaos.
- The Holy Foundation Pillar, with the major subpillars of Light, Heaven, Grace, Moon, Sun, and Judgment.
- The Fae Foundation Pillar, with the major subpillars of Volcano, Storm, Ocean, Glacial, Swamp, and Forest.
- The Archaic Foundation Pillar, with the major subpillars of Arcane, Void, Metal, Illusion, Alteration, and Time.
- The Harmony Foundation Pillar, with the major subpillars of Body, Mind, Primal, Chi, Karma, and Zodiac.
- The Machine Foundation Pillar, with the major subpillars of Hacking, Armaments, Integration, Mecha, Interweb, and Sci-Tech.

Your soul has been altered to properly utilize Unholy magics, miracles, and martial arts. You merely need to learn how to acquire such powers now. However, you will be forever barred from any of the Holy, Fae, Archaic, Harmony, or Machine Foundational Pillar categories and their subpillars regardless of complete understanding or not—due to the changes your soul has undergone. Please note that although some abilities you come across will have only the Unholy

Pillar requirement, their major subpillars and further specialized pillars may require a deeper understanding of their own attributes prior to utilizing the specialty types.]

[Dao advancement is partially locked until the pretutorial trials and the tutorial trials have been completed.]

The vision ended as abruptly as it'd come, and Riven found himself gasping when his senses returned.

Scrambling to his knees, he looked around—still struggling to breathe properly as his heart went wild at the sudden and impulsive rage that'd taken place within his body and mind. But it was done now…and he seemed to be all right, without any bad side effects.

Riven nodded with a small grin on his face, pleased with the outcome and having gone back on a gut instinct to find this statue. He felt like he'd downed three energy drinks simultaneously—and his body even flickered slightly with small yet noticeable currents of red electricity that occasionally erupted from his pores.

"Thanks, crow lady. I owe you one."

Riven gave the statue an awkward thumbs-up before heading down the hallway straight ahead like he'd originally intended to do. He began to jog, feeling the energy lighting up across his skin and spurring him on—and then he began to sprint. He went fast, then faster—sparks of red lightning surging in abundance across his skin the more he exerted himself. Despite how much he ran, Riven found that he wasn't even beginning to break a sweat. To his amazement, he was also running way, *way* faster than he'd ever originally been able to run. It was about twice the speed of his old all-out sprint. It would have been more than enough to very easily outsprint many of the collegiate sprinters he used to watch on TV.

Fuck, yes. This was more like it!

His body failed to tire as the blessing's power coursed through him. It brought about the question of what a "tier" was. But for now, he was too involved in the moment to care about it much. Of all the questions on his mind, this was one of the ones that least concerned him given his current situation.

For a short time, as the stone walls and mounted torches rushed past at high speed and the cool air brushed past him as he traversed the labyrinth, he forgot about all the other bullshit that'd clouded his recent events. The disappearance of his parents years ago, the introduction of the new world, the confusing trials he was part of—it all faded away as he was caught up in the thrill of his newfound power.

Until he tripped and fell flat on his face halfway through a turn that was just a little too tight for his own good.

WHAM

Cursing and wiping his bloodied nose, he groaned a bit and stood up—only to realize he was at yet another crossroads. This time, however, as he examined the passages in detail, he got no reward for doing so. Nor was there any sign to clue him in which way to traverse. But...as he chose the rightmost passage that led upward through a flight of stairs and then dropped back down through a hole in the floor into yet another hallway—he found himself staring at a door.

It was old, carved out of marble, and very out of place given the colors of the rest of the labyrinth thus far. A single, smooth door handle of a medieval make sat at chest level, and with a shrug, he pulled it open. He hadn't seen any reason why not to.

That, he found out, was a mistake. At least according to his nostrils.

A current of foul wind, heavy with the stench of the dead, pulled him in— sucking him inside like the hand of an angry god had come to grab him—only to slam the door behind as he fell into a pit of dried-up, indistinguishable corpses and innumerable statues...

There *were* two familiar statues, actually. There, on the floor in front of him in the flickering light of the torches...were two people he recognized from the group who'd made it to the top of the pyramid. An old man and a slightly younger woman—both turned to stone. Both missing their eyes and tongues... both having clawed bloody handprints into the back of the door immediately behind him. Some of their fingers were missing, and many of their toes were gone as well. Their faces were set into a silent scream, and it was probably one of the most horrifying things he'd ever laid eyes on.

"Don't be so dramatic with your gawking..." A deep and feminine hiss echoed out from behind him and farther into the room. "They just didn't have what it takes... You may not share their fate if you play my game properly... Maybe..."

Riven found that his jaw had been opened without him realizing it, and he shut it before slowly turning his head to look farther in—past the piles of dried corpses—past the two stone ones—and toward a...a medusa?

He cocked an eyebrow, curiously inspecting the scaled half snake, half woman figure that sat coiled upon an elevated stone platform in the center of a rectangular room. The torches here were far brighter, warmer, and even her smile seemed inviting. She was what he would consider beautiful, with the exception of lacking legs, but she was not hard to look at. The snakes that made up her hair were a bright green, her eyes glinted gold, and she wore no clothes as she sat coiled around her serpentine lower half with a sly smile.

Despite the eyeballs and tongues lying there on a plate in front of her while she tapped her clawed fingers on a glass table with a...with a chessboard?

"Sit..." she invited, motioning to a spot across from her on the opposite side of the table with two of her slender fingers. Immediately, a shoddy wooden chair materialized out of thin air to descend from a foot above the ground, gently touching down.

He kept his eyebrows raised, slowly coming to his feet and hesitantly walking over to the table while eyeing the chessboard. Then he glanced down to the chair, and then to her again where she remained smiling with wicked white fangs bared his way under beautiful golden eyes—eyes that he specifically avoided meeting. "You want me to play you in a game of chess?"

She didn't reply, merely waiting for him to sit as the snakes of her hair aggressively hissed and snapped at him. The way she looked at him gave him the feeling that he shouldn't trust her—screamed at him not to trust her—and his base instinct was to run… Unfortunately, there was nowhere to go. The way out had been sealed already, and he saw no other door beyond the piled, withered corpses of victims long dead.

Other than the chessboard, next to the plate with the eyeballs and tongues was a long, slender knife made from silver that was coated in blood down to the handle. The plate also had an odd, out-of-place set of words along the white ceramic rim, and the center of the plate acted as a mirror in the middle.

"Chess…is truly a game of wit…" the medusa hissed, her long green snakes shifting in unison as they looked him over with the occasional baring of fangs. Her slender fingers came down to the board, putting the tip of one finger on one of the splendidly carved wooden rooks and then gesturing to the other pieces. "White or black?"

His eyes narrowed. It'd been a long time since he'd played chess, but his father had made it a habit when he'd still been around. "White."

CHAPTER 5

The coiled medusa raised an eyebrow and slowly turned the board, positioning the black pieces in front of her before gently moving the first pawn two spaces and leaning in to rest her chin on her hands. "The other two chose black."

He grinned back at her, not meeting her gaze, and mirroring her own move in order to make way for his queen in the next. "Will you kill me if I lose?"

"Perhaps... Perhaps not."

"Then do you mind answering me a couple questions while we play?"

"It depends on what they are, little man..."

He furrowed his brows and crossed his arms thoughtfully. Little? He was by no means little. Was she being demeaning on purpose? He pushed the question aside for a more important one, though, and truly hoped she'd answer it. "Where am I?"

He moved another pawn forward to take one of her own, and a series of uneventful positionings was exchanged.

She let out a long, dark chuckle as a rook moved into position to protect a forward knight. She gestured for him to move next and then leaned back a little to observe him better. "How would I know? I've been down here for centuries just waiting for company...banished here by a lich who got the better of me."

"So you're not part of Elysium, then?"

She teasingly raised an eyebrow. "I'm not sure what you mean by that."

Then she placed two fingers on her queen and went in to take Riven's pawn. As soon as she took the piece off the board, Riven's right pinkie toe broke off in a gruesome and miniature explosion of blood and bone.

He screamed, collapsing out of his chair and onto the floor in a state of shock and horror as the serpentine woman began cackling in amusement. He clutched and stared down at his mutilated foot, then back up to the creature ahead of him. "What the hell is this?!"

She didn't respond but just laughed even louder, and as he reached out to grasp the knife, she abruptly hissed and reared up to her full height.

He paused, still sneering up at the monster, but slowly withdrew his hand. She in turn lowered herself down into a coiled position again, her prominent breasts on full display underneath a sly smile.

"Wise choice," the medusa eventually said with a nod while he grimaced and clutched at his foot. "I am bound by rules here; if you were to have stricken me, I could have killed you on the spot. Considering how weak you are…it would have been less than a hassle."

She gestured to the board, mockingly, and gave him an overly polite smile. "Now, shall we continue? Just try not to lose anymore pieces—you may lose some fingers and toes along the way if you do."

"When I took your pawn, nothing happened to you," Riven muttered in anger, sitting back down in the chair with a plop and grimacing. "How is that fair?"

Her smile turned into one of maliciousness. "Who said anything about being fair?"

He snorted, taking one of her bishops and then doing a quick exchange of two more pawns back-to-back as the pieces on the board grew fewer in number. Each time Riven took a piece, he merely set it to the side. But every time she took one of his pieces, a toe or finger would pop off in a miniature, bloody fireworks display to both the agony of Riven and the gleeful cackles of the medusa.

He could only hope that this trial had some real way of getting him out of here. It was pretty obvious to him that he stood little chance against her in a fight, so he'd have to bear with it and do his best to try and get out of this using his wit like the trial was designed to do.

He grunted, screamed, and occasionally dropped to the ground whenever he felt another digit explode. First he lost two more toes on his right foot, then three fingers on his left hand. His right pinkie finger and his left big toe next. He sat in a pool of his own blood, actively bleeding out as he became light-headed and unable to think as fast as he had previously—but he managed through sheer willpower to keep his wits about him and mentally pushed through the pain. Both players used their queens to push their advantages, neither of them willing to sacrifice their own queen in order to take the other's, the two prominent pieces dancing across the board. She was good, but he was better, and it was beginning to irk her. Her play style was too aggressive, and it cost her more than one time. Her smile began to fade, and slowly a frown appeared on her lips as she took more and more time to distinguish between the right and wrong moves available to her.

It was during one of these pauses that his eyes again focused on the words along the rim of the plate beside the bloody chessboard. He mentally strained to focus on the written symbols, doing everything he could to keep himself upright and silent while his limbs screamed in torment.

Reflect upon your opponent and see the truth amid the lies… This was what the plate said along the rim of the mirror. What did that mean, exactly? Was this a clue of some sort? If he was stuck in here with a creature obviously meant to test his wits somehow, could he really expect that all this trial wanted from him was to play a game of chess and win?

That didn't seem right, given the way it'd gone so far. Even if it was incredibly painful to undergo. In fact, it seemed very, very wrong. It was too simple, out of place, and didn't seem to fit the narrative of the labyrinth. He'd scanned the entire room many times over now, but was that even necessary? He could very well just be wasting time here while the other participants in this trial got ahead—leaving him behind to die if he didn't make it to the top one hundred spots.

Again, he was brought out of his thoughts by her melodic voice and sweet smile. "Well? Are you going to tell me what you're talking about?"

"Huh?"

"You asked me about being part of Elysium."

He humored her, pretending to consider his next move while trying to figure out what was really going on as his trembling hand shifted uncertainly over the chessboard—dribbling red liquid onto the game set. Frankly, he didn't know how he was even upright anymore, as he literally sat in a large puddle of his own body fluids. "Elysium…or perhaps the administrator these messages keep talking about. What are they?"

That…that got her attention—and he noticed the ways her eyes narrowed at the mention of the administrator.

"Oh…I have no idea what you're talking about."

"Sure you don't."

He was about to make his next move when the words finally registered. *Reflect upon your opponent and see the truth amid the lies…*

The stone figures, the plate's words…and the obvious power this medusa held over him. It definitely wasn't looking good. She'd conjured a chair out of thin air and had piles upon piles of bodies—both stone and withered beyond belief—littering her little nest.

The knife was there, too…but he felt like it had been put there on purpose to try and goad people into making a stupid decision, if this was truly a test of wit. He had little chance of killing her head-on, especially if all these people around him had once been other trial takers. Certainly one or more had tried the violent path out.

Then a random set of messages appeared in front of his vision.

[In order to identify enemies and items, say or think the word *Identify* with intent while simultaneously targeting your desired object. As an example, the identification information of the medusa in front of you is now being displayed.]

[Medusa, Trickster, Level ???]

Oh. Well, that was interesting.

He dismissed the holograms. Two more pieces were exchanged with pain that rocked his body, and he gambled by sacrificing his own queen to take hers.

"How unexpected…" came the soft voice of the woman across from him as she eyed him like a hungry predator—still not once having met him eye to eye. She placed his queen off the board after having taken it and then moved her rook into position. "Check."

He smirked, then took her piece with a bishop. He saw a path to victory, and his heart rate began to pick up. The pieces danced across the board. Two moves later, and as tension in the room began to rise, he announced "Checkmate."

There was a long silence, and then a slow clap followed his victory. Much to his surprise, and he almost looked up to meet her eyes as she laughed.

"Good show, young man. Good show…"

He put on his best version of a forced smile, one quivering and pained hand missing all but his pointer finger and thumb with bloody stumps where the others had been. "So am I free to leave now?"

There was another pause, and he felt the air in the room shift to a frigid cold.

The click…click…click…of her claws against the table caused him to flinch with every tap. His arms edged forward a little bit, and he lowered his head more. "Am I free to go?"

There was another muffled laugh that quickly turned into a hiss, and that hiss turned into a low growl of annoyance. "No, my dear boy, you were never meant to go. You are mine. LOOK AT ME, BOY! LOOK AT ME!"

She lunged at him and caused the table to nearly upend itself, the contents spraying into the air. The knife, plate, tongues, and eyes went flying.

Or…he thought she had lunged at him. In reality, she'd just slammed her clawed fists into the table and her snake hair had flared up—little eyes glowing red along each of the snakes as her own larger, golden eyes burned brilliantly with power in the next second.

He did the only thing he could think of, the only reasonable approach to this ridiculous situation, as he knew he couldn't fight her one-on-one. The only thing that made sense given his knowledge of the classics and the hint that was literally written into the plate itself. Without moving from the spot he'd positioned himself in when starting the game, he snatched the flying plate out of the air between two remaining fingers before it was able to get far. He'd been ready for it, anticipated such an action, and he'd bet his life on the one simple trick that he pulled now.

As fast as he could, with his new blessing speeding his reaction time and reflexes, he brought the plate down in front of his face with the mirrored center angled directly back at the medusa to show her a reflection of herself.

The clattering of the knife, pieces of the glass table, and the body parts hitting the floor sounded all around him as his chest heaved. Slowly, ever so slowly, he brought the plate farther down and peered from atop the edge...only to choke out a sigh in relief as his eyes met an enraged—yet very stone—medusa. She'd been frozen by her own power, killing herself in the process of trying to turn him into a statue, and the bet had paid off.

In an instant he felt a surge of energy as light gathered around his body, enveloping his flesh in a golden sheen that almost instantaneously repaired his losses. His toes and fingers all came back, and his wounds closed over as he remained sitting in a chair over a pool of coagulated blood.

He put his head down into his hands and slowly covered his face, shaking from the mental scar the torturous game had caused him. It felt a little surreal, and in some ways he counted himself one lucky idiot to pass this obstacle in such a way. It'd been a gamble, based on what he'd known about medusas from ancient lore and the clue on the plate, but it'd paid off. That, and his chess skills had been up to par.

Beyond the stage where he sat and farther along the wall on his left, another narrow passage opened up with the grating of stone and kicking up of dust. The dagger that'd clattered onto the floor vanished in a puff of smoke, and so did the mirror he'd used to backfire the medusa's gaze. Getting up from where he sat and letting out a snort, he checked the surrounding area for anything valuable. After not finding anything, he stepped around the shattered glass and made his way through the room toward the exposed hallway.

CHAPTER 6

Hours passed, and he found himself thrown into a bizarre mix of puzzle games, gates with solvable riddles, dangerous traps, and winding turns that seemed like they'd never end. He encountered a couple more bodies, one half-eaten by a large rat that he had to run from after it noted his presence, and it made him wonder just how many people were going to get past this stage in the quest.

His Blessing of the Crow had also run out of time, and his once-endless stamina and speed increase now faltered as his jogging came to a fast-paced walk. Unlike earlier, he now breathed heavily and had to take the occasional break.

He thus found himself sitting down against a wall to catch his breath in the corner of a small, dark room that was devoid of anything at all while massaging his aching legs. Dust covered the stone floor underneath him, and he hadn't seen even a trace of anyone else who'd been sent into this odd labyrinth ever since the stone statues in the medusa's room. It felt eerily lonesome.

"This is quite the situation to be in..."

Riven let out a small laugh, finding amusement at how ridiculous his situation was. Regardless of how tired his muscles were, he knew that most if not all the others must be even more tired. That gave him a little bit of hope that he'd still make it. He'd been going nonstop, and he'd had his free trial period of the blessing for the first hour of the trip...

What if the others had already finished the maze and he just didn't know about it? What if he was one of the ones who were sentenced to die now, to rot here in this godforsaken labyrinth, forever to roam until he died of starvation without a clue that he'd already failed, stuck here in who-knows-where without even realizing it yet? What if he were to remain here and live out the rest of his remaining days, withering away and slowly coming to the realization that he'd been left behind?

He shook his head. No, he couldn't think like that.

The cold stone at his back beckoned him to slumber. Yawning despite his best efforts not to and leaning to the side, he realized how little sleep he'd gotten recently. Folding his arms and refusing to let sleep take him just yet, knowing he couldn't sleep unless he wanted to die here, he decided to give himself just another minute longer...and he tilted his head farther out to lean against the adjacent wall for a little relaxation.

Or he would have if the wall had even been there.

With a start, he fell completely over. The illusion didn't hold his weight whatsoever, and he quickly found himself sprawled out in yet another room with a single green ball of flames hovering in the middle of it...displaying a large wooden chest underneath.

Curious, and remembering many stories he'd heard and games he'd played in the past, he quickly got up, brushed himself off, and headed toward said chest. It was old; moss had grown over nearly half of the wood, and a large, rusted lock decorated the front.

He repeatedly blinked, bit down on his tongue hard enough to elicit pain, and slapped himself once to try and wake himself up. Trying to get the lid to come off came with no results, and the chest was far too heavy to move by himself. Frowning, and walking around it while glancing up once more at the ball of green fire overhead, he came to the front yet again and began to examine the lock.

[Pick the lock to proceed. Failure after attempting this will result in death.]

In death? That was nothing new here. Captain Obvious to the rescue.

The system notification flared to life as another teal hologram in front of him just as the ball of flames above flashed a brighter green—trails of fire slowly dripping down to land on the chest itself, only to fade away, leaving behind five thin metal instruments.

He'd definitely done his fair share of lock picking back on Earth, but at first glance he'd thought these objects were some kind of odd bent pins rather than lockpicks he was familiar with.

Hesitantly he picked one of them up, examined it, and then tried to get a better view of the hole leading into the lock. Having no success there, either, he once more took a look at the pick in his hand and steadied his breath. Inserting it, he began to fidget around...and felt a snap when he applied a little too much pressure.

And as his initial attempt failed, a metal gate erupted from the ceiling to slam into the stone behind him—barring his exit completely.

Oh, no.

How ominous.

He rolled his tired eyes. The trial was trying to intimidate him, as if he wasn't already trapped here. Frowning and withdrawing the lockpick, he found it'd broken off. Fortunately he was able to fish the other piece out rather easily with the end he still had, but then his worry grew as he realized he'd just used up one of five total lockpicks.

He took another steadying breath and tried to clear his mind of the exhaustion he felt. It was safe to say that breaking all five lockpicks before the chest was opened would constitute failure. He had to do this...and do it carefully.

This time, as he picked up the second of the picks, he very gently inserted it—trying to make a mental image of the dimensions of the lock with the depth, height, and width. He put very little pressure on his movements this time, careful not to break it—and found that there were actually five tiny spring-loaded cylinders inside the lock that he could gently press upward on.

To his great relief, he found that the first of these cylinders clicked into place when he pressed up just right...and a large smile crossed his face as he knew how to proceed. He'd seen locks like this before.

Unfortunately, some cylinders were more sensitive than others...and after the first two cylinders had clicked into place, he found he'd gone too far on the third cylinder. With a snap and crunch, the cylinder slammed back down into the bottom of the lock—taking half of his lockpick with it and resetting the entire thing in one fell swoop.

"Damn it!"

The fireball above him flared slightly, growing in size as palpable heat began to descend upon him.

Becoming more aware of his impending doom, he withdrew the broken lockpick from the keyhole again and started anew. The third time went exactly as the second time had gone—the pick ending up breaking on the third cylinder.

He inserted the fourth lockpick into the hole and had to calm his nerves before proceeding so that his hand would stop shaking. When he'd finally steadied himself, he began again.

The first and second cylinders clicked into place just as they'd done so before, and he gave himself an internal pep talk to congratulate himself on at least a small victory in that regard. This time, though, when he came to the third cylinder, he used both hands to steady the advancing pick instead of one. Using it like a lever, he pushed up against the cylinder just slightly—taking it in second by second, until it, too, clicked into place. Sweating profusely and moving on, much to his delight, the fourth and fifth cylinders clicked into place far easier than even the first two.

[Congratulations, you have completed part two of three in Chalgathi's Lineage. Because you have found one of the hidden exits, please choose an additional prize before leaving. Do not choose more than one.]

With the mechanism audibly unlocking, the chest's lid was swung open to reveal two items at the bottom of the box. Delighted at having discovered a way out, and also having found a prize in the process, his face fell into confusion as he looked upon either object.

One was…a vase? A very small ceramic vase, painted white with ornate and wilting black flowers…and it had a lid that hid its contents, if there were any to be had.

Meanwhile, the other item was more typical of the fantasy-style world he now found himself in. Though it was certainly a little grotesque. It was a necklace of sorts…or a charm, in the form of a bird's withered foot that'd been encased in an amber stone and then strung up on a metal chain.

There was no explanation. No telltale sign of what either of them did. No notification to detail their usefulness, and even when he tried to identify these items like the system prompt had described with the medusa, there was nothing.

A little frustrated at the lack of detail, he decided to pick up the vase. It was a white porcelain aside from the black painted flowers, small enough that it fit in his hand, and the lid seemed to be screwed on—but before he could even try to remove it completely, the green fire above him flared to life.

In the next instant, he evaporated in a sweltering shower of pain and green flames just as he had at the top of the pyramid in the first trial. Less than a second later, all signs of his presence were gone—vanished from the labyrinth to move on to the third part of the quest.

Riven's mind stayed blank, but a prompt appeared, urging him to select from the following options:

[**For every level gained, you will be presented with a certain number of stat points depending upon both your class title, your race, and sometimes other unique factors that will not be discussed here. Currently you have no class title, and your race is set to Human. The human race has +5 free stat points per level. Please choose your starter class title, or if you'd rather, you may choose to change your race to one of the selected options, courtesy of Chalgathi. All supplied choices are unique to the individual, and remember that beyond this unique event, classes do not dictate your survival style—rather, in the future, your survival style will dictate what classes you are awarded beyond these base forms. The better your performance, the better classes you will be awarded upon evolution opportunities.**

Novice Necromancer (Class Title)—A strictly caster-class evolutionary pathway emphasizing the mass production and control of undead, such as corpses, skeletons, and ghosts. Unlocks ten minion slots for undead creations, +1 Willpower, +2 Intelligence, +3 free stat points per level.

Unholy Deacon (Class Title)—A divinity-using, faith-based evolutionary pathway, emphasizing the use of Unholy miracles. In order to get the most out of this class, you will need to choose a patron god to worship early on—but choosing this class now will also allow you to make contact with a deity for contracting their power. +3 Faith, +1 free stat point per level.

Novice Warlock (Class Title)—A pathway that leads to very high magic damage output in future evolutions, one that focuses on harnessing black magics and contracting with demons. +1 Willpower, +2 Intelligence, +2 free stat points per level. Enables demons to contact you of their own volition for contracts if your Willpower requirement has been met; up to two contracts may be filled with this class.

Novice Rogue (Class Title)—The beginnings of a class pathway emphasizing underhanded close-quarters and ranged martial art abilities. +7% bonus to all Stealth attempts or abilities and light armor attributes. +9% bonus to damage done by daggers. +2 Agility, +1 free stat point per level.

Ghoul (Race Change)—Ghouls are the most basic form of sentient undead and display a sincere lack of pain along with a vast increase in Sturdiness. A good choice for any melee fighter. +18 to base Sturdiness and Strength immediately upon evolution. +3 Sturdiness, +2 Strength, +1 free stat point per level.]

Riven blinked. *Class choices?*

Frankly, he didn't know what he wanted to choose. Being a necromancer sounded really cool; the idea definitely appealed to him, as he'd control minions to fight for him while he could remain safe on the back lines and dish out hard damage while at it.

Because of that, the Novice Warlock class also really appealed to him. It had an evolutionary pathway emphasizing a similar type of play style, but instead of undead it revolved around demons. Not only that, but it was the only class described itself as a path that would lead to "very high damage." That was a big plus.

Unholy Deacon sounded cool, but Riven wasn't so sure he wanted to get mixed up with any gods early on, either. He'd never been the religious type and didn't see that changing any time soon.

Rogue... Well, Riven had an Agility-based blessing ability. So that'd help with this class given the bonuses it gave to Stealth and Agility, but he wanted to use magic, too. Now that he'd entered some sick and twisted fantasy–sci-fi "multiverse," as the prompts had called it, he wanted to cast magic, goddamn it! So Rogue was out the window.

Then there was the race change to Ghoul. This was completely off the table, as Riven didn't want to be transforming into some sort of undead monster. Controlling them sounded interesting, but becoming one was certainly less appealing.

He thought about it some, regarding the choices of necromancer and war-lock before finally settling down with a nod. Thus, he selected Novice Warlock.

CHAPTER 7

[Part three of three in the Chalgathi's Lineage Quest now commencing. Death stalks the living as you tread down the path of the Novice Warlock. However, Chalgathi demands sacrifice to receive his gift… and the blood of your peers is the price he demands.

Notice: You have been granted early access to the class title Novice Warlock. One hundred participants in this trial now remain. Only fifty will leave here alive. Accept the class title, pick your starter pack, pick your bonded starter minion, and select two starting ability tomes to learn from. You will have a time-condensed period of five days to learn these two abilities. You must then kill your opponent to survive. If you have not figured out how to perform your chosen spells, miracles, or martial arts within the five-day period, you will go into the fight at a disadvantage. Good luck.

Uploading commencing. ETA for initiation—two minutes.]

He was standing on an island, and somehow he'd arrived wearing a thick, hooded, weathered cloak. He was certainly thankful for it, as the night wind was chilly upon his skin. The island was somewhat flat and grass-laden, with a brilliant moon illuminating the small amount of land in front of him. All around him were dozens of other islands equal to his in height with various slopes or flattened tops—all with their own singular inhabitants that he could barely make out when he looked around. These other islands also drifted among the reflections of the currents below, and just like his own plot of land, they each had a long drop down magnificent cliffs to a calm ocean underneath that shimmered under the stars and cosmos. Seagulls or some kind of other seafaring bird flew overhead, though their features were somewhat indistinguishable due to the dark of night, and little luminescent lights glowed down below where the ocean met the bases of the cliffs. Of particular note, all the islands were shifting—moving in various directions but not making contact with one another as they seemed to swim about the massive body of water while avoiding one another entirely, which made the entire scenario all the more odd.

The air was crisp, and he filled his lungs with a deep inhaled breath only to set his vase a little way back from the edge of the floating island to dangle his legs off the side. The sight was beautiful, and honestly—after all he'd been through already—he wasn't worried about the coming fight this notification spoke of.

If anything, he was just slightly confused. He didn't necessarily want to kill anybody, nor did he want them to kill him—but no matter what happened, he'd not hold back. He was a survivor, and he wouldn't balk at the idea of killing another person if it meant that he got to live for it. It had been a very, very long time since he'd felt this way…since he'd felt so alive, and he didn't want to let go of the sensation when all the excitement of joining this new world finally pushed him over the edge into wanting to live again.

Not just to live for someone else, but to finally live for himself.

It was weird to think about, but nearly having been killed numerous times now had made him come to the realization that he didn't want to give up. He didn't want to just roll over and let it all end like he'd thought about when his father had first disappeared. His father wouldn't have ever wanted that for Riven to begin with. His parents would have encouraged him, told him to try to move on and that they may see each other in the next life, if there was one, so that they might talk about the grand adventures he'd set upon.

They'd certainly have loved that.

He at the very least needed to try…and even if not for himself, then for Allie's sake. So that he might see the wonders of whatever this new world had in store for him and his little sister when he found her again. So that he could live through more moments like this…and appreciate the beauty of his surroundings—something he'd never before taken the time to do. So that he could appreciate the relationships he'd built up, and not be so confined to the loner mentality he'd secluded himself with. The same seclusion that had only let Allie and Jose inside his close circle of confidence and had never let anyone else get close after what'd happened with his parents.

He wanted to start over, and this was his chance.

But moving back to the present, he couldn't ignore what'd just happened. Looking over the title he'd acquired, he was excited to try out what powers the warlock-type character could give him.

[This chosen class title has been opened to you:

Novice Warlock (Class Title) (Trait): +1 Willpower, +2 Intelligence, and +2 other stat points of your choice per level. Social penalty: -5 base Charisma. Allows demonic contact; two contracts are available with this class.

Note: Choosing this class will enlist your very first demonic servant. You may only choose one demonic servant for the trial's purposes.

Do you wish to accept or decline this class title?]

Really? A social penalty? What did that even mean? It hadn't talked about that earlier!

But he picked yes anyway.

[Novice Warlock class received.]

[Starter packs are now available. Every starter pack comes with a crude cultist's robe, a cloak, a basic survival kit, and a backpack. Choose from the following:

—Dual Poisoned Daggers (iron)—12 damage, 30% chance to apply poison
—Basic Casting Staff—4 damage, 12% mana regeneration, +3 magic damage
—Crude Scythe—17 damage, +5 Unholy damage, 18% chance to apply Amplified Bleeding
—Minor Amulet of Protection—rechargeable, applies a temporary shield worth double wearer's health. One of one charges.

Starter ability tomes are now available. You may only select two, then your five-day condensed time period to learn these spells will begin. Choose from the following:

—Wretched Snare [Unholy], Tier 1—fire snares of black magic that deal damage over time
—Create Shadowling [Shadow], Tier 1—create temporary shadow beasts that attack your enemies
—Miasmic Bolt [Death], Tier 1—high-damage, high-speed, long-range attack
—Extradimensional Chains [Depraved], Tier 1—summon rooting chains from selected points in space to target your enemies

—Wall of Hellfire [Infernal], Tier 1—create a barrier of hell's flames

—Bloody Razors [Blood], Tier 1—summon spinning discs of crimson with minor lock-on abilities to slightly adjust for enemy movements

Starter minions are now available. Upon death, minions may be resummoned up to one day later by paying the blood price. You may currently only select one:

—Succubus, Unholy, Level 1—caster demon, good crowd control and debuffs, moderate damage. [16 Willpower required]
—Shadow Fiend, Shadow, Level 1—fast and mobile, stealthy, good for assassinations [17 Willpower required]
—Imp, Infernal, Level 1—mobile, physically weak but high ranged damage and a very high intellect [13 Willpower required]
—Cinder Soul, Infernal, Level 1—ethereal demon that can fly and is unaffected by physical attacks but must attack at close range [11 Willpower required]
—Shadow Monarch, Shadow, Level 1—caster demon, very high damage output, very long range, very high cooldowns on abilities [18 Willpower required]
—Ravager, Blood, Level 1—physically strong, passive regeneration, good for tanking, slow and dumb [10 Willpower required]
—Blood Weaver, Blood, Level 1—very fast arachnid variation of demon, stealthy, good crowd control, fragile, smart [14 Willpower required]

Each of the potential minions had a Willpower cost… Interesting.

And he didn't even know if he had enough Willpower to contract any of these creatures. Focusing on the words *Status Page*, he willed his own information into a hologram screen that appeared right ahead of where he stood…and he was a little surprised at how lopsided a lot of his stats were.

Go figure.

[Riven Thane's Status Page:
• Level 1
• Pillar Orientations: Unholy Foundation
• Traits: Race: Human, Class: Novice Warlock, Breath of Malignancy (???)
• Abilities: Blessing of the Crow (Unholy)

- **Stats: 8 Strength, 8 Sturdiness, 19 Intelligence, 10 Agility, 1 Luck, -4 Charisma, 3 Perception, 18 Willpower, 9 Faith**
- **Equipped Items: Basic Cloak (1 def)]**

He finished looking his status sheet over and frowned at a very particular part of it. Breath of Malignancy was listed as one of his traits, and it was completely unfamiliar to him. What was that supposed to be? The page gave not even a hint, even going as far as to have question marks concerning what it actually did.

Well, at least he wouldn't have any problems obtaining one of the minions. He was slightly disappointed that there weren't any martial arts, but spells were more than okay with him. He preferred magic over physical abilities anyway.

CHAPTER 8

He looked over the items list first, choosing the Crude Scythe for a couple reasons despite his regrets on wanting the mana regeneration from the staff or the protection of the amulet. Of course, this was all assuming that *mana* was essentially what powered *magic*—based on previous lore from Earth. The first reason was that he wouldn't have much mana yet, and if he ran out by spamming abilities, he'd be left with what—exactly? A stick or his fists if he chose the staff or amulet. The daggers would be nice in that regard, too, as they did good physical damage like the scythe, but they lacked range and Riven lacked any experience in really serious fighting besides a couple brawls or gang fights he'd gotten into over the years. It certainly wasn't significant enough for him to feel comfortable using daggers here where people could use magic. Also, the scythe gave a bonus to Unholy damage—which was a category he had now chosen.

—Crude Scythe—17 damage, +5 Unholy damage, 18% chance to apply Amplified Bleeding

That brought him to the next choices: his two abilities. He'd already decided what he wanted before he'd selected the scythe, and he was relatively certain it was a good combination.

The first ability tome he picked was both a crowd-control and damage-over-time ability.

—Wretched Snare [Unholy], Tier 1—fire snares of black magic that deal damage over time

This would hopefully give him some versatility and the ability to lock down opponents, especially if an enemy chose a tanking or close-combat minion to attack him. The scythe would also increase the snare's damage done over time by an average of five.

The second ability tome he chose was Bloody Razors.

—Bloody Razors [Blood], Tier 1—summon spinning discs of crimson with minor lock-on abilities to slightly adjust for enemy movements

He specifically chose this ability due to the lock-on effect it had. He was unsure of how accurate his aim would be, so this would hopefully compensate. He needed to make sure he actually hit his opponent instead of wasting all his mana missing when he'd had relatively no time to practice the spells.

[Tomes have been chosen and will be presented to you upon time warp. Please choose the rest of your selections. Once you have been introduced to your demonic servant, your time warp will commence and the battle between upstart Chalgathi's Chosen will commence.]

This brought him to what was probably the most important choice for his upcoming battle: a minion companion. As for which minion he wanted to begin with—the options that caught his eye most were Succubus, Shadow Fiend, Ravager, and Blood Weaver.

Honestly, he was ashamed to admit that he was very curious about how the succubus would turn out, but Mama didn't raise no simp. So…with a sigh…he declined the option. At least for now, because he already had one crowd-control ability of his own, and the message pertaining to the succubus seemed geared toward that category…even though it truly, truly caused him pain to turn the succubus down. His Latin maid and other related fantasies would have to wait for now.

The Shadow Fiend was very interesting to him, but looking around his flat, floating island, he couldn't see any real objects or obstacles the creature could use to its advantage pertaining to stealthy moves. Maybe that wouldn't matter, but he didn't want to risk it.

The Ravager was a really interesting choice. Riven could use a tank, as this class of his was probably very weak defensively. The Ravager even had passive regeneration! That was a huge plus, but the description also called it slow and dumb. So…it was basically a brutish creature of some sort. Slow was definitely a negative, but would being dumb be a huge hindrance to Riven if he was trying to use it as a meat shield? He wasn't sure.

Then there was the Blood Weaver. Riven didn't like that the description called it fragile, but everything else about the arachnid screamed *this is great!* to him. It was very fast, stealthy, smart, and had good crowd control. Surely that wouldn't be a bad pick, would it?

Truthfully, though, it was mostly a guessing game, as these descriptions gave very little in terms of information. Wanting them all, he eventually ended up choosing the Blood Weaver…and hoped that it wasn't a mistake that would cost him his life here in the next twenty minutes or so.

—Blood Weaver, Blood, Level 1—A very fast arachnid variation of demon, stealthy, good crowd control, fragile, smart

[You have selected Blood Weaver. Please choose from the two available Blood Weaver demons that have chosen to accept your request:]

In a flash, Riven was staring at a pair of realistic holograms of two different spiders. The first was a pitch-black spider the size of a hound with silver fangs, two red eyes instead of eight that looked like rubies, and similar red patches painted along its body. She had twelve long and slender legs, and they each came down to a sharp point. She looked very pretty, even though Riven had always hated spiders, and there was an elegance to it that he hadn't expected. Its name was Athela.

[Athela:
—Blood Weaver Demon, Level 1, Female
—Starting Skills: 1—Bloody Strings (crowd control), 2—Necrotic Venom (stamina-draining effect and damage over time)
—Trait gifted to you upon choosing this demon: Adrenaline Junkie— you find yourself teeming with energy, and your muscles pump blood faster than ever in response to the bodily change. +15% to Agility.]

The next Blood Weaver was rather different in its presentation. Its coating was black, with orange spikes down its back up to its head, and it was a little larger. It had an extra pair of fangs, one of which dripped acid, but it, too, had a pair of similar red eyes to Athela—and it, too, had twelve legs instead of eight. Its name was Veriksha.

[Veriksha:
—Blood Weaver Demon, Level 1, Male
—Starting Skills: 1—Bloody Strings (crowd control), 2—Acid Spray (ranged damage)
—Trait gifted to you upon choosing this demon: Thermal Insides—you have 90% increased resistance to cold weather and cold-based abilities.]

The choice was a rather hard one. Athela's starting skills were about the same as Veriksha's, though Veriksha did have a ranged attack and Athela didn't—Athela's blood venom and therefore close combat seemed to be more potent. At least that's what he got out of the description.

Veriksha's Thermal Insides trait was interesting, though he didn't look favorably on it when comparing it to Athela's Adrenaline Junkie trait. Thermal Insides would basically make him immune to cold weather or cold-based attacks, while the Adrenaline Junkie trait made him faster with an outright percentage. The problem with Thermal Insides was that it only helped him in very specific situations, and Adrenaline Junkie would help him all the time.

So that's what sealed the deal for him, and he selected Athela as his first minion choice.

[Your pact with Athela has been sealed under the watchful eye of the administrator. The demonic seal representing Athela will be etched into your flesh, and your body has been restored to perfect health. Congratulations on obtaining your new demonic minion.]

[Demonic contracts enable you to revive your demons at the significant cost of a blood price that will ever increase the stronger your servants become, but Holy resurrection magics won't be able to bring them back. Holy healing magics or buffs will have zero effect on them. You have two minutes to introduce yourselves.]

In a flash of light, the holograms were gone, and in their place a red pentagram with a spider in the center was etched into the ground in front of him.

Then he lurched forward, grimacing as light of a similar color began etching itself into his skin. He looked down, gritting his teeth as a numbing, chilling cold blossomed along his sternum. Again the symbol of a spider was drawn first, and it was then surrounded by a red pentagram that remained inked into his skin as he got yet another notification.

[The demonic seal etched into your flesh may be touched and concentrated on to unsummon or resummon your minion from the nether realms. This applies to any future demonic minions as well, and again, congratulations on obtaining your first demonic servant.]

The tattoo was rather neat now that he looked at it some more and the pain had gone away, but he didn't have too much time to appreciate it. A moment later, Athela began to rise out of the ground in the center of the pentagram. The creature was exactly as the hologram had depicted her—a large red-and-black spider that was a rather pretty creature for an arachnid, which was odd, considering how he'd always thought most spiders looked disgusting. Athela's blood-tipped legs tapped rapidly in excitement as she looked around, and as her two red eyes settled on him, she lifted the two front legs and spread her fangs while getting up on her hind legs. "Hi, there, Master! How's your day going?"

Riven was taken aback. The spider could talk? The voice was high-pitched, feminine, and was the equivalent to a soft summer's breeze or wind chimes—it was nice, pleasant to hear, and he couldn't help but chuckle. Not only was the spider very pretty for an animal, but even her voice was pleasant and friendly?

He gave Athela a mixed expression of confusion and amusement before getting up and walking over to the dog-size arachnid. Extending a hand and shaking one of her rather cold, sharpened front legs, he smiled down as she clicked her mandibles together. "You're rather cute. How'd I get so lucky with my minion choice?"

He could have sworn that the spider flushed pink for a moment before she shook his hand vigorously with dramatic affect.

"Now, now, human, I can't have you hitting on me right after summoning me. We're different species and it wouldn't work out."

Riven stifled a laugh, and he felt himself relax as he heard the clicking laughter of the arachnid when Athela got back down to all twelve legs. "Seriously, though, you're not what I expected. At least when concerning your...demeanor."

CHAPTER 9

Athela looked around the small island, gazing up at some of the other floating islands in the starlit sky and then down to the crashing waves of the sea below. Then she looked back up to him with a confused expression and poked him with a foot. "So… What is this place?"

Riven shrugged, put his hands on his hips, and yawned loudly. "Beats me. Something about the quest for Chalgathi's Lineage. Know anything about it?"

The spider raised a leg, paused, and then slowly retracted it while shaking her head. "No…no, I don't. I have never been to the mortal realms before."

"Well, apparently I'm supposed to fight to the death with another person here soon in order to keep my class."

"Oh, really?" The spider perked up and widened her mandibles with a malevolent hiss and a look that Riven could only describe as a spider smile. She used animated gestures with her fangs, abdomen, and legs to describe her next thoughts. She looked…hungry as she spoke the words that were turning into a growl. "Who do we get to kill and feed on? I'm starving! Let's GUT them, RIP out their entrails, DRAIN them of fluid, and LAY OUR EGGS in their carved-out corpses! WE WILL BE FEARED!"

She raised her front legs animatedly, continuing to laugh with that same clicking sound she made with her mandibles, and danced on her back legs in a circle. It looked a little bit like a ritualistic dance, but the sight was slightly ridiculous to behold.

Riven slowly examined the creature inch by inch with a mixture of startled disbelief and amusement, this time rethinking his first impression of her. "You really are a demon, aren't you?"

She immediately glared back at him over her little spider shoulder—red eyes sparkling in the moonlight. "And what's that supposed to mean?!"

[The time limit for introductions has come to a close. Time warp for study of tomes is now commencing. You have five days to learn your two chosen spells from the tomes provided: Wretched Snare

and Bloody Razors. During your time here, you will not experience exhaustion or fatigue, and you will not need to sleep. Failing to learn your given spells in the allotted time will result in a disadvantage during the upcoming fight for your life.]

BLIP

In less time that it would take to blink, Riven had been placed in a spacious room of white light, a high ceiling overhead, glowing walls, and a lukewarm interior.

He was quickly getting very tired of being zapped around to different locations at this point.

A timer of 120 hours started counting down in the ceiling above him, indicating the time he had left to learn these spells. In front of him was a long wooden table with two books laid flat: one, with a burgundy cover, was titled *Bloody Razors* with what looked like a circular, six-bladed red throwing star on the front of it, while the other was titled *Wretched Snare* and had a black-and-gray cover depicting something like an ancient fishing net.

A red velvet armchair appeared out of thin air seconds later, placing itself softly on the lightly glowing white ground with an echo across the cavernous room. Lastly, a target dummy made of clay appeared at the opposite end of the room from where the armchair, table, and books were.

Cocking his head to one side and glancing one more time around the room to make sure he wasn't missing anything, he pulled the chair out and took a seat at the table. He stared at the books one after the other before shrugging and picking up the *Wretched Snare* tome first.

The book was heavy for its size and likely held a hundred or so pages. Opening it and flipping through, he saw the yellowed parchment contained within was filled with schematics, drawings, explanations, and applications of the spell. It appeared there was not just one single use for this spell, but numerous ones depending on his own creativity.

What had him most interested though was the beginning of the book, where it described basic magical theory in detail. As he started reading, his excitement began to grow until he was fully immersed within the material set before him. An hour in, his excitement had spiked even higher. All the daydreams he'd had as a kid were finally coming true. Despite his possible impending death, if this was how he had to die, then so be it! He was going to be a fucking wizard!

Prologue: An Introduction to Basic Spell Theory

You have probably already acquainted yourself with the basic rules and tenets of spell casting by now. But I will nevertheless give a brief description of what is expected when undergoing spell casting of the Unholy variant.

If this is your first attempt to acquire a spell, know that as soon as you have succeeded in fully understanding the spell to the point of system acknowledgment, your soul will undergo a permanent change—one that necessitates acquiring mana to cast spells within the pillars of this universe.

All skills can be placed into one of three categories. Those that use mana, or spells. Those that use stamina, or martial arts. And lastly those that use divinity, or miracles.

Some abilities may overlap with one another. For example, Infernal from the Unholy pillar, Sun from the Holy pillar, and Volcano from the Fae pillar. Infernal abilities often utilize hellfire, Sun abilities often utilize blessed fire, and Volcano abilities utilize elemental fires. They may sometimes look the same, but their underlying properties and origins of drawing power are different. They stem from different sources of energy and have vastly different effects upon the body, mind, and soul. Each and every skill is assigned to one of the pillars or subpillars that create the foundations for the universe, and each pillar is a different pathway to utilize the pure-energy component of the soul.

Then there is the topic of cooldowns. Cooldowns are the time it takes for a pillar to reset itself after taking the form of a certain spell and utilizing that ability. Sometimes cooldowns can happen out of nowhere—meaning you'll activate an ability and suddenly find yourself unable to reuse the same ability for a limited amount of time. Other times you'll get lucky and be able to cast numerous times in a row as long as your mana, stamina, or divinity doesn't deplete. When a pillar takes a certain shape and releases that shape, it can become rigid and stagnant—blocking the flow of mana for a certain amount of time. This is the essence of what a cooldown is, and it can be worked around by utilizing different parts of the same pillar, casting smaller-scope versions of the same ability for decreased amounts of cooldown, or you can increase your resource expenditure and simply push through the cooldown limiter at the expense of more mana, stamina, or divinity being cast. Just know that for a beginner mage, you'll likely run into times when you'll be unable to cast repeatedly if your soul's pillars become too rigid after repeated use of various spells.

Magic tiers, or spell tiers, differ slightly from stamina-related martial arts or divinity-related miracles, so what knowledge is written down here only applies to spells.

There are seven tiers of spell casting, with Tier 1 being the most basic and Tier 7 being the most advanced. As the author of this book, I have only ever been able to acquire spells up to Tier 3, though I am sure if you were to find masters of a certain type of magic they could provide you with more knowledge on Tiers 4 and 5. Tiers 6 and 7 are the stuff of legends, and I doubt you'll ever even bear witness to one of those spells—much less cast them yourself.

Tier 1 spells are the easiest to learn, the fastest to cast, and they require three things. They simply require you to channel mana through your soul pillar. Not divinity, not stamina, but mana. Experiment if you must between the three to get a feel of what you need when channeling your soul's energy, but the spell you're trying to cast won't react if you have the wrong power source. Then, while having the proper vision of the spell you wish to create, you must have a key understanding of how the spell links to the astral plane around us. Mana channeling, vision—sometimes known as intent—and understanding are the three basic requirements of any and all spells, and without these things you will never be able to create even the most simple of spells.

For a proper mana channeling, you will have to focus on the pillars within yourself and draw the pure energy through those pillars like water through a sieve to convert the energy into the needed mana. Note that if you do not have the required pillar, it simply won't work. You'll need to acquire that pillar's blessing.

If the pillar even accepts you, that is. You'll need an affinity for the pillar as well, and though everyone has at least one affinity, it is never guaranteed which ones they'll be. You may want to utilize the Fae Foundational Pillar but could only have the Harmony Foundational Pillar available to you; sometimes it's just luck of the draw.

For proper vision—this inner vision is how you wish the mana to present itself when it exits your soul. This requires focus, a complex picture of what you wish to form through you as a conduit, but it is often the easiest of the three things needed.

Lastly, for proper understanding, this can be gained by learning through tomes of people who have perfected the spells already and opportunistic visions given to you by the system that may be deciphered. Upon leveling up, the system may reward you with such visions, and it will be your duty to understand them and learn from them as best you can. If you fail to do so, it is your loss, as they will likely not be presented again. There is a third way to acquire proper understanding, and this is through experimentation...but it is often a very dangerous road to take and can lead to one's death or worse.

Tier 2 spells aren't necessarily more powerful than Tier 1 spells, as the power of a spell in large part depends upon one's magic stat affinity as well as the amount of mana they pour into it, but the higher tiers are usually more potent, and they're definitely more complex. Tier 2 spells work the same way Tier 1 spells do and have the same previous requirements, plus one additional requirement. They, too, require mana channeling, vision, and understanding—but Tier 2 spells incorporate very specific movements of one's body that works very much like a key fitting into its lock. Though instead of a physical key being placed into a physical lock, you are using those motions to unravel certain astral bindings that relate to the spell you wish to use.

For most humanoids, Tier 2 spells are therefore cast with hand gestures. Hands are a perfect means of completing complex motions at a fast pace, but there are many other creatures or even monsters that use different aspects of their body to undertake the same motions at faster or slower speeds depending upon the caster. Hands are by no means a must; you could even cast with your toes or nose if you had the skill to do it, but hands certainly make it easier.

Tier 3 spells require the previous components mentioned plus yet another addition to the list. Tier 3 spells require mana channeling, vision, understanding, specific movements, and finally they require spoken recitals as well.

Think of a recipe in your mother's cookbook back when you were a child. It was a list of ingredients, a means by which you created that perfect pasta or cake. This is the same concept by which Tier 3 spells are performed. You speak the correct words in the correct order of spell casting, and you receive the proper end result.

As the last portion of this prologue: I will be discussing channeling and items that help you channel. These usually but not always include staves, charms, totems, scythes, pendants, crystal balls, and wands. These items have usually been enchanted with mana lines or inscriptions and have been shaped properly with proper materials of various affinities to create conduits that amplify spells in a certain way. Some amplify mana output, making your spells more powerful. Others reduce cooldown, allowing you to cast spells more frequently or cast more of the same spell at one time. Some are only oriented toward one type of mana, while others are oriented toward all types of mana. Some of these items can recharge your natural mana replenishment, while others utilize your mana at higher costs in order to perform specific functions such as special abilities innate to the item. Some of them don't even need to be held and can activate spells on their own.

Regardless of which it is, channeling conduits of various types will no doubt present opportunities to you that can be capitalized on. Staves, scythes, or wands can be used in place of your hands to perform gestures needed for Tier 2 and above spells as well, so do not think that utilizing a handheld item of this caliber will cause you to underperform at the higher tiers of spell casting. In many cases, these conduits can be used to even circumvent a portion of the hand motions or even chants of the Tier 3 spells simply by being held in your hand…if it is the right conduit for the job. In the end, creating one of these conduits yourself often takes a lot of practice but is very doable if you have the right skill set. If you do not, it is highly recommended that you find someone who does and use them to better yourself, as in many ways these items can increase your proficiency with spell casting, much like a pen can help you write better on a page than a stick could. Especially when you start delving into the high-quality conduits—that's where things really start getting tricky.

CHAPTER 10

Riven flipped yet another page, curiosity getting the better of him as he continued to read without pause or boredom. Allie and Jose would have loved this kind of stuff, and he couldn't help but wonder what they were going through right now. His mind began to wander, and worry set in about whether or not they were okay. They needed to survive their own trials in order to be reunited with him, according to the system's early message when he'd first split off, but he had no way of telling whether or not their trials were just as ridiculous as his own or if they were having an easier time.

No, he couldn't think about that. Back to the present, and he put his nose to the grindstone for learning. The prologue for the text had indeed been helpful, but there were still many questions concerning the actual spell he needed to learn rather than just the backbone fundamentals.

The spell Wretched Snare had a vision that he could produce easily enough just by the way the spell was drawn out in the book. Pictures of a black, sticky, needle-laced net of Unholy magic were drawn on the parchment rather well. However, the book also described how he needed to encompass the thought of burning, the thought of being sticky, the thought of ensnaring an enemy into the vision rather than just what one physically saw. Vision included not only sight, but also purpose and meaning—which was something Riven hadn't necessarily anticipated upon the initial description in the fundamentals section.

The channeling of his mana wasn't too hard to do, and that might have been due to the fact that he'd already gained the Unholy pillar via the blessing he'd received in the maze. Blessing of the Crow had imbued him with the pillar in a vision of what Riven now knew without a shadow of a doubt was the inherent changing of his soul. He'd inherently felt it might be that, but it'd just been guesses made upon introspection until now. What he hadn't known was that the pillar, that bustling orb of green, crimson, and black lights that had attached itself to the white core of his center self, was actually a type of converter. One that would convert his body's pure energy into mana that he could then use for the spell he was trying to learn.

He was curious about how the next spell would work, but at a bare minimum he assumed learning Bloody Razors would be harder to do because it was in a more specialized pillar. He had the Unholy pillar already, so a subpillar shouldn't be too hard to acquire? Or maybe it came along as a package deal since he had the major category already? Then again, he did have a high affinity for blood magic, at least according to earlier prompts. It was hard to tell from the pages of the book.

Thirty-six hours had passed in that well-lit room, and he was beginning to sweat with the exertions of pushing mana through his body. He'd identified the inner source of his power, his soul, through a good amount of meditation and direction from the book. He could feel it, a presence inside him that pulsed every time he tried to force forward the energies that'd been so foreign to him in the beginning—but now that this power was within him and available to him, it made its presence known as a stark outlier from how his body had felt previous to leaving Earth.

It was like he'd grown an entirely new organ, almost akin to lungs. But instead of air, they breathed power.

The energy had been very hard to deal with at first. He could feel it, twisting and turning as new mana channels were dug out and created through his physical body and his soul. It'd been painful, but he'd endured—and now the hot, smoldering collection of raw power that tingled at his very fingertips struggled to be let free against some mental barrier he couldn't quite place his finger on yet.

Again he pushed, sending out a wave of rushing power that caused his hands to convulse…but otherwise he got nowhere with it.

What was he doing wrong?

Riven closed his eyes in a meditative pose while sitting on his red velvet armchair, concentrating on his inner core and feeling the roiling energy within his soul vibrate upon his mental touch. Slowly, ever so slowly, he began to draw the energy through his pillar—converting the energy into mana. He drew the energy forward from his core, into his body, farther into his hands—and could literally feel it heating up the skin along his fingertips on either side.

All right…now for the vision again.

Within his mind's eye, he began to focus on what he wanted to create. A net of black, writhing needles that would ensnare his enemies, burn his enemies and keep them at bay.

The mana began to condense—welling up into shimmering black balls of energy that floated over either hand. Smiling to himself for at least getting this far, he began to push harder on his mana reserves.

The black balls expanded outward, ripping apart as tiny needlelike appendages began lengthening and withdrawing over and over again until the black mana had formed strings very much like a net. Each one of his hands contained a square, stringy, four-by-four-foot net of the Unholy power—and it continued to grow to an even greater size until at the very last second they each popped.

The mana dispersed into thin air. He hadn't been able to stabilize it again, and he felt the energy leave his body. It was yet another failed attempt at the spell that caused him to growl with irritation.

Something here was very wrong.

He began flipping through the book again. He was certain he was channeling correctly; his vision was good, too, so there must be something wrong with his understanding of the spell.

He came up with another hypothesis, which absolutely failed minutes later. Then he came up with two more ideas, both of which failed in turn over the next hour despite many attempts. But it was a passage from one of the very last pages of the tome that caught his attention in the end—something that he'd overlooked before.

He put his finger on the line and read aloud. "'Using this Wretched Snare, you must imbue your mana with the concept of pain. You must manifest pain into not only your vision, but also connect that vision with the true essence of what it means to be tortured with mind and body.'"

He blinked and repeated the last part of that line. "…with mind and body."

Previously he'd been thinking about how pain could be inflicted upon someone in the form of physical pain, focusing on back when he'd been a kid and burned his hand on a kitchen stove. He hadn't been putting much effort into imbuing the magic with the idea of what mental pain could accomplish through this spell…so it was time to give it a shot.

Moving through his memories, he didn't have to think hard on what the most torturous ones had been over the course of his life. There were three of them, each one a significant weight upon his shoulders that even now caused his body to ache when thinking about them. But it was the memories of his family going missing that instantly sprang to the forefront of his mind; it was the hardest to cope with as he sat there in sullen silence contemplating his life.

He quickly snapped out of it, though, using the remnants of those memories in conjunction with a physical burning sensation. He utilized proper channeling once again, forcing the soul energy through his Unholy pillar. Then he added vision, commanding the black orbs to begin forming nets above his outstretched hands. As they slowly expanded, he incorporated his new understanding of what this spell's purpose was…to imbue these nets not only with physical pain, but also to afflict his enemies with emotional pain as well.

Lo and behold, the magic stabilized.

With a low hiss, the nets of black energy expanded to over six feet in diameter and erupted from his outstretched palms. They shot across the room, landing two dozen yards away and splattering against the floor with an acidic sizzling sound while the black needles of the nets bubbled and writhed.

[You have successfully learned the spell Wretched Snare. Congratulations! This spell has been added to your status page.]

"HELL YEAH!"

Riven shot his fists into the air with a hoot and did a very brief victory dance with a self-satisfied nod. He repeated the spell once, twice, and then thrice while aiming at the clay dummy a little ways off. Each time the nets would expand after being fired, and the sticky needles would contact the dummy before biting in and wrapping around the object. When the acidic black magic ate all the way through the dummy a couple dozen seconds later, a new dummy would then appear.

It took him a while to get his head on straight after that. The excitement of being able to *really* cast magic was intoxicating, despite his fucked-up situation and the potential of a life-and-death battle headed his way. It was *insanely* cool, so at the very least he'd go out with a bang!

Riven settled back down and pushed aside the *Wretched Snare* tome, pulling over the other tome that read *Bloody Razors* with the six-pronged red throwing star on the front. The introduction to basic blood magic was overall the same as the other had been, with a few key exceptions to the earlier paragraphs. After that, it got more complicated.

Just like all other blood-related spells, the focus you should be keying in on is the concept of remaking blood in your body's own image. Cause the material within your blood to multiply, redistribute that blood into the environment, and cycle it into your soul's Blood subpillar to simultaneously convert it into mana. If you cannot focus in on the Blood subpillar, you may use the Unholy pillar as a substitute—though it may be harder to do it this way and is more costly in terms of mana consumption.

Like many of the elemental pillars, utilizing your blood abilities can actually allow you to create ambient mana from the surrounding environment. Namely, you can draw out power from the blood of your fallen enemies. If there are corpses nearby, use them. This allows you to cast spells in the Blood subpillar at a reduced or even free rate if your mana manipulation is good enough. This aspect of using your environment to benefit, enhance, or even pay the mana cost of your blood spells is the same reason why the elemental subpillars of the Fae category are so popular despite their rigid utilization and relative lack of diversity. Just like a water mage can use nearby water, so too can you use nearby bodies to fuel your blood spells.

Otherwise you're looking at creating mana-imbued blood from thin air. Creating it by utilizing your own body's crimson liquid as a blueprint is the easiest application of this branch of magic, but this will obviously be more mana-expensive than using the environment around you, such as using the fallen soldiers on a battlefield for a highly reduced mana cost.

But utilizing the environmental factors is a long time coming and will take a lot of practice. Probably years or even decades, especially if you're a beginner. In the meantime, rotate the mana and sharpen the mana's vessel in your vision for eviscerating your enemies.

CHAPTER 11

Ah, so he did have to acquire the subpillars one by one. Or if he didn't, he'd at least be utilizing these spells via the Unholy pillar and paying a greater price to cast them.

Riven immediately got to work. Now that he had a solid base of knowledge to work off in terms of spell casting, he was able to progress at a much more rapid pace.

Even without the Blood subpillar currently within him, he was still able to force mana out of his soul and into his palms along the mana channels that his initial pillar had carved into him. Though he didn't direct it through the Unholy pillar itself, rather, this new flavor of related mana skirted along the edges of the Unholy pillar instead. The mana channels were still there and the energy of his soul began to accumulate…albeit it had a different feeling to it than pure Unholy mana did. It was a little more…translucent? He couldn't really describe the feeling otherwise.

He'd bet on what the previous book had said, though. As long as he had a complete vision and a good understanding of what he wanted, the system should provide him with the correct pillar given his will. The system would find its proper match as long as his soul had enough space left for the proper pillar, provided he had the affinity for this blood spell type.

He closed his eyes, sitting cross-legged on the velvet armchair as he concentrated on the vision of what he wanted while the timer overhead continued ticking down.

Visions of what had been drawn in the book entered his thoughts first. A spinning disc of serrated, sharpened, solidified crimson. A willingness and wantingness to hunt down his enemies, to cut them apart with the blades he would summon. A sea of red, a battlefield of the dead, a liquid that gave life, and a pack of leeches swarming toward prey. These images were merged into one to create the essence of what blood truly was. He lastly combined all this with what he knew of blood and cellular molecules from basic biology back home: the shape of the cells, the oxygen they carried, the other components such as platelets and plasma. They began to settle, forming a complex, flowing tapestry.

Much to Riven's delight, the energy within his soul immediately began to respond. And to his utter bafflement, the Blood subpillar was incredibly easy to obtain. He was a downright natural—beyond natural, even, as it actually began to embrace his soul like a warm, long-lost cousin, and this blood magic seemed to be at home within his body, even more so than the Unholy pillar was.

[You have an impossibly absurd affinity toward the Blood subpillar, with a perfect affinity score of 100%, and it will accept your body as a conduit since you wish to utilize its power. You are now oriented toward the Blood subpillar, and your blood spells will cost far less mana and have much more power output than if you were to only utilize them through the broader-spectrum Unholy pillar.]

His mind went dark as warm tendrils of red light began to wriggle their way up and around his limbs, his chest, and his neck—creeping all the way into his eyes as he let out a silent scream.

He saw it again—the myriad of memories that were bits and pieces of his life. The memories that made him who he was—all jumbled together just as it'd been the first time when he'd received Blessing of the Crow and had acquired the Unholy pillar. Only this time, instead of a mixture of the crimson, green, and black lights that symbolized Unholy energy, this time the energy was a pure, bright red. The wash of crimson power slowly drifted through the pockets of memories that made up his life, casually forcing them aside until it entered the central pocket of his soul, where a bright-white orb of glowing light glistened in the very center. Attached to that brighter, larger orb was the conduit of the Unholy pillar—stabilizing the left side as it pulsed with ropes of its own energy connecting the two objects.

The Blood subpillar didn't bother stopping. Instead it continued to drift slowly onward, passing the Unholy pillar and his soul core effortlessly until it came over to the opposite side of his soul like a snowflake coming to settle down upon a silent, red-laden hill.

Tendrils of crimson came out and connected the Blood subpillar to Riven's soul a moment later, calmly stabilizing the connection between them as Riven's pain faded away into nothingness. Looking at it, he sensed a supreme state of calm... a sense of assuredness, as if the Blood subpillar had been waiting to embrace him for his entire life just to let him know that it was where it was meant to be.

His eyes flashed red for just a brief second when they snapped open, return-ing to the normal green an instant later as mana surged out of his soul's Blood subpillar and entered the energy floating above his outstretched hands. The energy immediately condensed, crystallized, and roared to life as two spinning discs of solid red bloomed before him. They blurred forward, orienting themselves on their own and adjusting course to make a direct impact with the clay dummy's head. The head was ripped open, flinging bits and pieces of the dummy everywhere. It was like a knife going through butter, and Riven was completely taken aback by just how fast and easy learning this new spell had been.

[You have successfully learned the spell Bloody Razors. Congratulations! This spell has been added to your status page.]

"Impossibly absurd affinity, huh?" Riven scratched his chin and raised his eyebrows, feeling rather giddy with himself and not being able to hide his growing smile as his heart began to race. "I suppose 100 percent affinity is a rather rare thing? What about my other pillars—what are their affinities?"

Unfortunately for Riven, he didn't have an answer to that question just yet.

He spent the remaining two days practicing with the new spells he'd acquired. The Wretched Snare could travel somewhere in between ten and fifteen yards accurately before completely misfiring or falling to the ground, and his Bloody Razors would travel three times that length before losing momentum at his current level. By the end of it, he felt a true sense of accomplishment. Frankly, he couldn't believe he was actually casting magic, and his newfound excitement over being a mage was far outweighing the minimal unease he felt about the upcoming battle. And as the last few seconds of his time in the alternate space fell away, he finally found himself back where he'd previously been on the drifting islands. It was still nighttime, as it'd been when he'd left, but the spell tomes he'd been using to practice his magical arts were now gone, as if they'd never been there in the first place.

[You have successfully acquired the spells Wretched Snare and Bloody Razors.]

[Two minutes until fighting begins.]

Athela the Blood Weaver demon was back with him, too, though the dog-size red-and-black spider was blinking at him curiously with both of her eyes like she'd just asked a question to which he'd never given an answer.

Now that he'd selected his options and obtained his spells, his promised outfit began to bloom around his body as a series of items were put into place. The crude cultist robes he'd been given were exactly that—a worn, dark outfit that was very fitted to his body. It covered his arms down to his wrists and had an additional hood attached to the back, with a flaring gown and cloth pants underneath. The robes fit nicely underneath his cloak, though he had to tuck the new hood into his first one so it wouldn't scrunch up.

He got some boots that were well fitted, too—though they looked ragged and worn. Next an oddly styled backpack of brown leather flashed into existence along the ground. The way it sat made it seem full, and a quick look confirmed that it did indeed have a basic survival kit: including a fishing net, a bronze hatchet, flint and steel, bandages, a vial filled with red liquid that he could only assume was a health potion, and a small rolled-up blanket.

In his hands he felt a sudden heaviness, which was accompanied by the materialization of a long, rusted scythe about five feet in length with a thin, curved blade at the top measuring about two feet. Taking the weapon in both hands and waving it around, he found the balance to be what he'd expected—but it was a little more awkward than he would have liked. It was leatherbound around the middle of the wooden shaft, devoid of any real decoration otherwise.

[One minute until fighting begins.]

"Oooooooohhh!" Athela crowed, rapidly tapping all twelve arachnid legs with excitement as the notification popped up in front of her as well. "LET'S DO THIS! FIGHT TO THE DEATH, YEAH!"

He spared the demon a glance. Athela didn't seem to know Riven had been gone all that time. At least she didn't ask any questions about why he'd been gone or where he'd gone to. The five days of his practicing may have only been seconds here.

He steeled his nerves.

It was time, and just to make sure that everything was working right, he gave his spells a final try outside the practice room. Raising his free left hand and aiming across the small floating island, he thought, *Bloody Razors*. Instantaneously, two spinning, serrated discs of crimson each about a foot in diameter materialized in the air on either side of his outstretched hand and shot out in the direction he was pointing.

They were pretty damn fast, and they left thin trails of red liquid in the air behind their blurring paths for brief moments until they slammed into the earth twenty yards away—leaving the grass there torn to shreds in little patches around an indentation the magic had cut into the ground before fizzling away into the air.

They were pretty brutal weapons, and he was eager to see what they could do. Even if it meant killing someone else, he wasn't about to die here in this strange place. Not after just having his world open up with the potential for magic. No…he was going to live.

[**Time is up. Your fight to the death is commencing now. If no winner is announced within ten minutes, both participants will die. If you have bonded companions due to your class choice, upon death your minions will be sent to the nether realm to try and find new masters for further exploration in Elysium.**]

"BRING IT!" his Blood Weaver screamed when she saw the notification and waggled a red and black spider foot his way. "I don't want to go back to the nether realms! We'd better win, you hear me?!"

"You're damn right we're going to win." He gave her an encouraging nod and adjusted his stance to ready himself, but he hadn't noticed the other looming island closing in until right before the two land masses hit.

The cliff faces made impact with a thunderous clap of noise. Rock slammed into rock with a huge boom, shaking both islands in a spray of debris. The ground shuddered and caused him to almost lose his footing, but he planted down firmly and waited for the shock waves to pass. When the dust settled, Riven found himself by some stroke of luck looking at the same bald asshole who'd shoved him and told him to *move it* in the second phase of the trial.

Why is it that bald people were always assholes?

Bald people are the worst.

Riven knew it was petty. He knew it wasn't a good reason to kill the man, but his reason was already set. Riven wanted to live, and even that small amount of injustice, rudeness, and arrogance made it all the easier to grip his scythe more firmly with deadly intent.

The larger bald man had surprisingly enough chosen a caster's staff…but he also had an amulet. Something that Riven didn't understand. How could he have two choices from the items list? Riven had only gotten the scythe. His enemy's staff was long, about five feet in length, and had a gnarled knob end to it. It wasn't anything special, but what Riven found really odd was the necklace around the sneering man's neck. It had a small circular pendant made of white ivory, depicting a carved dragon with emeralds for eyes. The pendant was held up by a black cord of some kind, and the artwork was rather ornate.

Was that really the Minor Amulet of Protection from the items list? Looked rather fancy to be minor.

Aside from that, the other man had chosen a minion that hadn't ever been presented to Riven. Perhaps it was because the other man had chosen necromancer or something similar?

It was a huge, skeletal, zombie wolf. The creature was large, as big as any other wolf from Earth, but it had only patches of rotting flesh or fur with bright-white eyes on glistening bones. The breath from the creature's decrepit lungs came out as a gaseous cloud of green through fangs as it was snarling at Riven with a keen hunger. It looked alien and formidable as it circled its new master protectively. Just by looking at the creature, he guessed it might be able to crush his own spider minion rather easily—being two to three times Athela's size.

The older, taller, balder man sneered Riven's way and spat on the grassy ground between his feet. "We meet again, *pig*."

CHAPTER 12

The words Riven's opponent spoke were rough and filled with intent to kill, though Riven thought the choice of insult rather odd. Still, the look of disgust on his enemy's countenance illuminated by moonlight was more than enough to let Riven know he wouldn't be given any mercy...which again only made the things he had to do easier for Riven to go through with.

But the bald man wasn't done speaking. Or rather, the man was shouting due to the distance between them. He stepped forward to point at Riven with an accusatory posturing while chill winds rustled both men's robes. "You probably have no idea what's really going on here, do you? To think that I would be paired with these worthless fools. How was it that any of you got through the labyrinth to begin with? Has Chalgathi become complacent in who he admits into his chosen? Was it not supposed to be us true cultists who received his graces?"

Riven gave his opponent across the grass a blank stare in return, only shifting slightly when the crisp night breeze blew hard enough to whip his cloak about. This...wasn't going as Riven had expected. It appeared Baldy knew who Chalgathi was? That was weird. And a cult?

Riven knew he had cultist's robes on, but he didn't think that qualified as being a cult member. This guy, though—he was actually claiming to be part of one? How intriguing.

The larger man angrily spat in Riven's direction at the lack of reply and then scoffed in utter disgust. "You probably haven't even figured out how to bring up your status page yet, *have you?* You probably never even experienced *real* magic before this; you're probably one of those people who concentrated on your nine-to-five desk job instead of truly living and thriving in the gift that Elysium sent us as a divine sign of things to come. Pathetic. Utterly pathetic that I spent so much time learning the ins and outs of it all, to be only one of a mere ten within the cult's ranks to make it to the last round. The rest of you are not deserving of this gift, are not deserving of such power in this new world. You all deserve nothing but death, and after having prepared for this moment with years of study to completely master both of my chosen spells, I am confident in my ability to send you into the afterlife. I doubt you were able to master even a fraction of a single ability in the minimal time granted to learn, so perhaps I'll grant you a final gift before your death and allow you to see what a real sorcerer can truly do! Say your last prayers, worm, and balk before my majesty!"

Riven raised a skeptical eyebrow, thoroughly unimpressed with the rambling. It really hadn't been *that* hard to learn those two spells. But a head start? That was rather unfair, though Riven could see no reason why the man would lie to him. Had this guy really taken a years-long head start to learn just two of them? Hmm. That's what it sounded like. Was it supposed to be bragging? Was that some kind of great feat? Riven cocked his head to the side in confusion, briefly opening his mouth to reply but not finding the words. Regardless, now things were definitely on an entirely different level of weird with the monologue. This guy was basically telling him in some insanity-driven speech that he was part of a cult and had been preparing for this weird-ass situation? Upon studying the man's words and attitude, Riven definitely could make out that he was genuinely angry…and the venting seemed more directed to the world around them.

So Riven said the only thing that came to mind and opened his mouth to speak again. "Your potato head shines in the moonlight. There, I said it."

"Huh?"

"You heard me, you bald old fuck."

There was a long silence after that as the other man considered Riven's words with a confused glare, but he then shook his head with a snarl and began to summon magics to his bidding. "I'm only thirty-six! I am nowhere near old, you fucking idiot!"

"More's the pity for your baldness then, you poor, cursed man."

"Silence! I have perfected both spells given to me by Chalgathi far in advance of this trial! You will succumb to my power, and I will bathe in your blood!"

"Well, that's not very nice." Riven frowned to consider the mental image of a literal bloodbath just when shadows began erupting from the man's staff and the brief monologue ended. Condensing and reforming into one another, the shadows quickly created two skulking, terrier-sized quadrupeds from shadow mana. Their bodies flickered in and out of existence, each with two red eyes glaring at him and claws extending as they hissed his way.

Was that the Create Shadowling spell?

[Create Shadowling [Shadow]—create temporary shadow beasts that attack your enemies to do damage. Shadowlings are faster and stronger in dark places.]

Then, remembering how he'd acquired his own first unique ability from the second phase of the quest, Riven grew just slightly more confident.

[Blessing of the Crow (Unholy): Activate this ability up to once per day for an hour's worth of increased Stamina regeneration with a significant boost to Agility.]

It was his only movement ability. Hopefully this would give him a mobility advantage that he could utilize, especially with Athela's new trait imbuing his body with even further speed.

Red sparks of electricity began to flicker to life across his clothes and skin when he mentally activated the blessing. The power began pulsing and shifting to light up the area around him in a sinister shade of crimson, and his body felt invigorated beyond what any stimulant could have done for him back on Earth. The boost empowered Riven with immense amounts of stamina regeneration, speed, and agility—his muscles were literally electrified with might beyond natural human boundaries—and he glared back at the man he'd have to kill just when the shadowlings stopped halfway between them.

The bald man, not recognizing the ability, gave Riven a confused frown, and his features became even angrier as fights began to break out all around them on other floating islands nearby. Blue, red, black, orange, teal, and purple energies began lighting up the night sky around them as screams, explosions, and bestial roars echoed around the chasm between land masses.

The fights had finally begun.

"DIE!" the shiny, hairless man screeched with an angry roar as he finally went on the offensive. Pulsing, neon-teal mana was conjured and then condensed into the size and spherical shape of a baseball, then was flung at a shrieking speed past the two shadow beasts and in Riven's direction.

Riven was rather surprised at just how fucking fast the attack was going, startled even, but he had expected the attack and instinctively pushed mana into the ability of his blessing to empower it further. His mana channels surged with warmth, the crimson lightning arcing about his body radiated outward beyond its stabilized form, and he blurred left.

Thus his body flashed out of the way just in time, and his opponent's spell crashed into the ground a couple feet to the left of where Riven now stood. It was also where Riven had just been. His strained movements emphasized the red lightning trickling along his skin, though the mana pull started to decrease as he calmed down. But he was definitely surprised at the result; he'd never pushed that amount of mana through his channels before, and his knee-jerk reaction to force mana into his activated ability far outweighed his previous sprint through the maze.

The earth and grass exploded and withered right where he'd been a moment before, five feet to his right, and the neon-teal glow faded away to leave a moderately sized hole in the ground that smoked with the remnants of his enemy's mana.

Riven spared the impact site a very brief glance. Was that the miasmic bolt spell? If not, it was at least something similar.

The bald man hissed in disbelief, now sporting a bulging vein across his forehead and focused eyes. "You should not be able to move that fast!"

Athela began to chitter and screech, rushing forward only to be stopped with a hand gesture by Riven. The demon did stop, though she gave him a confused sideways glance. Yet another two miasmic bolts rocketed toward Riven as he tested the waters of his enemy's strength and let him whittle down his mana reserves. Both miasmic bolts left smoking holes in the ground behind him, both of them were dodged even more easily than the first, and then yet another bolt soared past into the air to make impact with another island far off.

It truly was a long-range attack, but this time it was a little too close for comfort. His spells didn't go nearly that far, with the Wretched Snare traveling maybe a dozen or so yards accurately while his Bloody Razors went about three times that length. The distance between the two casters, though? It was farther than that.

Still, if Riven hadn't activated his blessing, he was utterly sure he'd have been unable to dodge these attacks. Riven dodged yet another magical bolt while he got a handle on adjusting the power output for his blessing, and meanwhile he considered his enemy. What the man had said was right—he normally shouldn't be able to move that fast—and even now Riven wasn't 100 percent confident in his ability to continue dodging if they kept on coming or if he was caught up fighting the summoned shadow beasts. Even if it did mean whittling down his enemy's mana, Riven didn't know just how much mana his enemy actually had. It would pose a problem if the man had more mana than Riven did, and although Blessing of the Crow didn't use any mana at a base level, it did utilize a lot of it if he pushed himself to elevate his speed further. So he quickly decided to switch tactics and stopped experimenting. In large part he also attributed his success at dodging the shots to the very animated way the crazed caster would prepare the attacks, basically broadcasting it every time he made a move before he even started channeling the spell.

Not only that, but the combatants were a good ways away from each other—giving Riven time to dodge that he wouldn't have had up close. That being said, his spells were both shorter range than the one this caster was flinging at him, so he'd have to bridge the gap.

With a grunt Riven pushed off—vaulting ahead in a burst of speed and then keeping his blessing at a base level to preserve mana. His Blood Weaver, who'd been watching him curiously after he'd activated the crow's blessing, screeched and raced ahead with him—far outstripping him in speed even when utilizing his boost and passing him by with excitement in her eyes. The fun little Blood Weaver was gone, and in its place was a feral hunter—silver fangs flashing.

"SHRREEEEEEE!"

Panicking at the speed at which the arachnid was gaining ground, the other caster fired off another miasmic bolt that was easily and expertly dodged by the creature. Athela's alien screech hit a higher pitch as the large zombie wolf lunged forward with a roar—trying to snap at the arachnid's legs only to find empty air. Glinting crimson strands of blood silk wrapped around its neck, and the undead creature was yanked back hard to flip over violently when the spider's threads met an end.

Immediately, the spider demon was on top of the wolf's back—and the two monsters were at each other's throats with hisses, roars, shrieks, and flashing teeth in a tumble over the dirt and grass.

Despite the battle going on to Riven's right, he focused on his own opponent. He pushed onward, sprinting faster and faster ahead. He dodged another projectile of glowing miasmic power that seared his cheek, rolled to duck under another, and fired off two Bloody Razors that whipped forward through the air with arcs of crimson flowing out behind them. The caster cursed and, to Riven's amazement, launched an intercepting attack that took one of his razors out midair before getting nicked by the second attack. The caster roared in outrage, and blood started leaking from a deep cut where he'd managed to turn his body at the last second, though the wound in his arm was certainly ugly to look at.

Riven took that opportunity to close the gap even farther and summoned the spell Wretched Snare. Black magic erupted from Riven's outstretched hand as a small globe of black that quickly expanded into a net of cruel needles. It was only partially dodged when the other man frantically kicked off to the left, his trailing leg being hooked by the net's edge. The man screamed as the sharp pieces dug through his pants into his leg, and both his body and mind were assaulted with waves of unholy pain.

The rest of the net slammed into the ground, sticking to both the man and the dirt below like glue as Riven's enemy repeatedly shrieked and tried to fling it off him, to no avail. The black magic was burning the target like acid, and smoke billowed up where the needles of the net had buried themselves. Riven grinned victoriously amid his sprint forward, focused on ending the fight as fast as possible, and his mana channels expanded with another surge of power. He leaned left, kicking off to bypass one of the small shadow beasts, and prepared to cast Bloody Razors when the two black shadow beasts he'd been trying to get around lunged. Their sharp fangs and claws wrapped around his legs, and the power he'd been building up across his fingertips fizzled out in an instant.

WHAM

He slammed face-first into the ground, dropping his scythe and screaming in horrified pain as the temporarily summoned little minions clawed at his ankles and bit into his feet.

"SON OF A BITCH!"

Cursing and kicking at them, he managed to get one off just as he saw another miasmic bolt being shot his way. Unfortunately he didn't have time to dodge and took it to the shoulder, screaming even more loudly as a chunk of his deltoid was ripped out and fried in a spray of blood.

CHAPTER 13

A second later and Athela was there, flashing by and rapid-firing hardened *Bloody Strings* from her abdomen that pierced the shadowlings like needle-shaped red missiles. The tiny shadow beasts shrieked and withered into puffs of black flame before the Blood Weaver demon turned around to reengage the undead wolf that'd followed her, nimbly dodging the snaps of the zombie and burying her silver fangs into the wolf's neck bones.

The wolf furiously roared and blasted a green toxin cloud around its position to shake the demonic spider off. Meanwhile, necrotic venom from Athela's fangs was injected into its spine in a counterattack. The venom from her silver fangs was black, creeping along the joints of the zombie's exposed vertebrae and causing pieces of bone to rot off, while the cloud of toxic gas seemed unable to affect the demon at all. The larger zombie managed to roll Athela off and leaped back to try and buy itself some space—but it found itself entangled time and time again with strands of sticky red webbing that latched onto its feet, neck, and thorax.

Meanwhile, Riven snarled despite his mangled shoulder and dodged yet another miasmic blast of neon mana that rocketed by his left ear—only saving himself due to his enhanced body under the power of the crow's blessing.

WHOOSH

The bald man was snarling in disbelief at yet another blur of motion on Riven's end, rage filling the sorcerer's features while blood seeped from the burned-off portion of his pants where Riven's snare had entangled his bloodied legs. "YOU LITTLE BASTARD!"

Two more shadowling summons began to form amid dark mana that spilled out of the sorcerer's staff, coming to life and giving shape to animated quadrupeds yet again. The shadows molded, folded in on themselves, and then solidified to glare out at Riven before shooting ahead with a fervor.

This time, though, Riven was ready.

His mutilated feet ached under the strain, but he shot forward anyways and unleashed two razor discs of crimson. The spinning blades of blood mana rocketed ahead to meet the charging shadowlings, which were both too close and too slow to dodge. One almost escaped the attack, but when the small creature went left, the spinning blood magic went left with it. This particular spell had minor lock-on abilities, and the blood magic adjusted to the direction its target was moving in and cleaved the summoned creature cleanly through. The sleek blade of magic caused the small monster to burst into another puff of black fire. It never even stood a chance.

"INSOLENCE!" the bald man screeched, and he raised his staff to cast yet another miasmic bolt but paled when nothing happened.

Simultaneously, Riven grinned. He must either be out of mana or the man had finally triggered a cooldown. Riven's muscles flexed, and he dived forward to take advantage of the situation, ignoring the pain of his wounds. Blood seeped through his boots and along his shins, over the torn musculature of his right shoulder, but the blessing kept him going and red electricity pulsed along his skin to drive him toward greater speeds.

Then he conjured a Wretched Snare, and a black ball erupted from his left hand where he held the scythe. The magic surged and spread out, evolving and expanding into another net that slammed full force into Riven's enemy. This time there was simply no room to dodge even part of it now that the combatants were so much closer to one another, and the spell caught the sorcerer's entire body within the rooting black magic.

The bald man screamed, flesh and mental barriers alike burning and tearing underneath the damage-over-time effect of the Unholy net. Writhing, burrowing needles of the snare dug farther in second by second, ripping pieces of the man's body apart and letting loose streams of blood under their strangling, tightening hold. The enemy caster dropped his staff only a second later, and his knees hit the ground while his lungs took in deep, rapid gasps. He struggled frantically in a pained panic, trying to get out of the rooting snare and simultaneously trying to stop his body from going into shock, but was only able to tear off small pieces of the Unholy magic at a time. With each piece he tore off, so too came a chunk of his own flesh, and he was far too slow trying to get the snare off before Riven finally got there.

With a roar of anger, Riven swung his scythe down, cleaving deep into the man's thigh. The thigh wasn't necessarily what Riven had been aiming for, but he'd take the hit without complaint after the sorcerer jerked his leg up to protect his vital organs.

The blade sank deep, but Riven was kicked back despite this and staggered to the ground as the man regained his mana and fired another miasmic bolt. The magic tore a hole through Riven's billowing cloak, but the sorcerer's frantic attack had missed the target's body in his terrified state of mind, and the shot had gone right under Riven's good arm.

Riven fell back a ways to put some space between them and whirled. The scythe was still embedded in the man's thigh, left there after Riven had stumbled backward, but Riven raised up his good arm and drained what little mana he had left to cast his final spells. He could literally feel the rest of his mana leave his body, emptying it like a drain would a bathtub, and he released the magic upon his enemy with a bloodthirsty smile.

Not two, but four Bloody Razors formed ahead of him and shot forward like spinning crimson bullets aiming for the other caster. The blurring magical projectiles left ribbons of blood trailing their paths through the air, but Riven found his spells slamming into the undead wolf when it jumped in front of its master and took the hit for him.

The wolf was already damaged. It was somehow missing a front leg and had obvious signs of necrosis along its neck and thorax even beyond its original state to the point that its bones were cracking all over its front. Strands of Bloody Strings were flowing out behind it where it'd broken free from Athela's ability, too. Now, though—as the sharpened discs of razor-edged blood mana crashed into its body—the undead creature made a final yelp and was shot down midair to slam atop the master it served.

It lay there, twitching, until it died a true death only seconds later.

Riven could barely move despite his blessing. His entire body screamed at him in protest, but he willed it to keep going and continued to push himself forward. He shakily managed to take another couple steps until he fell over again and forcibly let out an expulsion of air when he hit the bloodstained grass in a daze. He was bleeding out, slowly dying while the holes in his limbs poured out his own bodily fluids. He looked right, seeing a piece of muscle hanging on to his shoulder by a slim flap, and was disgusted when he realized it smelled like cooked meat.

The thought of it made him literally gag, and he felt bile climb up his throat.

But his thoughts were interrupted by the chittering laughter of Athela. The spider had crawled over to him, missing a leg of her own. Pale-green ichor dripped from the wound—but otherwise she was in great condition.

"You did well to stay alive! I'm super proud of you!" the Blood Weaver said with genuine happiness as she sweetly stroked his head with two sharpened arachnid feet. "Let me finish this. We both participated in the kills, so we'll both get XP. I think we may even grow a level or two after this! Be right back!"

The spider's ruby eyes turned, and Athela menacingly stalked toward her prey with a loud, evil cackle. The other mage, who continued to screech at the top of his lungs in agony as the net burned away his skin, had only managed to partially get himself out of the tangled mess... But when he looked back over his shoulder to see the demonic spider making its way to him, the sorcerer went into a full-blown panic attack.

As for the demon? Athela's next words were filled with excitement and a thrill for the kill. "C'M'ERE, BITCH!"

Riven's breathing became shallow and time began to slow down, or at least it seemed that way to him when his mental faculties started to shut off. He watched in silence, his vision slowly fading while the other man's helpless screams of terror and pain reached new heights. He watched as Athela tore into the man's stomach and began ripping out his intestines. Watched as she loudly mocked the sorcerer amid his begging pleas. Watched as she sprayed webbing all over the man's face to keep him quiet while she ate him alive, and watched as she did another ridiculous happy dance atop his corpse when the man finally fell silent in death.

This spider was a goddamn kill-happy psychopath.

[Part three of three in the Chalgathi's Lineage Quest has been completed by slaying your opponent in a one-on-one battle to the death.]

[You have gained one combat level. Please visit your status page to assign stat points.]

[You have become one of Chalgathi's chosen few. You hold no allegiance to anyone but yourself, and Chalgathi in turn is interested to see where you will take this path and how far you progress in your new life within Elysium. Perhaps if you tread carefully enough, you may even find further favor...and further power.

That...that is to be determined through your own actions.

Good luck, young Novice Warlock. May your kills be many and your dominion be swift.]

A flash of light surged across his body. Suddenly Riven could breathe normally again, and he took in a long gasp of crisp, fresh air. Riven's expression of eager happiness increased in magnitude when he felt the wounds along his body clear up and saw his clothes visibly repair, but the expression faltered and turned into yet another frown when he read the texts. His situation sounded rather ominous, and he found it hard to believe Chalgathi didn't expect anything of him after this. He didn't know who or what Chalgathi was, but every action had a reason behind it.

The stars overhead gently twinkled down onto his sprawled-out form, and he took a moment to get a grip on what he'd just gone through. It didn't last long, however, not with all the distracting noise his victorious demon was making.

Pushing himself up with a strained groan, he looked at the still-dancing spider while she chittered and clicked her mandibles atop his enemy's corpse—waving the man's intestines around in the air like pom-poms or batons... Riven studied the bound demon for a few seconds with a blank stare, and then he couldn't help but laugh. It was a sour, cold laugh, because he'd nearly died and the sight was rather gruesome. But he was alive...and that damnable little spider had without a doubt saved his life.

"Good job, Athela. I think I owe you one."

CHAPTER 14

The Blood Weaver turned around, dropped the intestines and scurried over to him. Wrapping her two front legs around his own right leg, Athela nuzzled up against him with her face. "WE DID IT! I WAS SO WORRIED WE'D DIE! Mother would have scolded me if I'd died right after my first summoning."

[Special event and starter quest Chalgathi's Lineage has come to an end with successful completion. You will be recycled back into mainstream events two minutes from now. Please gather your equipment, as you will only take with you what is on your person.]

Shaking his head at the injustice of being yanked back and forth through various realities, he sagged his shoulders and bent down to give Athela some petting—which she very obviously enjoyed before she went back to eating the corpse nearby. Then he walked over to the dead man to search his bag. He took the health potion from the dead man's pack, an extra hatchet, the wooden caster's staff, and the circular ivory necklace depicting the dragon with emerald eyes.

Elysium's administrator gave him no information about the necklace when he tried to identify it, and he was still skeptical as to whether or not it really was the Minor Amulet of Protection. If it had been, it would have saved the man's life there at the end to buy him some time...but it hadn't done so. What was this necklace doing here, then? Had the man found it like Riven had found the blessing or the vase?

He tried to identify these items numerous times, both the vase and the ivory amulet, but attempting to do so simply didn't work.

Why was that?

Was there some kind of stipulation on these particular items? Or were they just too high a quality to be identified by him?

Hopefully he'd be able to figure it out soon. He really wanted to know what they were and how they worked…but for the meantime, he'd just stuff the vase into his backpack and slip the amulet over his neck. Hopefully the amulet would give him some passive bonuses if the other items he had were anything to judge by—even if he wasn't aware of them for the time being. Then, rearranging his supplies and making sure that strange vase was in a secure position inside the leather bag where it was least likely to get damaged, he nodded to himself in affirmation.

[Your time is up. Starting area confirmed. Commencing upload.]

WHUMPH

[Welcome to Elysium's multiverse tutorial—Earth Origins, section 239,342.]

Earth? Did he read that right? Was he back home?

Riven found himself standing in a sprawling meadow covered in wildflowers and rolling green hills under a cloudless midsummer sky. The chill breeze had become a very faint gust of radiating warmth. Far ahead of him in the distance was a snow-capped mountain range, a radiant green forest was far off to his left, a coastline that expanded into an ocean of shimmering blue waves was farther to his right, and immediately all around him were hundreds of other people in the nude.

The stark difference between him and the others drew a lot of attention when he arrived. He had a full set of gear, while the rest of the people here were utterly naked and thoroughly confused, just like he'd been when initially starting Chalgathi's starter quest. That, and his Blood Weaver demon—Athela—was latched onto his back.

She looked around excitedly with rapidly transitioning orientations of her head, clicking her mandibles and eyeing the discouraged, frantic crowds of people around him with genuine curiosity. "So many meals to feed on! Can I eat them? Can I?"

He face-palmed as one of the women nearby shrank away with a scream at seeing the huge spider, and he muttered under his breath so that only Athela could hear, "No. Don't ask again, and play nice."

If the spider could have frowned, she would have. Instead she just smacked herself atop her own head with one of her front legs. "Ah, damn. Okay…if you insist."

Although she was cute, Athela was truly a ravenous monster in every sense of the word. It hadn't taken Riven long to figure that one out.

[Welcome, participants, to the new chapter of your lives. I am Elysium's administrator, the core essence of Elysium itself, and for all intents and purposes I am the multiverse your new reality is run on.]

Riven frowned when he read the words and glanced around again. It looked like another introduction scenario, much like the one he'd already been through. Were these people really just getting into the multiverse now? He knew he'd been given a unique opportunity, but had it actually been a head start as well?

None of the others that'd been with him in Chalgathi's trials were here now. None of the people around him had any sets of items or clothes at all. Had he been put inside Chalgathi's Lineage Starter Quest early and ahead of schedule? The people he saw around him were agitated, confused, upset, or downright in awe of their surroundings. Sometimes a mixture of all those things. Some people were grouped together as families, while others appeared to be friends. Fewer people were like him, those who stood alone amid the mutterings and questions being thrown around while the people of Earth oriented themselves to this new area they occupied.

[Please note the basic functions of Elysium over the next few minutes. Only bare-bones hints and explanations will be given, so pay attention.

First, Elysium is built on a leveling system that functions on Dao pillars and classes.

Second, your world is not alone in this integration. Beware.

Third, guilds are an important part of Elysium's event structuring.

Fourth, you are able to interact with objects in the world around you by accessing system commands. By focusing on the word *Identify* with intent, you can get basic descriptions of objects and entities alike. Identify for the sake of learning in the early stages of integration will present to you as if you had the lowest-tier identifier class, but your version will change later on to a more basic form of Identify later. You are also able to read your own information in detail when focusing on the words *Status Page*.]

This... This was a repeat of the stuff he'd already learned. When he'd first been told about Identify, it'd been in the medusa's lair playing a chess game. Nevertheless, Riven glanced down at his scythe. Then he turned his attention to the staff he'd taken off the self-proclaimed cultist, and then focused on his robes one after the other. He hadn't really taken the time to evaluate them in much detail earlier, because he'd been rushed into a quick decision right before life-and-death combat.

"Identify."

[Basic Casting Staff, 4 damage, 12% mana regeneration, +3 magic damage]
[Crude Scythe, 17 damage, +5 Unholy damage, 18% chance to apply Amplified Bleeding]
[Crude Cultist Robes, 1 defense]

Riven nodded in appreciation as these particular items did indeed pull up status pages, and he leaned into the scythe to alleviate some of his weight. Should he have gone with the staff after all? That other warlock had been able to cast more spells than he'd been able to. Had it been the amulet? Or the staff?

Chances that the amulet also had magic regen properties were slim, so he had to guess that the staff was the reason why. If that was the case, and it probably was, he'd actually done himself a disfavor by going with the scythe after all. He'd only managed to get one real swing in during the duel with the sorcerer and could have definitely made better use of actual spells.

So from here on out he'd probably be going with the staff after all, or at least until he found something better. After he came to that decision, he then started checking out the people around him.

[Human Woman, Level 0]
[Human Man, Level 1]
[Human Boy, Level 0]

Interesting. Focusing on the words *Status Page*, he was rather surprised to see his available stat points had changed from zero to seven, with other class-based points already having been applied. One point had already been applied to Willpower, two to Intelligence, with five free points coming from his race and two free points being given from his class.

Seven free stat points to assign from leveling up, eh?

"Hey, Athela, just to clarify something—Intelligence is what we use for increasing magical damage, right?"

"That's right! It also increases your mana pool, so you can cast more spells."

He assigned all seven to Intelligence without a second thought, increasing his mana pool as well as his magic damage output and bringing it up to twenty-six. He might branch out more whenever he finally got ahold of some martial art abilities, if it suited his future build, but in the meantime he was a pure mage.

[Riven Thane's Status Page:
• Level 2
• Pillar Orientations: Unholy Foundation, Blood
• Traits: Race: Human, Class: Novice Warlock, Breath of

Malignancy (???), **Adrenaline Junkie (Blood)** (+15% to Agility)
- **Abilities:** Blessing of the Crow (Unholy), Wretched Snare (Unholy), Bloody Razors (Blood)
- **Stats:** 8 Strength, 8 Sturdiness, 26 Intelligence, 10 Agility, 1 Luck, -4 Charisma, 3 Perception, 19 Willpower, 9 Faith
- **Minions:** Athela, Level 2 Blood Weaver [14 Willpower Requirement]
- **Equipped Items:** Crude Cultist's Robes (1 def), Basic Cloak (1 def), Crude Scythe (17 dmg, +5 Unholy dmg, potential Amplified Bleed debuff), Basic Casting Staff (4 dmg, 12% mana regen, +3 magic dmg), Chalgathi Cultist Amulet (???), Leather Boots (1 def), Backpack of Supplies]

He glanced at a nearby man, who was angrily yelling at his nearby peer about needing to repent and how they'd reached purgatory or some other nonsense. He shook his head. His thoughts drifted back to Allie and Jose. Mostly Allie, actually. He was confident Jose would probably come out just fine given his aptitude for survival in the past, but Allie was another matter. His little sister was frail, weak, and he loved her more than anything. It sincerely worried him thinking that she might be undergoing similar events, but he hoped that Jose would keep her safe in Riven's absence. Still, he couldn't dwell on the matter. It'd only cloud his mind with worry and would cause him to lose focus of surviving himself. If what the system had said was true, he'd be reunited with her as long as they both survived. He had to believe that she would live, and he had to make it to her after this was all said and done.

He blinked to clear his head, then he sighed. While the rest of the people in the field were still panicking and trying to figure out what was going on, there were two more items in particular that Riven wanted to try and identify again. It wasn't like he had any real clue about what the hell was happening, either, but he wasn't going to get all worked up about it.

The first was the ivory amulet around his neck, and the other was the sealed vase he'd taken from the pyramid as a reward for finding that hidden room and picking the chest's lock. Now that he was out of Chalgathi's trials, perhaps restrictions on what they were had been lifted? After rummaging through the bag's contents, he brought the vase out, and then scoffed in disbelief as both attempts for either item came up rather empty-handed.

The item descriptions were still locking him out.

[Chalgathi Cultist Amulet: ???]
[Strange Ceramic Vase: ???]

CHAPTER 15

He tried opening the vase by unscrewing the lid along the top, but it wouldn't budge after a certain point. Not wanting to break it, he just grimaced in irritation and placed it back in the bag before hefting the bag over one shoulder while smiling at a kid who accidentally bumped into his leg.

"No worries, man!" Riven stated calmly as the little boy apologized profusely and began to slink back over to his wary parents a few yards away.

"HISSSSS! Begone, peasant child! *BEFORE I EAT YOU!*"

He had to slap Athela on the thorax to get her to stop hissing at the terrified kid.

This spider was going to get him into trouble if he didn't teach her not to antagonize people. There were already people yelling at one another and trying to gather everyone up, seeing what anyone knew about this situation and trying to figure out where they were or why they were here. No one really knew what to think, from the conversations he overheard, and it quickly became apparent that he'd been correct in his initial assessment. These people were all just now getting here from when they'd entered their own pillars of light on planet Earth to escape the monster swarms.

[The tutorial event is about to begin. The tutorial provides randomized insight into different aspects of Elysium. You may reengage the rest of your fellow earthlings alongside other participants originating from your two merged sister planets when you reach the end of the tutorial.

Please form a tutorial group of up to ten people to proceed. Simply willing yourself into another's party or willing an invitation to another person in close proximity will allow the party interface to form. If you have not selected a group within the allotted time, then you will be sent into the tutorial on your own.

Tutorial part one of two: Crafting will begin within twenty minutes; you will be given limited time and supplies to create items to help you in part two. Part two of the tutorial will be Battle, which will be a fight for your lives centered in a tutorial dungeon. Countdown commencing now.]

The unease of the place erupted into a panic.

"We have to fight for our lives?!" a middle-aged blonde woman yelled out in utter disbelief while hugging her teenage daughter to her. "This is utterly ridiculous! This isn't funny! Where are we?! Why am I naked, and how did I get here?!"

Another man, who was growing red in the face and shaking his clenched fists, spat onto the ground and began screaming up at the sky. "WHAT THE HELL IS THIS?! Why am I here?! What happened to my friends?!"

The sentiment was the same from much of the crowd, many of whom were already anxiety-ridden or still in denial of what was happening.

[As a warning of the severity of your situation, nonbelievers and skeptics of this situation will begin to die off one person per minute until there are none left. Cooperation is in your best interest.]

Off to Riven's left, a man's head abruptly exploded, sending his brain matter all over his wife, who began to scream. It was the shock they all needed to get it into high gear.

Mass anxiety immediately turned into a clusterfuck as hasty negotiating between groups commenced amid wails of despair. Most people tried maxing out the number of people they could take, but the larger families with young kids were in particularly poor spots, because each child counted toward their number cap. People were avoiding grouping up with these families altogether, and they were often left alone entirely despite trying to match with others just as fiercely as everyone else.

Riven, on the other hand, had no problems whatsoever getting offers, and he was blatantly inundated with requests as people came his way to try and get him to come along with their groups. Out of everyone there, he was the only one with any equipment. He was also an obvious outlier given that he was the only person here at level 2, whereas everyone else was level 1 or 0. It was something most people around him noted quite fast upon using their Identify ability.

On a related note, something he pieced together almost immediately was that all of those rated as level 0 were rather petite women or children—along with a disabled guy who couldn't walk very well. Every single one of the other adults was now starting at level 1.

Despite the spider hissing viciously and turning on people while poising to shoot blood silk in their direction, people were not entirely deterred. In fact, many of them were intrigued about the enraged but beautiful dog-size spider riding on his back that began chittering at them and actively threatening them. They'd obviously never seen or heard a spider talk before.

Athela waved her two front legs rapidly in front of her toward a nearby brunette woman who deemed it wise to approach. "I'LL CUT YOU, PEASANT BITCH! COME CLOSER AND I'LL RIP OUT YOUR INNARDS!"

The woman faltered.

Thus it was a muscular tattooed man in his twenties who was the first to approach Riven head-on instead of calling out to him—but the man still kept a wary distance from Riven's back, where the hissing spider was still perched. "Uh…we already have three other guys about our age. Why don't you come along with us? Your pet can come with you, too…if you want."

"I AM NOT A PET! I'M A PRINCESS!" The spider whirled to glare, hissed at him with an animated wave of her front legs, and blasted the poor guy with red silk from her abdomen that caused him to fall back in surprise. "I'LL CUT YOU!"

Riven decided to merely wait and watch as the confrontation between the crowd and Athela unfolded, partially in amusement, while he considered what his best course of action would be. If not anything else, his eyes began scanning the crowd for potential options that weren't approaching him on their own. He needed someone capable if there was a battle section and didn't want another close call like it'd been in the Chalgathi trials. Even if he did feel bad for the weaker members and families with kids, he needed to get back to Allie and Jose.

"I'll work to pay you back if you take me with you!" an older but very pretty raven-haired woman urged, pulling on Riven's cloak to bring him closer away from the others surrounding him. She then winked and slid her hand down his thigh. "I'll pay you back in more ways than one!"

The spider reacted poorly. "FUCK OFF, BITCH!"

Athela's silk hit the yelping woman straight in the face before Riven could even think to respond, and he had to double-check to make sure she could breathe before he fended off even more offers while trying to get out of the crowd.

Jesus, Athela really wasn't as friendly to others as she was to him—that was for damn sure. Even though he half-heartedly asked her to stop underneath a poorly hidden grin, the spider either did not hear him—or just flat out was ignoring him on purpose. In fact, it looked like she was even having fun, randomly spraying people that got too close and laughing like a maniac with that high-pitched, chittering, feminine laugh of hers.

A set of large, rough-looking, raven-haired bearded men who were obviously twins stopped him when Riven managed to pull his sleeve away from another pleading woman with a scowl. They both looked like they lived in the mountains or cut trees down for a living, were both significantly bigger than Riven was, and were covered in thick patchy hair along their thighs, chests, and arms.

"You're coming with us," one of them said while squaring his shoulders threateningly, his brother in the background glaring Riven down. "You've obviously got a head start of some sort. You're going to tell us how you did it. You're also going to tell us how you got a pet class already; we can tell this is going to be like one of those fucking video games your generation plays and we want in on the secrets."

The guy's twin nodded, then aggressively jabbed a sausage-like finger into Riven's chest. "I suggest handing over your shit, too, before things get messy. That includes the pet."

Riven had been busy trying to respond to the numerous other requests, and this new threat kind of caught him off guard.

Nor did he get a chance to reply.

"FUCK YOU VERY MUCH!" The arachnid leaped through the air like a missile, screeching a battle cry while tearing into the first man's face. "I'LL CUT YOU, BITCH! I'LL CUT YOU AND YOUR MAMA!"

WHAM

The big man screamed and reared back, and Riven watched in fascinated horror while the utterly batshit-crazy spider demon he'd bonded with tore off the man's nose with her mandibles and swallowed it whole in front of his very own eyes. Athela's victim struggled to get her off him and was obviously in terrified agony. "GET IT OFF! GET IT OFF ME!"

The man's twin, who was utterly dumbstruck by the sight, frantically grabbed ahold of the giant spider and got an upper body full of red threads. Only that instead of the normal kinds she usually produced, these were sharper and solid, like the ones she'd used to kill those shadow beasts the necromancer had summoned.

WHAM-WHAM-WHAM-WHAM-WHAM

The sharp, slender pieces of crystallized blood silk shot out of her abdomen like a miniature nail gun, slamming into him and causing him to reel back, screaming. He clutched at his own face this time and tripped to fall backward onto the grass, gripping the solidified blood webbing and yanking on it to pull the spikes out with agonized cries and curses.

Riven dived for the spider, ripping her off the first man's head amid the man's screams while she struggled to take another bite.

"C'M'ERE!"

Though she was cackling like a lunatic and wiggling her twelve sharpened legs around in a crazed frenzy that dug bloody trenches into the man's flesh when she was pulled off, Riven finally succeeded in wrenching her free. She gave the men a quivering, crazed stank-eye while being held in Riven's arms and specifically pointed one of her front legs at her first victim while literally spitting venom.

"FUCK YOUR MOTHER AND YOUR COUCH!"

He had no idea what that even meant. Fuck the guy's couch? He'd have to ask her later.

Riven was slightly bewildered, and he saw just how bad the wounds were as the two men rolled around on the ground sobbing and cursing at him. They shouldn't have come to threaten him for his minion and his stuff, but goddamn, she'd gone ham. The first twin was missing his nose and his face was completely mutilated now, and the second twin had piercing projectiles sticking out of his upper chest, shoulders, and even two that were lodged in his lower jaw.

The horrified looks of the other people around him told him that they'd overstayed their welcome. Without another word, he held Athela to his chest with one arm and ran out of the crowd while wondering what the fuck he'd just gotten himself into with a minion like this.

But he was amused rather than angry and not really feeling too sorry for the thugs who'd just tried to shake him down. He continued on. Pushing his way through the crowds and away from the wounded men, he began to chuckle slightly. If they came at him again, he might really end them by unleashing the little demon in his arms and wouldn't think twice about it. No doubt the strange situation they found themselves in had jaded many of the survivors, and people would be very ambitious in trying to get ahead in the new world now that they all had nothing. Thinking about it as he walked across the field, he came to the conclusion that he should expect this kind of behavior more often than not—and would have to be careful about whom he aligned himself with in the future.

CHAPTER 16

Nobody stopped him to ask or plead again as he made his way to the perimeter of the populated area. Most of them kept their distance, though others still looked longingly his way in hopes that he'd see them and would make an offer himself. A lot of them were scared, and rightfully so, in his opinion. He had a maniac spider with him, after all.

The countdown timer continued to tick down. Eleven minutes remained.

He let out a slow breath of contentment and stretched his arms while he sat. The sun's rays felt rather nice, and the grass of the field between his fingers was soft. He leaned back to watch the chaotic scene unfold, letting in scents of the grassland fill each intake and dwelling on why he hadn't been a more outdoorsy person over the course of his life. Meanwhile, he was calming Athela by giving her pets…which she accepted grudgingly while muttering about cutting people and keeping her two red eyes in the direction of the two men who'd threatened Riven.

He still couldn't decide whether or not to thank the demon or to scold her… so he just said nothing and continued to sit. He'd also left the scythe behind in the madness and had only managed to pick up the staff. He didn't see himself using the scythe again any time soon after his telling battle with the other caster, though, deciding mana regeneration was worth far more than the silly blade at the end of a stick. So he didn't bother going to get it. No doubt other people would have use for the scythe over him. Setting the staff down beside his right thigh and pulling his backpack around, he rummaged through it to pull out the vase.

The painted black flowers along the porcelain refused to reflect any light whatsoever, and he turned the sealed object around in his hands. With a humph and inspecting the lid, he tried to twist it off along the sealed corkscrew top—but was again met with resistance even when bracing the item against the ground. It would turn just slightly if he put enough effort into it but would jam every time he got to a certain point. Curiously, he turned it back and forth—trying to get it open, and finally he even considered breaking it to see what was inside.

The vase was far too heavy to be empty, and when he shook it, he could hear something muffled hit the sides of the object with every movement. Riven guessed that there was padding or packaging of some sort, or perhaps even dirt, and it was infuriating that he wasn't able to find out. The one thing that stopped him from smashing it open right then and there was the idea that maybe it was the vase itself that was valuable and not the object within it…if the vase had any value at all. He assumed it did, though, due to finding it in an event where, out of over fourteen hundred people, only fifty survived. He'd also found it in a goddamn treasure chest, of all things!

There was no way it was just trash.

His attention was diverted when another bunch of people in front of him began to throw punches and tackle one another amid shouts, quickly evolving into a full-scale brawl between two groups of at least a dozen different members each. With a huff of irritation at the blatantly irrational behavior between the men and women in front of him, he stored his vase and got back up to his feet to move somewhere else with his pet spider in his arms.

And that was when he saw them.

It was a family of three a little ways off. They all had red hair with pale-white skin and freckles, obviously of Irish descent. There was a mother, a son, and a daughter, with the daughter being about Riven's age and the son being in his early teenage years. The teenage son was on the floor. He was the skinny young man Riven had seen get knocked out cold with a fist that'd clipped him along the forehead right when Riven swiveled their way. Their mother was likely in her forties or fifties, with slight wrinkles on her face that suggested she smiled a lot, though she wore a terror-stricken scowl on her face as she screamed for help right now.

Yet nobody moved to help her and her children. Not a single soul.

She was desperately trying to shove off another group of four dark-haired white men who'd taken it upon themselves to begin dragging the two screaming and crying women off into another group of their comrades that waited eagerly nearby. Many of the men were obviously…excited, yelling and laughing about how they needed to "protect" the girls in the upcoming trial.

"Come on, ladies! You'll be sure to *love* the company!" one of the men crowed while he laughed and tugged at the roots of the daughter's hair.

Oh, how this *Lord of the Flies* scenario was already starting to play out. Riven could only see this going one direction with the way the men groped the young woman and laughed while another of them took it upon himself to start beating the struggling mother savagely with his fists before he straddled her.

The son remained passed out cold, having stood no chance against the older, fully grown adults who'd seen fit to take his mom and sister away.

Riven had watched end-of-the-world or postapocalyptic movies in the past, and he couldn't say that he was surprised at this kind of behavior. Humans were usually dog-shit creatures, and that's why he'd been a loner most of his life, even aside from having to drop out of high school to take care of his sickly mother before she disappeared like his dad had done. People who got a little taste of power always tried to take it a mile, and without strict punishments for their behaviors, there was little holding back much of society from straight anarchy. He'd seen it many years ago on the news as well, when New Orleans had a hurricane pass through and looters ravaged the city in a lawless state during the aftermath. He remembered a news report about how some of those people had even shot at a police helicopter trying to help the survivors, and this in many ways was not very different.

But those thoughts only stayed mere moments before Riven's heart began to speed up with adrenaline. It also very much reminded him of something more personal that'd happened to Allie years ago. Post-traumatic stress disorder was not always something that made people violent—in fact, it didn't affect most people that way. However, in Riven's case…he was prone to lashing out.

Riven's eyes briefly flashed a bright shade of crimson, unbeknownst to him, and his breathing rapidly increased while previously sheltered memories berated his mind. Even with his current abilities and his little demon…he would likely be unable to take on a group that large to stop them. Aside from the four men who were dragging the younger woman away or the two beating the mother's face in, there was the large group of their friends waiting expectantly nearby. Most of these men had identifying gang tattoos that matched one another on their arms, chests, or backs. When they pulled the young woman inside the perimeter of their crowd, the screams and pleas from the girl only intensified amid the laughter of her aggressors. Others nearby slunk from the situation, putting distance between themselves and what was happening so that they wouldn't be the next targets, and still others just dumbly watched with blank expressions.

"Athela."

His voice was shaky, heated, and his entire body became rigid. It did not go unnoticed by the demon, either.

"Yes?!" Athela turned onto her back like a dog wanting a belly scratch in his arms, but instead of asking for that scratch, she lifted her two front legs and placed them on either side of Riven's cheeks. Her tiny legs were cool to the touch, and she brought her spider face up to him to stare into his eyes and speak to him with that smooth, silky voice that sounded like a wind chime on a midsummer's day.

"Are you okay?"

Power rippled the air along Riven's skin, and despite the spider trying to pull Riven's face toward her own, he did not let his eyes leave the sight of the two women being attacked. Emotions roiled inside him, and he shifted his posture to turn in their direction.

Slowly, he started to walk. "We're about to kill a lot of people."

"OH, REALLY?! How splendid!" The spider cackled and hopped down onto the grass, excitedly tapping her feet in anticipation. "I assume you want to play hero to those fine li'l ladies? Your body language is easy to read. I'll keep you safe, don't worry! I didn't leave the nether realms just to be put down by a bunch of cocksuckers like these guys!"

Mental anguish racked his mind, and pain very briefly etched itself into his facial expressions. He barely computed her words, beginning to pick up pace while memories of Allie on that night all those years ago caused him to literally shudder. He'd been too weak, and they'd been too many. His sister had cried for his help. It was a mental scar he'd never get rid of. But today things were different; today he had the power to do something about it—even if the odds were not on his side due to a massive number difference. His body stilled and ceased its shaking, his blood ran hot, and his lips curled back in a sneer.

With an ever-rising fury fueling him, he began to channel mana into his fingertips.

Riven paused for a few moments to watch, however, when a single man of African descent barreled into the group like a truck. He was big, huge even, and looked like he worked out twelve hours a day, seven days a week. Large tribal tattoos covered his arms and legs, and he took out the first of his opponents with a roar and a single swing of his fist.

The jaw of the first man who'd dragged the young woman over to his buddies cleanly broke under the force of the dark-skinned man's knuckles, causing the opponent to let go of the young woman and whip around—spinning to the floor unconscious. Immediately after that, the scene was chaos.

Four others immediately began attacking the newcomer, two of them tackling him while the others began to slam their fists and feet into his body while he struck back out at them and tried to maintain balance.

"Please…" The mother begged a ways off from her daughter, spitting blood when she was slapped hard across her bruised face.

The man over her just sneered down, a poorly shaved mustache turned into a sour frown. His hands gripped the older woman's neck and began to squeeze. "Shut up, you dumb whore! I didn't—"

Two discs of razor-sharp, crystallized blood cleanly ripped through the man's neck and left a trail of ribbonlike crimson through the air as they passed. The man's speech was sharply cut off—Riven's magic cleanly lopping off his head, severing it from the body with a single attack. The head flipped into the air, spraying the others nearby with red fluids as it bounced along the ground to settle in front of the other would-be defiler waiting his own turn with the older woman. He looked up from his prey, bewildered, just when another razor ran itself through his right eye and partway into his skull.

SHUNK

The man screamed, reeled back, and only managed to choke out a single cry for help before a booted foot slammed into the protruding piece of blood magic—lodging it deeper into his brain. He flopped backward, sprawling unceremoniously onto the grass in death, and began to twitch.

Fatality.

Those nearby paused or gawked at what had just happened, many of them in a state of shock or simply just in denial of what had just occurred. But others were quicker to react.

Riven held up his staff in his left hand to whirl about, using the object to point at his next victims when they rushed him. A net of black energy erupted forward, spreading out while it went and slammed into the crowded bunch of three men to catch them in sticky, burning, needlelike barbs. The magic pierced their bodies and tangled them up like glue, smoking and tearing into their skin and sending torturous thoughts of agony through their conscious minds. His targets were flung off their feet into the air before hitting the ground hard, and their bodies began to rip more and more due to their struggles while they cried, flailed, and screamed.

Riven stepped forward, animatedly crunching onto the neck of the twitching second man he'd killed. He then aggressively leaned forward with a malicious sneer, conjuring condensing pockets of blood magic in the air around him. *"Kill them all."*

CHAPTER 17

A chittering cannonball of fury rocketed over Riven's head when his Blood Weaver leaped forward, sinking her mandibles into one man's neck and injecting necrotic venom that quickly spread across his throat in a blanket of black. She left him in shock, clutching at the spreading, rotting arteries until his eyes rolled back into his head and he died in the grass beneath Riven's shadow.

The loudly crying, shaking young woman the gangbangers had been pinning down was let go when they came to help their comrades, but Riven's enemies had quite the fight ahead of them. The spider zipped around their feet with speed far outstripping their own—tripping them with silk made from enchanted blood that wrapped around their ankles. Then she went for their throats, too, one by one ripping out flesh or arteries in a gruesome display of violence amid curses and shouts for help.

Riven held his hand out and rapidly launched six more Bloody Razors at the foremost enemies who tried to respond, not giving them a chance to even get close. The repeated use of magic continued to surprise everyone, and the projectiles torpedoed through the air at a speed far outmatching what anyone here—aside from Riven—could dodge. It ripped open chests, guts, legs, and skulls—mutilating the surprised, screaming men in sprays of bodily fluids. His targets either died instantly or fell screaming to the ground, maimed with grievous wounds that were sure to be the end of them.

He turned, absolute rage still building in his heart, and he approached the three men he'd snared. Making it up close and personal while they squirmed and agonizingly wailed in the Unholy net, he rapidly slammed the butt of his staff into the faces of the three clustered men until their broken skulls showed brain matter on the ground while his demon kept the others busy. Then he raised his hand to send another set of spinning crimson discs out at a rather bulky guy who'd ended his fight with the African man in order to head Riven's way. They'd seen Riven was the bigger threat here, and they still hadn't given up despite their losses.

The discs ripped through the bulky man's stomach and left him partially disemboweled, writhing on the ground, only to be met with a sharp *SNAP*. Riven's boot slammed into the side of his face and twisted his neck back at an abnormal angle, quickly ending his life.

The fury in his heart propelled Riven forward. He didn't yell, didn't frown, didn't even make any facial expression when he realized he was out of mana and there were still more people to kill. It was a big group—what could he say?

He mechanically flung the staff to his off hand to keep his mana regeneration going and ripped out the hatchet at his side to hold in his right hand. Driving forward into another man who'd been preoccupied with his minion, he felt a rib snap when the metal axe blade pierced his screaming target's lung. Riven hacked again, and again, and again, sending blood flying out of the gasping man's back while he lay in shock on the ground.

Athela turned and skittered to the next victim with a loud screech and chittering cackle of amusement.

"Come on, you bastards—HEY! DON'T YOU DARE FUCKING RUN!" Riven lunged ahead, shouldering another injured and rather rotund enemy that tried to flee and knocking the man over before bringing up the hatchet with both hands. There was a dead look in Riven's eyes while glaring down at his intended victim, and the man screamed and begged to be given mercy.

"PLEASE, DON'T! I'LL LEAVE, I SWEAR!"

Riven only considered the man's request for an instant.

What if this had been his own mother being handled like this?

What if it had been his sister again?

He snapped the hatchet down into his target's blocking arms, hacking away at the forearms of the horrified, screaming man until Riven was able to find the man's chest. It was almost like chopping wood.

CRUNCH

CRACK

SNAP

He slammed the weapon home while standing over his victim, chopping repeatedly into the fat, the ribs, and then the heart until the rotund man's body went limp and his struggles evaporated.

The thought repeated itself in his head over and over as he hacked, slashed, and threw out another net of binding magic when his slowly refilling mana allowed it. Meanwhile others came off the African man they were beating to death to deal with him instead.

But Athela was there in an instant.

Shards of peppering blood crystallized from her webbing blasted them in waves. Threads of mana-imbued silk wrapped them up and pulled them away or tugged them in close toward snapping mandibles.

Riven fought alongside her, taking more than a single punch but grunting and bearing down while dodging a man's tackle and bringing the hatchet down into the back of a cervical spine.

Holy shit. He was actually winning this.

His heart was racing; blood was everywhere; the screeches of his demon and the screams of the wounded filled his ears.

He whirled and met a fist to the face that sent him sprawling backward. Cursing and rolling to the side, he avoided a foot stomping down onto his gut and summoned another disc of swirling blood mana that exploded against the shins of another enemy, carving into the man's bones and slamming his opponent's face into the ground. Then the target's ankles came down at an odd angle with a snapping sound, and his screams quickly ended when Riven drew his hatchet back and flung it in a spiraling arc to embed itself in the man's face.

What if that had been his sister who'd been getting attacked?

The next minutes passed by amid a bloodlust that encompassed Riven's mind, the question still repeating itself over and over like a broken record in his head while he finished off the wounded enemies one by one. He continued to stomp on their necks, chop at their hearts or heads, and blow through whatever mana made itself available to him as soon as he got it over the course of the fight. He did not blink or hesitate even once.

Then at the end of it all, the timer indicated five minutes left before the launch of the tutorial events.

[You have gained two levels. Congratulations! Please see your status page to assign stat points.]

The vase in his backpack began to vibrate briefly before calming again. A faint whisper of power and pleasure drifted through the air, originating from the vase itself, but he was way too far gone to notice.

Riven's mind slowly cleared from the fog of rage that'd overwhelmed him. He was covered in viscera and blood that glistened under the bright sunlight; sweat poured down his face, and his heart madly beat in his chest. His clothes were absolutely ruined, and even the backpack would have to be cleaned or replaced after this. The bodies of somewhere between fourteen and eighteen tattooed men were all still in death, pools of bodily fluids collecting underneath them, and the younger woman had rushed over to her mother where she lay badly beaten with swollen black eyes and a bloodied face.

He was actually a little bit surprised that he and Athela had been able to kill all these people.

He glanced about at the carnage, seeing mutilated bodies and body parts strewn everywhere. It was a scene straight out of a slasher movie. All around them, for the second time since getting here less than an hour ago, dozens of other people on the outskirts stood horror-struck at the sight and maintained a healthy distance.

All except for one.

The huge African guy who'd first dived into the fray was covered in shallow cuts and large bruises, but he stood tall and limped over to where Riven was panting. Holding out a hand of friendship, he bowed his head in appreciation. "Thank you for doing what others would not. You are a good man. What is your name?"

The man's voice had a thick accent, Nigerian, maybe—but Riven couldn't be sure.

Riven gingerly collected the hatchet from the corpse at his feet, casually smiled, and took the man's handshake with a nod of thanks. He had to look up just slightly in order to meet the man's eyes, even though Riven himself was over six feet tall. "Riven. My name is Riven...what's yours?"

"FEARRRRRR MEEEEEEEE!"

The dancing spider was hopping up and down on her six hind legs while wiggling her front ones up in the air and gnashing her teeth. Athela was chittering loudly as she did it, bouncing around, moving her butt up and down, and hissing every couple seconds while decorating herself with the innards of the men she'd killed. She was wearing a headdress made of intestines, and all Riven could do was look away and pretend not to know her.

"Hakim," the man said with a small smile, releasing Riven's bloody hand without a second thought. "You were very brave. Is that your pet?"

"Nope. I don't know her."

"Are you sure about that?"

"Uh... Yes. I mean, no. Okay, she's mine. Don't call her a pet, though, she doesn't seem to like it."

"Should I call her a demon then? Identifying her says she's a level 3 Blood Weaver demon."

Riven gave the spider a sideways glance. "You guessed it."

CHAPTER 18

Hakim waved his hand at the carnage around them. "I must admit, I was surprised to see you using magic like that. I wasn't sure if my eyes were playing tricks on me at first, but this is a strange situation we find ourselves in. I guess I shouldn't be too surprised."

"Well, you saw it right." Riven nodded in acknowledgment, then cocked his head—and sent Hakim a request to join his party by purely his will to do so. "It indeed was magic."

[You have invited Hakim to join your party.]

[Hakim has joined your tutorial party—two out of ten spots filled. You are now able to share gained XP, divided among the group with the majority of XP going to those who get the final kill or put in the most effective effort.]

The bigger man grinned, and then bowed his head in appreciation yet again. "Thank you for the invitation."

"Do you have anyone else with you?"

"No. I am alone, or I was until now."

Riven nodded absent-mindedly. There were three minutes left, and Riven was surprised to find the teenage boy now picking himself up to stumble over to where his sister and mother were. The boy sported a shallow cut where a fist had clipped his forehead, and he shot Riven and Hakim a wary glance. Then he paled when he saw all the death around him, eyes becoming wide while he tried to maintain his balance after being knocked out for a short time. Still, his focus was primarily on his badly beaten mother, and a look of concern was evident as his sister frantically tried to wake their mom. The older woman's breathing was shallow, and her eyes were swollen; bruises were evident on her neck where she'd been roughly choked, and frankly, it didn't look good.

Riven sighed and pulled his backpack around, finding what he was looking for only a moment later. Wiping the blood off the two glass bottles containing both the potion he'd received and the one he'd looted off the cultist at the end of the Chalgathi trials, he identified them and smiled at being right with his initial assumption.

[Minor Healing Potion: use this item by drinking it or pouring it over wounds for a small healing boost.]

The two vials of strawberry-colored fluid were exactly the same, and he gave Hakim a hesitant look before starting over toward the family of three. As he approached with Hakim on his heels, leaving his spider to do her thing, Riven came to a slow stop when the freckled, redheaded son whirled on him with nearly a hiss and held up a hand to stop him from coming any closer. His lips quivered and his green eyes were shedding a steady stream of tears while he put himself between Riven and his family in a stance of defiance.

"Go away," the young man said with a shaky voice. "Please, just go away."

Hakim frowned. Meanwhile, Riven moved over to the right and got a good look at the young woman's mother. Her breathing was worsening by the moment, and she lay on her back on the grass.

The young woman, the older of the siblings, pushed past her younger brother and gripped Riven's leather vest with both hands. She was almost a mirror image of her mother but much younger, with green eyes and red hair coming down to her shoulders. She was covered in bruises, but nothing nearly as serious as the other woman. "Can you help her?! You cast magic earlier—do you have anything that can help?"

The woman's voice was weak, even desperate.

Riven pushed gently past them without saying a word, uncorking the first potion and kneeling down in the grass. The woman's gasps for air were shallow, and her swollen eyes didn't allow her to see anything at all—but she gripped her son's hands tightly while she struggled to cling to life.

Opening her mouth, Riven poured the first potion into the woman's mouth—letting the berry-scented red liquid trickle in and down her throat. As the last of the potion finished and she managed to take in the liquid more easily, she gasped. The swelling along her neck and eyes began to dwindle, and a rib snapped back into place that Riven hadn't even noticed had been out of normal orientation moments ago. The color in her face began to return from bruised back to normal, and she opened her eyes to stare up at him—and then her children—with a mixture of emotions.

Her kids immediately began to sob openly as they flung their arms around their mother, chests heaving and tears streaming as they consoled one another after the trauma they'd just undergone.

Riven took the time to stand up and distance himself, giving them some space and feeling good about being able to help. But as he went to walk away, a hand caught him by the sleeve and caused him to turn. Glancing over his shoulder, he saw it was the daughter.

"Thank you," the young woman shakily stated while wiping a tear away. "Thank you so much."

Riven nodded and silently shifted his gaze to the son, who still looked rather confused and disoriented from being knocked out. Thus it was the mother that introduced herself first. Her daughter had been whispering into her ear to tell her what was going on even with her eyes being swollen shut for much of it, but she straightened herself and tried to keep her composure. She got up with the help of her children and bravely walked to stand in front of Riven, though Riven could tell that she was nervous by the way she clasped her hands tightly against one another.

"My name is Tanya..." The mother shifted her weight nervously with some effort to stabilize herself and took another look at the gore-strewn battlefield. Then her green eyes fell on two other men far off, wearing the same kind of tattoo as many of those Riven had just killed. The two of them slunk back into the crowd and quickly disappeared from sight when they realized they'd been spotted, but her face turned pale.

It was obvious Tanya had a lot more to say and many questions to ask, but there was one thing above all else that she needed to ask most. "Would it be all right if my children and I came along with you? I promise, we won't get in the way."

No one else seemed to want to deal with the blood-soaked Riven after the encounter, not for any reason, and their group remained at five of ten spots filled when the countdown timer finally hit zero. Riven's minion ended up not counting toward that number. Perhaps people had gotten the wrong impression of what'd happened, or maybe they'd only seen the end and not the beginning. Perhaps they thought him a crazy magic-wielding murderer, but Riven knew he'd done the right thing. The smiles of appreciation he and Hakim got from the three they'd saved were testament enough for him, though the teenage son still gave Riven an occasional wary glance.

Tanya, their mother, was still a little bruised despite having taken the healing potion, though she was in far better shape than she'd been minutes ago. She was in her late forties and had been an elementary school teacher. Julie was the daughter, being twenty-three years old, and had just graduated from a university with a degree in marketing. Tim was Tanya's son at nineteen years old, which surprised Riven because he thought Tim looked much younger than that. Tim had been attending the same university his older sister had gone to the year prior.

They admitted to their obvious Irish heritage when he asked about it, but Julie managed to roll her eyes and laugh at the question while saying they got that question all the time. They hadn't actually lived in Ireland and had lived in New York before this abduction off-world had taken place.

Hakim had also opened up in the short amount of time they'd had before the tutorial's crafting section began. He was from Ghana but had spent years in the States while getting an education and playing football. Then he'd graduated, and at the age of twenty-eight he'd been a financial adviser and a personal trainer before coming here. He was rather easy to like and promised to share more stories of his home right before the time ran out and the world around them turned white.

In a flash of power, they were taken from the sunny field and into a large, well-lit cave with torches at regular intervals along the walls. The cave looked hand-carved, with smooth and polished rock all around the perimeter and numerous skylight holes dug through the stone in the roof. Each of these skylights showed twinkling stars high above them, with occasional sound of crickets somewhere up above and outside their cave. There were also six different stations sporting large tables and various types of equipment at each of them. Farther down the cave was a single iron door, barred shut, and right beside them was a clear pool of water with a series of ordinary wooden cups and flat plates of food.

As for the food? There were grapes, cuts of smoked meat, carrots, and freshly baked loaves of bread. It smelled utterly amazing, and Riven's stomach immediately rumbled as he stared down upon the food in bewilderment. "We get snacks?"

His Blood Weaver was more enthusiastic. "SNACKKKKSSSSS!"

The demon hopped off his back where she'd parked her head on his right shoulder and scurried over to start devouring a slab of meat, unsettling Tanya and Julie by the way she moved so rapidly as they gave the blood-covered demon an uneasy set of looks.

[Tutorial part one of two: Crafting has now begun. This tutorial is only a small taste of the options you'll find out there in Elysium.

Here in this tutorial we have prepared a randomized sampling of six different crafting pathways with basic supplies and needed tools. Each table will have a small crafting book that describes the fundamentals of each, though you will be unable to take these books with you when you leave the tutorial. Experimenting upon the given knowledge will also bring about potential boons.

Here, for your individual tutorial group, we have prepared the following crafts:
—Smithing
—Cooking
—Clothes Making
—Mapmaking
—Totem Making
—Prophecy

You have seventy-two hours from now to learn and create as much as you can. It is suggested that you concentrate on things that would benefit you in a fight or a trek through the dungeon, though that is up to you in the end. After seventy-two hours, part two of the tutorial, Battle, will commence. The iron door at the end of the cave will open and you will begin your descent into the tutorial dungeon—or you may stay here and starve.]

CHAPTER 19

With a sigh, Riven dropped his backpack to the ground and landed on his ass next to Athela with a grunt. Shaking his head and scratching, he sniffed. The food just smelled too enticing to leave alone, and even though he was still covered in blood, he really didn't give a shit. He plucked a grape from a nearby plate and began to chew.

It was goddamn delicious.

With an eager smile, he scooped up the flat plate next to the glistening pool of water and began to devour the food like he'd never eaten before. He'd been stressed and overwhelmed up until this point, and he was surprised to find a single tear trickling down his face as happiness bloomed from a stupid smile while he chewed. "Jesus, this is good…"

That earned him a small laugh from Hakim as the other man sat next to him and picked up a plate of his own. "Good enough to cry over, eh?"

"Shut up."

The two of them shared a grin and then burst into laughter, feeling relieved and relatively safe while knowing they had another three days of peace before more craziness unfolded. As they stuffed their faces, the family of three nearby eventually sat down to eat as well…though a little more hesitantly than Hakim had. They were still traumatized after what'd happened and even sat at a small but comfortable distance from the two men while they talked in hushed voices or occasionally shot Riven, Athela, and Hakim glances.

"Don't worry about them," Hakim said cheerfully in a hushed whisper of his own while he tore the loaf of bread on his plate in half and shoved some of it into his mouth. Licking his fingers, he burped and smiled politely Riven's way. "They're just shaken. I would be, too, if I was them. They'll come around."

Riven nodded, absent-mindedly chewing on a slice of smoked meat, which he assumed to be ham, and taking a moment to swallow. "Yeah. That was rough, and I don't blame them for wanting to be somewhat alone. You doing okay, by the way?"

"Yeah, just a few deep bruises, but I'll be fine." Hakim patted his stomach and leaned back, taking in a long breath of air and exhaling slowly. Looking up to the rays of starlight leaking through the holes in the cave roof, he seemed to relax. He was also very respectful concerning Riven's story and his minion, not pushing the subject at all and waiting for Riven to be the one to open up about it. So instead, he asked about something else.

"Now that we're here in this odd situation, what craft are you going to take up?"

Riven chuckled, setting his plate to the side and cracking his fingers before downing a swig of chilling water. "You seem to be adapting to it rather fast compared to most of the others back in the field. As for a craft? No idea. Prophecy sounds really neat, but I don't know how that's supposed to be a crafting class. Do you craft prophecies? I'm not sure how that'd even work."

"There's always that book the system talked about you could take a look at."

"Yeah. At the very least, I'll take a look and get a better idea of how it works. It'd be very useful, that's for sure…" Riven turned his head to look at his bloodstained bag, then stuck a hand inside and pulled out the white vase with black flowers again. He spun the vase around in his fingers, curiously observing the ceramic craftsmanship for some time before speaking. "Though…I may actually take a brief glance at totem making as well. Not sure what that's about, but it sounds interesting. Hell, who knows, maybe this thing is a totem and I just don't know it."

"TOTEM MAKING?!" Hakim let out a bellowing laugh, truly amused, but bent over and extended a hand. "That'd be a long shot if it was. A vase doesn't come to mind when I think of the word *totem*. Mind if I see that?"

Riven nodded and handed it over, gently placing it in Hakim's outstretched palm. "I have no idea what it is, but I got it in a pretutorial event that was pretty brutal, and I think the vase is valuable. When I identify it, it comes up with 'Strange Ceramic Vase' and a bunch of question marks. Are you able to get any other information when you try?"

Hakim slowly shook his head, turned it around, and tried removing the lid—but failed as well. Then he handed it back to Riven with a grunt. It was also quickly obvious that he considered Riven's talk about the pretutorial event as a green light to talk about how he'd come to get his head start. "I get the same message. You'll have to tell me about that pretutorial event sometime; I'm curious. I thought the tutorial was the beginning for all the people in our group, but you already had a class before you arrived. I went straight from the gym to whatever world we're in now…I hope my family is okay. I don't talk to them much anymore, but I can't help thinking about them if this is happening to other people around the world. Oh, and what about guilds? The system talked about guilds for like half a second and then didn't speak of it again."

Then before Riven could get out a response, Hakim pointed to the ivory dragon-depicting amulet around Riven's neck. "What does that do? I can't identify that, either."

Riven considered the question and shrugged, palming the circular pendant that hung around his neck, and looked into the emerald eyes of the carved dragon. "Neither can I. I took it off a dead guy when we were forced to fight to the death at the end of the trial."

Hakim's eyebrows raised. "That happened? You don't think we'll be forced to do that here, do you?"

Riven let out a curt laugh. "No, I don't think that'll happen here. The event I got this class from had selected over fourteen hundred people that met some sort of hidden requirements, and only fifty of us made it out alive. I guess I just got lucky, but this tutorial we're sharing right now seems more geared toward preparing us for what's to come...and doesn't seem like it's designed to cull the people participating like that first event did."

"There were more than fourteen hundred of you? And only fifty made it out?"

Riven nodded again, but he wanted to change the subject and lifted the cup to his lips again. "Yeah. It was brutal. So...I've gotta ask. What do you make of all this?"

Riven waved his hand around the room, settling his gaze on Athela, who was munching on some meat to his right. "Magic, demons, a tutorial event teleporting us around, and some kind of system intervening to bring people from all over the world into one of many thousands of groups. At least that's what I assume given our tutorial group was labeled **'Earth Origins, section 239,342.'** I got a quest, of all goddamn things, to finish that event just before the tutorial, and the very first notification I ever got on those weird holograms talked about not only magic—but miracles and martial arts, too. Doesn't this all seem a little bit crazy?"

Hakim shifted his posture while sitting on the floor and hunched a little more—flexing his muscles while the tribal tattoos on his arms rippled under the minor exertion. He wore a perplexed frown, and eventually he shook his head and placed his wooden plate of food on the floor in front of him. "I do not know, nor do I attempt to understand it. I am very surprised this is all happening, but it's rather refreshing in some ways. In other ways, it scares me. The old world was mildly boring, but at least it was comfortable. It was safe. I don't know what we're going to be facing or where we'll even be going after all this is said and done. What's the purpose? Is this God intervening in our lives? Or is it some other force that we know nothing about?"

Hakim shook his head and let out a deep sigh with a heave of his broad shoulders. "Frankly, it is beyond me, or any of us, really. I'll just roll with the punches and do my best to live a happy life while I'm still breathing. What about you? You seem to be getting on well with magic this early."

Riven snorted with contempt—though it wasn't directed at Hakim, rather, the contempt was directed at the system that'd brought him into the first set of trials at the beginning. "Getting on well is one way of putting it. But yes, I agree. Not sure what to make of it all. Athela—do you know what's going on here?"

The large red-and-black spider quickly shot him a glance before turning back to her meal and gobbling down more food. Between mouthfuls and low hisses of delight, she scrunched up her shiny legs and let out a hybrid burp-hiss. "Your world is being integrated into the system."

"The system?" Hakim asked, eyebrows raising.

"The multiverse, as the prompts have stated," Athela replied flatly. "I can't tell you more than that at the moment, though. The system forbids it, and I don't feel like being smitten by that damnable thing. It's a real stickler with its rules. Don't worry, though, you'll figure it out eventually even without my help."

Riven and Hakim shared a glance with one another but remained silent for a few minutes after that to mull over what the spider demon had said.

"So what do you wanna be?" Riven eventually asked Hakim, steering the conversation back on track to the near future. "Any idea now that we're going exploring into no-man's land?"

Hakim's response was quick. "Baker."

Riven spewed the water he'd been drinking out of his mouth and all over the floor as he choked amid his laughter with the grin Hakim was giving him. "Cut the shit."

Hakim threw up his hands to either side. "I don't know what's out there. I see the system describes you as a Novice Warlock, but I haven't seen much about classes yet. I don't even know how to get one."

"Surely you have some idea. Do you want to pursue the *Dungeons & Dragons* fantasy lifestyle? Or do you want to settle down and live peacefully? Is being a baker really what you want to do?"

Hakim rolled his eyes and gave Riven a look. "Adventuring sounds fun if you're talking fantasy, though I never played *Dungeons & Dragons* before. Maybe a warrior of some kind? That is, assuming this is really a magical realm we're entering given the types of crafts and context clues I've seen. Despite the danger, I believe it would be a good fit for me. Who doesn't want to do that kind of thing?"

"Figured you'd say something like that. You're definitely built for it."

They continued eating in silence for a time, and Riven took the opportunity to more thoroughly inspect his surroundings. In doing so, he was easily able to identify which crafting station was which.

The smithing station had a furnace, an anvil, bellows, hammers, tongs, ingots of various metals, a firepit, and numerous other medieval smithing tools or materials littered about a rather large and solid stone table. The cooking area had rows of meats, bottles of spices, pots, pans, cutlery, roots, powders—the list went on. The clothes-making station had numerous textiles—though they were all rather plain, consisting of a couple archaic sewing machines, thread, needles, leather straps, some hammers, of all things, and a variety of odds and ends Riven couldn't recognize to save his life. The mapmaking station contained a miniature replica of the room, along with a hologram that flickered on and off in various patterns and a bunch of blank sheets with an inkwell and feather pen. The totem-making section displayed another small furnace with mounds of clay, a variety of sharp and dull tools, some odd metal pieces laid out as insignias, wooden boards with a nail and hammers, some feathers, and paint. Meanwhile, the prophecy corner sported a couple cushions with floating wisps of light that danced among the air.

"Welp…" Riven muttered, getting to his feet and turning with a thumb hiked in the direction of the prophecy area. "I'm going to go check these things out. Maybe it'll be therapeutic after all the bullshit. Catch you later."

Hakim gave him a wave, then settled back down on the stone floor to lie facing up at the ceiling. "I'm going to take a nap. Don't stab me in my sleep."

"I would never. I'd have the crazy spider do it."

They exchanged grins, and Hakim closed his eyes while Riven took his backpack and marched past the small family of three. He paused, though, remembering that he had a blanket in the bag. Taking out the quilt and then removing his cloak, he handed both of them to the two nude women with a nod and a brief glance that did not linger. They seemed startled at the act of generosity, but before they could say anything more, he'd already left them to start for the prophecy area.

Coming to a stop at the table in front of the cushions and floating orbs of light, Riven acknowledged that this was the most barren of the stations. By far. A single book was set on the table, with only a small crystal ball present otherwise.

He glanced up at one of the lights that floated over and reached out to touch it, but his hand passed right through it, giving him nothing but a warm sensation. The blood vessels and musculature of his hand did light up as it passed through, though, so that was kind of cool.

Picking up the book, which had the sigil of an outstretched hand and an eye painted along the hand in black ink, he opened up to reveal the first paragraph. It was all written in English in the same black ink as the cover but had more of a curvy text style than normal letters.

[*The Basics of Prophecy:* Written by Oralmius Mephator, third sage of the White Tower]

CHAPTER 20

[*The Basics of Prophecy:* **Written by Oralmius Mephator, third sage of the White Tower**]

Oralmius? Weird name. A little bit on the grander side of things. Though just reading through the man's writing over the course of the next while, Riven could tell he was a pompous asshat and the name fit him quite well. He obviously had a thing against peasants to boot.

As an introduction, let me first say that most of you peasants will never be able to fully grasp even the basics of this ancient art. Most of those who do have a gift simply acknowledge it as déjà vu and carry on with their lives not knowing their potential. Most who seek potential do not find it. Most of you looking this book over probably can't even read and are as intelligent as the sheep and goats we feed on.

You fucking peasants usually smell just as bad, too.

The first thing to note about prophecy is that the lines of fate either choose you or they don't. You will be able to use prophecy, to mold it, or you can't at all. There is no helping it, no changing it, no rhyme or reason as to why you may or may not have the gift. For one out of every ten thousand that do have a minor grasp of this art, I applaud you and highly suggest you keep reading. Having this gift is a great boon that will reward you for the rest of your life, and developing the skill of crafting prophecies and fate to fit your own desires is a worthwhile goal for very obvious reasons.

The art of creating prophecy is just that—an art, one that you can bend and shape to your liking at varying and limited extents. It means you can occasionally see and therefore slightly change the future, but only if you have a strong grasp on fate. It is certainly not foolproof, though—even the greatest of prophets cannot read into everything. For those that don't have the gift, there is no way to change this, and you might as well stop immediately after finding out.

In order to find out the easy way whether or not you have the gift, I suggest you find a crystal ball. They can be created by various types of mages and enchanters, so hire one if you need to—but otherwise just buy one from a guild. Many high-ranking guilds employ prophets to tag along on their expeditions, and you could perhaps even use one of theirs for a fee. Crystal balls are a method of channeling, a conduit, for both scrying and prophecy. By just touching one, if it reacts to you—you will know that you have some form of the gift. So before reading any more: go find a crystal ball. I say again! If the crystal ball doesn't react by lighting up, there is no need to read any farther, as there is no changing your potential and you should go back to humping donkeys or whatever it is you filthy peasants choose to do in your spare time.

Was this guy serious? Riven scowled at the book with distaste, but then glanced back at the crystal ball on the desk. Shrugging, he reached out and placed a hand on the glass orb and waited.

And waited some more.

And then he waited even more.

He even tapped the glass a couple times with his finger, and then he tried squeezing it, but nothing happened.

Riven sighed and shook his head. Taking the author on his word, he put the book down with a thud. "Guess it just isn't meant to be."

A little disappointed and with a sour frown, he turned to the next in line and made his way over to the smithing table—though he had no intention of being a smith at any point. He just thought he'd get a general idea of what each book had to offer him.

What he failed to see as he walked away, immediately upon averting his gaze, was the accumulation of the deep crimson cloud within the orb after he'd left. Simultaneously Riven's Blood subpillar, the one attached to his soul, began to radiate small pulses that gave Riven momentary pause with a sincere confusion. He looked down at his hands, which had both begun to tremble. He wasn't sure what that tingling sensation was, but it certainly felt...energizing.

Even beyond this new, unknown sensation and at that very same moment: in Riven's bag, the ceramic vase he'd been unable to open or identify began to shudder ever so slightly.

The crimson power grew within the glass orb. It accumulated seconds only after he turned his back, being not quite what one would expect of a bright light that the reading described. That crimson coloring stayed there for just a few seconds longer, marinating in Unholy magics, and even caused the orb to crack slightly. The sound of chipping glass caused Riven to cast another glance back over his shoulder from where he now stood at the furnace, but as if sensing his gaze, the Unholy power immediately faded away before he could catch even a sparse glance of the crimson hue.

There was a long pause.

"Everything okay?" Hakim called out curiously, scratching his chin and frowning at Riven's wide-eyed expression.

Riven stared at the crystal ball, stepping closer toward it and seeing that the glass ball now had a splintered chip in the base. He picked up the small piece of splintered glass, spared a quick glance Hakim's way, then turned back to the crystal ball with growing concern and leaned over the item with furrowed brows. "Yeah…I just had a very strange feeling. Don't mind me; it's nothing important."

Hakim blinked twice and shrugged, returning to his meal.

Meanwhile Riven continued to glare down at the orb in the flickering light cast by torches on the cave walls and stars from the skylights overhead. He turned his back to the others, steeled himself, and hesitantly reached out to touch the crystal ball one more time.

His mind erupted with blinding pain, his vision flashed red, and an internal shrill scream so high-pitched that he thought his head would explode pierced his thoughts. His pupils immediately dilated, and a feeling of dread overtook him amid a rapid-fire spike of his heart rate. Crimson light flared in the glass and ripped through his arm, sending jolts of silent electric currents through his fingertips that set his very skin apart to split open his hands and expose his bone.

He wanted to yell, he wanted to shriek out in horror and call for help, but he couldn't move a muscle and stood lock-jawed with pupils expanding out to become so wide he didn't even look human.

"You are not ready. Not yet."

The voice was a ghostly whisper he could barely make out, so far away from him but simultaneously able to touch his consciousness with ease. It left a sense of intent, of foreboding, a warning not to try to touch the orb again. The electric currents rapidly dissipated, his hand rapidly regenerated to soak up all the blood and fleshy bits that'd ripped off moments before, and he found himself gasping for air over the table. He watched in real time as the crystal ball repaired itself, as the crimson light faded away, and sweat began pouring down off his chin to splatter onto the wooden table beneath him.

Rapidly he backed up, breathing heavily and staring at the crystal ball with an unexplainable fear. He didn't know what the fuck had just happened, but even looking at the glass orb gave him an impending sense of doom.

The same could be said for the book on prophecy, and despite all logic telling him he should go open it up again to scour its pages and discover if there were any clues, there was some kind of mental block that absolutely refused to let him do so. A mental block that told him exploring this avenue of power would cripple him should he try to master it too soon.

He internally battled with himself, one part fighting to go and reach out again. To touch the crystal ball one more time and learn more of why it'd reacted that way. To read the words written on those pages and perhaps piece together whether or not what'd just happened was normal, but he instinctively knew it was not. It was anything but normal; even in this new world of fantasy it was not normal, and the other half of him absolutely screamed for him to just walk away and not turn back.

Riven wiped the sweat off his face and hands, realizing he was drenching the already bloodstained outfit he wore, and took in a shaky breath. Letting out a long exhale and straightening himself, he gave the glass orb a final long look before reluctantly gritting his teeth and turning away. Whatever or whoever that voice in his head had been, it hadn't been hostile. That much he could ascertain just by the way his consciousness connected with it in a brief moment of time. It was concerned for his well-being, and he wasn't going to play Russian roulette with powers he didn't understand. Hell, it'd even started to rip his goddamn arm off! The voice had also said he wasn't ready *yet*, so theoretically he'd broach this matter again in the future. And as much as his curiosity nagged at him, he put the matter aside with a tinge of regret to carry on—not saying a word to any of the others about what'd happened in order not to concern them. He was already concerned enough as it was and didn't need other people flipping shit about ghostly voices in his mind or ominous powers surrounding his situation.

After a few minutes to calm himself down, and another small snack of freshly baked bread for stress-eating purposes, he settled on checking out the other stations in the cave.

Riven learned a little bit more about each of them as he passed them by. Smithing was a bit obvious, though Elysium's mechanics had very different avenues and a wide variety at that. Crafts grew by tiers, rather than levels, that signified immense differences at each step above the previous tier. Each tier title somebody acquired made huge leaps and bounds in what perks they could offer, and if someone was good enough, they were even offered a noncombat class title concerning the craft that would expand those horizons even farther. Crafting classes were definitely an option; they often added in different unique stats and leveled up through progressing on that given class—but they would completely replace any combat class someone had. Thus if Riven wished to pursue a craft, he'd want to acquire as many crafting tier titles as possible but absolutely refuse any potential classes he might acquire options for on potential class evolutions.

Smiths could upgrade weapons based on what type of ore they had, build mana veins for enchanting items with the cooperation of an enchanter, have unique signatures that would employ special bonuses specifically based on what attributes their soul had, and could utilize various environmental ores that weren't ever present on Earth. Those who practiced smithing apparently couldn't utilize many of these special elements without massive drawbacks. Examples the book included were Lava-Forged Battle-Axe and Scimitar of Windsong. The Lava-Forged Battle-Axe could be created using an element called Molten Ubsrid, which was apparently a very rare material found at the bottom of volcanoes. The Scimitar of Windsong could be created using crystallized fairy dust intermixed with steel. The book even mentioned extremely talented smiths creating varieties of living weapons, though these were often the rarest and very hard to come by.

The cook, baker, or chef classes were rather unique as well. Most of it was based on a support role, where they were able to create foods that could give buffs, blessings, and resistances to those who ate them. Some foods could be created to keep a person from going hungry for weeks, and other, more valuable foods could even amplify one's health and vitality by threefold over the course of an hour. The better and rarer ingredients were often sold for massive amounts of money, too. The book was quick to state that nobody could even utilize the cooking skill for these bonuses at all without having the class—meaning that in order to even begin to create such extravagant meals, you absolutely had to take up the cook class. Which was unlike most other crafting classes that could take on combat classes and do the craft on the side with lesser bonuses than one would get with the actual classes oriented to the craft, and it made those who chose the cooking classes a fairly appreciated bunch.

CHAPTER 21

Beginning to see a trend, Riven wasn't surprised when the clothes makers, seamstresses, and tailors had similar advantages. They could create articles of clothing that self-repaired or self-cleaned, perfectly fit whoever wore them, smelled certain ways, camouflaged the wearers, or gave various buffs and resistances. There was even a thermally heated blanket one could make without electricity, which in Riven's opinion would be a great Christmas gift if he ever celebrated Christmas again.

Mapmaking...now, this was where it got weird. There were different types of maps to be made, and they required different ingredients and materials to create, as well as what the Elysium administrator considered a semiperfect knowledge of the area being scouted out. Sure, someone could just draw a map on a piece of paper and call it a day—but mapmakers specialized in creating maps one could utilize in different ways. Some of them could track your movements between towns. Others could be edited to your liking as blank slates. Some could be incorporated into your peripheral vision, and others were even three-dimensional or a combination of all the above. This one caused Riven pause, and he seriously considered stopping there to take a deeper look at it—but then realized it required a lot of advanced math. Riven was by no means stupid, and he'd never been bad at math while he'd been in class, but he had dropped out of high school to take care of his dying mom before her vanishing act. So he doubted he'd be able to understand the concepts here after looking them over.

Then, coming back around to the last of the bunch, was totem making. Frankly, he found it hilarious that totem making was even a crafting option at all. What kind of benefits could someone get from that? What kind of game world would invoke that, of all things, as a craft? Was the administrator being serious about this?

But then a remnant thought concerning channeling items crossed his memory—one brought up by the spell tomes he'd used to learn Wretched Snare and

Bloody Razors. Totems were one such channeling item that he could utilize to emphasize his spells…and his interest was immediately piqued.

He also hoped the book had some information he could use concerning his porcelain vase. It was a small hope, one that probably wouldn't yield results, but he had little else to go on. Placing the object on the table beside the book that had a pot drawn onto the front in black ink, he opened it up and began to read. Surprisingly, what he found…was rather fascinating.

Totem Making—The Blessings of Fae and The Curses of Devils: Author Unknown

Totem making has long been used as a basic means of creating decorative monuments, household apparel, and things to keep evil spirits out as a focus of old wives' tales, and it wasn't originally such a lucrative or useful craft in the beginning. This is likely due to the disgust many mainstream mages hold for shamanistic practices despite its usefulness, and it is often referred to by great scholars across this land as "barbaric" for its affiliation with forbidden nature magics and the dark arts.

The key to understanding the basics of totem making is essentially understanding that it is an alternate path of enchanting. Enchanting requires a lock-and-key mechanism via runecraft and mana distribution through a conduit—the conduit being the person who is creating the totem, who must have the proper affiliated type of magic. The runecrafting is very similar to how one casts a spell with hand motions in Tier 2 and above spells. But the key differences between totem making and enchanting are twofold. First, that totem making requires an imbuement of a soul or soul shard, and second, different lock-and-key sets are utilized. To create a true totem with one step beyond an enchantment, it requires either death magic or specialized fae magic to do so. Fae's Foundational Pillar has multiple specialized subpillars that represent the embodiment of life magic, most specifically in the realm of its major subpillar—the Forest subpillar, but it is not limited to that alone. With death being the opposite of life, both the Death subpillar and multiple Fae subpillars deal in the realm of souls.

Not only that, but totems require certain amounts of Willpower in order to control and utilize properly. Shamans, druids, necromancers, and warlocks therefore tend to use them more often than anyone else. Those affiliated with the Holy Foundational Pillar, Harmony Foundational Pillar, and Archaic Foundational Pillar along with their subpillars have tried creating totems in similar fashion, as told by the history books, but they have all failed to my knowledge.

Regardless, those who consider themselves totem artisans are often nothing more than that—artists who come up with fancy designs meant to scare children for the holidays. The true craft comes into play when we imbue these materials to create what are called influence fields.

Totem making is often used in conjunction with various runes or symbols of power, wards, and enchantments to create stable and consistent magical effects that we term influence fields. These influence fields are essentially a type of interactive enchantment that the soul shard imbued into the totem can control. It incorporates runes but is different from normal runecrafting, as influence fields use a different subset of locks and keys including the shapes and materials of the totem makeup. Why might this be, you may ask? What purpose is there to having different lock-and-key mechanisms in the sigils? The reason is that enchanting is a static thing, unmoving and unbending, while influence fields are ever moving and even become alive. It is also why influence fields that totems use are able to be controlled by souls you imbue the totems with, whereas an enchantment is not inherently able to be controlled by such an attached entity.

Totem making is thus the step between normal enchantments and awakened items—which are an entirely different type of category altogether. The three categories of magically enhanced equipment are therefore defined by the following:

Enchantments or enchanted items are rigid and unbending, and they lack the ability to be controlled by anything other than the direct user. This category also includes cursed or blessed items.

Influence fields or totems are fluid and are able to fluctuate or change under the influence of a soul.

Awakened items are entities that have their true consciousness bound to a physical item without any actual soul.

All three have different lock-and-key sets, or different runes or rules, that are bound by the system. All three have their own unique downsides or perks. They are three different parallel pathways to creating items of power, even comparable to how mana, divinity, and stamina differ from one another in their own abilities. But now we are getting off track. Back to totems and influence fields:

Influence fields can be anything from a pleasant smell to seduce the opposite sex to an electrified floor to a defensive barrier—the commonality between them being that they are bendable, fluctuating spell alignments and are contained within a physical object that we call totems. Specific combinations of the right materials, right ingredients, right incantations, the right soul shard, and right runes or symbols in just the right way can create truly potent effects. The important part about this is that the one who makes the totem must have the correct attribute in order to imbue the totem with a spell. If the mage creating the totem gets the symbols, materials, and shape right but fails to have the specialized Forest attribute—they will fail to imbue the totem with any forest magic regardless of how perfect the totem otherwise is. The same goes for Water, Blood, or any of the subpillars of Fae and Unholy. As Forest is a subpillar of Fae and Death is a subpillar of Unholy, you will only ever find totems enchanted with categorical magics underneath the Fae and Unholy pillars. Fae, Volcano, Storm, Ocean, Glacial, Swamp, Forest, Unholy, Blood, Shadow, Death, Infernal, Depravity, and Chaos will be the only types of totems you ever run across. Well, that and their more specialized pillar types that evolve from the major subpillars. Additionally, those affiliated with the Unholy pillar may never be able to wield totems affiliated with the Fae pillar and vice versa, as pillar orientation is needed to command the soul shards and totems after they're imbued properly.

With the right knowledge and attributes, you may place the right runes or paintings in the right patterns to provide a magical webbing of sorts. Creating the right shape of the totem is also very important, as they act as a key to a lock in conjunction with the runes you place upon them. If the runes, shape, pictures, or patterns of the vase are incorrect, the key won't fit the lock correctly, and the effect won't take hold. Sometimes even the coloring matters. Sometimes if you do a half-assed job, you'll get a half-assed effect. That'd still be better than no effect, though.

Moving on to examples of what such things I have seen as a master totem maker, you would likely be surprised. I have created vessels that burn with fae light, illuminating the darkest of places as beacons to the world. I have created vessels to seal away the greatest of demons, placing them in forbidden tombs to keep them at bay from the civilized world. I have created totems that poison enemies around them and heal those who are marked as friendly, totems that capture the sickness from those they touch and towering bastions that bless farmland for miles around them over decades to come.

Many once scoffed at me, laughed at me, told me I was a fool for pursuing this very abstract and often disregarded profession. In the end, though, it was I who laughed, and as I sit upon a mountain of treasure and bathe in the gifts that kings shower upon me, I often ask my many wives if they'd have another man, to which they of course say no.

"Well, goddamn, he's living the life!" Riven snorted a few laughs and smirked at that last sentence, then flipped through the pages some more. It was time to expand his horizons.

CHAPTER 22

There were various chapters on different types of runes one could implement, how to collect souls or soul shards from the beyond using Forest and Death magic, and types of wards he could erect with the right application of knowledge. Looking over his shoulder, he found that literally everyone else had fallen asleep—obviously exhausted from recent events after having traversed from one world to the next. Even Athela had fallen asleep and was—to Riven's surprise—curled up next to Julie with the woman's arm draped over the spider while she wore the blanket he'd given her.

Just how long had Riven's head been in the books to not notice that one?

But this was good. It was a good thing that they got some time to relax... He was sure the small family especially needed it.

Turning back to his book, he began to read some more. Time passed like a blur as page after page flipped over in his hands, and soon the daylight hours overhead turned to night and starlight through the holes in the cave roof—leaving only the burning and crackling torches to light the pages in his hands.

He dreamed of his long-gone dog that night. She'd been a half basset hound, half terrier mix with stubby paws and floppy ears and a bark that was far too deep for a dog her size. He remembered how she'd been just a puppy and they'd taken her from a family friend of his father's who owned a farm, and how that family friend's dog had gotten frisky with a stray to produce the litter of puppies Riven got to pick from.

He'd known she'd be called Shadow even before he'd met her. Back then, as a kid, he'd thought the name was cool, and that'd been the sole reason for naming the dog that. Funny, because she wasn't even a black dog...she'd been brown, a deep chestnut-brown color. But he hadn't cared, he'd liked the name. He remembered how she'd whimper and cry at night in the kitchen while being potty trained… She wasn't trusted to sleep on the carpet back then because she'd pee everywhere, like all puppies do. He remembered taking out the big blue mat his parents kept in the closet, dragging it out into the kitchen and hiking his legs over the little latched gate…putting that mat down next to Shadow and letting that cute little puppy snuggle up next to him late into the night before he had to get up the next morning for school.

She'd lick his face to get him up at the urging of his little sister as she laughed and laughed before dragging him to the car and making him say goodbye… Then he'd get back home and do it all over again the next night.

God, how he missed those days.

But here and now…in the dream state he was in, he found himself happy again. Finally happy again, with his mom laughing off to the side as Shadow licked his face to get him up for school…

Riven snapped out of his slumber amid the laughter of the others, coming face-to-face with Athela's two ruby eyes as the spider demon licked his face with a short, stubby tongue between those massive fangs of hers as he drooled onto the desk.

He'd fallen asleep reading that damnable totem-making book.

And now he was being licked all over his face by a dog-size spider while she made obnoxious hissing noises and rapidly tapped her feet on the desk to the amusement of the others.

Cool.

Hakim was the only one not laughing, but even he was grinning at the ridiculous display of mock affection while he leaned back against the smithing station with a bowl of water and another plate of food. Tanya and her two children, Julie and Tim, were guffawing loudly—obviously prodding the spider on with their laughter as she went in for what Riven could only guess was a kiss.

He abruptly shot up and whacked the spider atop her head, resulting in an irritated hiss from Athela when she failed to go in for the finishing insult, and he wiped away the drool on his face. "Is this my drool? Or is it yours?"

"Both!" Athela hummed musically. "I was cleaning you off!"

"Is that all you were doing?"

The spider gave him what was probably the most sheepish look a spider could ever give. "Would I lie to you?"

"Goddamn you, Athela."

"Huzzah!" The spider cackled and raced off to jump into Julie's arms, the young woman catching her easily and without hesitation.

Riven rubbed his forehead, wiped off his cheek, and made a gagging impression that made everyone else burst into even more laughter—this time including Hakim. He glared at them, and then to Athela, with less amusement than they had by far. "I didn't realize you were all so chummy with her. She wasn't playing very friendly back in the tutorial's beginning area—didn't think she'd like anyone other than me."

Tanya fished out a wet rag from God knows where and walked over to Riven's face, wiping it down in a very motherly fashion and smiling down at the younger man. "Your demon is very, *very* nice. I have no idea how anyone could ever *not* get along with her!"

Riven let the woman finish cleaning him off and gave her a polite smile of thanks, then raised an eyebrow and cocked his head at the purring sounds Athela was giving Julie while she was being petted. "You did see her rip through..."

He didn't finish the sentence, not wanting to bring up yesterday's memories when they appeared to be doing so much better than they had been the last time he'd been awake. Whatever Athela was doing, she was doing it well...in terms of getting their spirits up, anyways.

Instead, he just smiled and yawned, then noticed the plate of food and water next to him on the table.

"That's for you!" Julie said while brushing her hair out with a comb that she'd gotten...from where, exactly?

Riven looked around. Then, knocking his head with the side of his fist twice, he realized that they were all semiclothed, too. He recognized pieces of his cloak stitched with pieces of the blanket he'd given them, sewn into various other articles of clothing that'd likely been taken from the clothes-making station not far off. It was all very crude, but it covered up all their private parts rather well and made moving about pretty easy.

"I was a seamstress once upon a time," Tanya stated proudly with a grin, placing her hands on her hips. "A bad one, but nevertheless I had training. I figured I'd get everyone properly modest while we're here together. It was awkward...walking around naked in here with men we don't know. I'd make you something, too—if you want it, but you already had clothes...so..."

She trailed off, and Riven gave her a thumbs-up of understanding.

She nodded. "Thanks for the blanket and cloak. I appreciate it."

"*We* appreciate it!" Julie said with a small wave Riven's way. "For the blanket and cloak, but also for yesterday, too. I've got a question, though; did you really find a giant undead wolf that breathed fire like a dragon?"

All eyes were focused on him now, and Riven's slightly ajar jaw hung loose as he looked from one to the other. "Huh?"

"Athela said you ran away screaming like a little girl while she had to defend you from a thirty-foot wolf zombie that breathed fire," Tim stated, matter-of-fact, with a concerned frown, softly stroking Athela's head as the spider continued to purr curled up in his sister's lap. "Don't feel bad about us knowing, though, I would have likely screamed, too—right before dying. I'm just glad you made it out alive!"

"She said you pissed yourself," Hakim said with a loud chuckle, not being able to retain his grin. "She said she was carrying the team on her back."

Riven's jaw dropped even farther. "She really said all those things?! Athela, you little ingrate! That wolf wasn't thirty feet tall, it never breathed fire, and I sure as shit didn't piss myself!"

The room burst into laughter again and then went into an uproar as Athela wiggled a spider foot dismissively his way, stuck out her stubby tongue, and went back to being pet by Julie and Tim with a dramatic, feminine humph.

He felt their mother, Tanya, nudge him from the side, and looked up from his sitting position in the chair. He saw the older woman lean down to whisper in his ear. "I can't believe Athela is a demon. She seems so nice...are you sure she's really a demon?"

Riven shot Athela a glare. "Based on my limited interactions with her, I'd say definitely yes."

Tanya nodded thoughtfully and straightened back up again, watching the dog-size spider with renewed admiration. "That's so neat. This whole situation is so...just so bizarre. The tutorial messages talked about 'earthlings' and 'incorporation into the multiverse.' What does that even mean?"

Bizarre was one word for it. However, neither he nor anyone else here had any real answers for Tanya. No one *truly* knew if this was just a group of them or if the entire planet was somehow involved in this event...but if he took things at face value based on notification pop-ups, he could only believe it really was a worldwide event. More than that, even, with mentions of other planets being merged with Earth. Also seeing people from all sorts of cultures back in the tutorial wasn't very promising for this being a limited and secluded event.

He was curious as to how merging with other worlds would end up after he got out of this tutorial.

The next few hours went by, and everyone got to work. Tanya went with Tim to start showing him how to sew and fit people with clothes, Julie and Hakim worked together to figure out the basics of smithing and hoped to craft some crude weapons for themselves before the dungeon opened, making the place echo with their hammering, and Riven worked to figure out more on totem making.

The time spent crafting kept their minds off the upcoming dungeon crawl, and the others were all rather uplifted by the fact that Riven and Athela were there with them. This was supposed to be a tutorial dungeon, and Riven was already a level 4 warlock with a level 3 demonic minion.

Thinking back on it, Athela had likely done just as much as he'd done in that last fight against the men they'd killed...but she'd told him that he likely got more experience for taking the final blows using his hatchet on a lot of the ones that she'd incapacitated and tied up on the ground. He apologized to her for it, but Athela had actually insisted that this was a good thing, as keeping him alive was a priority over herself. Simply put, she could respawn and he couldn't. She also told him that he needed to put some points into Sturdiness from time to time as well, despite the talk about the majority of his points needing to specialize in growing his Intelligence and Willpower.

"The reasoning behind this is simple. You don't want to die, and Sturdiness will help you stay alive by enabling you to take a harder hit," Athela said as he took a break from reading the lore on the most basic runes and the shapes of various totem figurines concerning different lock-and-key mechanisms the gods used for ritualistic summonings. "Every time you level up, you acquire more health, mana, and stamina. Depending on what Elysium deems you needing most and your fighting style, you get different amounts of each. It isn't always exact, either. Unlike many of the other stats, health, mana and stamina are all hidden stats concerning how much you have. So we won't ever know what your exact health Points, or HP are…but we know they're there. Putting an occasional point into Sturdiness will help you stay alive and increase the amount of damage you can take for every point of HP you have. Each point in Sturdiness will decrease the amount of HP you lose from attacks and decrease the amount of Stamina you lose from physical activities, such as running away. Many mages like you fall into the pathway of becoming glass cannons, then they get one-hit killed by an assassin who slips in past their minions and that's it—poof, gone. Don't be one of them. Oh! Almost forgot, since you've been given a class title of Novice Warlock already…you may have other demons approach you from the nether realms over time. This generally happens for one of two reasons: to form a minion contract if you have available slots and enough Willpower to contract them, or to make deals with you for one reason or another—as demons can't usually contact ordinary mortals under normal circumstances. It probably won't happen until you're out of the tutorial, though, with stipulations and all that."

Riven took the message concerning Sturdiness to heart with a nod, knowing full well he could die just as easily as all those people at the pyramid with Chalgathi's starter quest. However, he was still early in the workup of his power schemes, and he wanted to concentrate more on his other stats first before applying any to make himself tankier. The best defense was a good offense! He'd grown two levels since assigning stat points, and he got five points per level for his race. He'd also gotten one Willpower, two Intelligence, and two free stat points for every level gained thanks to his class title. That meant a total of fourteen free points, two Willpower, and four Intelligence for the two levels he got. After assigning nine of his free stat points to Intelligence, one into Sturdiness, and the other four into Willpower, Riven came out like this:

[Riven Thane's Status Page:
- Level 4
- Pillar Orientations: Unholy Foundation, Blood
- Traits: Race: Human, Class: Novice Warlock, Breath of Malignancy (???), Adrenaline Junkie (Blood) (+15% to Agility)
- Abilities: Blessing of the Crow (Unholy), Wretched Snare (Unholy), Bloody Razors (Blood)
- Stats: 8 Strength, 9 Sturdiness, 39 Intelligence, 10 Agility, 1 Luck, -4 Charisma, 3 Perception, 25 Willpower, 9 Faith
- Minions: Athela, Level 3 Blood Weaver [14 Willpower Requirement]
- Equipped Items: Crude Cultist's Robes (1 def), Basic Casting Staff (4 dmg, 12% mana regen, +3 magic dmg), Chalgathi Cultist Amulet (???), Leather Boots (1 def), Backpack of Supplies]

CHAPTER 23

"So, acquiring new abilities and spells... Any idea how to do it? I just want to clarify that what I read about getting them in the book from Chalgathi's starter quest was accurate," Riven asked with a sideways glance at the spider beside him. Then he started writing on a piece of provided scratch paper with a quill pen—adding to the start-up notes of usable totems, one he could take with him when the tutorial ended. The system message had claimed they couldn't take the books, but given that this station had allowed him two pens and a couple papers, he could assume that he could take down notes and draw out the runes, a means of utilizing soul shards, and totem shapes along with ingredients as long as he could fit it on the provided material.

So far the list of Unholy variant totems the book knew about was rather small, only having come across two very basic totems he could personally use as most of the book talked about theoretical situations or Fae pillar totems. Even so, these were two totems he could create here and now before they entered the tutorial dungeon. They included a Minor Totem of Murk that slowed down enemies that entered a certain radius with an Unholy mist, and a Minor Totem of Leeching that sucked life out of creatures at a steady rate in small amounts.

Athela was busy playing with her threads and took a while to respond to his question on the topic of spells, but she glanced up at him in between fiddling with the red silk ball she'd made and grunted an answer.

"There are a couple ways to learn new spells. The first way is at random times by gaining combat levels; the system will reward you through visions that you must decipher. Whether or not you decipher the visions properly is up to you, and often it is heavily oriented toward whatever class you have. If you don't have a class, they're usually oriented toward what your goals may be or how you've performed over your life. There is a saying that your combat style will influence the way you are presented classes, but the opposite can also be said to an extent, because the system will award ability visions you may or may not decipher depending on your combat style or achievements—but also on the class you have, even if it isn't one you want to keep. The system isn't always fair at how it distributes these... Sometimes the world will present visions to you after gaining three levels, sometimes it'll present it to you after twenty-four levels. Some people think this is purely due to luck, while others theorize it depends on your own actions and environment. You can also find a grimoire that explains a new spell and study the magic that way, find a teacher who is more experienced than you to explain how the magic works, or study the magic that you've got by experimentation. You can also find or buy spell scrolls that work the same way the abilities given by the system do—just read a spell scroll if the magic is within your given attributes and accept the 'learn spell' prompt to collect it into your abilities list. However, these scrolls are very, *very* expensive, hard to make even by master mages, and they often fail if you don't quickly grasp the understanding it is trying to bestow upon you."

"Can I create my own spells?"

"Absolutely, though it takes someone who fully understands the magic to do this. The worst mages are the ones that depend solely upon the spells given to them by their class visions, and the best mages end up having a solid fundamental knowledge of the magics they're working with to better their spells or create unique ones. The system rewards creativity and hard work that way. That even applies to martial arts and miracles."

"You seem to know a lot about this stuff after being stuck in a nether realm all your life."

"I only know the basics. This is common knowledge among the natives of Elysium... Okay, fine. Maybe I did some studying back there in preparation for when I got a warlock master, so I lied. Why don't you create a disc of blood for me, just a single one?"

Riven frowned in the dim light of the cave, then folded his arms. "I'm not sure I can do that. Every time I cast the spell Bloody Razors, I get two discs of crimson per cast. Though if you mean conjure two of them and use one, I can do that."

Athela stopped playing with her red silk ball and got up on all twelve legs, pointing one of the black-and-crimson appendages directly at him and prodding him in the chest. "No, you definitely can. This is exactly what I'm talking about. You are only using the basic programming of the spell you were given and not thinking about manipulating its potential. That time you summoned four blood discs? You used the spell twice over instead of just once while pooling more mana into the single cast. I saw and felt you do it. It cost you time and additional mana for the start-up cost. If you want to be an elite among your peers—which I intend you to be because I want to stay here as long as possible and hopefully forever—you'll need to learn these things. When we leave this tutorial, I'll be giving you regular lessons on how to cast properly, effectively, how to consider cooldown times with combinations of your skills, and how to manipulate the magic you do have while learning how each other's tricks work. This will all be secondhand knowledge, though, because I don't actually use spells myself."

His eyebrows raised, and he leaned in with a little bit of excitement evident in the smile he gave his minion. "You're saying you'll teach me? Can we swap our blood skills?"

"No, I just meant that so we can fight together better. I utilize martial arts—my body's abilities are drawn out of stamina rather than the mana you use. Bloody Strings is a stamina-inducing ability. Your stat points are focused on Intelligence, building a mana pool with every stat you apply to it, while you have very little stamina pool to draw from. Not only that, most martial arts scale off physical attributes like Agility or Strength. There'd be no point even if we do share the same pillars of Unholy and Blood…unless you wish to become a hybrid-type fighter." Athela quickly held up one of her spider legs and scrutinized him with two narrowed eyes. "And a word of advice—do *not* become a hybrid fighter."

Riven's brows furrowed in confusion, and he held out his hands to either side. "Why not? Seems like it'd be a good idea to diversify."

She huffed. "It's just my opinion, but utilizing a pure build is better. You have enough diversity as it is with the number of spells you'll be able to acquire, and the higher up you go, the more experience or XP it will take from killing enemies or training to level up. Each level will become harder and harder to acquire, and if you don't push your stats into a more narrow selection for your build, then you'll end up finding yourself weaker than your peers who are of a similar level. Because although you may have lots of different miracles, martial arts, or spells at your disposal, they all build off different stats and all will be weaker, and that isn't good if you end up wanting to continue growing levels and power at a steady rate. Hybrid classes always take far longer to level up—just look at your average paladin."

"What about your average paladin? I'm from a planet without magic and whatnot—definitely no paladins in the average neighborhood, if you catch my drift."

Athela did a spider version of a facepalm and shook her arachnid head. "Ugh. All right. Back to the basics. So there are three general pathways to power: your martial arts that typically key in and scale on Strength and Agility. The second path to power is magic or spells that scale off Intelligence and in some cases Willpower. You in particular will be using Willpower for more than just magic, though, because I'll be needing more Willpower from you as my bonded slave in order to evolve."

Riven ignored the *slave* comment completely, even with dramatic pause and an amused hiss on Athela's part.

"Willpower will also be needed by any other minion-contracting classes, such as beast tamers, angelic summoners, or necromancers…but we're getting off topic here. The third pathway to power is through miracles, which scale off Faith mostly—but there are a lot of miracles that also have the Luck stat incorporated into how they work."

"Truly? You're meaning to tell me that casting miracles can require points into Luck?"

Athela shrugged. "Yup. So again: the bare-bones foundation for martial arts is Strength and Agility, for spells it's usually Intelligence and sometimes Willpower, and for miracles it's usually Faith and sometimes Luck. Getting back to paladins—these hybrid idiots try to spread their limited stat points on four and sometimes even six different main stats. This usually leads to the majority of would-be paladin start-ups dying really early. Still seems to be a popular choice, though."

Riven frowned. "Popular with who?"

"The other people of Elysium's multiverse, of course."

"Other planets?"

"Yes."

He scratched his head. "Can you tell me more about these other planets? That's so fascinating, thinking that I may be eventually meeting people from elsewhere in the universe. That's just crazy…"

"Sorry, can't do. Against the rules. I don't want any punishment dished out my way, no thanks. I can't give any advantages concerning specific knowledge of the multiverse until one year in, so ask me in a year. Even now what I'm telling you with the general stuff is pushing my luck, but telling you about the other people already integrated would definitely get me a one-way ticket back to demon time-out for a century or two."

Athela gave a helpless shrug when he glared at her, but eventually he sighed and just accepted it. It would be a stupid thing to lie about, and there was no reason Athela would gain from doing so here—at least no gain that he could immediately see. "Fine. Then why would anyone want to become a paladin if they're as bad as you say they are? Surely it can't just be for the diversity…"

Athela paused. "Well… There is one upside to choosing hybrid specializations. If you manage to get a good class title from the system, if you earn it from the system, you'll find that they give out large percentage bonuses or scaling bonuses that make up for the spread-out stat points. It's an equalizer, but getting one of those class titles is very hard to do, and it takes a lot of time, dedication, and grinding through the lower-tiered classes in order to get a paladin class worth a damn. Later on in the leveling schemes, the paladin classes are actually really good or even some of the best, but most people die before getting to that stage in the attempt. You have to survive long enough to make it worthwhile."

"So you're saying that paladins and hybrid classes are typically really weak early on and scale much later if they earn an evolved version of their class?"

"Yes, but we're talking many evolutions down the line—not just one. You're a Novice Warlock right now, for example. It's a base class, which is really good in the early tiers, so your survival chances are high, and you'll have a wide variety of evolution options depending on how you fight or progress. Some options may be better than others, and the system gives out better class titles to those who display competence in the lower tiers. How you behave, environmental factors, and how well you do determines what options you get. You could even stop utilizing magic entirely and start fighting with your fists, and the system would probably consider giving you some sort of brawler class completely devoid of any magic perks. It's complicated."

Riven frowned, rubbed his forehead, and sighed. "Right."

"Just concentrate on putting your stats into Willpower for minion power-ups and Intelligence for your own magical pool. Then, as I said earlier, occasionally put points into Sturdiness so you don't die so easily. At least for now, until you figure out a more specialized build specific to your fighting style. You'll always want to put a couple points into Sturdiness here and there to keep you alive, or Perception to make sure you're not entirely snuck up on all the time, but generally focus on Intelligence and a little less on Willpower. Trust me on this. Okay?"

"Fine. What awaits us after this tutorial, by the way? I have no idea what to expect…and so far everything has been less than friendly. Other than you, of course."

Athela gave him a chittering laugh. "That's for both of us to find out. All I can say with confidence is that it will likely be a version of your world."

The demoness spider flinched as if she'd just gotten a mental shock, and she shook her head back and forth with a hiss. "That's just a guess, though—every integration is different, and the system won't allow me to say more than that without punishing me—and I have no intention of defying the system. Sorry."

She paused. "Moving on to another topic I was thinking about… I know that you said, 'Mama didn't raise no simp,' and you didn't choose the Succubus because of it, and mark my words, I'm happy you didn't, because you got me! But crowd control specialists—like the Succubus—will become very valuable to you in the future. Warlocks and most other mage types generally aren't very mobile, and they don't have many defensive skills unless you get lucky or reach the higher levels. In order to reach the higher levels, you need to live through the lower ones, and leveling up fast requires killing things. Therefore, your best bet to survive would be to utilize crowd-control minions that can stop your enemies from getting to you in the first place while you use your high-damage ranged attacks.

So a Succubus would have actually been a very good first choice for a warlock, if you hadn't picked me instead. That idiot with the zombie wolf had no clue what he was doing, choosing not only an undead starter minion that's supposed to be used for hunting and tracking, but also utilizing a poor combination of skills along with a class meant to utilize numerous weaker minions when there were no resources to raise them. If he'd been smart at all, he'd have chosen at least one crowd-control ability, just like you did, and would have chosen a different class specializing in one-on-one combat before transitioning to necromancer later if that was what he really wanted. Or he would have capitalized on a minion that had long-range attacks to compliment his miasmic bolts, because he already out-ranged you and probably would have outranged anyone else, too. Fortunately for us, he wasn't the brightest."

This was actually making a lot of sense, and Riven rubbed his chin thought-fully as the spider continued to talk. "Just to clarify, since you're a demon under my control… Does this mean you don't have your own stats?"

Athela shook her head and plopped her abdomen back on the table to sit. "No, I have my own stats. You can look at my status page for more clarification on the matter."

The spider summoned her own stat page and flipped it around to show Riven what she was talking about, and he immediately realized that as a minion, her stat page was a lot shorter than his own, with a few different descriptors.

[Athela's Status Page:
• **Level 3**
• **Pillar Orientations: Unholy Foundation, Blood**
• **Traits: Race: Blood Weaver Demon, Class: None, Adrenaline Junkie (Blood) (+15% to Agility), Naturally Agile (+7% to Agility)**
• **Abilities: Necrotic Venom (Blood), Bloody Strings (Blood)**
• **Stats: 12 Strength, 7 Sturdiness, 10 Intelligence, 38 Agility, 5 Luck, 23 Charisma, 18 Perception, 4 Willpower, 1 Faith]**

Huh. So her base stat for Agility was thirty-eight, but the 22 percent bonuses she had from her traits made it really top off even higher at forty-six. That was eight free stat points.

Interesting. For her, Agility was a stat that scaled faster than the others just because of the bonuses alone…and he could see why she'd concentrated her stat points there because of it. He was even lucky enough to have one of those two bonuses, though his path on magic was already set and he wouldn't be transition-ing anytime soon.

Turning back to the scratch paper he'd been working on and glancing down at the instructions for the two totems he wanted to create, he tapped his finger on the yellowed parchment and kept a solid gaze fixed on Athela. "But this craft, if I choose to pick it up…will my Intelligence stat affect it? Or would it not?"

Athela paused, read over the description in the book, then nodded and slammed a spider paw onto the picture Riven was pointing at. "Yes, the more magic you have, the better you can make the totem. I think. A Blood attribute is needed to create this Minor Totem of Leeching as well. These things bind and unbind to the people with the required prerequisites of Willpower and pillar affinity to distinguish ownership. Totem making is actually a very rare craft, from what I've gathered, and you got very lucky to have it randomized to this tutorial. If it's a craft you want to pursue, it would be both very useful and lucrative."

"And very interesting." Riven nodded in agreement with his hands clasped in front of him. He winced as Hakim slammed home a rather loud hammer strike from across the room and frowned their way, getting a laugh from Julie and a sorry wave from Hakim when they caught his glance. "I could definitely see myself doing this. Would you mind helping me, Athela?"

Athela nodded in contemplation atop the wooden table, then flipped the book around with one of her legs. "Sure. I'll have to catch up because you've got a few hours on me, but I've read about these in minor detail before."

"Yeah, that works for me—go ahead and start reading up to that point. In the meantime, I'm going to leave you to the book and try to have a go at making the totem of leeching. All the materials are here, so hopefully it won't be that hard."

The spider gave him a shining spider grin. "Don't be so sure of yourself. There's probably a reason it's a rarer craft… despite the poor stigma it has, most people would still find totems very, very useful."

Unfortunately, the spider proved right. Totem making really was hard, far harder than he'd anticipated.

The Minor Totem of Leeching he was trying to make was about two feet tall and made out of wood. It had to be carved into a cylindrical shape, so using a small tree stump or something like that could have probably worked, but that was just the body for it. Riven found himself using a chisel and mallet, along with occasionally pulling out his hatchet, to hollow out the totem until he could see the opposite end of his wooden cylinder and stick his hand through it. Then he stuffed a few small quartz crystals inside, which he'd actually found underneath the table in one of many drawers he hadn't noticed earlier, dribbled some of his own blood onto the quartz crystals, nailed flat circular boards over the top of the crystals to keep them in place, and painted it red all the way around.

Apparently for this particular totem, red coloring was a necessity. It didn't have to be painted, but it definitely had to be red.

Then after the paint dried, he attached yellow feathers, which he took from a nearby crate, around the top of the totem with a sticky resin and flour mixture. The resin dried after a while into a tar-like substance, and he switched to a yellow paint to add two additional symbols to either side of the totem—each a hollow teardrop shape with a line from the center down the middle of the bottom. When he completed the sigil, he carved divots at regular intervals in a ring around the top and bottom.

Then he took another look at his notes, placed a hand on the totem, and concentrated while attempting to channel his blood mana into it by focusing on the image of what he wanted.

Nothing happened.

He did it again, trying to focus on a pool of blood within his mind's eye.

Nothing happened.

Frustrated, he tried to force mana into the totem—focusing on the feeling he got when he used magic but simultaneously picturing an actively bleeding corpse of one of the men he'd killed not long ago. This time, he got a prompt.

[Would you like to infuse this totem with the Blood attribute? Yes? No?]

Smiling widely at his sudden success, he selected Yes. Then he immediately turned that smile upside down as the totem literally exploded up toward the ceiling in a shower of blood as the top blew off, pelting both him and Athela in disgusting remnants of his laborious attempt. It was far more blood than he'd actually put into the totem himself, which confused him, and then another prompt appeared.

[Totem creation has failed.]

Riven muttered under his breath, wiping blood off his face and onto his clothes as he got looks from around the room and chuckles from the spider.

He did this again, taking another hour to put it back together properly, and ended up getting a notification saying he'd placed the runes improperly. Athela pointed out that they needed to be opposite from one another on each side, and he took her advice to get yet another prompt when he tried to infuse mana—saying the runes he'd drawn with the yellow paint were not adaptable to blood magic.

Looking his yellow runes over, he found that one of them had actually dripped paint down the wood before it'd dried, and it didn't look like the original rune anymore. When he finished with this one, instead of exploding out the top, it just started leaking blood all over the countertop and remained inert without any real effect otherwise.

[Totem creation has failed.]

It was hours later, after a light lunch with the others and on his next attempt, that he finally got it to work. Well…work better than it'd been going, anyway.

[You have created an incomplete Minor Totem of Leeching. Soul shard is still required for complete autonomy and movement; enchantment and runecraft is intact. Incomplete Minor Totem of Leeching has been bound to you; unbind this unfinished totem to transfer ownership to another.]

[Incomplete Minor Totem of Leeching: Slowly whittles away at health, dealing one average blood damage per second, drawn from a single nearby enemy, eighteen-yard sensing radius. Since this totem has no soul shard, you will need to place this totem in a secure position or on ground and command it to activate for use. Targets any enemies you would consider hostile. Uncommon tier. Requirements: 2 Willpower, Blood subpillar.]

The totem's yellow runes began to light up, turning from yellow to a dull orange glow with a few red strands of power encircling the totem in slow intervals. It was a spherical pattern that traveled through the wood of the table as if it weren't even there and was rather mesmerizing. Riven definitely felt pride swell up in his chest at having created it. Even though he'd had a handbook guiding him through the process, even though the damage rating was rather pathetic, it was still an accomplishment to be proud of.

"The totem knows who I would consider hostile?" Riven asked curiously as he showed her the system message. "And why does this totem have a damage average on its attacks when my spells don't? I thought that was only for items."

Athela looked up, putting the book concerning totem making down on the table and folding her front legs sagely. "I don't know how the totem knows. As for the average damage per strike, that's because the runes, mana input, and materials you used were good or bad enough to average out that way. If you made another Minor Totem of Leeching, it'd probably be around the same damage but may not be exactly the same. Same goes for the sensing radius."

Athela jabbed a foot into his chest. "The reason why your spells don't have those numbers is because it largely depends on how much mana you channel into them. Like I was telling you earlier, Bloody Razors can come in ones, twos, threes, or any number, really, if you have the mana during the channeling. However, they can also be flung at faster speeds, can have their shapes manipulated, can become more mana dense, depend on your magic level… The list goes on. Therefore spells usually don't have an average damage on them when looking at a status page because it depends on who the user is and how they manipulate it on a given casting… But if you really wanted to know how much damage you're doing with a spell, there are items you can acquire that will measure the damage for testing purposes."

"Got it. How do I test this totem out here and now, though? We don't have any enemies around yet."

The spider demon chuckled, then crawled off the table and walked over to an area of the room devoid of anything fragile. Turning, she waggled her arms at Riven and danced on her back legs. "Think for just a moment that you want it to hit me and see what happens! I don't know if this will work, but—"

Riven didn't let her finish as the totem's glowing orange runes lit up brighter on either side. In less than a second, a strand of red light pulsed and shot out toward the Blood Weaver with respectable speed.

The spider easily dodged it, though, being far too fast to hit, but she was surprised when the strand of red light took a U-turn and followed her around the room. For a few seconds, the totem and the demon played a game of cat and mouse where the strand of red light continued to zigzag through the air as Athela dodged left and right, before she eventually went out of bounds and left the totem's eighteen-yard radius zone. She bobbed up and down and looked at the spot on the ground where the thread of red light had smashed into the stone floor. Then she looked back up at Riven, both eyes sparkling, and literally jumped into the air with a screech of excitement. "THAT'S SO COOL!"

"I KNOW RIGHT!?"

Riven had also jumped up, and the two of them laughed as they did a ridiculous dance together and galloped in a circle.

"WE'RE GOING TO BE AMAZING!" Riven yelled over the clanging of the hammers.

"I KNOW! I KNOW!"

"MASTER ARTISANS!"

"WIDOWMAKERS AND BABY STOMPERS!"

Riven immediately stopped dancing and looked down at the excitedly shaking spider. "Baby stompers?"

"I was just kidding."

"All right, just making sure. Stomping babies isn't what I ever intend to do. Like, ever."

"What if you…like…theoretically had to go to sleep…and a whiny baby was keeping you up at night? You *really* wouldn't stomp it?"

"Athela. I better not catch you ever attempting to stomp a baby because, so help me God, I will strangle your little arachnid neck."

"To be fair, when I have stomped babies in the past, it was more of a poke because my feet are so small. They didn't die or anything like that."

"…what the actual fuck are you talking about? Haven't you been stuck in the nether realms?"

CHAPTER 24

The next two hours were spent making another of the incomplete leeching totems. They worked step by step right until Tanya called everyone in for a break. By this point Riven was confident in his ability to remake the totem given the right ingredients, and there were even substitutions for the quartz crystals he could use via other types of gemstones, but he was still unsure about adding the soul shard. That was going to be the hardest part and would require him to utilize the Death subpillar—which he still hadn't bound to his soul yet. The description in the manual had a lot of theory behind it that he didn't quite understand. But he was still very excited to see what would happen when these incomplete totems eventually acquired their soul shards. It would be a venture for another day.

Tanya passed around snacks she'd made, having cooked some more meat they'd taken out of an equivalent refrigerator left by the system for food storage that was fueled by water magic. They had the day-old bread as well, and it still tasted just as great as it had twenty-four hours prior without having gone stale at all.

Julie was excitedly explaining to her younger brother and her mother the specifics of the forge that she and Hakim had learned about through the tutorial book, along with trial and error of their own. She was sweaty, covered in soot, and her hands were starting to blister before she'd wrapped them—but she was obviously enjoying the work. "We're trying to make knives, because we don't have all that much time. I don't know how long it's supposed to take, but we just finished a knife each..."

She held up her own finished product. It was made of solid iron and wasn't perfect by any means—but they could tell she was proud of it. The edges weren't entirely sharp and the leatherbound handle looked a little too big for the blade, but it was definitely a knife, all right.

[Crude Iron Knife, 5 average damage.]

Julie beamed as everyone clapped, setting it down in front of her with a smile. "The hand-forging of the blade, then grinding them to refine the shape…we had to make all the fittings, handles. Had to harden and temper them, then sharpen it again. It took a long time, but at least I have a weapon for the dungeon now!"

Riven thought about the extra bronze hatchet he'd taken off the sorcerer he'd killed and picked up his bag. Going through it, he quickly found the hatchet, then slid it over across the stone floor to Hakim. "Forgot I had this. Go ahead and use it if you want."

[Bronze Hatchet, 10 average damage.]

Hakim wiped sweat from his brow, still breathing heavily from exertion, and looked at the knife he'd made for himself.

[Poor-Quality Iron Knife, 6 average damage.]

Passing his own knife to Tanya, he picked the hatchet up with a nod of thanks Riven's way and pointed to the totems. "What are those?"

Riven raised an eyebrow. "Have you tried identifying them yet?"

It was a simple thing, but they were still getting used to the idea that they could interact with most things in their environment just by identifying them. Some things had lots of descriptions, while others had none other than a name. Other things were unable to give them details, being too high-quality for them to assess…like Riven's flowered vase or the bone amulet around his neck.

But he could tell that Hakim got the detailed message regarding his totems when his eyebrows lifted and a large smile crossed his face.

Showing off his creations next, boy did he get a reaction from the others. It was just unfortunate that only he could use them, because none of the others had any Unholy-related pillars. Or any pillars at all yet, for that matter.

[Five minutes until tutorial part two, "Battle," commences. Upon countdown ending, the door to the tutorial dungeon will open and you will be permitted to enter. There are multiple ways out of the dungeon and into Elysium, but it is up to you to find out what they are. The only option given at face value for exiting the dungeon is killing one of the dungeon bosses or minibosses. Good luck.]

Riven had created a third incomplete blood-type totem after yet another failure since his initial two were made. He'd also tried twice to make the other type of Unholy-oriented totem that slowed enemies within their radius, the one called Minor Totem of Murk, but had been unsuccessful both times and no longer had any more time to spare. He'd have to figure out what he was doing wrong later, because the system's tutorial had stopped giving him hints after his third failure.

Still, coming out with three semicomplete totems that drained health from his enemies was something he was not only proud of, but they would possibly come in handy if he utilized them right. He'd created leather straps for each of them and tied them around the middle to more easily carry the objects and was finally ready to go now that the dungeon was opening.

As for the others, Tanya and Tim had successfully stitched together some additional clothes: namely some very basic shirts, skirts, and shorts. They'd also been able to make plain sandals with some guidance from the tutorial book and the materials given to them, while Hakim and Julie had provided three daggers. There was one for each of the small family, and then an additional small wooden buckler for Hakim, who also wielded the hatchet he'd been given by Riven.

It was better than nothing, that was for sure, but everyone felt rather disappointed at the lack of success concerning the prophecies. Not a single one of them had touched the crystal ball with a reaction, and they'd all given up on day one after trying.

Except Riven, of course, who was still very wary about what'd happened with his own experience concerning the crystal ball. That was some information he'd be keeping to himself, at least for now.

Everyone except Riven and Athela was nervous and shared wary glances with one another while they waited. Even Hakim, who was trying to put on a brave face for the others and was a hulking monster of a man, was obviously a little on edge while tightly gripping his shield and axe.

[Two minutes until the tutorial dungeon opens.]

Meanwhile, Riven was cram-studying what he could from the totem-making tutorial book at a last second run-through. He'd already stuffed the two papers he'd scratched down instructions on for the two totems he'd be able to use, along with the theory notes on soul-shard acquisition and utilization, but he hadn't found anything usable in the pages of the book beyond this. The rest of the totems were based in Fae magic and the subpillars like Water, Air, and Forest, because the author of the book had been a fae specialist himself.

"Totems will provide experience points toward leveling up if they are used in taking down an enemy, even at a distance. However, this XP is at a significantly decreased value from what would normally be gained by participating in combat yourself."

Riven nodded, with the final tidbit of knowledge tucked away in his brain, snapped the book shut, and he was about to place it on a nearby table when it simply evaporated from his fingers in a cloud of warm, glowing white smoke.

[Tutorial dungeon is now opening.]

The large double doors in front of them creaked, the hinges on the heavy, rusted iron breaking and snapping open while dust and dirt fell to the floor. Swinging open and coming to a stop, the doorway lay wide-open before them.

It was the entrance into an abyss, a shadow of black that had no end. There was just a whole lot of nothingness on the other side of the door, and a deep chilling sensation ran through Riven's bones when the cold air hit him.

"What the fuck?"

WHOOSH

In the next second, a howl of wind ripped him and everyone else off their feet, sucking them into the open entrance without warning. They went screaming into the yawning oblivion, the doors snapping shut behind them—blotting out the light while they fell.

Falling through the endless void of nothingness had Riven's heart doing somersaults in his chest as his limbs flailed about him. He was internally cursing his luck, and that enraged cursing grew to even greater heights when a new and very unexpected message appeared in front of him.

[As one of the few who made it through Chalgathi's Lineage Starter Quest to gain early access to the warlock class, you have once again acquired the attention of this entity through your various actions in the brief time afterward. Chalgathi has intervened in the tutorial process and has drawn you along with your comrades into his abyssal realm. You have one of two choices, and you have sixty seconds after reading this message to choose before immediate death sets in.

A Choice of Selfishness: Your four recently made allies (Tim, Julie, Tanya, and Hakim) will remain banished here forever, lost souls unable to escape the shadow they are secluded to and unable to sense anything but the darkness around them. Your selfish choice will benefit you, however, in that sacrificing their souls to Chalgathi's realm will gain you four legendary-tier pieces of soul-woven warlock armor—the Soul-Woven Warlock Hood, Soul-Woven Warlock Pauldrons, Soul-Woven Warlock Robe, and Soul-Woven Warlock Boots—to complete one of the best early-stage outfit sets currently available across your world. You will then be placed back in the normal tutorial dungeon to complete it as the Elysium administrator deems fit.

Or, the next option...

A Choice of Selflessness: You choose to save your newly found friends and take the hard road yourself. Choosing this option notifies them of what you have done, the choice you had to make, and pushes them into a safe room within the dungeon: each given an early combat-type starter kit geared toward their chosen style of combat. They will each also receive an additional one ability tome to learn from, similar to the way that your first spells were taught, an event that will be given to them immediately. The catch is that choosing this option will separate you from the group and insert you into a minor hellscape dungeon of Chalgathi's choosing instead of a normal tutorial dungeon. This hellscape dungeon will be much harder than the basic tutorial dungeon but will also have more opportunities for you to progress faster. Just like the tutorial dungeon, this hellscape dungeon will also have exits into Elysium that you must find in order to leave. That, or you must kill a dungeon boss or miniboss to leave.

The countdown to choose begins now. 60... 59... 58... 57...]

CHAPTER 25

[You have selected: A Choice of Selflessness. Your previous allies have been notified and have teleported to a safe room within their tutorial dungeon. The road to hell is paved with good intentions; just make sure that yours don't get you killed while visiting.]

The warm, musty air filled his lungs as they expanded; the wooden bench he was sitting on felt grainy to the touch. His eyes adjusted to the light while his pupils dilated. His body felt…different, and the texture of everything was very focused as the transition ended.

He found himself alone in an old, dusty room with crimson rays of light leaking in through ancient wooden shutters showing signs of rot. The entire place had a very creepy haunted-house vibe going on. Cobwebs lined the corners and interior of the room, with ancient stone walls on all sides. There was also an old coffin, a rotting old chest, three glass vials on a rickety table, and blood-stained embalming equipment next to them. Then there was a rickety old door leading out as well, with signs of rust accumulating on the hinges and doorknob.

As he looked around, another hologram notification appeared in front of him.

[Special Event: Chalgathi's Hand of Fate—You and your minion, Athela, have both started in a relatively high-risk, high-reward, minor hellscape dungeon as an introduction into Elysium. Normally you would be able to unsummon and resummon her to your side by focusing on the commands Summon and Unsummon or touching the pentagram emblazoned on your skin, but due to the nature of this trial, you must physically find her first before summoning options are available again. Athela has started out many miles from your current location, despite pairing up with the initial drop.]

[New Quest: Find Your Spider Princess—Meet your minion, Athela, at the center of the city next to the large statue of the bearded, axe-wielding man, without dying, to receive a reward. Dying would be less than ideal, for obvious and permanent reasons. But let's be real, you probably *are* going to die here, little warlock—so pucker up! Also: if Athela dies in this dungeon prior to bonding with you again, she will be permanently killed, despite her status as your demonic minion. WELCOME TO HELL!]

His brow furrowed in sudden worry. Worry turned to frustration. Frustration turned to anger, and he momentarily closed his eyes to calm himself down. So that's why he'd spawned alone... If he'd known choosing this option would put Athela at real risk, he'd have just sacrificed the others, as callous as that sounded. But he hadn't known, there was no way he could have known, and the notifications concerning his choices were not as clear-cut as they appeared to be. Perhaps if he'd taken the selfish option instead, he may have very well ended up in this same exact situation—just in a different place with really neat warlock gear...

It's easy to be a Monday morning quarterback.

Riven let out a long exhale, rubbing his fingertips against the dusty wood and then against his skin. He sat there, trying to control his breathing on the bench that looked like it might collapse under his weight at any second now. "Goddamn it. What does Chalgathi find so interesting about me, anyways?"

He stood up and moved around, gingerly flexing his muscles and stretching before grabbing his gnarled staff and brushing dust from his crude black cultist's robes. The backpack was still there, so at least he still had his things other than the missing minion.

He took a couple minutes to adjust to the new reality of his situation just as hope had been swept out from underneath his feet—yet again being thrust into a lonesome life-and-death situation. He was here, in an alternate version of Elysium's tutorial dungeon that he knew less than nothing about. He was currently alone, now even devoid of his bonded familiar, who could die permanently if he didn't find her fast enough.

God forbid he died himself. More than anything, though, he was concerned for Athela. She was certainly capable, but she was physically weak, and if she got caught in the wrong circumstance, she'd be gone just as fast as she'd come into his life. Being a minion, she had a vested interest in his own success and wouldn't betray him like so many others had in the past. She was funny, though obnoxious at times, and she put herself on the line for his own sake. Even though he didn't know her that well, she was a friend. He needed to find her before it was too late.

He chuckled, thinking that she was likely having similar thoughts about him. Or at least he hoped she was.

[You have entered Dungeon Negrada. Other in-area participants: one.]

His eyes paused upon coming to the other one in-area participant, and he frowned. Were he and his minion the only ones here?

Or did Athela not count as the other in-area participant?

He sat there for a good five minutes, seriously contemplating what the actual fuck had just happened, rubbing his forehead vigorously as he tried to make sense of it all. Eventually he shrugged and stood up. He'd had so much tomfuckery going on with this Chalgathi character and Elysium's multiverse that he was beginning to just roll with the punches. He would succeed, just like he had before, and not only succeed—but he would excel. He had no choice.

And first order of business was inspecting the rather creepy room around him.

He walked over the cold, dry floor toward the rotting chest first. A howl of sour-smelling wind whipped against the old wooden shutters of the window, causing them to creak when he got on his knees and put his hands on the unstable wooden box.

Pulling gently, he heard a snap when one of the rusted hinges on the back of the box immediately gave way without so much as an effort on his part—but the other one held firm, and the lid swung open awkwardly at an angle to reveal a set of clothes. They were poorly preserved, light brown in color and made of some sort of cloth with numerous holes in them. He stood up, holding the pants and tunic out in the dim lighting to get a better look at them, and grunted when they weren't in his size anyway.

[Old Sinner's Pants]
[Old Sinner's Shirt]

Identifying them as being nothing special, he just put them back in the box.

Then he turned around and headed for the table next, where he saw some embalming equipment and three glass vials—the three inactive totems he had with him rattling against one another. He ignored the glass vials entirely, as they'd be utterly useless to him, but picked up one of the bloodstained, rusty knives that glistened in the dull crimson light and curiously looked it over. It was very simple, about a foot long, and was made of iron with a blade dulled from use.

Though it was still the sharpest of the tools here.

[Rusted Embalmer's Knife, 3 average damage]

It did just as much average damage as the staff did. Not what he'd expected for a blade. Regardless, he was sure that this world had rules he was unaware of concerning damage output and didn't question it much—so he held the knife loosely at his side as he moved through the room. Having another means of protection was still crucial just in case.

He looked underneath the table and underneath the bench, only to find nothing. Coming over to the window, he stood on his tiptoes to get a better look at the outside through a crack in the shutters where dim light was streaming through. There he found a strange, red, midday mist right outside his perch that obscured everything within three feet of where he looked out.

"Well, that isn't creepy. Nope, definitely not."

Riven scratched the back of his head with the handle of his knife and turned around to get a better look at the coffin. It was the only remaining thing in the room he hadn't taken a good look at other than the door leading out, and he wasn't about to leave just yet without having opened it up.

There could be loot in there, after all. This *was* a dungeon…right?

He came around to the side, where he saw a good-size metal clasp locking the lid in place. It was in slightly better condition than the rest of the metal around the room, and he didn't have a problem flipping it up before yanking.

With a creak, the lid flung open and banged against the floor on the other side. Years of dust bloomed into the air from where it'd settled on top, and Riven had to cover his mouth and eyes with his robe to stop coughing.

When the dust finally settled and another shriek of howling wind caused the window's shutters to quiver, Riven pulled his robe down and evaluated the contents of the coffin more closely. There was a very frail-looking body, poorly mummified, with bandages yellowed with age. The skin was pale, gaunt, and wrinkled beyond recognition underneath the wrappings. It'd probably been a woman once, due to the bone structure of the corpse, but time had been unkind, and he really couldn't make it out for sure.

He inspected the mummified old corpse thoroughly, gently folding the arms to make sure nothing was underneath—but frowned when he saw nothing but the wooden bottom of the coffin. The body was surprisingly soft, yet crusty to the touch, and pieces crumbled off underneath his fingers. He patted it down, trying to figure out if there was anything he was missing—and eventually came to the mummified left hand.

Feeling something hard underneath his touch along the pointer finger of the mummy, he quickly used the rusty embalmer's knife to cut away the digit. With a crunch and a snap, the finger came off—and he gingerly unwrapped the decaying old appendage to reveal an emerald-studded silver ring alongside another smooth wooden ring that he really didn't take a fancy to. The emerald ring was identifiable and titled Witch's Ring of Grand Casting, while the other ring he got basically no information on, just like the necklace he wore.

[Witch's Ring of Grand Casting, +26 points to Intelligence.]

[Old Wooden Ring: ???]

He almost began to drool at the sight of the emerald-studded witch's ring. Multiple levels' worth of stat points to Intelligence? Seriously? This one ring was about two-thirds of his current magic-boosting Intelligence points.

Gaping at his magnificent find, he took both of them off the finger but flinched as a painful shock lit up his hand when he touched the wooden ring particularly. He dropped it by accident and in surprise, but when he tried picking it up again, he experienced another painful, similar shock.

Riven raised an eyebrow in confusion, and even when he tried using his foot to prod the wooden object, the same thing happened again. Only this time the pain was far stronger, and he even yelped slightly before stepping back. Nothing like this had happened before, so he didn't know what to make of the item's reaction.

He reached out one more time, and upon attempting to retrieve the item, it vanished in a puff of teal-colored smoke that fizzled away through the air.

[You are now haunted.]

He blinked.

"You've gotta be fist fucking me."

Riven checked his status page, with no luck. There was no change there whatsoever, and he didn't feel any different. He looked around to make sure no enemies were coming after him but didn't hear or see anything noteworthy. Still on edge, he discarded the decaying finger and turned the remaining emerald-studded item around in his hands a couple times to admire the craftsmanship. It was just beautifully made, with multitudes of tiny dragons encircling one another as carvings in the metal—and the green gem itself was neatly cut into an octagon.

He put it on, then took it off, but became delighted as he felt the warm surge of power rush into him each time he wore it. The effect was immediate, and he could literally feel the power vibrating as it stabilized throughout his body with the item attached securely to a finger.

His thoughts were rudely interrupted by a creak from the coffin, and his green eyes tore back to the corpse.

Had it just moved? He could have sworn he thought he saw the head twitch, and his heart began to quicken slightly. But instead of waiting to see whether or not he was right, he immediately jammed his knife into the skull of the corpse with a brutal downward stroke that cut cleanly into the decayed flesh despite the poor condition of the knife.

The thing he'd thought to be a corpse wasn't as dead as he'd initially thought. The old woman's mummified corpse shrieked and spasmed, flailing its arms to grasp at him as he stumbled back in surprise. It abruptly flipped right over the coffin's side to land onto the stone floor with a thud in response to his attack, let out a croaking and hoarse howl of hunger, and began lurching forward a short ways at a time in a slow but determined gait.

"Unimpressive." Riven backpedaled, slapping away the grasping hands of the zombie that'd come to life right before his eyes as it moaned and reached for him—but was very slow. And given the way pieces of its body were falling off... it was still in a very poor state of decay.

How curious. Riven cocked his head to the side and circled around the room to keep his distance from the slow-moving creature while watching its gait pattern and ripples of teal death mana occasionally licking across the edges of its open wounds. If only he could study the monster and learn how to create something like this himself...

The undead monster suddenly lunged forward, nearly getting a hold of his left arm before he brutally rammed his knee into the creature's face on reflex— sending it stumbling back momentarily with an audible crunch and giving himself some room to summon a Wretched Snare.

The black magic bloomed in front of him like a flower, expanding and encasing the creature with its needlelike net that tangled the howling undead up in a frustrating, flailing attempt to break free while it burned into the creature's flesh with sizzling sounds.

Riven stood there, curiously examining his new enemy in silence despite the continued wails of the zombie. "You are quite...interesting."

He watched the creature die slowly in the webbing of his own creation. The magic seemed slightly thicker along the needle-filled black net, and he could have sworn that it had gotten bigger with the cast after putting the ring on.

Looking down at the emerald-decorated ring on his hand, he curiously stared and then summoned two Bloody Razors, rapidly spinning to either side of his staff-wielding hand. Just as suspected, they'd also grown in size—though not by much. With a casual flick of his wrist, they shot out and tore into the trapped creature beneath him.

The creature born of hell screeched even louder as the two spinning discs of blood magic tore off an arm and severed part of its neck, black blood splattering along the stone ground and wall with a final ear-piercing shriek. The partially decapitated zombie's reaching hand slowly fell downward while burning on the snare entangling it, and soon the creature's entire arm fell limp as it died—jaw ajar as pieces of its rotted body continued to fall off like cooked meat from a bone.

"You're also one ugly bitch." Riven held up the gnarled staff in his right hand and slapped the dead creature's dangling head with it out of irritation, also kicking it along the way as his magic faded and he bypassed the corpse with a humph.

CHAPTER 26

Riven hadn't realized it until just then, but the words coming out of his mouth were not in the English language. He was speaking…something else…and it was downright natural. It was as if he'd known this language his entire life. Confused, and not understanding how or when this particular bunch of knowledge had transplanted itself, he added it to the list of system tomfuckery that'd been going on over the past little while.

With a creak, Riven turned the doorknob and pushed. A dust cloud came up off the ground a few feet into the air as the door came open, and in front of him, a long dark hallway led to a staircase going down.

Not creepy at all. Nope. Nothing about this wonderful joyride had been creepy in the slightest, and this dark, ancient hallway definitely didn't fit that bill, either.

He walked in silence, only pausing to inspect the immediate surroundings of his hallway. All of this…it was downright fascinating to him. Sure, he might be stuck in hell, but he'd been an atheist all his life. Exploring and sightseeing might not be such a bad idea while he was here, and this ruin seemed as good a place as any to start. There were occasional scratch marks carved into the walls to form crude demonic hieroglyphs. Little skulls of oddly shaped rodents were scattered along one side of the hallway where an alcove into the hallway had been built—or what he assumed to have once been rodents. An ancient halberd rusted with age that'd been snapped in half during a battle millennia past was placed directly in his path along the dust-covered floor—and those were only some of the things in the increasingly clutter-filled hallway. Decayed books, overturned tables, and a charred human skull were added to the list—but nothing of true value other than the ability to stimulate his curiosity was found. Soon he came to the end of the dark, dry, and nearly lightless hallway to peer down the set of stone stairs. At the bottom, about thirty steps down, was yet another hallway that was already partially illuminated from here—this one a lot less cluttered than the one he'd just left.

His boots stepped softly against the ancient stone steps, and he found himself on another path with glass windows that branched out into three different directions straight ahead at a crossing point. The thick glass windows were mostly smudged with layers of dirt and grime, but still high enough above the ground to give him a real view of what he was looking at despite the clouds and occasional layers of mist.

It was not what he'd been expecting when he'd been placed in a dungeon.

The sun above him wasn't a sun at all, but rather it was a deep red, unblinking, lidless eye wreathed in flame. Above him an abyss of crimson sky spread out from horizon to horizon, with lightning intermittently flashing in the distance many leagues away and giant flying monsters farther off encircling the skyscrapers of an ancient stone city.

He was standing on an enclosed catwalk hundreds of feet above the ground. Far below him, down on the broken cobblestone streets below, were piles of rubble and wreckage from another age. Broken wooden carts covered in mold, crows overhead, scattered skeletons and bones, and pieces of collapsed stone walls were everywhere. There were alien or goth-styled structures such as citadels and temples with high steeples, and far expanses of wreckage in between were in abundance. All about him were the other towering stone skyscrapers opposite his own—some with caved-in rooftops. The red mists and scattered clouds of black smog stretched skyward in various patches. And as he stood there watching, gawking even, the light of the flaming eye was soon overshadowed by one of many slow-moving smog clouds.

More worrying were the lumps of barely recognizable old corpses that'd been strung up and hung in various areas from the rooftops or undersides of buildings. The bodies were of many species that included humans, and they'd been completely skinned. They'd also been eviscerated, leaving their intestines to hang out of their bodies in a gruesome display of malevolence. There were random bouts of flame that cycloned through the air from time to time out of small holes in the ground, but they were far and few between while alien bellows echoed out across the tainted landscape. There was even a large, bloody pentagram drawn on a distant temple front.

Occasionally movement could also be seen in the streets or between buildings, but he couldn't get a good look at whatever it was that was living down there…and Riven got the eerie feeling that he was being watched.

"Well, fuck me sideways."

He turned right, looking down the new hallway where it came to a catwalk's crossroad while giving his staff a tighter grip. Hesitantly walking over and stopping at the intersection, he saw paths continuing out in all three directions… each one disappearing into darkness where they connected with other towering skyscrapers.

But he didn't see any giant statue of a bearded, axe-wielding man when looking out the windows... So, without further internal debate, he kept on going straight ahead and hoped that he'd chosen well.

An hour later he was still wandering the dark halls of the ancient building he'd entered. It was huge, with numerous rooms full of wreckage and stairways, some of them partially caved in, closets full of cobwebs, and many musty halls to traverse. Rotting old furniture, broken windows, and, worst of all, the dusty remains of people numbering in the hundreds with rotted, shredded clothes still on the remnants of their bones.

What the hell had happened here? To have so many bodies scattered about like this...it must have either been some kind of massacre or some sort of very abnormal and deadly event that he couldn't quite comprehend. The thing was, most of the bodies had their skeletons intact without any signs of sharp or blunt trauma...sometimes even with their clothes 100 percent intact—and that really weirded him out. Whoever these people had been, it was as if they'd all just simultaneously dropped dead...

To boot, he was absolutely lost.

"KAJIT HAS WARES!"

"AAAHHHHH! SHIT!" Riven nearly had a heart attack when the high-pitched, feminine voice of an old woman screeched out at him from a little nook in the wall where pieces of brick were missing. There, in the dim light of the crevice, stepped out a familiar figure.

Neon-teal mana rippled along her decaying skin in random intervals. Black ichor leaked out of a goofy smile that was missing most of her teeth. Bandages old and yellowed with time lay wrapped across her body at odd intervals, and matted gray hair came down over the taut gray skin covering her face. However, the finger he'd broken off one of her hands was now replaced again, and the bodily harm he'd done by killing her earlier was nowhere to be seen.

"You again?!" Riven said with a dumbfounded, gawking stare. "And you can talk?!"

"Of course I talk! I sell you goods, yes?!" The zombified woman from whom Riven had originally taken the ring he now wore was standing...no, hovering before him. She drifted slightly off the stone floor with minimal effort, and upon inspecting her more closely, he saw the body she now occupied was very slightly transparent.

Riven blinked twice and took a step back, cocking his head to the side and scratching his head. "Didn't I kill you once?"

"Yes, death is bad for business. But for you I make special offer, special price!" The zombified ghost's toothy grin only grew wider, and the ichor leaking out of her mouth dripped onto the floor, only to disappear completely without making contact.

Riven shifted his gaze from the ghost to the spot on the floor where the black ichor had disappeared, and then back to the ghost. "This is about that wooden ring and getting haunted, isn't it? All right, what's this about you having wares? What was it, Kajit? Is that your name?"

The ghostly, decrepit woman folded her arms with a huff—the eye sockets in her semitranslucent skull narrowing. "You say it Khajiit—it is Kajit. Say it right, numbskull, or I leave with my wares and never return!"

"That's what I said. Kajit."

"YOU SAY KHAJIIT!"

"Jesus fuck, lady." He pointed an accusatory finger the floating woman's way. "All right, Karen, explain yourself! What are you doing here and what do you want?! Didn't you try to kill me earlier?!"

"I say I make a special price for one and only!"

"Don't you ignore me, damn it! You tried to kill me!"

"YOU STAB ME IN HEAD FIRST, UGLY BOY!"

"Ugly?! Take a look in the mirror! You're hideous!"

"I use special salve that make my skin extra-shiny gray. It all rage in hellscapes, you know. Do not be jealous. If you take salve, too, you may get real man arms."

"Huh?" Riven inspected either arm, though he kept a ball of Wretched Snare in one hand ready to release it just in case this creature decided to stop the crazy old lady act and go feral again. "What's wrong with my arms?"

"They are noodly appendages. So skinny, cannot get girlfriend save life. Barely fit for baby."

"Hey! That's rude! My arms are average, okay?!"

"Average for paralyzed stork!" The zombie ghost humphed and glared down at him from where she continued to drift upward at an ultra-slow, steady pace. "Do you want special price or not?!"

"Special price for what, though? I have exactly zero dollars."

"What is dollar? NO! I have special price! Special price on special item?!" The ghost suddenly faltered, then seemed confused, judging by her own expression. She clicked her tongue, however a ghost did such a thing, and then started mumbling to herself under her breath.

"I know I have it here for special price. Where it go... I..." The ghost trailed off, her voice becoming distant and faded, before her body blipped out of existence altogether in a flash of neon-teal light.

"..."

The deafening silence was sudden, coming just as quickly as it'd left. Riven took a few steps forward and inspected the area she'd vanished into, but nothing was present at all. "Hello?"

There was no response other than his own voice echoing slightly down the dark halls of the ruined city.

"Kajit? Spooky ghost lady?"

There was still no response.

He waited around for another couple of minutes, then assumed she wouldn't be coming back. Or at least, wouldn't be coming back anytime soon. He could safely piece together what was happening here after the "Haunted" notification had afflicted him. He'd never had a notification saying he wasn't haunted anymore, but he'd originally assumed killing that creature back in his starting room would solve that issue. He'd assumed wrong, apparently, and it very much looked like he had a tagalong ghost lady who was trying to sell him some sort of wares…

How odd. Nevertheless, going on what he knew, he could assume that it didn't matter where he went—she'd probably be able to find him.

Shaking his head and stepping over another set of skeletons while praying to God that these things weren't undead like the haunted zombie he'd come across earlier, he came around and into a large ballroom.

He could tell that it was once a ballroom at first glance just by the look of it. A huge chandelier many times his size lay crashed in the center of the room with pieces of glass scattered across the floor. Broken tables and chairs were littered about the outskirts of the enclosed area, and dim rays of light filtered in through the roof where patches were missing due to what he'd assume was water damage from the mists…though he wouldn't expect it to rain here anytime soon, given what the outside world looked like.

Glancing up, he noted another human body hanging from a ceiling strut. It was completely still, with a long chain looped around its neck, and unlike the bodies outside, this one was decayed with one leg missing and a small swarm of flies whirling about it.

What in the literal hell were flies doing in a place like this? Then again, he'd seen crows, too. And…flying ghost ladies he'd murdered trying to sell him goods. Hadn't been expecting that last one, either.

He turned his head right, and then left, seeing another hallway leading out of the ballroom on the opposite end…but also noting a single, closed wooden door to his left. The difference with this one when compared to the others he'd passed, and the thing that caught his attention most, was the gleaming, intact lock along the front.

That kind of thing hadn't been present on any of the other doors he'd come across thus far, not a single one, and a small smile turned up at the corners of his lips. If that didn't scream *loot*, he didn't know what did.

He nimbly stepped through the haphazard sprawl of shattered glass and debris, passing by the chandelier and moving hastily across the room until he stood at the door. He gingerly took the handle in his grip and then pulled down.

It didn't budge; the lock was definitely still intact. He got down on one knee for a better look; he couldn't see worth a damn due to the crappy lighting...

He looked about. There was a ray of light nearby, and with a bit of quick thinking he scrambled over to obtain a piece of glass that lay on the floor—one of many pieces of the broken chandelier not far off. Coming back to the door and using the glass to reflect some of the ray's light into the lock, he began to get an idea of what he was working with.

It wasn't like the one he'd picked back in the pyramid; this one was more familiar. Back on Earth, he'd had a minor amount of experience picking locks as a hobby...so he was happy to see that this particular lock was just what he expected it to be—and pretty simple upon inspection.

It was just a knob lock—meaning the cylinder for the lock was located in the handle itself. He could go about picking it, and that would have been his choice in any normal situation to avoid any noise, but here...

Here he could simply knock the damn thing off with something heavy.

That, and he didn't have any lockpicks anyways. Finding or creating a makeshift lockpick would be a real pain in the ass, comparatively. If all else failed, he could try to blast the door off with magic, but it looked rather sturdy, and he wasn't too confident in that plan.

It only took him a second to find a suitable item to work with. It was a heavy iron bar, thick and short, that had likely once been part of the ceiling's support structure before falling to the floor below.

Riven smiled at the small victory, then walked back over to the door. Dropping his staff and raising the bar overhead, he quickly brought it down to slam into the handle.

The knob completely broke off on the first strike, tearing out a chunk of the rotting wood and making a loud ringing sound that hurt his ears. He grimaced but dropped the bar and removed what was left of the doorknob from the door. Then, pushing it open, he came into another, smaller and comparatively well-lit rectangular room.

He walked inside.

There was a large, intact window overlooking a river of shimmering red liquid running through the middle of the ancient, ruined city below that stretched out for miles, but he still couldn't see out into the beyond for too long before the obscuring film of mist shrouded his vision on and off.

Was that a river of blood?

Wow.

Anyways, it was an awe-inspiring sight, even if it was slightly disgusting. Therefore he took a moment to admire the view despite the spooky factor before looking around the room again.

There was a bed on thick wooden stilts, a nightstand about two feet across, an oddly shaped lantern with a bell curve to it, and a boxy chest. It was all in fairly good condition considering what the rest of this place looked like, but still looked rather old. The bed had a wrinkled velvet blanket atop a well-made mattress, and two slightly moth-eaten pillows were laid neatly at the headboard. The nightstand was redwood, just like the bed, and had two books sitting atop its surface next to the metal lantern. Then there was the chest, a container that could have likely fit him inside and made of planks that had a simple clasp to seal it shut.

"Not too shabby."

CHAPTER 27

WHOOSH

Riven's feet were swept out from underneath him as the floor abruptly lit up with green runes and gave way, a hole forming directly underneath where he stood. His eyes went wide, and he had mere moments before his body reacted to gravity's pull, which sucked him downward into darkness.

SPLASH

Gasping and coming up for air, Riven found himself enveloped in a large pool of blood similar to the river he'd seen outside. Only this one was stagnant and placed in the middle of an enclosed, squarish room with pillars and passageways leading out along the walls. The ceiling overhead was surprisingly well lit with yellow crystals, showing that even the passageways leaving the room ended in dead ends and rubble. Overhead was the hole he'd fallen through many dozens of yards up, but nothing else of note was around him. He frowned at his misfortune, obviously having fallen into a trap set down by the dungeon. He should have expected such things, but this was really the first time he'd encountered anything like it. Considering what options he had and treading the red liquid, he began to think of a way back up.

That's when he felt something large and slippery glide across his leg, easily brushing him away and causing ripples in the otherwise still pool of blood he floated in.

"What the fuck?!"

His heart sped up. He couldn't see beneath the surface, but something was definitely there, and this time it slammed into him—sending him spinning through the pool into a nearby wall with a hard thud.

He gasped, his backpack rattled as the vase inside nearly cracked, but he was more worried about staying afloat with an injured left arm than he was about his belongings. He whirled while treading blood in the pool, summoning spinning crimson blades and firing them at random into the depths to scare off whatever had attacked him.

Nothing happened. Only silence and occasional ripples in the red liquid remained. Meanwhile, his breathing only became more ragged, as he simply couldn't see what was down there. Whatever had attacked him could likely very easily kill him due to surprise alone, because if he couldn't see, he couldn't dodge or fight back. And even if he could see, he was very much at a disadvantage treading liquid here and not being able to move properly.

"Shit… Shit, shit, shit!"

His left leg was abruptly tugged under, causing him to scream and flail, only to have it released again. Was this creature toying with him?

Regardless, he took the opportunity to swim frantically back up to the surface to gasp for air again. His clothes, hair, and skin were drenched in red, and he coughed the lukewarm blood up out of his lungs after having accidentally taken some in during the panic.

This time he let loose. Unleashing net after net and dozens of conjured Bloody Razors, firing randomly into the depths, he burned through his mana with an enraged and simultaneously terrified scream of defiance, splashing into the depths one after another. However, whatever it was down there that he'd hit…it didn't seem to like that very much. The pool beneath him almost immediately turned into a torrent of madness as magics clashed with something very large, something very angry, that lived in this strange room amid the ruins.

BOOM

The room shook when a giant tentacle five times Riven's body length crashed into a pillar opposite from where he floated. Debris and dust began showering him from the ceiling above, but there was simply nowhere for him to go. He looked to the tunnels in a mad panic and began swimming toward the nearest one despite the dead end, but they were already in a state of disrepair and began to collapse as one after another of newly emerged monstrous red tentacles began climbing out of the depths while a groan of some unearthly god erupted from beneath his feet.

The room and his body shuddered amid the cacophony of noise, and his eardrums began to bleed. He screamed, covering his ears in sheer agony as this beast from the beyond clambered upward to find the man who'd dare injure it.

THUD

THUD

THUD

Riven tried to unleash another spell in desperate attempt to discourage the creature, but he'd already unleashed everything he had in his original volley. The magic didn't want to come to him; his soul reservoir simply didn't have the stored energy anymore. Meanwhile, the blood pool was billowing upward to make way for the huge bulk of some enormous creature—sending waves of blood in all directions with a rising pinnacle in the center.

THUD

THUD

THUD

The sounds of climbing through the depths were growing louder, as was the echoing groan. More of the tentacles reached up, this time all around him, climbing and clambering across the pillars and walls toward the ceiling, where suckers each a few feet in diameter stuck to the stone and pulled the monstrous weight behind it.

THUD

THUD

THUD

Cursing and using his staff to leverage his body, he managed to finally get a poor hold on a ledge where one of the pillars had been cracked by one of the passing monster's weighty appendages. He pulled himself up, reeling, just in time to see the numerous fleshy red tentacles all slowly withdraw and sink into the pool.

He paused, heart beating faster than it ever had before. Dead silence descended upon the room like the call of the grave, a foretelling of his impending doom that lasted for more than a dozen seconds before the pool finally stopped rippling. Then, in the center of its flat surface and under the yellow light of the crystals above, a figure began to emerge at an incredibly slow rate—but the face that came up was focused solely on him.

It was a bulbous, smooth, fleshy head with alien features that Riven could only describe as disgusting. Fishlike eyes on a smooth, semirounded maw—a cross between a giant fish and a frog—pulled out of the depths, revealing itself to have large rows of teeth. Blood dripped down its mouth that was easily big enough to eat three of Riven in a single bite. And even though it was so large, it now made absolutely zero noise while it pulled its ugly head up out of the pool to stare at him with a hungry, open mouth.

Riven was awestruck. He dropped his staff to the ledge, feeling his heart drop with it, when he suddenly realized that this was it. He was going to die here. No matter how many spells he threw at this thing, he was nowhere near powerful enough to come even close to killing it. This was a monster far, far beyond him, just by sheer size and bulk alone, and upon trying to identify it, he didn't even get a name. Rather, all he got were question marks. There was also no way out, nowhere to go, with all passageways out being dead ends and zero ability to get back up to the ceiling where he'd dropped down—he was truly and utterly fucked.

"RRRRRAAAAAAAAAAAAAAAAAAHHHHHHHHHHHHHHHHHHHHHHHHH!"

The room and pool around him vibrated and shook underneath the monster's bellow, shattering what remained of Riven's right eardrum right before dozens of smaller tentacles blasted out of the water to latch onto his body, clothes, and items. Some scoured his belongings, tearing off his clothes and backpack before tossing them aside. Others began burrowing into his newly exposed flesh, leeching off his blood as he felt a sucking sensation from numerous areas where the monster had merged with his bloodstream to begin feeding on him alive.

The sucking sensation made him vomit immediately, and he wanted to scream afterward when one of the red tentacles crammed itself down his mouth and began draining blood from the veins in his throat next.

His eyes rolled back, and he experienced pain unlike anything he'd ever felt before via a multitude of pinholes that burrowed through his flesh. His body quickly atrophied while the fluids of his tissues were drained out, though, surprisingly enough, he didn't immediately die. Though he looked like some kind of skeleton within a mere twenty seconds of being tortured alive and fed upon, his body was somehow regenerating without any explanation of how or why.

The creature was equally confused by this and moved in closer while maintaining its constant sucking that leeched blood from his arteries at over three dozen points.

Riven remained like this for some time, in a state of near death where his mind went hazy and he felt the lifeblood of his body being sucked out in droves…until primal rage and desperation finally overcame him. His body tensed, his Blood subpillar vibrated violently, and his eyes blazed crimson as he shrieked through the red tentacles crammed into his throat. Everything became a base-level instinct, and he desperately began fighting for his life.

[You are severely underfed and require the blood of mortals to satiate your hunger. Insanity takes hold of your mind until you feed.]

RIP

Fangs ripped out of his mouth, and Riven bit down hard, easily tearing into the appendage with a twist of his head and swallowing it in one go. His muscles began to pulse, and a hunger for blood rippled through him as his own screech was joined by the monster's while its bitten-off tentacle flailed about and rapidly retracted.

The monster roared, erupting from the pool and lashing out at him with larger and more sinister-looking bladed tentacles that cut through the air like whips.

The appendages inside his body, draining his lifeblood, exploded as his Blood subpillar resonated with a torrent of power—calling out to the lake of crimson liquid in front of him. His red eyes shot wide-open and holes throughout his body immediately mended. A fountain of blood tore through the air to intercept the squid-like appendages immediately thereafter, though he was still far too underleveled to be blocking an attack like that.

A razor edge ripped cleanly through his leg, severing it at the knee, only to be stitched back a second later as crimson liquid blazed and lit up—condensing around his body, pouring into his throat while he sucked it down, and repairing his wound over the course of seconds. Meanwhile, he smashed down on another tentacle with abnormal amounts of strength, and he became the equivalent of a frantic, hard-to-kill cockroach for the monster as it dealt out serious punishment.

CRASH

He lost an arm, only to stitch it back together while ribbons of red tore out of the pool to answer the call of his vibrating Blood subpillar.

BOOM

He narrowly dodged another blow that would have surely ended him, stone in the wall behind him having shattered under the crunch of another tentacle.

[You are severely underfed and require the blood of mortals to satiate your hunger. Insanity takes hold of your mind until you feed.]

[You are now well-fed. Your insanity fades.]

[You are severely underfed and require the blood of mortals to satiate your hunger. Insanity takes hold of your mind until you feed.]

[You are now well-fed. Your insanity fades.]

Meanwhile, his mind went in and out of consciousness, sanity and insanity battling with one another. Every time his body took in an influx from the blood pool, he'd regain his clear thinking. And every time he suffered a large wound or breaking bone, more of the blood pool was ripped out to repair his body.

But his regeneration speed was slowing down, and the pool of blood was rapidly being drained. It appeared he had serious limits on this kind of healing. Despite the massive amount of environmental resources, it was taking huge quantities of the stuff to regenerate his limbs, and he could feel his Blood subpillar starting to slow down its vibrations.

He was still going to die here if he didn't get out very soon.

[You are severely underfed and require the blood of mortals to satiate your hunger. Insanity takes hold of your mind until you feed.]

[You are now well-fed. Your insanity fades.]

He began to brainstorm. During one of these moments when his sanity returned and his unnatural strength briefly left him, he finally came up with a plan. Bone snapped, limbs and guts ripped, ribbons of blood poured out of the pool to keep him alive amid the creature's barrage that tore chunks out of the stone wall and splattered it with Riven's body—but through sheer willpower, he persevered. Even though his body wasn't healing nearly as fast as it had been even a minute ago, even though the pain was immense and he felt like he was dying a thousand deaths, he still persevered.

The answer was a simple one.

During one of the instances when he was free of being pummeled to death by the brutish monster in quick lashes that would crush any normal man, his hand shot out and produced a black net. His mana by this time had recharged enough to cast a few of these things, and he launched himself onto the wall in a mad scramble upward.

The surprised creature behind him missed and shattered rock again where Riven had just been standing. It roared, sending another tentacle upward to latch onto his ankle, only to have a Bloody Razor appear to snip the appendage off at the tip.

He scrambled even faster, firing one net after another to make a sticky ladder out of the Wretched Snares one by one up the side of the wall. He'd been wary of the idea at first but found that the magic didn't burn him at all, as it was his mana. He was able to manipulate the magic and actually grip the needles in one hand, and they'd just melt into a smooth cord instead. Yet they remained sturdy upon his will. Thus when he rapidly reached a point farther up and close to the trap hole he'd fallen through, he was able to combine multiple snares into one casting. He was able to stitch one end to another, and then another, and then another, and he flung it up at the ceiling. He stuck the snare to an area adjacent to the hole in the floor, barely swinging out of the way from another tentacle strike from far below, and allowed himself to climb up in a mad dash.

UMPH

He breathed heavily and slammed into the floor of the room he'd fallen through earlier just as another tentacle skimmed the tips of his toes. He grunted amid a screech of outrage, still exhausted from the bodily trauma. Passing the threshold into the room, he let himself fall with a light thud onto the stone floor and let out a loud groan. "This place is the worst!"

His body shuddered, his lungs gasped, and he peered out over the edge of the hole to see the monster roaring back up at him.

Its large, unblinking, fishlike eyes scoured him up and down, watching in a hungry rage. But as it glared back at Riven's sneering face, one of its other eyeballs was directing other appendages to dig through Riven's things—and when it came to the vase in Riven's backpack, it simply snapped the thing open when the porcelain wouldn't budge on its own.

And that was the creature's fatal mistake.

A shock wave erupted from the vase, shearing Riven's peering face clean off along with one of his eyeballs, which was sent splattering across the ceiling

above—even if he'd made it all the way up. So, too, did it destroy all the appendages trying to trail up the sides of the pit, vaporizing most of them instantly with
a wave of darkness and causing the creature to shriek in rage.

The monster reared up, exposing a long, tubular neck that connected to a
thicker body near the base where thousands of tentacles swirled about its core.
Its large maw hissed and roared, but when another shock wave of raw Unholy
power directed solely at the monster buried itself in the creature's face and then
sheared through its brain like a razor through cheese—the monster simply died
on the spot.

The abomination twitched animatedly three times over, the top half of its
skull rolled off the rest of its neck and splashed into the pool, and then the rest
of the monster crashed into a nearby wall to start sinking back into the depths
from whence it came.

Riven, still somehow conscious, began to see again as a mixture of both
shock and disbelief overcame him. His body hung halfway over the hole he'd
been looking down, pain screaming through his muscles and skeleton. His shaky
hands came up to his face, one of them intact and the other completely devoid of
almost any flesh from where he'd tried blocking the pulse of power on instinct...
until it started to regenerate new muscles, bone, ligaments, and skin right before
his one remaining eye.

His eyesight came back to 100 percent again and he felt his face, which was
also healing up. For the first time, he actually realized his body was somehow
drawing on the blood of the pool beneath the ledge he lay on. It finally clicked,
and he slowly lifted a finger up to touch one of the now-receding fangs that
had sprouted from his mouth. Yanking out what remnants of the wriggling
appendages still buried in his skin with grunts of pain and disgust, he saw those
remaining holes close over, too. But he froze when his eyes lifted, still in a state
of shock, to settle on where the porcelain vase had shattered only moments ago.

There, staring directly at him from below, was an eyeless, ethereal maw with
sharp canines and a wicked grin. It carried no body with it, fading in and out of
reality by the millisecond. It was made up of a swirling vortex of black and red,
and just looking at it made his bones creak with what he could only describe as
an immense hunger. The hunger was unnatural, unbearable, unignorable, and
all-consuming, and the longer he stared at it, the longer he felt it...resonate...
within his soul.

It resonated with the hunger he'd felt after being drained. The hunger for
blood.

[Your racial bloodline's unique additional aspect, Breath of
Malignancy, has found a compatible Shard of Original Sin: Gluttony.
Shard of Original Sin: Gluttony has initiated contact. Core of Original

Sin: Gluttony will begin forming in your soul now. Estimated incubation time for core completion: unknown. You have lost your racial bloodline's unique additional aspect, Breath of Malignancy, and may no longer bond with any other Shards of Original Sin. Other aspects of your racial bloodline are still partially locked.]

The essence of the maw let out a demonic scream, far louder, longer, and with a presence far greater than the monster had exuded many times over. The very air around him quaked with raw power, and his soul screamed back. Red light erupted from his chest and ripped through the visage, drawing the Shard of Original Sin into his body with a flash of power that both stung and enthralled him down to his soul core. Heaven and hell, hope and despair, pleasure and pain—he experienced all these things in that one instant.

He shuddered, clutching his head as these emotions drove themselves into his psyche with an ever-gnawing hunger. His body fluctuated, muscles bulged and shifted, bones cracked and snapped, only to return to their normal form moments later. This repeated over and over again, and it was during one of these shifts that he felt his neck snap for the briefest moment, causing his head to slam involuntarily into the nearby wall—which ended up knocking him out cold.

Standing there, invisible to Riven's eyes just a few feet away, another man with similarly crimson eyes glared down at him. Hooded and cloaked, he dispelled the invisibility and snorted with displeasure. "I'd hoped the monster would kill him so that I could take the piece of sin for myself… How unfortunate."

The man glanced up to the sky and sighed, internally fuming at how close he'd come to acquiring Gluttony for himself. But he knew he could not act, not directly, not when the system itself would slam down the might of ten thousand suns and burn his soul from the inside out if he intentionally intervened in a system tutorial without permission. Integrated populations were protected for certain amounts of time dependent on situation, and Riven here was no different.

Growling and grumbling to himself, he turned around and headed out the door. Perhaps one of the other denizens of this hellscape would finish the boy off for him. Then, and only then, via death not brought about by his own hands, would he be able to strip Gluttony off Riven's soul to take for his own. Not only that, but the one who sent him would also be furious if he were to strike Riven down now, even if he could get away with it by the system bylaws. Which he couldn't.

"Poor luck and misfortunate follow you, youngling." The man glared back over his shoulder from under the hood of his cloak, eyes blazing with bright crimson light. "May you die a quick death."

CHAPTER 28

Riven woke up on the floor of the room, next to the hole he'd fallen through, to see the large pool of blood beneath him was almost entirely drained. It left a long drop down, hundreds of feet, into a chasm where the body of the creature that'd attacked him was half submerged in what little of the blood remained. Where that blood had gone, Riven had no clue, but it'd simply vanished to reveal nothing but a holding pit for the monster without any real areas of interest otherwise. Perhaps he'd drained it in his sleep?

That in itself brought a lot of questions. He'd grown fangs, regenerated over and over again at extreme rates—albeit using the blood pool to do so—and had lost his mind numerous times. He'd been told he was "underfed" and required the blood of mortals, yet this blood pool had seemed to satiate that hunger and calm his mind. The implications of all this were less than good.

He groaned, being utterly exhausted, and pushed himself up while blinking rapidly to clear his head. Curiously enough, his clothes and belongings were all right beside him…undamaged. His wounds were all long gone, having mysteriously healed without any flaw or imperfection. He lifted the hand that'd been stripped of flesh and flexed it, feeling it out to make sure there wasn't any lingering damage. He felt his knee where his lower leg had been severed cleanly and felt around his abdomen, where his guts had been ripped out. He was satisfied with the results.

He felt slightly different, but not by much. More than anything, he could feel that his soul structure had changed. It was similar to the way his pillars had attached themselves to the soul core, but now as he looked inward, he was able to tell his soul had a dual core on top of the original. The one he was familiar with, that ball of brilliant white light with his Unholy Foundational Pillar and Blood subpillar attached to it. Then there was…another, partial orb. This one was pitch-black instead of white, was slightly smaller, and orbited Riven's original core at a slow, monotonous pace. It wasn't entirely solid, though, and pulsed in between a ghostly ethereal black to a more solid void black—no doubt because it was still under construction. He could feel a gnawing sensation of hunger from the core. The same one that'd supercharged his body when he'd seen the visage of a maw.

Thinking about it, Riven curiously extended a tendril of mana toward the unfinished core of original sin. It immediately and thoroughly rebuked his attempt, letting him know that he wouldn't be able to utilize this newfound power until whatever it was doing was completed.

Hopefully that'd be sooner rather than later, judging by the monstrosity this untapped power had utterly demolished.

Riven shakily started putting his clothes back on. He packed up his things— well, what was left that hadn't been tossed away in the battle—and was thankful that the majority was still present. Glancing up toward the hole in the ceiling, he scratched his head and frowned.

Allowing himself some time to breathe, he continued to let the light of the fiery sky eyeball warm him from beyond the large clear glass window making up most of one wall. Then, reorienting himself to his surroundings again, he picked out the details of the room he'd so briefly encountered before.

The comfortable-looking bed with moth-eaten pillows and velvet covers looked quite nice given his current state. An oddly shaped bell-curve lantern sat on a short nightstand nearby, alongside two thick books, and a rectangular wooden chest was at the foot of the bed. Huffing and getting up off the ground, he started back at square one.

He walked over to the chest and flipped the clasp, then began to pry it open. It held fast at first, but he managed to grunt and heave enough that it gave way... when there was an audible click from inside.

He immediately dodged left and dropped the lid as a bolt shot past his ear— missing him by half an inch and landing to embed itself in the wall behind him.

His eyes went wide, though he wasn't necessarily surprised. Riven cleared his throat and adjusted his robe before turning back to the box. He'd been half expecting it to have mechanisms like this after what'd already happened to him. Still, it had been a close call. This time, a little more carefully, he lifted the lid again and revealed the contents inside.

A spring-loaded redwood crossbow had been rigged to fire and was set on a stand in the middle of the large box. Now that it'd been released, it lay dormant and unthreatening—but it looked to be in good condition. On the right-hand side was a belt attached to a quiver with over twenty steel bolts, and a sheath on the opposite side of the belt held a knife. On the left-hand side was an empty backpack, a leather vest, and three thick scrolls, each about the size of his hand and made from aging yellowed paper...but they each let off a very low glow of various colors.

He scratched his head, confused. "That's definitely strange…"

He hesitantly picked the scrolls up, becoming more confident as they didn't burn or shock him like the wooden ring from the embalmer's room had done, and set each of them on the bed. However, he did note how warm they were to the touch…and the way that warmth spread up his hand and forearm while holding them.

He unfurled each of these scrolls, smiling when numerous runic symbols lit up along the paper. They failed to furl back up and each stayed as straight as a board. One scroll was written in red lettering, a projectile of some kind depicted on the front that read "Blood Lance" in bold letters at the top. Another was written in dark gray and had a foot with wings on it and was called "Quickstep," and the last one was written in a light gray with an arrow on the front that read "Calculated Shot."

[Spell Scroll: Blood Lance (Blood) (Tier 2)—Channel power into your arm and unleash it at your enemies with a chance to pierce through. Very long range, medium casting time, medium cooldown.]

[Martial Art Scroll: Quickstep (Chi)—Envision the path you want to take in a straight line from where you stand, and blur ahead at great speed. May be used in any direction. Instant cast, high cooldown.]

[Martial Art Scroll: Calculated Shot (Chi)—Highlight vulnerable areas on your selected target, speed your reflexes, and slow time to perfect your aim as you fire. Must have a bow or gun in hand to use. Instant cast, medium cooldown.]

His eyebrows raised. Really, now? A Tier 2 spell? And they were scrolls as well, being far more valuable than tomes in the aspect that you could immediately learn the spell, but less valuable in the aspect that you couldn't repeatedly learn from it, and it would disappear after use.

According to Athela, anyways.

From what he'd read, Tier 2 spells required hand gestures alongside the image, intent, and all that other jazz he'd need for basic Tier 1 spells. Huh. And he'd been here less than a day before he'd found some ability scrolls already. Lucky him? Maybe, but it was yet to be seen whether or not he'd even survive this area. After all this was a higher-stakes, higher-rewards tutorial dungeon…and it was yet to be seen whether or not it'd pay off or get him killed.

Or get Athela killed.

He shook his head to clear his head of that last thought. He was lucky to stumble across something like this. The idea of having found additional magic so soon, and knowing these things were likely very valuable to sell even if he couldn't use them… It was a huge boon.

The key factor here was that these were actually ability scrolls—what Athela had said were incredibly expensive and very hard to make. They could imbue him with knowledge far faster than needing to learn out of a tome himself, but they were almost impossible to come by for those who didn't pay a hefty price, from what the spider had told him. Not only that, but he'd gotten incredibly lucky that one of them was usable with a subpillar he already had—Blood. He couldn't use the two Chi-type abilities, but he could definitely save them for later and give them to someone else if he ever got out of here, and if he didn't end up selling them.

He set the other two scrolls down to pick up the one that applied to his class. The scroll sparkled in his grip, and the warming sensation he got while holding the other two magnified with the touch of the scroll for Blood Lance.

He could safely say he just hit the jackpot.

Shutting the door and peering out into the ballroom through where the doorknob had been one more time, he didn't even bother inspecting the other stuff yet and got to work mentally willing the first of the scrolls he'd picked up to activate.

[You have the proper pillar orientation to utilize this scroll. This is a one-time-use item and will be destroyed upon use. Do you wish to use the spell scroll: Blood Lance? Yes? No?]

He nodded. "Yes."

[Are you sure? Yes? No?]

Again, he selected Yes.

[You have learned the Tier 2 spell Blood Lance.]

Not a second later, the spell scroll in his hand began to shimmer along the red lettering—and his mind immediately went haywire. Knowledge began to burn its way into his brain as his eyes lit up white—and he began to scream.

It was not nearly as pleasant as the first time acquiring abilities, when he'd learned them the hard way, that was a certain fact.

CHAPTER 29

Two hours later, Riven's head hurt like crazy as the influx of knowledge was downloaded directly into his subconscious brain. Motions, internal activation sequences, and basic knowledge about the new spell flooded his mind and were implanted into his subconscious brain. The feeling was like a killer migraine, or better yet—like he'd been a ping-pong ball put into a glass jar and shaken around frantically for a good long while.

He clutched his forehead after finishing the scroll and groaned, but he couldn't help but smile despite the pain as the newfound ability was registered into his character sheet. Not only did he see the new ability, but he had an entirely new section solely concerning his new core of original sin—which was still currently under construction and otherwise didn't provide details yet.

[Riven Thane's Status Page:
- **Level 4**
- **Pillar Orientations: Unholy Foundation, Blood**
- **Core of Original Sin—Gluttony: (Under Construction) (???)**
- **Traits: Race: Human, Class: Novice Warlock, Adrenaline Junkie (Blood) (+15% to Agility)**
- **Abilities: Blessing of the Crow (Unholy), Wretched Snare (Unholy), Bloody Razors (Blood), Blood Lance (Blood) (Tier 2)**
- **Stats: 8 Strength, 9 Sturdiness, 39 Intelligence, 10 Agility, 1 Luck, -4 Charisma, 3 Perception, 25 Willpower, 9 Faith**
- **Minions: Athela, Level 3 Blood Weaver [14 Willpower Requirement]**
- **Equipped Items: Crude Cultist's Robes (1 def), Basic Casting Staff (4 dmg, 12% mana regen, +3 magic dmg), Chalgathi Cultist Amulet (???), Leather Boots (1 def), Backpack of Supplies, Rusted Embalmer's Knife (3 dmg), Witch's Ring of Grand Casting (+26 Intelligence)]**

He took in a deep breath. Patience was a virtue.

The information was burned into his brain now, and he could summon the new spell at will. He knew what they could do, how he could do it, and he was just dying to try it out. Thus he waited another five minutes for the headache to clear, pushed off the wall with a grunt, and walked out into the ancient ballroom again after flinging the old door to the side.

He looked around the dimly lit room for a clear space, but there wasn't much to be had. So instead, he got up on one of the rickety tables—making sure it could bear his weight—and stood up straight. He concentrated and began twisting his fingers with an inward clawing motion using his conjuring hand. This clawing motion, via body parts or instruments, was the specific motion required of this particular Tier 2 spell.

The spell scroll hadn't lied—this ability did indeed have a medium time to cast. Unlike his other spells, where he could cast instantly, this one took a few seconds to charge up after the initial hand motion. As he channeled the magic into his arm, red wisps of liquid magic rose off his skin like soft, slow-moving ribbons, all the way from his fingertips to halfway down his bicep. When those wisps of energized blood reached his bicep six seconds later, the spell discharged—ripping through the targeted table like it was wet paper and impaling the stone floor behind it in a flash of red energy.

The attack itself was shaped like an elongated, spiked lance, hence the name, and the shaft of magic was probably five feet in length, with the width being slightly smaller than Riven's forearm. The end of the glistening red spike sticking out of the floor that wasn't halfway embedded into the stone was also incredibly sharp. The projectile had pierced a couple feet into the stone structure underneath him but hadn't entirely gone through... Even so, it was significantly more powerful and faster than his spinning blades of blood.

Trying to cast it again with a bit of excitement bearing down on him, he unexpectedly felt the magic resist, and a cooldown sigil indicating Blood Lance appeared in the top right-hand corner of his vision.

Raising an eyebrow, he felt something inside him click into place a solid nine to ten seconds later and was once again able to cast the spell.

Meanwhile, he was able to repeatedly fire off discs of Bloody Razors almost one cast after the other with a very short cooldown, if it even activated a cooldown at all—each not having any casting time at all. The discs of serrated blades formed by blood were created immediately instead of having to charge up. When compared to the power of the Blood Lance, though, the serrated blades only scratched the surface of the stone or shattered on impact without penetrating.

Interesting. He'd experienced cooldowns only a few times since acquiring spells, but he knew it when he saw it. Still he repeated his experimentations with this new spell, continuing to charge and fire them off intermittently between his other two offensive spells—the snare and razors. He spent quite a while doing this, figuring out that although cooldowns didn't always kick in with his Blood Lance, they occurred far more often when compared to his Tier 1 spells. From what he remembered, cooldowns basically occurred because his channeling pillar became rigid after pushing an influx of mana into a particular part of it. He also knew that the power of the spells would increase and the cooldowns of those same spells would decrease as his Intelligence got higher, so perhaps one day in the future he'd be able to fire off numerous Blood Lances simultaneously without any cooldown kicking in at all.

[Blood Lance (Blood) (Tier 2)—Channel power into your arm and unleash it at your enemies with a chance to pierce through. Very long range, medium casting time, medium cooldown.]

He read the spell description again and nodded while slowly rubbing his chin. He walked over and inspected the hole his last lance had left in the stone floor after the magic vaporized into thin air and then looked about at the other holes decorating the ruin floor. Damn right, his spell could pierce through things! This attack was incredible! Faster, stronger, and more lethal…with the downsides of having a charge-to-cast time and a cooldown time after that. Between the two, he'd have to charge up the Blood Lance, fire it, wait for the cooldown, if he got one, and begin to charge again before a second one could be fired. That was currently somewhere in the realm of fifteen or sixteen seconds between shots, and he could fire off eight rounds of two Bloody Razors apiece for sixteen razor attacks in those sixteen seconds. That fire rate for the Blood Lance was doubled when he charged both arms, each hand creating a clawing motion to initiate the spell as red wisps traveled across his biceps, forearms, and hands when the power built.

He'd also have to use this spell sparingly, at least for now. Not only would it take time to cast—and it felt like it cost more mana, too—but he would also be broadcasting his upcoming attack immediately after the enemy knew what those red wisps crawling up his arm represented. They'd be able to anticipate the move. However, with some further experimentation beyond the normal basic information that'd flooded his mind, he found out some pretty unique things concerning the spell. Through trial and error, he was thankfully able to stop the immediate discharge and hold the spell there within his arm for minutes at a time once it charged. This meant that although they'd know he had it at the ready, he'd not have to immediately fire it off and could wait until the opportune moment to let the magic go. He was also able to discontinue the spell, and canceling it sent the mana flowing back into his body with only a very small amount of the mana actually being lost in the transition.

Getting another idea, he decided to try and channel the Blood Lance through his arm while using his staff-wielding hand to conjure Bloody Razors by creating a curling sweep in the air with his weapon. To his absolute delight, it worked—and the mana actually channeled through his fingers and into the staff before discharging the Blood Lance amid an onslaught of power across the room.

However, he was only able to keep this up for a short time before he'd run out of mana completely. He could tell in the three levels he'd grown that he could already cast more frequently than when he'd been level 1 in the duel versus the necromancer from Chalgathi's quest line, but the change was minimal, and he definitely had limits. Still, if he'd progressed this much in just three levels in terms of how often he could cast spells, then by level 40 or 50, he would be able to cast consistently without having to fear running out of mana—unless he was in a prolonged battle.

He continued to use the scattered skulls, chairs, and various pieces of furniture around the ancient ballroom as target practice while diving, ducking, and running. All the while, he continued casting and trying to get a feel for combining his new abilities. He knew after talking to Athela that many types of mainstream builds for casters generally lacked mobility...so he needed to make up for that weakness by practicing firing while on the run. Athela had mentioned to him that casters often met their demise because they stood in one place while channeling spells or thinking themselves safe on the back lines of a group, and he was determined not to be one of those fatalities.

He spent the next hour practicing, becoming more confident with his timings between the cooldowns of his spells when they triggered and finding that the Wretched Snare spell required about the same hidden mana cost as his Bloody Razors, and it had about the same cooldown when it happened. He could spam the Wretched Snares rather easily, but the problem was it was far shorter of an attack than either of his other projectiles. In his duel with the necromancer in Chalgathi's quest line and when using it on the would-be rapists in the tutorial, he'd been rather close in proximity while using the sticky, burning snare. Here, though, he quickly realized it had half the range of his Bloody Razors and about an eighth of the range of the Blood Lance. Standing at one end of the ballroom, he could fire a Wretched Snare halfway across the large chamber before it fell to the ground. The Bloody Razors made it the entire way across and out the windows before they started to sag and decline in height. Meanwhile, the Blood Lance completely went out the opposite wall, through an open window halfway up, and into the next tower over.

This was, of course, just using the base spells for each of them. If he imbued them with even more mana per cast, he was able to make them each go farther or hit harder or even grow the size of his projectiles.

Oddly enough, Blood Lance also made very little noise when it struck an object. It was *almost* completely silent, unlike the snare, which hissed and burned, or the spinning razors, which trailed out ribbons of blood in their path or shattered in explosions of red upon impact with harder surfaces. But the power behind it was far more deadly, and he could only imagine how it'd affect a person's body.

He also took an hour to try and figure out how to manipulate the spells he did have in various ways. Athela had told him that he'd be able to conjure just one disc of a Bloody Razor at a time, and she had mentioned that spells did different amounts of damage dependent on the mana spent. So he used what she'd said concerning mana as a clue to try and change how much power he put into every spell, instead of the standard amount he naturally prescribed.

Upon his first two tries, it didn't work.

The amount of mana for his Bloody Razors didn't change, but on the third attempt, he was able to decrease the mana amount significantly as he fired a spell and saw the spinning, razor-like discs of crimson decrease in size by two-thirds. This was exciting to him, because he'd never altered a spell to this degree before. Combined with how he'd used his snares to get out of the trap room, this was another testament that he could change and alter given spells in various ways to find different combinations or uses for each basic form of the spell.

He concentrated harder, trying to do the same thing again and again, and finally got the hang of mana manipulation—being able to reduce or increase the size of his Bloody Razors based on how much mana he placed within them. The bigger the size, the more apparent damage they did to the targets they struck. However, it was much harder to figure out how to change the actual *number* of razors, and that's where he got stumped momentarily. At first the razors would crack and break; other times the spell would just fizzle out completely, and yet another hour passed before he was finally able to figure out how to fix it.

The trick had been visualization. He'd had a certain vision of what the spell should look like, ingrained in him through reading of the tome that'd first taught him the spell. When he changed that visualization and used it as a new template, he was able to create one, two, three, four, or even five spinning discs of razor-sharp blood magic before it became a problem when he tried to up it to six. So he remained at five or fewer for now, after repeatedly failing to conceptualize a number over that properly and seeing his magics fizzle out or shatter when he tried too hard. He knew he'd probably end up being able to do it with practice, but each disc required a small amount of individualized concentration upon the summoning, and it was temporarily beyond his ability to do so with more.

Another thing he quickly realized was that the amount of innate mana he used was less with single casting when compared to multiple casts of the same spell—and he did this by feel. He could literally feel his hidden mana pool empty each time he used a spell, even though he had no visual tool to help him monitor it. When using his blood magic and creating four simultaneous discs of the same size—compared to using two castings of two discs or four castings of one razor disc—he realized by feeling out his mana pool that the single casting of four discs cost less than the two castings of two discs, which in turn cost less than the four castings of one disc. It appeared that each initialization of the spell had a base cost to it despite what the actual spell was, so he would be able to utilize his mana more efficiently by using fewer individual casting initializations. He also decreased the number of cooldowns he got simply by casting less frequently and in bulk, so that was yet another reason to cast as much as he could all at once versus multiple casts of the same spell.

During this time, he was very pleased with his results, though more than once he suffered from a complete lack of mana that occasionally gave him a severe migraine. He even got a decent feel for when his mana pool was about to hit rock bottom, and he tried to avoid it in order to avoid the spinning visual auras and headaches that sometimes accompanied mana expenditure.

He decided to wrap things up and was just about to head back into the room for a final look around, specifically to see what those two leatherbound books on the nightstand were about, when he heard a noise from behind and down the near hall leading out of the ancient wreckage of the ballroom.

Riven paused, his blood running cold as he heard again what he thought to be metal-on-stone grinding along the floor...echoing distantly off the stone walls. He turned to the hallway he'd initially come from, staring down the dark corridor as the sound became progressively louder...and louder...and even louder. He didn't know what would make that noise, but his mind went wild with possibilities... He glanced up at the corpse hanging overhead, remembered the skinned bodies strung up in the streets of the city below, and he immediately looked around for a place to hide and watch.

CHAPTER 30

Thinking it foolish to seclude and potentially trap himself in that small, one-entrance room, he avoided it entirely and moved to hide behind an overturned table. His breathing was quickly steadied, and he charged another Blood Lance across his right arm as ribbons of red started peeling off his skin while he peered out around the edge of his concealment.

Then, he waited.

The swarm of flies overhead buzzed around the deathly still corpse. His heartbeat picked up. His eyes narrowed as he silently watched from cover, pumping himself up in case of a coming fight, as the sound of metal scraping against the stone floor grew louder. While it neared, he began to hear the thud of feet against the ground, too, and soon saw the creature making those noises enter the room from the hallway he'd originally come through himself many hours before.

It was a grotesque humanoid monster—an *abomination*, if no other words were used to describe it. It was pale, naked, bald, and lidless, with enormous yellow eyes that scanned the room when it came in. It had an unmoving and creepy smile with lips peeled back to show sharpened yellow teeth—literally from ear to ear—that set his hairs on end. One large, veiny arm on its right side dragged a huge, lusterless, and battle-worn claymore behind it, while a shriveled left arm just dangled uselessly at its side, displaying cracked yellowing nails that were far too long for its own good. There were four slits along the front of its face that it used to breathe like nostrils, and its thorax was abnormally elongated into a hunched position.

Even so, it stood well over seven feet tall, and its long, scrawny legs were just as out of place as the left arm in comparison to the roided-out right arm that carried the claymore.

Riven slowly exhaled, never letting his eyes leave the creature while remaining in his concealed position. "What in the southern cousin hillbilly marriage is this thing?"

[Mutated Ghoul Berserker, Level 7]

Another undead? Perhaps he'd be able to take this thing out with the new ability he'd obtained. However, it looked rather dangerous considering how tall it was and how muscular that one arm was. It'd probably be able to crush him easily if it got ahold of him, and it certainly looked far more intimidating than that little zombie he'd fought earlier… Did he really want to chance it before meeting up with Athela?

No, he didn't. It was too risky to fight this thing by himself when he didn't even know how the basics of this world worked yet or what kind of chance he stood. So he'd just sit his pretty little ass here and wait for that thing to walk on by.

The metal dragging along the stone floor continued as it leaned back and forth, back and forth, coming down the center of the ballroom and heading toward the opposite end that Riven hadn't ventured down yet—when it abruptly stopped.

Slowly, the ghoul turned to face the room Riven had just partially looted… where the wooden door Riven had opened was still ajar. The creature seemed to know something about that door was amiss, and if it traveled these halls frequently, it'd probably never seen that door open before. It cocked its head with that sickening smile it wore and began to visibly salivate, drool dripping from its yellow teeth to splatter along the ground.

With a sudden scream and echoing roar, it rushed forward with a lumbering waltz straight out of a horror film that shouldn't have been as fast as it was considering the way it ran. The monster barreled through a pile of furniture, crushed skeletons underfoot, contracted its veiny muscles, and slammed its large claymore into the side of the ancient stone wall adjacent to the room's doorway.

Riven went pale when he saw part of the unstable wall give way under the creature's strength and collapse in on the small room: crushing the bed, books, and the nightstand in a shower of rubble as the large undead bellowed thrice in a deep, guttural bark. The ghoul probably wouldn't have been able to take the entire thing out with that one swing under normal circumstances, but given how old things here were…Riven wasn't too surprised after the initial shock evaporated.

The ghoul waited for the dust to settle, looking right and left expectantly with its large, yellow eyes—searching for the creature that had violated its hunting grounds…only to find nothing.

When the confused ghoul whirled around and scanned the ballroom, Riven skirted around the edge of his concealment to place himself on the other side. He could hear it breathing, loudly and rapidly sniffing like a dog on the hunt as its footsteps began to close in on his location.

Wait…

Could this thing smell him?

Oh, fuck.

His mind raced, as he couldn't imagine how it'd feel to be struck by a claymore as large as he was. It'd probably be the last thing he'd feel if it came down to it. Or worse yet, he might be eaten by this thing. It certainly looked carnivorous with those sharpened Willy Wonka teeth.

God, it was even uglier than the haunted zombie he'd killed earlier.

So despite his level disadvantage, he committed to a plan. He only had one life to lose, and he'd be damned if he died here while not putting up a fight. Picking up a small piece of rock on the ground in the hand that still shimmered with writhing black shadows, he threw it across the ballroom toward the chandelier at a low angle so that the ghoul wouldn't see the toss.

The rock hit true, loudly shattering one of the still-intact pieces of ornamental glass.

Immediately the sniffing stopped, and the ghoul let out a low growl before turning it into a scream. Its large gray muscles flexed and sent it barreling past Riven's hiding place and into the fray of glass.

The huge arm and claymore came up, then swung back down—delivering a shattering blow to the remnants of the huge chandelier. Shards of it flew in all directions while the ghoul repeatedly beat the area around it in a downright violent temper tantrum.

Riven watched, partially in awe and partially in confusion while the rampage continued. Either this thing was incredibly stupid, or it simply wasn't hurting itself doing what it was doing. But...judging by the way the glass shards were cutting into its body and causing it to bleed—he could safely assume that it was just stupid.

Really strong, but also really, really stupid.

Well, that made him feel a little bit better, but why was this undead bleeding red when the zombie he'd killed earlier bled black? Was it because it was mutated? Weren't undead supposed to be devoid of actual blood, from the stories and books he'd read?

He waited just a little bit longer, taking aim and waiting for the jumping, hacking undead creature to stop its rampage—before Riven stood up and aimed.

Red magic exploded out of his right arm, rocketing with immense speed toward the ghoul and ripping through its body to pierce where its heart should have been. Blood and flesh sprayed out the front side with the shock of the intense energy tearing away to leave a large, gaping hole.

The ghoul stumbled forward, shocked and gasping as bodily fluids ran out the front and back of its thorax. It bent down, screamed at the floor in rage, and dropped the claymore with a clatter of metal. It whirled, wide-eyed, looking for its attacker, just when Riven dived back into cover.

How the hell is that thing still standing?!

In a fit of madness, the monster left the claymore it'd dropped and began to bulldoze through the room—throwing debris, skeletons, and furniture to the left and right as it went. It didn't know where the attack had come from, exactly, but it knew the general direction and was quickly approaching Riven's position when he scrambled to set down one of his three unfinished wooden totems. He had yet to use them in real combat and wasn't sure how effective they'd be, but when the first totem was set firmly on the floor, he got a quick notification asking whether or not he wanted to activate it. He selected Yes, then popped out of his hiding place and engaged.

A Wretched Snare bloomed in front of him as he held his staff at the ready, the dark magic turning from an orb into a net as it shot through the air—but the magic was significantly slower than his other attacks, and the ghoul easily dodged right in its advance with a snarl of fury. Yellow eyes bulged and locked onto him with primal hunger, and the creature renewed its efforts in bulldozing through everything in its path.

Cursing as the infuriated undead rushed him, Riven activated the Blessing of the Crow only to realize his Blood Lance was still on cooldown.

Red lightning sparked across his skin, and his body was blessed with new-found Agility. It was Agility that he'd very much needed, because he barely managed to dance backward in time to avoid a crushing blow that shattered the table he'd been hiding behind—sending splinters flying as the creature roared at him with yellow eyes wide. Blood covered the creature's lower body, continuing to seep from the hole the Blood Lance had made, but Riven now saw that the hole was very gradually starting to seal itself up…and he knew it was not going to be a fatal wound.

The creature screeched in annoyance and pain when the totem Riven left behind summoned a ribbon of red power just over the top of the wooden object and shot it at the ghoul—hitting it in the side of its right arm. It began continually beaming health from the undead monstrosity, ticking away small amounts of damage every second it remained latched to the slow-moving, stupid monster. The creature whirled, hissing at the blood magic leeching off its primary limb, and crushed the totem with repeated strikes of rage. This was more than enough time to buy Riven space, though, and his now-enhanced body leaped backward again. The blessing significantly increased his speed, and he rushed across the room far faster than a normal human ever could. He slid over another table while simultaneously firing a flurry of five decently sized discs of sharpened, solidified blood aimed at the undead. The spinning discs tore into the screeching creature while it followed, burying into its body and shattering in sprays of red shrapnel while leaving parts of the ghoul ripped or bleeding and forcing it to slow down.

[You have inflicted an Amplified Bleeding debuff on your enemy, and it will now take damage over time.]

[Bloody Razors (Blood)—summon spinning discs of crimson with minor lock-on abilities to only slightly adjust for enemy movements. Targets hit will experience damage to stamina and a slowing effect, and a high chance for Amplified Bleeding damage.]

"RRRRRAAAAAAAAAAAAAAAAAAHHHHHHHHHHHHHHHHHHHHHHHH!"

The unearthly, rage-filled scream chilled Riven to the bone as he rolled to the side and narrowly dodged an incoming strike that sent vibrations through the floor. Riven's body blurred left when he empowered his blessing with another large infusion of mana, then he somehow managed to awkwardly flip backward and came to a rolling stop to avoid yet another strike from the ghoul that landed in quick succession and shattered a nearby chair. He couldn't continue to move like that, though, and needed to keep his blessing at a baseline level lest he completely run out of mana and be defenseless.

He kicked off from his kneeling position after the roll and lunged backward to try and put some room in between the undead monster and himself again, but the creature was almost as fast as he was even with his amplified speed. The monster lunged ahead and clipped his shoulder, but Riven retaliated while holding his staff in his left hand and casting another snare that hit the ghoul point-blank. Meanwhile, while his right hand sank the dagger he'd picked up deep into the rolling muscles of the creature's bicep.

They crashed into one another when the undead pivoted, and the ghoul briefly snickered at him mockingly while ignoring the burning magic wrapping around its body. For Riven, time seemed to slow as he realized he was in deep shit. The creature's mouth dripped saliva onto the ground from its sharp rows of teeth in that moment, and the ghoul abruptly backhanded him a second later to interrupt his casting. Simultaneously it ripped through the entangling snare with little effort and screeched. The blow was enough to knock the air out of Riven completely, and he was flung five feet backward to land on his back with a thud.

Coughing, catching his breath, and reorienting himself to the threat, he quickly realized that the ghoul was now standing over him with its large, muscular arm raised above its head for the killing blow. It had acidic burn marks all along its decrepit flesh from where the snare of Unholy magic was still wrapped around it, hissing as smoke sizzled off the undead's body, but the magic simply wasn't strong enough to hold it in place. Nor did the creature appear to feel any pain. Compared to the necromancer he'd fought or the men he'd killed in the tutorial, this thing was an absolute beast. They couldn't even hold a candle to it.

With a final roar, the ghoul brought its huge fist down just as Riven screamed in defiance and sprayed another five Bloody Razors out in front of him to blind the monster. He simultaneously just barely rolled out of harm's way to the left. The blow slammed into stone beneath the undead's fist, blood from its wounds seeping down its body to pool around its feet, and the creature's head and neck were slowly oozing from bloody wounds. Spikes of red were sticking out of its upper body and head—the left eyeball completely blown open with one of Riven's sharp magical projectiles sticking out of the eye socket, and numerous shards of glass were stuck into its thorax and legs…but the bloodied ghoul didn't even seem to notice.

What it did notice, though, when it raised its fist to look at the spot where it'd hit—was that there was no victim. There was no body, there was no meat to feed on…it took a solid couple of seconds for the stupid creature to realize, but the prey had escaped in the hail of crimson that'd blinded it.

It cocked its head in confusion and stared dumbly at the spot for another fifteen seconds, not understanding what had just happened as Riven channeled red ribbons of mana up his right arm for the second time when his hand gestured a clawing motion.

Riven was pretty sure a rib was broken and his ankle was injured, making him lean on his staff for support. His nose was bloodied, and he had a killer headache, but he was still very much alive and hell-bent on bringing this creature down. He grimaced hatefully at the stupid creature when they finally made eye contact and then gave it the finger with his noncasting hand.

Its one remaining, large yellow eye dilated upon seeing him, and its sharp-ened teeth clacked and clattered together as it threateningly gnashed them in his direction with the promise of pain.

"DIE!"

The air in front of Riven split apart. Ribbons convulsed and tore away from his outstretched arm, ripping through the air and into the undead creature's skull in a splatter of brains and bone. The magic continued out the other side to make impact with the far wall and it, too, exploded with rocky debris a ways behind Riven's target.

A wet, sloppy *splat* was heard as the remnants of the creature's skull hit the ground; the ghoul's body staggered back as if in surprise before the huge mass of grotesque, gray flesh slowly fell backward to crash into the stone floor.

[You have landed a critical hit. Max Damage x 4.]

[You have gained one level. Congratulations! Please see your status page to assign stat points.]

Riven was panting at this point, red sparks of lightning still streaming along his skin at random, and he dropped his quivering right arm to the side just before turning and vomiting to his left. He puked again, his heart rapidly beating into his chest, and his body ached…but he was alive. He shook his head, sank to the floor, and wiped off his mouth while spitting at the creature's body.

But then he grinned, and slowly he began to laugh.

CHAPTER 31

Pain flared across his chest like a hot iron, causing him to cringe. Yup, his ribs were definitely broken in at least one spot. It was painful to stand—let alone move around. It especially hurt when he leaned forward at all, so he did his best to keep his back straight and stiff as he walked over to the corpse. But, to his surprise, his body slowly started to regenerate. Small cuts and scrapes started to mend before his very eyes, his rib snapped back into place with a *pop*, and his ankle stopped swelling.

Riven was baffled. This was the second time this had happened today alone. Was it because of the fragment of Gluttony he'd absorbed? But he'd been kept alive before he'd actually absorbed it, when that creature had been sucking him dry like a sponge. Did it have to do with his bloodline that was still "partially locked"? He didn't know why or how this was happening, but whatever the reason, he was glad for it.

Using his foot to roll the remnants of the creature's face, he wiped his bloodied face off on the sleeve of his robes before kicking the mutilated skull across the room.

"God, that guy was tough…"

He was seriously glad it hadn't full-on hit him. The hit Riven had received was half-assed and a sideswipe just meant to stun him for the follow-up killing blow. Even *one* of those real strikes would have easily ended his life in an instant, claymore or not, and he'd been lucky enough to come out with only a rib fracture. That rib and the bloodied nose left him in enough pain as it was.

Well, he was gunning for a mage-type class, after all. He'd have to be more careful about getting into close-combat encounters like that. Not that he hadn't tried to in this circumstance, but he was hoping for a build that would eventually allow him to keep people at bay while he did damage from a safe distance. That included either more crowd-control abilities or more abilities involving maneuverability…or maybe even more minions that could tank for him and protect him.

He cleaned off his embalmer's knife after ripping it out of the corpse, wiping the ghoul's blood on his pant leg—then leaned back on his caster's staff to support his weight, as his legs still continued to shake slightly due to exhaustion despite the healing he'd received. It'd been too close a call not to get his adrenaline going, and he'd come within an inch of death.

He inspected the claymore the ghoul had dropped amid the wreckage of the chandelier after he'd first blown a hole through the creature's back and chest. The weapon was very, very large and looked ridiculously heavy. It had chips along the blade's edges all the way down its surface but was made of a thick metal that was slightly darker than iron. At first he'd thought it just to be dirt and grime from ages of use, potentially even bloodstains, but upon a closer look he was absolutely sure that this metal was just outright different from the things he was familiar with.

"Identify."

[Damaged Orchalium Claymore, 58 average damage, two-handed for full effect, 89 Strength requirement.]

This was the first weapon he'd seen thus far with a stat requirement—albeit he hadn't seen many.

And eighty-nine Strength? That was *way* more than he had. Riven only had eight! He placed his wooden staff on a nearby pile of rubble and bent down just to get a feel for the weapon. Even when using both hands and straining, grunting, and getting red in the face—he was unable to pick it up more than a couple inches off the ground.

Then it started to slightly shock and burn him to the point that he definitely felt pain. The weapon got hotter and hotter to the touch, beginning to feel similar to the wooden ring back in the room he'd spawned in, until it became downright painful about ten seconds later.

"Holy shit!"

He let it go before his fingers broke off, and the weapon crashed into the ground with a bang. Flinging his hands out to the sides a couple times to get the blood flowing back into them, he just shook head in amazement. "Ridiculously heavy, by God."

Reading the item information for the claymore did bring up an interesting question, though. It had a requirement, specifically the eighty-nine Strength to wield it. Was this burning sensation he'd felt the system's way of telling him off for not meeting the Strength requirement and trying to use it anyways?

He could safely guess yes.

Regardless, the other weapons he'd seen up until now hadn't had any requirements at all.

Pausing, his thoughts drifted to Jose and Allie. He really hoped his friend and little sister were all right, but he'd been trying very hard to block those thoughts from his mind. He needed to survive himself, and dwelling on something he could literally do nothing about would only damper his own mind when he needed to remain sharp. If what the system had said was true, as long as they all survived, he'd be reunited with them after the tutorials.

He shook himself. Glancing over at the caved-in room he'd been in just prior to this, he frowned at losing the books. He didn't know if they were valuable or not, but now he'd never know. There was no way he was digging through all that rock just to try and find them, and he wasn't sure he even could if he tried.

At least he still had the two scrolls he'd found. Maybe he could sell them to other people when he eventually found a way out of here... He certainly couldn't use them. Athela wouldn't be able to, either, as she was also bound to the Unholy Foundational Pillar and its subpillars. The Chi subpillar was in the realm of the Harmony Foundational Pillar.

[Martial Art Scroll: Quickstep (Chi)—Envision the path you want to take in a straight line from where you stand and blur ahead at great speed. May be used in any direction. Instant cast, high cooldown.]

[Martial Art Scroll: Calculated Shot (Chi)—Highlight vulnerable areas on your selected target, speed your reflexes, and slow time to perfect your aim as you fire. Must have a bow or gun in hand to use. Instant cast, medium cooldown.]

Regardless, he really needed to get the hell out of here to find that statue, and the longer he fucked around, the more of a chance Athela had of dying.

Yet he didn't feel entirely guilty for spending time acquiring a new spell or experimenting with his abilities, as these things were the keys to helping him navigate this strange, dangerous place to find Athela. Without them, he had a good idea of what would happen—and it involved something similar if not identical to the numerous hanging corpses scattered across the ruins. He might have even ended up as a lunch for the creature he'd just encountered if he'd not come across the spell scroll for Blood Lance when he did.

Based on these few experiences he'd recently had, this was an area infested with undead—and that first zombie he'd faced had been quite weak in comparison to the ghoul he'd just fought. He likely wouldn't last here too long if he stayed in these ruins, and finding Athela was still at the top of his priorities list.

Speaking of that zombie, where was his haunted saleswoman, anyways? Hadn't she said she'd been looking for some kind of item she wanted to give him a *special price* for? She'd only been gone a few hours, though, so who knew when she'd show up again. He needed to find Athela and get out of this dungeon as soon as possible.

Riven palmed the polished wood of his staff and hoisted it up. Remembering he needed to distribute his stat points from his recent level gain, he pulled up his status page and placed them into Intelligence and Willpower and one point into Sturdiness. His boots crunched on shattered glass as he walked until he reached the opposite hallway that led around a dark bend. Taking one last look at the corpse behind him with a backward glance, having a minor amount of pride in his recent kill, Riven vanished into the depths of the stone skyscraper like a ghost in the night.

One day later

Screeches of the undead echoed through the halls, and Riven's feet pounded against the stone panels, pushing him ahead with everything he had. Sparks lit up across his skin and his muscles contracted to their fullest, kicking himself up over an overturned crate with spilled-out pottery from another age and toward the exit.

"OHS VRASHAMA TU VASKI!"

Whatever language these skeletons were screaming at him in, it didn't sound very pleasant. He rolled under a hole in a rotting double door and launched himself back to his feet just as skeletal hands slammed into the ground behind him, clawing at the ground and battling one another to try and fit through the hole he'd just gone through.

Riven sneered and spun in midair, launching a Blood Lance backward that shattered three charred skeletons with glowing teal eyes. More of the undead took their place, though, and the wave of enemies slammed into the remnants of the thick wood, causing it to splinter right before it burst. He swore and continued running, pushing harder than he'd ever pushed his legs before, and turned a corner while more of the bone walkers rushed him with deathly wails.

[Bone Walker, Level 3]
[Bone Walker, Level 4]
[Bone Walker, Level 1]
[Bone Walker, Level 3]
[Bone Walker, Level 2]

Hundreds of the monsters were hot on his tail like an ocean wave, having been waiting in ambush for prey in one of the larger citadel rooms he'd passed through. They'd nearly killed him in a mad rush when he'd first entered, and now he was struggling just to stay ahead of them while launching projectiles and counting on his blessing not to run out just yet. He'd been running for God knows how long, but the undead had almost never-ending stamina that kept them moving far longer than any human would have usually been able to match.

BOOM

The wall in front of him shattered, and he made an abrupt right, skidding along the hall and almost crashing into two minotaurs that bulldozed through the rubble in an attempt to figure out what was making all that noise in their domain. The huge nine-foot demons had rippling muscles, brown fur, curved obsidian horns, large double-sided battle-axes in their hands, and blazing orange eyes that shifted from Riven to the swarm of skeletons screeching down the hallway in a roiling swarm.

The monsters collided with one another, the two larger minotaurs taking sweeping swings that crushed dozens of the skeletons into the bulk of the swarm before they, too, were overrun by a tidal wave of ravenous, bloodthirsty bones that sank their teeth into the demons to begin sucking life force away.

Riven didn't stay to watch, continuing down the ancient stone hallways, past grime-covered windows, over broken altars, and up a spiral staircase toward the top of a tower. He cursed when he saw that there were still dozens of the undead creatures following him, but he had nowhere else to go, and if need be he'd try utilizing his snares to drop off the side of the tower and stick himself to the outer wall. It was the best plan he had.

His heart pounded in his chest, his feet thudded against the stone steps, and he nearly slipped on the corpse of some imp-like creature that was sprawled out on the stairs with a cracked neck. He kicked it down for the undead to feed on, successfully drawing the forefront of them away from his flight, but more were coming, and they clambered over their undead counterparts in a primal hunger with bones clattering together in a mad rush.

Another undead latched onto his right leg, and he spun around to kick with his left, taking the skeleton full on in the face and sending it crashing backward as he landed on the steps. Frantically spinning and blasting another two of the undead with four of his Bloody Razors, he continued racing up the stairs to finally come to the top of the tower minutes later.

The top of the tower was flat, the sky above him red with clouds of black smog partially obscuring the flaming eye overhead. Battlements to his left were still intact, but on his right they'd been crushed or torn off by some great beast in millennia past, and it was here that he set his sights.

"Here goes fucking nothing!"

Dodging another swipe of a skeletal hand and wincing at such a close screech from the monster, he raced ahead of the swarm, and without even bothering to look and see what was over the edge, he launched himself off the building.

The ruined city was far below him, and he felt himself free falling with screams of the bone walkers behind him growing more distant the longer he let himself go. He'd always been afraid of heights, but he found himself letting out a sigh of relief while he plummeted hundreds of feet toward the ground.

Conjuring a multitude of snares and still being far up above the ground, heading toward a chasm splitting the earth of the hellscape apart, he wrapped his Unholy magic around his waist and then launched the other end at the side of the skyscraper he was falling from.

The snare stuck, and he felt an abrupt tug around his midsection when the magic stretched. He came to a brief stop and violently slammed into the side of the building for a moment, then sailed back upward like a bungee jumper. Thankfully he'd only been badly bruised by the impact, though he had probably shattered some of his smaller bones, which he assumed would heal due to recent experiences, but otherwise he hadn't taken much damage. Bouncing a couple more times and watching three of the bone walkers fall to their deaths past him due to their zealous chasing, he eventually lost his momentum and hung along the side of the enormous stone ruin while laughing his ass off and catching his breath. This place, these experiences, the fights he endured: they were changing him. He was becoming somewhat fearless, and honestly, he was even starting to have a good time despite the many near-death experiences. It was thrilling to come so close to death, against such odds, and still survive due to his own efforts.

Turning and watching the screeching creatures explode into various bony pieces when they hit the ground, he saluted them with a grin and planted his feet on the tower wall. "It was a good run, lads. On to bigger and better things!"

CHAPTER 32

His searching had resulted in failure. He'd escaped the swarm but had then been chased again three times after that. The calm he'd initially experienced when first presenting here in the hellscape dungeon was now replaced with fight-or-flight situations every couple hours. First he'd run into a pack of red-skinned, fire-flinging imps; he'd he managed to kill three before getting out of dodge—and he picked up a level while doing it. Then he took a dive in the river of blood to get away from a pack of hell bears, which were essentially flaming grizzlies twice Riven's size. Then he ended up running into patches of other patrolling undead similar to the ghoul he'd killed, although they were all scrawnier and less misshapen than the one he'd encountered in the ballroom. He'd picked up yet another level there as well, after having plastered the floors and walls with ghoul guts numerous times over. If someone were to have asked him, he'd say he was getting pretty good at killing things by now. He'd stuck most of his stat points into Intelligence, some into Willpower, and a few points into Sturdiness to keep himself alive, so he was feeling pretty good about himself.

[Riven Thane's Status Page:
- Level 7
- Pillar Orientations: Unholy Foundation, Blood
- Core of Original Sin—Gluttony: (Under Construction) (???)
- Traits: Race: Human, Class: Novice Warlock, Adrenaline Junkie (Blood) (+15% to Agility)
- Abilities: Blessing of the Crow (Unholy), Wretched Snare (Unholy), Bloody Razors (Blood), Blood Lance (Blood) (Tier 2)
- Stats: 8 Strength, 13 Sturdiness, 57 Intelligence, 10 Agility, 1 Luck, -4 Charisma, 3 Perception, 33 Willpower, 9 Faith
- Minions: Athela, Level 5 Blood Weaver [14 Willpower Requirement]

- **Equipped Items: Crude Cultist's Robes (1 def), Basic Casting Staff (4 dmg, 12% mana regen, +3 magic dmg), Chalgathi Cultist Amulet (???), Leather Boots (1 def), Backpack of Supplies, Rusted Embalmer's Knife (3 dmg), Witch's Ring of Grand Casting (+26 Intelligence)]**

Worry about Athela, Jose, and his little sister, Allie, kept him going at a fast pace, though. He had to find Athela to make sure she didn't die a permanent death, and he had to believe Jose would keep Allie safe until he finished the tutorial. These thoughts continued to haunt him little by little until he'd ended up passing out from exhaustion while looking for the statue his quest spoke of.

But that had been hours ago, and this was now.

[Arise.]

His mind flashed with Athela's image, and an impulse rushed through his body, sending him into a spasming and uncontrolled fit while he remained asleep on the floor. Possibilities and potential events clashed with one another in a battle of fate within his soul structure, reorienting his soul pillars and even altering the course of his Gluttony core for a few moments before it resumed its normal cyclic rotation. Images of his bonded minion in a cage, of her death at the hands of some obscured enormous monstrosity, and then of her escape with her small body in his arms all plastered themselves against his semiconscious mind. They presented themselves as conflicting scenarios, directly opposing one another before evaporating with a single remnant feeling being left in their wake.

He needed to get the fuck up.

Riven abruptly woke to a shrill scream of panic—a sound that could have been pulled from his very nightmares—and he sat up abruptly while clutching his staff. Blinking a couple times and rubbing his eyes, he tried to settle his heart rate by taking in long breaths and exhaling slowly, and then oriented himself to his surroundings again.

He was in a dark closet from an age past strung up with cobwebs and layers of grime. He'd found it last minute before the lidless eye in the sky completely vanished, bathing the area in darkness without warning a couple hours ago when he'd been searching for a safe haven to get some shut-eye anyways. This had happened more than once now, and he assumed this was the dungeon's version of nighttime.

The closet was very small and cramped, but big enough for him to curl up and lie down while shutting the door behind him. The stone floor was uncomfortable, but it was a lot better than being out there in the open.

Another scream, and the sounds of begging and crying echoed up through the adjacent hallway. It sounded like both men and women, human voices, but Riven couldn't be sure at this distance. That was odd, because usually the ruins were devoid of sound other than the occasional roar of a monster.

Were there really other people here? If so, they were in obvious danger…and not only that, but they'd be the first true contact he'd had with his own kind since arriving in this dungeon. They might even be able to help him.

And beyond that, a feeling was tugging at him that he needed to move now. It was an impulse, something coercing him to not wait any longer, and trying to ignore it only caused a sinking feeling in his gut.

His heart rate began to spike with mixed emotions of excitement, curiosity, and worry, but he slowly opened up the door. Thankfully it wasn't nearly as creaky as a lot of the other doors that remained intact in this godforsaken place. He took a look left and then right, making sure the hallway was clear before he slipped out into an almost equally dark hallway. The path was poorly illuminated where he stood now, other than a few windows that let in the pale light that emanated from pools of fire in the distant cityscape, but farther down the hallway from where the screaming was heard… here was another faint orange glow from around a corner.

Fluidly going heel to toe in the direction of the noises and charging another Blood Lance across his right arm, he passed by another couple rooms that he hadn't gotten around to checking yet. Most of the doors were already open, showing signs of recent activity and a lack of dust layers that much of the rest of these ruins had, and the ones with shut doors he didn't bother venturing into just yet. He had more pressing matters to attend to.

The begging, crying, and shouting were getting louder now—and he rubbed his eyes again to clear his sleep-deprived vision. He was still really, really tired, but his adrenaline was starting to kick into high gear as he peeked his head around the corner.

It was another long and windowless hallway, but this one was a little odd. There was a mounted torch that hadn't been there when he'd gone to sleep—flickering yellow and orange light from flames that danced not far off. It was stationed in an iron rack off to the end and left-hand side, and it only had one exit point—the door that the torch was set up next to. This door wasn't wooden, rather, it was made of metal and had a trail of recently spilled blood splattered across the ground leading up to it. There were also bloody handprints along the front, and as Riven crept closer, he saw that there were also smear marks along the edge where fingers had been desperately trying to cling to the door before being pulled off.

A sinister, deep laugh rang out from the other side, followed by muffled voices and another shrill scream of a woman before she was abruptly cut off into silence. Then there were some crunching sounds, some ripping sounds, and another muffled round of cackling laughter.

As quietly as he could, Riven slowly placed his hand on the bloodied door and turned his wrist. The handle was utterly silent, as was the door when he very gingerly pulled it back to see through the slightly ajar opening. His eyes went wide, and his jaw dropped.

There, sitting just a little ways away from him, was a monster the size of a bus. Its skin was red with twenty insectoid legs, two clawed arms coming off a humanoid upper half, three curved demonic horns, eight buggy eyes, and a gaping mouth full of rows of teeth. Dark rows of spikes were stationed on its forehead, and its long body below the waist snaked around to curl up about itself. It was male, or at least looked male by the more recognizable features, and was chewing on a bare humanoid leg. Blood and fleshy bits dropped to the floor, splattering against the ground below where half of a head was resting—brains and all, with one strangely pointed ear still intact.

The door led out to a slightly elevated platform off the rubble-strewn ground beyond, not a room, and the mists swirled around them under the dark of the night sky. Torches illuminated most of the large and rectangular platform rather well, though, being placed in racks a lot like the one outside the door, and there were three shorter, lanky, hooded figures dressed in black that stood together near a number of large metal cages. They probably stood at four and a half feet tall each and had arms as long as their legs, which made them look apelike. Their skin was red as well, and they each had a third eye perched along their foreheads between sets of small black horns. Thick white beards that came down across their chests were knotted or braided in various patterns, and they all clutched small staves while chuckling through sharp teeth.

Just beyond the platform at a five-foot drop was solid ground, though Riven had no idea how he'd gotten to the bottom level in all this time. He'd thought he was far above the base level, or perhaps he was just on the edge of a cliff. Running around in the maze of ruins was definitely an easy way to get disoriented.

There were ten cages in total when he counted, and scattered around them were barrels and boxes of various sorts. All the cages had thick metal bars, and two of them had a total of three occupants. The occupants had been stripped naked, with thick metal collars around their necks that glowed with green runic markings. One of them was a blonde human girl with long hair who looked to be about twenty years old, maybe even younger, and the other was a young human man sporting silver hair bound into a medium-length ponytail behind him.

Then, lastly, there was his Blood Weaver minion.

Athela and the man were opposite from each other in the same cage; the man was obviously more afraid of her than she was of him, but the spider, for whatever reason, was still in that cage with him and had three of her legs missing with green ichor leaking out of fresh wounds. She was battered and bruised, shaking and curled up in the corner in an obvious state of pain and fear. There was also a long gash across her thorax…but she was definitely alive.

Riven's heart melted at seeing Athela like that, wanting to scream out and tell her he was here to help, and he had to quickly suppress the urge to sprint out there toward her.

He took a deep breath, clenched his fists, and thought hard about how he was going to approach this. All of them were utterly terrified, and the blonde woman was outright sobbing as she shook and wrapped her arms around her shoulders while in a cage of her own—secluded from the other prisoners.

"Please! My father will pay you if you let me go! He'll send you more sacrifices! I promise!" She was desperately pleading with the robed creatures, who simply ignored her and continued to speak in hushed tones as the larger ate nearby. "PLEASE! I DON'T WANT TO DIE!"

[Lurker Demon, Level 45]
[Jabob Demon Cultist, Level 14]
[Jabob Demon, Level 9]
[Jabob Demon, Level 11]
[Human Hunter, Level 2]
[Human Priestess, Level 4]
[Athela, Blood Weaver Demon, Level 5]

Demon cultists? Really?! *Why* were there so many goddamned cultists in this new multiverse?!

Riven gritted his teeth, nerves climbing high as his eyes latched onto his minion again. She'd obviously gotten into a few scuffles since their time apart and had plainly failed to escape this lot. He tried to think of what to do, but all he could think of in that moment—in that scrambled state of mind—was to harshly whisper to himself:

"You've gotta be fist fucking me!"

CHAPTER 33

The highest-level Jabob demon had even acquired a class title of cultist. What was the difference between his own novice warlock class title and the cultist class? Damn it, he should have done more research on this stuff when he'd had the chance. All of them were likely much, much stronger than Riven, too. Even before identifying the largest creature, he knew that trying to fight that enormous lurker demon alone would immediately result in his death.

No way he was getting into a fight with that thing and coming out alive.

However, he obviously wasn't about to let his minion die here. He was going to save that batshit crazy spider if it was literally the last thing he did. She'd saved his life in the Chalgathi trial, and he wasn't going to let her become lurker food.

His chest swelled, and a surge of determination flooded through his veins. Even if he died trying, he'd give his best shot in trying to get Athela out... He just needed to wait for the opportune time, if there was any to be had. The others, though their plight tugged at his heartstrings, would only be bonuses if he succeeded.

Though even just getting her out alone was looking rather unlikely.

One of the short, lanky, Jabob demons who'd had enough of the blonde girl's pleading turned around and raised a hand. The beard swayed, and the three eyes narrowed. Its voice was snakelike, with a hoarse hiss to it, and it almost sounded like the creature had smoked far too many cigarettes over the course of its life. "Shut your ugly mouth, mortal wench! I've had enough of your sniveling!"

Blue fire flared to life from the small demon's hand, and in an instant the woman's face exploded with flame.

She screamed even louder, reeling back and rolling around on the ground to try and put out the fire as the other two demons laughed. It made Riven want to rush in, to save her and kill all the creatures participating in her torment. He wanted to play the hero, to save the day and come out victorious. But real life was not like those fairy tales where the knight in shining armor battled against all odds to win. Real life was brutal and cruel, even before this multiverse had swallowed Earth. The strongest made the rules, oftentimes taking advantage of those weaker or less fortunate. This was no fairy tale; if he walked out there without any kind of advantage and tried to fight them in a full-on confrontation, he'd no doubt die a quick death as nothing but a fool.

So, no, despite his internal struggles concerning this unknown woman's situation, he would not rush out to save her. Not when Athela's life was on the line, and dying meant Athela would die, too. No, he would wait until he either had an advantage or opportunity of some sort presented itself, or until he was forced out of hiding when Athela herself was targeted.

"You are spoiling my meal." The unusually deep voice of the fleshy lurker echoed throughout the large room, putting the laughter to silence immediately. "I told you, I want my sacrifices fresh…not charred."

The Jabobs simultaneously bowed to the much larger demon they served, and the one who'd attacked the girl spoke up while stroking his beard anxiously underneath his hood. "I'm sorry, Master Rhemvish. I will correct my mistake at once."

With a snap of his fingers, the girl's face stopped burning…though the charred and smoking skin, the burned-out eyes, and the violent weeping-shaking combination were all testaments to the damage that'd been done.

And yet…while he watched the cultists continued to talk with one another jovially, as they completely ignored the scared, bawling young woman, a ball seemed to drop into the pit of Riven's stomach. This was just cruel. These creatures were downright evil.

[Optional Quest: Save the Prisoners. You have stumbled across a small cult of demons sacrificing people to their master. If you are able to save either of the remaining prisoners aside from Athela and stay out of harm's way for eight consecutive hours, you will be rewarded. Time remaining: Unknown.]

Riven frowned and pulled back away from the door as he went over the new notification. It wasn't like he didn't want to save them. But both of them? The girl was in a separate cage. How was he even going to approach saving his minion in the first place? When he made his move, it had to have a chance and couldn't be a stupid blunder based on emotion. A dead Riven was no good to anyone…

That's when he heard the begging start up again, and another shrill scream as the woman's cries hit a new pitch. Riven glanced back up from his deep thinking to the slightly ajar door and peered through the crack, going cold with anger as he saw two of the Jabob demons dragging the burned teenage girl out. She was sobbing, thrashing about, and trying to free herself. Terror was evident in her cries, and the remnants of her scorched facial features were contorted with absolute fear.

This was horrible.

She was seriously injured, blinded, and for whatever reason wasn't using any of her abilities. If she even had any…but she was labeled as a priestess and had to have acquired a class title because of it. Didn't this mean she had related powers? Perhaps the glowing collar around her neck was suppressing her abilities? Or maybe she didn't have any offensive capabilities?

THUMP

Riven's eyes dilated, and the world around him was tinged in shades of black, red, and gray. He felt as though he wasn't actually standing on solid ground any longer, and an unfamiliar yet resonating cold mana rippled across his skin.

"PLEASE…GODS! GODS, PLEASE HELP ME! PLEASE, I DON'T WANT TO DIE!"

The blinded, naked young woman continued shrieking, struggling, and began to hyperventilate as the large, clawed hand of the monster wrapped around her torso. The cultists let go just as the lurker abomination picked her up and held her ten feet off the ground, and it eyed her with meager amounts of interest for a time as it held her there.

"Please…I'll do anything…I promise… My dad will bring more sacrifices…" The young woman sobbed, shaking and shuddering in the firm grip of the predator. "Daddy… Daddy, help me… Don't eat me… I—I want my dad… I—AHHK—"

Her words were cut off with a sharp, high-pitched shriek and the audible crunch of bones as the abomination abruptly squeezed. Riven's eyes went wide with horror as the girl's arms at the shoulders snapped inward at an odd angle, and she began to kick around frantically with her dangling legs. The crunching continued as the girl squirmed and tried to form words, but all she could do was gurgle and flail until another abrupt snapping sound saw a fountain of blood belch out from her open mouth.

WHAT THE FUCK KIND OF PLACE WAS THIS?!

Her eyes went wide, her face turned purple, and blood continued running down from her mouth as death took her.

Riven had seen death before, but that was a bit much for him. Rage entered his soul like a flood for being so helpless as he watched the giant creature rip off her head, toss it along with the metal collar aside, and stick a snakelike tongue out into the bloodied hole where the neck had been.

And…it began sucking. The sloppy sound was accompanied by more crackling as the monster squeezed the priestess's corpse like a little boy would squeeze a juice box. Even from here, Riven could see that forked tongue of the scaly beast work through her innards and pull them out in chunks and pieces as it garbled her insides down with relish.

"If you do not like it... For something so small and insignificant, you have the power to change it..."

THUMP

An unfamiliar voice whispered into his mind. Riven's heartbeat literally stopped in his chest, and ice began to flow through his veins. His eyes dilated again and began to turn a bright-crimson hue, his breathing slowed to a crawl, and he found himself back just two minutes prior. The girl was still in the hands of the monster, head intact, though she was about to be eaten again.

"PLEASE...GODS! GODS, PLEASE HELP ME! PLEASE, I DON'T WANT TO DIE!"

The blinded, naked young woman continued shrieking, struggling, and began to hyperventilate as the large, clawed hand of the monster wrapped around her torso. The cultists let go just as the lurker abomination picked her up and held her ten feet off the ground, and it eyed her with meager amounts of interest for a time as it held her there.

Riven blinked rapidly, not entirely understanding what was going on—but he was reliving these moments. This time, however, the world was no longer in shades of black, red, and gray. They were normal hues and felt far more real to him.

Had he experienced a vision? Thinking back to the crystal ball in the tutorial, he couldn't come up with any other explanation.

"Please...I'll do anything...I promise... My dad will bring more sacrifices..." The young woman sobbed, shaking and shuddering in the firm grip of the predator. "Daddy... Daddy, help me... Don't eat me... I—I want my dad..."

The world froze, right before the lurker abomination was to crush her body. Everything around him came to a standstill, and his soul apparatus quivered violently.

[Malignant Prophecy has activated; previously unrecognized heir has been found. Qualifications have been met, link established, royal lineage recognized despite tampering and suppression measures. Imperial system has officially recognized Riven Thane as a prince of the empire, thirty-seventh in line for the throne. All citizens, nobility, clergy, and leadership of the empire have been informed.

Desired Action: low-tier manipulation of fate. Current Willpower stat: 33. Barely sufficient Willpower to perform desired action. Performing this act will put your Malignant Prophecy on cooldown for significant amounts of time. Do you wish to proceed?]

What the fuck was this about being a prince? And what empire?! A manipulation of fate? Goddamn it, he hated this place. If Riven could have furrowed his brows, he would have looked like an enraged orangutan. But he couldn't—he was frozen in time and space, so he mentally just shouted out, *What desired action?!*

> [Desired action: save unknown woman from death. Malignant Prophecy's only available option for this pathway is as follows: Influence the lurker demon into taking the young woman up on her offer and letting the young woman go.]

CHAPTER 34

Riven took a moment to realize just what was being said here. Now that the initial shock of the new notifications had worn off, he pushed away the many unanswered questions to focus on only one.

This was a question of morality.

His sight shifted back to the girl being held in demonic claws at his left. Through the crack in the door he could tell that she was utterly terrified, and his heart truly hurt for her. How scared she must be, knowing she was mere moments from being eaten alive.

The question was, if he did sway fate in her favor, would she really go back to acquire more sacrifices? Would she uphold her end of the promise to this creature after it'd burned her face away? Or was she lying?

On one hand, he didn't know what the situation had been prior to getting here. She might have been in league with the demons the entire time, only for them to betray her. On the other hand, there was a very good chance she was outright spewing bullshit just to save herself, desperately thinking up ways to keep on living in the face of certain doom.

There was yet another question: Would she even be able to hold up her end of the bargain? He didn't know enough about demonic summonings, despite being a novice warlock, to know whether or not she could safely reach this destination again. Did she have some means of summoning them to her world? Did she create a portal to get here? Did she know about the exits out of here? Or did she enter the dungeon in a similar way he'd been thrown in?

If she knew the exits out, that was a reason alone to save her. He desperately wanted to skedaddle out of here as fast as humanly fucking possible, but then again the silver-haired man in Athela's cage might know just as much as she did.

Then there was the question of what reward he would get for saving her.

[Optional Quest: Save the Prisoners. You have stumbled across a small cult of demons sacrificing people to their master. If you are able to save either of the remaining prisoners aside from Athela and stay out of harm's way for eight consecutive hours, you will be rewarded. Time remaining: Unknown.]

Hmm. Saving both humans alongside Athela would be preferable for the quest alone; he had no idea what he'd get, but he was sure the reward would at least double in value if he saved two instead of one. Right?

Yet there was another thing to consider. He'd be putting this new Malignant Prophecy on a significant cooldown by using it to sway fate. Why it was called *malignant* was unknown to him, but any power that could literally change fate was fucking badass, and putting such an ability on cooldown for someone he didn't know was...

Ugh. Allie would have him save the girl.

The thought stung like an annoying splinter in his side. How was he supposed to look Allie in the eyes and tell her about this if he didn't save her? Truth be told, he was pretty convinced this "priestess" was just blabbering in order to get out of being killed, and he probably would have lied through his teeth, too, if he was in her situation. He would be selfish not to help.

He sighed internally, then peered back at the quest prompt and grudgingly accepted the action. At least he'd be getting an increased reward for it, so there was that.

[Desired action has been selected: save unknown woman from death. Influence the lurker demon into taking the young woman up on her offer and letting the young woman go.]

Immediately time unfroze, and he could feel his heart beating again. The red-skinned, apelike cultists cackled and laughed at the young woman—but the larger lurker demon suddenly paused.

Confusion marred its face while its open mouth let a forked tongue droop to the side, its muscles bulged and flexed, and it cocked its head in thought before gradually putting the naked woman down. "I have reconsidered your offer, little priestess."

The cackling and laughter from the smaller subordinate demons abruptly stopped. They gave each other incredulous looks, their features outlined by the firelight of the torches outside and along the walls before the platform they stood on ended into an expanse of ruined city.

"Uh... Master? That seems very unlike you." The highest-leveled of the Jabob cultists began, but he quickly shrieked and backed up—beginning to grovel when the towering level-45 monstrosity crackled with obsidian power and gave him a tyrannical grin.

"One more word out of you, ape…" One of the armored centipede legs of the lurker slammed into the platform's floor, showering those nearby in sparks and jagged pieces of stone. The lurker pointed a long-clawed hand at the Jabob and sneered. "I'll have your guts in her place. Understand me, maggot?"

The Jabob demons all quickly nodded, glancing hesitantly between their lord and the still-sobbing woman in a kneeling position not far off. The lurker turned, then waved a hand over the blonde girl as red lights began shimmering all around her.

The lights pulsed twice, forming balls of blood magic, from what Riven could tell, and launched themselves at the girl.

The priestess screamed as the magics ripped into her body, but while she began to writhe on the floor, her face began to change. The burns that'd been there were now gone, her wounds healed, and soon she looked up in bewilderment before nearly slamming her forehead into the ground with a bow and as a sign of respect. "Y-you are actually s-sparing me after all?!"

The woman quivered, and the demon looked down at her with disgust—but motioned with a claw as if to shoo her away.

"Yes…but I expect you to keep to your word. I will deliver to you a token in seven days that you may use to speak with me, then we can discuss how things will proceed. Perhaps having someone on the outside of this hellscape would be a boon after all… Remember: seven days, lest I become enraged and visit your world to devour you and your entire family. Do you understand? Now, leave me. I have things to attend to."

The young woman blinked, getting looks of disbelief from everyone else there, and stood on shaky legs. She quickly bowed, then gestured to her collar. "Could I get this off? Making it to the dungeon exit without my abilities—"

"No. Nor may you have your belongings." The lurker demon sneered down with a vile grin, and then chuckled when he saw her face pale. "If you cannot get there on your own, I have no need of you. Begone, mortal, and show me that you have the drive it takes to succeed."

Shit. She *did* know where the dungeon exit was! *And she was now running away!*

He watched her abruptly nod and catapult off the stone platform, sprinting as fast as she possibly could with eyes darting left and right until she disappeared into the darkness of the hellscape. He cursed his luck; she hadn't even attempted to stay around and see if the huge demon changed his mind. Which Riven understood, but Riven couldn't leave himself until he got at least Athela out.

After the demons watched the girl vanish around another tower, one of the lurker's large hand searched behind it and pulled up another headless corpse.

Beginning to feed and suck on this new body, it made content gurgling sounds while it lapped up bodily fluids.

There was a long pause after that.

"Ahem." One of the Jabob demons cleared his raspy, hissing throat and tapped his misshapen wooden staff onto the stone floor. He nervously stroked his long white beard and glanced around. "I believe it is time. We've finally acquired the necessary tools and souls needed for summoning your future partner, and it has been a very long road in obtaining the means to acquire such a creature. I may be hasty in asking…but may we proceed?"

All the cultist got in response was a brief nod from the lurker before it turned back to sucking on its meal.

"Very well." The Jabob speaking, obviously the superior of the other two hooded cultists, began to walk ahead. He then whispered something that Riven couldn't hear and motioned for them to spread out. As the other two did as he asked, the short demon raised a bony, red, three-fingered hand out in front of him and closed his eyes. "Abtala Rhukshash Ver Klonsik Azmoth."

Meanwhile, Riven was scouring the place for any signs of a key, anything he could use as a lockpick, or some way to get Athela out of her cage.

Riven didn't understand the gibberish of the summoning nearby, but soon a spark of black and red mana flared to life underneath the demon's small, outstretched hand—and a circled pentagram of crimson light began carving itself into the stone floor below. The other two hooded cultists raised their own hands out in front of them as the first had done and began muttering the exact same words. One by one, they threw materials into the center of the pentagram from sacks at their sides: a scalp of thick black hair, a couple eyeballs, a myriad of different types of teeth, a couple differently colored crystals, two fingers, and a runic stone that glowed green. All these things dissolved and were absorbed into the mass of black and red mana accumulated a few feet in the air—and soon, shrill screams of the dead began to echo throughout the platform as wisps of light shot out from their outstretched palms toward the mana as well.

Were those the souls that demon was talking about? Holy shit…

"Abtala Rhukshash Ver Klonsik Azmoth."

"Abtala Rhukshash Ver Klonsik Azmoth."

"Abtala Rhukshash Ver Klonsik Azmoth."

Riven watched, fascinated, until he realized that this could be his moment to act. He didn't know when he'd get a better chance. While they were summoning whatever it was they had in mind, all but the lurker had their eyes closed…and he mentally prepared himself over the next few seconds to make a sneaky break for Athela. At the very least he could inspect the cage and see if there was a way to open it from the outside, and if not—he would improvise.

He had to. He had no other choice.

CHAPTER 35

[Your manipulation of fate has gained you one Malignancy Point. Current total Malignancy Points: 1]

Riven blinked. Well, that wasn't good...probably?

Regardless, he began to move. With the cultists doing whatever weird summoning magic they'd set their intentions on and the lurker demon sucking a corpse dry—it was time. He slipped out of the door after slowly pushing it open and thanking God it didn't creak. There were boxes and barrels to his right on the way over to the cages, and this is where he headed with heel-to-toe movements to reduce his noise as much as possible.

The large lurker demon was rather enjoying the meal and continued like that over those next couple of seconds. It didn't even glance his way, and Riven's heart was pounding in his chest amid the chanting of the apelike summoners to his left when he finally reached the nearest crate and let out a sigh of relief. However, the peace was interrupted when an abrupt series of crazed roars arose from the darkness, and dozens of shadowy figures began to rush out of the dark mists from thirty to fifty meters out.

"SSSHHREEEEEE!"

"VRRRAAAAAHHHHH!"

"RRRRHHHOOOOO!"

Riven rubbed his eyes, and his jaw dropped at the fortune luck had sprung on him.

They were ghouls. Mutated and larger ones, like the first he'd fought in the ballroom. Not like some of the weaker versions he'd seen wandering around at random among the rest of the ruins. There were dozens of them, all of them looking disfigured and grotesque—but each of them slightly unique in its own way. Some were a necrotic black or gray, some were sickly green, some were missing limbs, and some had extras. They were all disfigured, yellow-eyed, and ravenous, though, and the Jabob Cultist Demons immediately dropped what they were doing just as a flash of light from the pentagram burst open through a rift along the ground. The Jabobs swore in a language Riven didn't understand and began to meet the charge with loud, high-pitched squeals of rage.

"AMBUSH!" one of the three-eyed, red-skinned demons screamed as it sent a roaring blue fireball soaring out into the oncoming pack, exploding upon impact and taking out three of the undead before they got to the platform's edge. This time they spoke a language Riven understood on instinct, though when he reevaluated it, he realized it still wasn't English.

The demon quickly whipped his head back and forth, eyes growing wide at the sheer number of enemies that'd managed to make it this close without being spotted. "I THOUGHT WE CLEARED THEM OUT OF THIS AREA! WHY ARE THERE SO MANY?!"

One of the other cultists spat in response to his comrade as a circlet of blue runes lit up on the ground in front of him, and another creature the size of a small dog—a purple-skinned, black-eyed, and sluglike demon with multiple long stingers—slithered out of the summoning circle to begin belching out high-velocity globs of acid that ravenously ate through the incoming undead's flesh. "Who cares why?! Just shut up and kill them! Negrada will have our heads if we allow the enemy dungeon to interfere!"

The lurker abomination glanced over at the oncoming horde, unconcerned, but stuffed the rest of the human's corpse into its mouth to hurry up and finish eating. It belched loudly, showering the ground with blood as it wiped its gory face with the side of an arm, and turned to meet the new enemy. Black balls of swirling power began to form and spark on either side of the lurker before blasting forward into the oncoming wave, obliterating numerous enemies at once before the huge monster rushed forward along multiple armored insectoid legs to meet the charge.

Riven was awestruck by the offensive might of the large demon while it tore through the undead like they were children's toys, and he nodded to himself. "Yup. Glad I didn't go in to try and fight that thing…"

And now that the battle between the two sides had commenced, the demons all had their backs turned to his position.

He quickly rushed forward past a break in the wall of crates, then ducked down behind one of the barrels and clambered over two stacked sacks of who-knows-what. He slid around to the right while trying to keep his steps muffled, around the outskirts of the cages with the wall to his back, until he eventually came to the one with Athela and the unknown man still inside.

BOOM

CRASH

The ground shuddered and the walls reverberated with the brutal violence of the battle nearby.

The silver-haired young hunter was staring toward the battle, hands gripping the bars and a hopeless expression on his face. He was of a medium build and a little taller than average, and he had burn marks along his left shoulder. In the bottom of his cage, a puddle of piss had collected at his feet, and he was breathing heavily. Meanwhile, Athela just remained curled up in her corner of the cage while continuing to shake.

An explosion of green light rocked the platform, and one of the cultists went down screaming before he hit the ground—shriveled and dead upon impact after just having released another blast of blue fire. Apparently the ghouls had back-line casters of their own—but the majority of the horde was focused on bringing the large lurker down while the ghouls died by the dozens in an attempt to swarm the gigantic alpha monster.

For just another second, Riven paused to watch in fascination as the battle commenced. The lurker was putting in real work, but the undead just kept on coming as they rushed out of the darkness and into view, replacing their fallen comrades even as the undead corpses began to pile up. Another flash of sickly-green light rocketed forward, blasting through an erected arcane shield that one of the Jabob mages had constructed and toppling him backward—though not completely killing him, as the shield took the brunt of the attack. It did, however, eradicate three of the nearby slug demons that'd been summoned. Even as they died, though, more of the sluglike purple creatures continued to pour in from portals that the remaining Jabob cultists were creating between offensive blasts. Soon there were dozens of the small stinger-equipped, acid-spewing demons, and some entered melee combat while others stayed onstage to support the lurker from afar.

The force of another green blast from the undead side immediately drew Riven's attention over to the caster. It was a hooded, robed skeleton with glowing blue eyes that carried a long black staff. It was slowly walking forward through the fog, and Riven wasn't even able to identify it properly.

[Minor Lich, Level ???]

Bodies ripped, screams rose, magics roared, and weapons hacked amid spraying clouds of acid that ate away ghoul flesh in abundance. This area of the dungeon was obviously way out of his league.

Riven knocked on the cage bars from behind with his knuckles, startling both Athela and the man as they turned around. Riven gave a brief glance to make eye contact with the unknown human before smirking in Athela's direction. "Hey. I can get you out of here, but I need to know where the key is. Any idea on where that would be?"

The unknown man stared his way, his sharp features set into a blank look of confusion as Athela uncurled her body and reached through the cage, gently touching his face with an outstretched limb while the spider continued to tremble. But if spiders could smile, she would be now, and she visibly began to relax as her arachnoid leg caressed his skin. "Riven...you found me...and yes, the cultists! Hurry, one of them has the keys!"

Riven glanced over doubtfully. One was already dead, but the other two were alive and well as they blasted magics while loudly screeching and summoned more sluglike minions as time went on. "Are you sure that's the only set of keys?"

"Please!" hissed the young man, becoming frantic as he glanced over his shoulder. "This disgusting monster is right! I—"

"Shut the fuck up," Riven interrupted with a hostile stare. "Now."

The man looked blankly back at him, and Riven snorted with distaste, but his green eyes focused on the red-and-black spider demon a second later. "Are you okay? You're injured..."

BOOM

The ground shuddered as the lurker demon ripped through the pack of undead and barreled into a wall. Debris began to fall from the tower, and pieces of stone began falling from the site of impact.

"Don't worry about it!" she hissed, her mandibles clicking as she gave a worried glance over to the battle—then twisted her head to show him a small black-and-green collar of her own. "We don't have time! You need to get the keys so we can leave. Then we'll get this suppression collar off and you can bind to me again, sealing the contract so that if I die I'll respawn. Just be careful not to get caught in the fighting!"

The other man, who was gripping the cage bars and listening to them talk, frowned deeply. Something akin to a sneer crossed his lips, and he gave a resigned sigh while putting his head up against the cage wall. "Oh. You're a fucking warlock. Great. I might as well just kill myself now."

CRACK

The mood immediately grew even more sour than it already was, and the ground shook as another blast of magic rocketed past them—tearing across the stone platform in a shower of rubble amid the screams of combatants.

"What's your name?" Riven hissed in irritation with a sideways glance toward the nearby fighting.

"Jalel," the man stated half-heartedly, his excitement at potentially being saved long gone.

Riven gave him a brief nod, then jabbed a finger into Jalel's chest as his right arm continued to simmer with wisps of blood magic. "All right, Jalel. Do me a favor and shut the fuck up while I save your sorry ass. Got it?"

Without looking back to see how the prisoner would react, Riven began to make his way around the barrels back the way he'd come for a better angle on his approach with a final head nod of encouragement from Athela. Riven felt the wisps of blood magic radiating up his arm and summoned four Bloody Razors that hovered in the air—spinning around him silently just in case the creature turned around during his act of thievery. Mentally preparing himself for a very brazen and out-in-the-open attempt to steal the keys right from under their noses, he took in a deep breath. His success depended on a lot of factors.

Sure, the little red ape he was targeting was behind the dozens of acid-spewing scorpion slugs and in the back line—so that was a plus. The battle was also raging rather fiercely now, and it was very loud, but there were a lot of eyes that could turn his way to alert his target. He'd be out in the open with no cover whatsoever, only using the distraction and noise of battle to conceal his movements, so he'd have to work fast. He also cursed his inability to use his blessing, because it was on cooldown for another twelve hours.

Keeping low to the ground, he broke free from cover and began sneaking forward as swiftly as he could. His radiating right arm itched with vibrating blood magic, and he thought about how great it would be to kill this bastard in front of him. Of how satisfying it would be to see the light leave his eyes after Riven had witnessed the creature burn off that girl's face, but doing so would certainly alert the others. If for whatever reason he was detected by a stroke of poor luck, then he could blast the bastard before trying to flee—but otherwise he'd have to let the demon live if he wanted to get himself out of there alive. The kill would not be worth the risk of drawing the attention of both demons and undead his way, and not only that…but if he died before he bonded her, Athela would die permanently as well.

SPLAT

One of the smaller acid-spewing abominations in front of him exploded, and a green shaft of neon light rocketed past Riven's ears as an undead mage from the foggy back lines loosed another spell. He squinted and covered his eyes so the bodily fluids wouldn't blind him, and a ghoul warrior's upper half launched skyward from the brawl to land a couple feet away with a crunch.

Riven kept moving, though, his boots rolling gingerly against the stone with every step, and his breathing became light as he got within ten feet of the cultist he was targeting. Then it was five, and then he was standing right behind him. The four razors floated ready nearby, spinning rapidly—two on either side of where he stood and ready to launch. He could smell the blood on his target's robes and feel the wind on his face whenever his target briefly changed stances while casting. The bearded little shit was cursing and screaming at the top of his lungs as he continued to throw blue flames out at the undead, occasionally erecting barriers to block incoming projectiles or enemy magics—but he was completely unaware of Riven's presence even if Riven was close enough to feel the heat of the mage's fire.

Riven did his best to get a good look at the cultist's pockets before moving in for the grab, and to his relief, he immediately saw a ring of keys exactly where Athela had told him they'd be—in the right-hand pocket of the demon's robes.

He waited for the shorter creature to adjust his stance so that the weight of the keys would be off his thigh, and when the time came, Riven struck like a viper. With nimble fingers that writhed with crimson magic and quick reflexes, he fluidly extracted the keys and, holding his breath, he turned around.

Good shit.

His heart pounded. He made as fast a retreat as he could manage without making sound and quickly oriented himself toward the nearest cover. Coming around the side of a rickety barrel, he let out the breath he'd been holding in. Dropping his head into his hands with a relieved grin, he took in a few more calming breaths as the screams and rage of battle drew closer. Looking back around the barrel, he saw that the swarming undead were still battling the infuriated lurker demon, but a couple of their number were now clashing with the smaller red-skinned casters and slug summons in close combat as they scrambled up onto the platform.

One particular ghoul, a three-armed creature with patches of scattered, rotting flesh and its intestines hanging out the front, tackled the cultist Riven had just pickpocketed like a linebacker. The short, screaming Jabob demon went down onto his back while blasting flames into the undead monster, but the ghoul still managed to sink its teeth into his neck while they rolled around on the floor amid the chaos. Some of the smaller sluglike minion summons jumped in to try and peel the flaming ghoul off their master, using their acid, stingers, and teeth to tear off pieces of the monster's flesh, and the brawl thusly spilled onto the platform.

"RRRHHHHOOOOO!"

Riven whirled and slammed his radiating fist into a large, green-skinned ghoul's rotting face. Simultaneously he let loose his charged Blood Lance, and the effect was devastating.

The blood magic exploded from his punch and blasted the ghoul's skull right off, sending the remnants of its body somersaulting across the platform.

Two more gray-skinned ghouls that'd been circling around rushed him, one with five arms and another with a sharpened tongue that whipped out like a knife.

Riven dodged the tongue lash with a quick sidestep and ripped through both monsters with the summoned razors—tearing one in half entirely while the other just staggered and roared.

Shit! They were going to give away his position!

WHAM

He slammed his staff into the roaring mouth of the ghoul, silencing it as he crammed the wooden shaft down its throat. Simultaneously he dropped to the ground and kicked its scrawny legs out from underneath it before blasting it with another summoned Bloody Razor.

The ghoul gargled and ripped the staff out of its mouth before flinging it to the side, but the razor lodged itself in its throat and caused it to stagger back.

Riven kicked out with his boot and made contact with the ghoul's skull to stun the monster and tried to summon another Bloody Razor, but he went pale when he realized the portion of his Blood subpillar associated with that spell had become rigid. His Blood Lance wouldn't respond, either, also being on cooldown, so he created the only spell still available to him.

Black mana erupted from his hands and formed a net, condensing into a rope upon his will just when he went in to grapple the stronger, larger monster. He took advantage of its momentary stunned state and managed to get on its back, away from where its numerous clumped arms couldn't easily get to him, and yanked back to securely fasten his Wretched Snare around its neck.

The rather stupid monster bucked and flailed, but he continued choking the creature while it scrambled around and tried to claw at him. He rapidly wrenched the black magic back and forth, scraping away flesh every time he yanked to one side and then the other. Sharp, burning needles dug into its flesh and then into its spine—scraping away bone while he used it like a saw to separate the monster's head from its body.

The ghoul thrashed, but because its many arms were so bunched together, it couldn't reach behind its body while Riven had his feet planted into its back.

He gripped his snare with everything he had and sawed right, then left, then right again, and finally felt the Wretched Snare rip through the cervical spine. The ghoul's head flew into the air, spraying black blood all over Riven's face and letting the body fall to the stone ground with a thud.

[You have gained one level. Congratulations! Be sure to visit your status page to apply points.]

He hit the ground with a thud. Riven spat and coughed the viscous liquid out of his mouth, gagging slightly due to the rancid smell, and then rubbed his eyes while evaluating his surroundings. The battle was still raging, and the demons hadn't even noticed the scuffle behind them. Checking that he still had the keys in his pocket, he picked his staff back up and started running toward the cage.

CHAPTER 36

As Riven moved back to the metal cage where Athela and the young man were still waiting with excitement in their eyes, they began to urge him on to be faster. Athela's face lit up with laughter while Riven produced the set of keys and came around to the front to try the lock, and he gave his minion the equivalent of a fist bump to one of her outstretched limbs while cursing under his breath amid the screams of battle.

"You did so well!" Athela said with a chittering guffaw. "I can't believe you came back for me! You know, you could have just summoned another minion if I died... What you did was stupid. But you came for me!"

Riven stopped what he was doing only briefly to give her a flat look. "I'd never leave you behind after what you did for me, Athela. You're my partner now, and I'm going to see you out and alive."

He started working on the lock again, cursing as he tried key after key. However, he did notice the abrupt change in his minion just a second later.

Athela had started crying tears of previously suppressed emotion. She'd stopped shaking, though she was still in obvious pain due to her wounds. Riven had never seen a spider cry, and it took him aback, not having expected it at all. Her face was pushed against the metal bars as Riven worked. "You're a maniac! But I suppose I am a princess, after all, so I can understand why you came to save me. I take back all those things I said about you being a useless warlock or a smelly human! Good job!"

"You said those things?!"

"Possibly."

Riven rolled his eyes at his minion while shaking his head and began fumbling with the metal pieces in his hands. Riven tried another key without success before cursing and moving on. The ground shook as the overconfident lurker demon was finally taken down with an air-shattering roar of pain, and a backward glance told him that it was being eaten alive with horrible wailing sounds and continued thrashing while dozens upon dozens of ghouls raced over their numerous defeated comrades to pile over it.

Karma was a bitch.

"Fuck!" His curse came out as a whisper, but he managed to get the second key into the lock as the two occupants of the cage silently watched him—helpless to do anything themselves.

The lock clicked a second later, though, and the cage door swung open, with Riven giving himself a silent congratulations.

"Let's go."

The new guy didn't hesitate and pushed past Riven, lurching out of the cage and over to where two large linen bags were sitting next to a crate. He tried picking both of them up, but the combined load was obviously far too heavy for him to lift. So he turned around and frantically motioned to the second bag while he picked up the first. "One of you, help me take these!"

Riven immediately grew angry at the suggestion. Athela was in no way able to pick up a bag that size in her current condition, and he was already occupying himself as he gingerly picked up the injured minion and cradled her in his arms. "Get fucked and leave it!"

"No! We take it with us!"

Riven scowled even more deeply, feeling anger simmer up in his face as he turned and tried to balance the spider in his grasp along with the staff he carried. He had no idea what was in those two bags, but it was obviously important enough that Jalel chose to stop in the midst of a battle with an oncoming swarm of enemies to get them.

Meanwhile, Athela's sparkling ruby eyes gazed up into his face unwaveringly—mesmerized and shaking slightly in her master's arms.

With a grunt of irritation, Riven rushed forward toward the exit and completely ignored the silver-haired man, shoving past the sack Jalel tried to give him. "I told you to get fucked. I'm not carrying that—it should be obvious I have my hands full!"

"Leave the spider and take this instead!" the man hissed with anger evident in his eyes. "She's a fucking demon, and she even said you could summon another one if she died! Leave her! This stuff is valuable back in the core systems!"

Core systems?

Riven had half a mind to kill the man right there for suggesting Riven leave Athela behind, and his grip around Athela tightened ever so slightly.

What a prick.

The bag in Jalel's grasp clinked together with the sound of metal on metal of some sort, and he was obviously struggling just to carry the other one alone, but Riven couldn't care less. He gave Jalel a final glare along with a middle finger, rushed right on past, and didn't say a word while he made his way for the door.

Then he felt a small spider foot repeatedly jab his shoulder at lightning speed, and he looked down at the minion, who was eagerly pointing off to their right with enthusiasm unbecoming of her injured state. "HURRY AND GRAB THAT STONE!"

She pointed to something behind him, and he whirled, half expecting to see an enemy lunging at them by the way she seemed so frantic.

That's when he spotted what she had been pointing at. Not even twenty feet away, over the spot where those Jabob demons had been conjuring something from a summoned pentagram, was a glowing red orb. It hovered over the stone tile, sparking with occasional bursts of bright-crimson light and displayed another pentagram on its surface. Demonic runes were etched into the edges of the orb surrounding the pentagram as well—and a feeling of uneasiness overcame him as he stared it down.

"GET IT! GO, GO, GO!" Athela screamed over the din of battle, starting to slam her little spider legs into his shoulder again, and then she began to wriggle when she thought he was going to ignore her and take her out the door anyways. "WE NEED THAT SHINY THING!"

They were beginning to draw attention from the remaining combatants not far off…but Riven didn't have to be told a third time. With a sideways glance at the battling demons and undead, Riven rushed toward the altar. His heart pounded hard, echoing in his eardrums as one of the bearded combatants finally noticed him and let out a hate-filled scream.

"THAT IS MINE, HUMAN SCUM!" the last living Jabob sneered, turning to raise a hand in Riven's direction only to have his arm batted away by one of the ghouls he'd been fighting a second before.

The apelike red demon roared and went down under the ghoul's weight, quickly forgetting Riven. Meanwhile, the warlock came to a stop right in front of the floating red orb. A quick look over the thing at close range gave him the heebie-jeebies, and he could literally feel heat radiating off it.

Riven hesitated just a moment, seriously reconsidering touching that glowing, floating orb etched with demonic symbols after remembering what'd happened when he'd tried picking up the wooden ring or the claymore just a day ago. This item, whatever it was, was surely far beyond his current level—and one try identifying it clarified his thoughts.

[Dark Arts Miracle Stone (Unique) (Filled): The prayers to Jograz Metz have been heard, the blood price has been paid, and he has answered with this gift. Using this particular miracle stone provides an infant B-grade demon species: Hellscape Brutalisk (Inherent to the Infernal Pillar) as a demonic familiar upon binding. Requirements: five thousand of five thousand souls sacrificed,

ingredients for summoning met, favor for your chosen dark god complete. This familiar requires a contract prior to binding and must be contacted to agree upon a contract prior to use.]

"Riven! Hurry!"

He snapped out of his trance and snatched the stone out of the air a second later. Turning heel, he handed the orb to Athela, who placed it between her mandibles, and he began running as fast as his legs could carry him amid the nearby screams of battle.

Jalel gave Riven a loud groan of complaint when Riven passed him by, not wanting to leave the other bag behind—but he picked up his own sack and took off with what he could carry. Not long after, all three of them were through the metal door leading into the building, and another minute had passed by the time they were running down an adjacent hallway to put distance between them and the battle they'd so narrowly escaped.

The first crimson lights of this dungeon's version of dawn began trickling in through the open window of the ancient, musty tower they'd set up residence in. The lidless, flaming eye was back, and it was glaring down upon their floating island of the abyss with mindless scrutiny. The one entrance leading down from the highest level they now rested in was closed and deadbolted shut in five different places, and although it'd made him feel somewhat secure, it also made Riven question what this barren room had been used for in the past. The red mist was still somewhat present, obscuring the ruined gothic city that sprawled out for miles in all directions, but the dulled rays of the flaming eye overhead were still a warm welcome compared to the dark night.

Riven was still groggy, exhausted, and uncomfortable on the stone floor, but he was happy to be alive. Turning his head, he saw that Athela had nestled up against him and was fidgeting with that stone again. He grinned at the spider and remembered with fondness the notification that'd appeared when he'd taken her suppression collar off last night.

[Quest Update: Find Your Spider Princess—You have found and rescued Athela! After taking the suppression collar off her, and due to being in close proximity, your bond to your minion has been restored to normal. Her death will no longer result in permanence, but rather a temporary banishment as per the normal contract. However, you will still not receive your rewards for finishing this quest until both you and Athela travel to the axe-wielding statue in the center of the city as described before.]

The suppression collar itself had shattered when he'd taken it off, the collar not recognizing him as its bonded owner even though he'd used the key for it. They must act like Riven's totems did...or at least similar to them—the totems bound to him as their specific owner, too. Either way, Athela had explained that those suppression collars each had nullification abilities that would stop someone from using abilities of any sort, and oftentimes they weakened the captive physically. After Athela had gotten into a fight with some kind of werewolf, she'd been injured and easy pickings for the cultists to clean up—which was how she'd gotten into that situation in the first place.

The other guy—Jalel—was still asleep, but Riven gave Athela a wave when he rubbed his eyes to clear the sleepiness away.

"Morning, Athela!"

She beamed up at him, chittering lightly and pushing her face up against his own to rub against him. "Good morning! Feeling blessed?"

Blessed? What the hell was Athela talking about? Riven felt anything but blessed, and it was an odd question to ask considering she was a demon. Then again, considering he had an Unholy blessing himself, he could assume *blessed* didn't necessarily mean *holy* or what have you.

He pushed himself up to his knees and then to his feet, extending a hand over to his minion, and paused as he got a better look at the stone she was carrying in her spider paws. The glowing red orb with the demonic symbols etched into its sides was pulsing slightly. She rubbed it with her newly regenerated legs—regeneration being a perk of the contract between minion and master—and Riven's eyes narrowed.

"Ready to try again?" Athela asked, pushing the bauble into his lap and lightly tapping it with a red-and-black foot. "I'm so excited!"

"Are you now? Just how good is a 'B-grade' demon, anyways?"

Athela shrugged. "Decently good. Not anything super special or overpowered, but for a beginner warlock? I'd say it's a pretty decent boon. I'm a C-grade type demon myself, if that puts things into perspective. The thing is, you weren't supposed to be able to bind another demon until we left the tutorial, but this?!"

She indicated the miracle stone with one pointed foot. "This will circumvent that problem and allow you to get another familiar now instead of needing to wait!"

Riven's face fell, and he sighed. He'd tried using it last night three separate times at her urging but had failed to get ahold of whatever demon was kept inside there. Apparently Hellscape Brutalisks were pretty solid choices for tank-type demons, and the chance to get another minion was definitely a nice find.

He glanced up again to meet her eyes, and she gave him a mischievous cackle.

"I don't think it'll work," Riven stated with a frown, rolling the bauble in his hands and feeling the warmth enter his body. "I already tried three times, Athela. It isn't responding to me."

She flippantly waved a foot his way, and her arachnid abdomen bobbed up and down in excitement. "Then try again! Maybe he or she was just having a bad day."

CHAPTER 37

"Or maybe the demon knows we stole the miracle and won't present itself to us."

The spider cocked her head as if deep in thought, then shook it vigorously. "No...no, that's definitely not it. It would have arrived and killed you in the contract ceremony if it had any ill will against you."

"It can do that?"

"Oh, yes, and frankly, I doubt I'd have been able to help you much against something this strong. It's always a risk to take on summoned demons, and this particular breed is not known for their kindness. It would jump at the opportunity to eat you if it didn't wish to bond with you."

Riven's eyes narrowed. "How the hell do warlocks survive if they risk dying every time they summon a new minion?"

Athela sighed. "There are different ways to contract with demons. One is by having a class that allows foreign contact at certain intervals or milestones. Another is by creating a miracle stone or summoning circle, which are more dangerous than the class-contact route, which is protected by the administrator of Elysium. Miracle stones and summoning circles are completely on your own, meaning the administrator won't interfere if the demon tries to kill you. The demons you can bind with through the administrator's system cannot harm you upon picking them. Usually demons contracted through a miracle stone like this are very rare until you reach well over level 100, especially with such a singular and powerful breed, so this is a unique opportunity. Dying is worth the risk for extreme gains and great power."

"Is it, though?"

"It is if you want to live a fulfilling life! You're a Novice Warlock, Riven! Warlocks are supposed to be risk-takers!"

He gave her a doubtful look. "Are we, though?"

"Definitely!"

"Uh-huh."

"You took the risk to save me, didn't you?"

He paused at that one, then gave the spider a small smile and a nod as she beamed up at him while happily tapping her legs on the floor in rapid fashion. "Fine. I'll give you that one."

Sighing and closing his eyes, he cupped both hands over the stone like Athela had shown him previously. He formed an image of the bauble in his mind and tried to channel mana into the gem by directing a spell—any spell—into the space it presented.

There was a connection, just like last night, with each of his three attempts… but nothing beyond that. The mana interlinked with the glassy, glowing orb… but he got nothing else. No attempt at contact, no other change, and Riven eventually gave up again after sitting there for fifteen minutes while slowly pouring his mana until it almost drained away completely.

He shook his head with a frown. "No good. Are you sure it's really in there?"

Athela considered his words while pacing back and forth across the room, ignoring the sleeping man nearby and his sack of wealth, which he still hadn't opened up to share yet despite Riven having saved his life. The spider eventually came to a halt, though, turned on Riven, and padded up to him. "I believe it is testing you."

"Testing me?"

She nodded. "The brutalisk is likely watching you and waiting to see if it wants to bind with you or not."

"So it can see me?"

"As long as you are within proximity to the stone, yes, it can."

"I see." He pulled up the information on the item again.

[Dark Arts Miracle Stone (Unique) (Filled): The prayers to Jograz Metz have been heard, the blood price has been paid, and he has answered with this gift. Using this particular miracle stone provides an infant B-grade demon species: Hellscape Brutalisk (Inherent to the Infernal Pillar) as a demonic familiar upon binding. Requirements: five thousand of five thousand souls sacrificed, ingredients for summoning met, favor for your chosen dark god complete. This familiar requires a contract prior to binding and must be contacted to agree upon a contract prior to use.]

Pushing mana into the stone did nothing. Not a single thing. Trying to touch it mentally also resulted in failure, and he turned back to Athela after reading it for the fifth time—shaking his head. "Will this Jograz Metz be angry that I stole his miracle?"

Athela burst into chittering laughter almost immediately, her legs tapping wildly as her abdomen bobbed up and down in amusement. Her laughter rose, and it took a little while for her to calm down until she settled into a low hum. "Jograz Metz will find it funny, if nothing else. He is a well-known elder god that we demons worship, and he enjoys acts such as thievery just as much as the sacrifices those Jabob demons took in making the miracle stone in the first place. They may have put in the effort, but Jograz Metz will certainly have no qualms with you stealing the stone he made as payment for their work."

Riven couldn't help but grin at that one. "Sounds good to me. And are you still sure you've never heard of Chalgathi before?"

Athela seemed to frown, though he couldn't completely tell. "Riven, I have told you numerous times now—I have no idea who Chalgathi is. Perhaps he is simply beyond my knowledge, or maybe he is an archdemon of some sort. Few have the power to manipulate the administrator's rules, though, and intervening with the tutorial is exactly that. Even his initial quest line was outside the administrator's jurisdiction, so whoever he is…he must be both powerful and foolhardy."

He raised an eyebrow, palming the warm orb in his hands. "Why foolhardy?"

"Because if he pushes the boundaries too much, the administrator of Elysium—what people sometimes call 'the system'—will destroy him mercilessly. Even the gods must be careful not to tread outside the rules too often, as the last one to overstep too many times was publicly destroyed for all creation to see. It was a very one-sided fight, if you'd even call it a fight. It was more of an execution."

"Wow, okay. Got it." Scratching his head, he looked down to the amulet he was wearing with curiosity settling in. "Do you know what this is or does? I don't think I've asked you yet. Have I?"

The arachnid had climbed up into his lap like a dog, but she turned her head to examine it. "No, you haven't, and no, I don't know what this is. You may need a professional identifier to glean information on it."

"Damn. Well, it was worth a shot." He reluctantly tucked the amulet away and huffed, leaning against the wall as his spider demon climbed up onto his lap again to snuggle in. Stroking her head, he let her play with the glowing bauble some more.

The spider eventually broke the silence and pointed over to Jalel's sleeping spot. "We should kill him and eat him."

Riven stifled a bewildered laugh, stopping his stroking pets as he did. "Excuse me?"

"I'm hungry."

"That doesn't mean you get to eat him."

"Why not? We can take his stuff, too!" The spider excitedly got up to all twelve feet, salivating as the red mists from outside showing through the windows caused her eyes to gleam a similar red in the unnatural light. "He probably tastes really good…"

He flicked her thorax with a scowl. "Stop that."

"Ugh. Fine. You're no fun."

Athela passively bobbed her head from side to side. Dim red light still trickled in through the open balcony window on her left, and she began gazing out into the fog with a distant look as she drifted into recent memory. "I'm looking forward to leaving and getting into Elysium's mortal realms. I'm excited to see what your new world looks like! But this place? This hellscape dungeon?"

She held up her two front legs to either side. "I hate the nether realms, but the hells are even worse."

Riven snickered, then put his chin in his hands. "You'll have to tell me the difference between the two sometime."

"It wouldn't interest you. It's rather boring stuff."

Riven rolled his eyes and then frowned Jalel's way. The sleeping man nearby had undergone a mental breakdown last night; he'd seen all his companions die, so Jalel really hadn't been in a talking mood.

Or...at least that's what Jalel had told him. Jalel had *claimed* to be upset about his comrades, but Athela was rather convinced he was upset about losing the other bag of loot. The one Riven had refused to take because he was carrying the spider. Often last night, Athela had caught Jalel giving her cold glares—and she'd wanted to kill him numerous times already.

Riven couldn't necessarily disagree. The man seemed slightly shady and had guarded that bag of...stuff...without letting Riven or Athela take so much as a peep at what was inside.

Perhaps he should have left Jalel back in the cages to rot. Perhaps that was an overreaction. Only time would tell.

Then again, maybe Jalel knew a way out of here. Jalel had given him a little bit of a backstory—he was apparently from somewhere in the "core systems" of Elysium. He'd come here treasure hunting with friends before it'd gone terribly wrong and was wanting to make a big break by finding valuables to sell in the markets. When Riven had told him that he was undertaking the tutorial trial after his world had just been introduced into Elysium's multiverse, Jalel had gone into *a loud laughing fit*...and had refused to explain why. He'd also given the same reason that he couldn't talk about it to Riven that Athela had given Riven in the past—that if he told newly integrated people secrets of the system too early, he'd be punished by the system itself. The only thing Jalel *had* told Riven was that this dungeon might be a trial for Riven, but for other people it was a lucrative yet dangerous surface-level hellscape dungeon connected to numerous planes along a multiverse of innumerable different worlds. One of those planes of existence was Jalel's home—another planet entirely.

Funnily enough, Riven took it at face value after all the ridiculousness he'd experienced thus far.

"Well, hopefully he can get us out of here. This isn't a place I want to spend much time in…"

Standing and stretching his muscles, Riven yawned and wondered how Tim, Julie, and their mother, Tanya, were doing. He'd thought much on Allie and Jose, but not about the others until now. He hoped they were all right and wondered what they and Hakim were up to now. They'd probably already finished their own tutorial dungeon, if he had to guess, and from afar he wished them success in their future endeavors.

To his left and out the window overlooking the ruins, a silky black raven with glowing orange eyes flew by, then doubled back to gracefully land on the windowsill looking in. There was no glass here, and the fog was drifting through in minor amounts to coat Riven's skin in a fine layer of dew. The bird was no different in that regard—its feathers were extra shiny as it ruffled its body to let loose some of the moisture that'd collected.

Putting his hands on his hips, he grinned at the odd bird. Those orange eyes were very…strange and gave it an almost alien vibe. Otherwise, though, it looked like just a simple bird. Ravens were supposed to be rather intelligent creatures, and he'd fed them as a kid with the spare bread he had—which often wasn't much, considering how poor he'd been. "Kinda misty. Nice day for a passive shower, eh?"

The bird cocked its head to get a better look at him, then looked to Athela, who was eyeing it hungrily, but it didn't move when Riven made his way forward to the edge of the large window a couple feet to the left of where it was perched. He looked down a steep drop in front of him, going down thousands of feet to the city streets below.

"Leave the poor bird alone, Athela."

Riven ran his fingers through his chestnut-colored hair and over his ears, took in a deep breath to expand his lungs to the max, and exhaled with his eyes closed. The air just a few feet away was a lot less fresh than when he stood here on the edge of the tower, and it felt good on his senses to remain there in the morning light.

Athela sprang up and rushed over to the ledge with a hiss in the raven's direction, but with a sharp look from Riven, she didn't attack it and instead crawled up his back to peer over his shoulder. She looked over the stone ledge and whistled at the steep drop beneath, leaning into Riven and placing her head firmly against his arm. "I'm glad I bonded with you. Thanks again for saving me."

He merely smiled back.

There was a long moment of silence as they looked out over the ruined, partially obscured city, where pools of fire glowed at scattered intervals in stark contrast to the mist surrounding them.

"I'm glad you're okay," Riven eventually said while gripping the waist-high stone barrier. "I can say the same about how you saved me, back there in the duel. I know you were being self-serving, but you've been very helpful, and I know I wouldn't have made it without you."

She chittered a laugh and pointed at herself. "Without me? You'd definitely have died, silly human. Bask in my presence!"

He forced his smile back, not wanting to encourage her further, and pretended like he hadn't heard anything she'd just said. Opening his eyes again, Riven scanned the obscured horizon as low-lying clouds and fog drifted across and through the jagged streets, catwalks connecting buildings, pools of fire, slews of strung-up bodies, and ruined gothic temples clustered around them. This tower was certainly not the absolute tallest in the area, but it was one of the tallest—and although it was narrow, there was another catwalk connecting this building to another just three stories down.

"This dungeon really is a maze..." Riven mused, catching sight of a large citadel partially obscured by the city's mists farther in—and then straining to see a distant forest of dead black trees off in the opposite direction when the fog briefly parted. "Oh! Finally, something other than these damnable ruins."

A groan from behind them caused Riven to turn, and the orange-eyed raven that'd been watching him took off with a squawk to soar up into the air and away from this blasted place...but it gave him one long, sideways glance before it made its final retreat into the fog.

Riven frowned as the other man got up and rubbed his eyes. "Hey, Jalel. Sleep well?"

Jalel, the silver-haired young man, glanced over to him warily and gave him an appraising look before sighing and shaking his head. He took a moment to regain his senses from the grip of slumber and stretched with a deep-set frown as he looked around the large tower room. "Not at all. This...this is the worst possible outcome."

CHAPTER 38

"Wrong!" Riven said cheerfully, trotting over and taking a seat a couple feet away with his legs crossed. "Worst-case scenario is you being dead. You got out, didn't you?"

Jalel looked up to Riven and then suspiciously to Athela, but gradually he shook his head no and tried to rub the sleepiness out of his eyes again. "No. I am still here, damned to this dungeon until I am able to buy my way out by finding something of value. There are still many questions that I have for you...such as why you chose to leave all that treasure behind. We lost a fortune because you chose to save that spider instead of taking the bag last night."

Treasure, huh? Jalel had been very nonspecific about what was in those two bags, but Riven's anger spiked yet again at another negative comment about Athela.

His eyes darkened, and he took an aggressive step forward with a quickly souring mood that was not unnoticed by Jalel. Riven's voice lowered threateningly, coming out as almost a growl. "You ungrateful little punk. I'll only say this once, Jalel, so listen very carefully. I don't know you, and I don't know what you went through to get here. I don't know anything about your situation where you have to buy your way out of this place. However, if you keep talking about Athela like that, I'll give you something to *really* cry about. I'll leave you crippled, alone, and I'll take that bag for myself so I don't have to hear you whine like a little bitch about it every five seconds. Or I'll just let Athela eat you. Got it?"

Jalel's face quickly paled, and he slowly nodded his head in acknowledgment of the very real threat.

Athela, on the other hand, seemed to brighten up with newfound admiration, staring at Riven through those widened ruby eyes just like she'd done last night when he'd saved her from becoming lurker food. "You'll let me eat him?!"

[Optional Quest "Save the Prisoners" completed: You have saved two of two prisoners aside from Athela and have acquired half of

**potential rewards based on performance. You have gained two lev-
els, a specialized dagger upgrade, and twenty-five Elysium Coins.]**

**[You have gained two levels, one for each victim saved.
Congratulations! Be sure to visit your status page to apply points.]**

A sack of coins abruptly fell onto the floor in front of him, much to everyone's surprise, and he opened it to see twenty-five bronze coins with an insignia
of a sunrise imprinted on the metal. Ah. Nice, the eight consecutive hours must
have just passed…and these must be the Elysium coins that the system had just
spoken of.

Then, seconds later, a popping sound occurred, and Riven saw his embalmer's knife being drawn out of his belt and into the air toward a small constellation
of crimson-colored moats of light. They shifted and swirled in the air between
the room's three occupants, changing angulation and orientation relative to the
people but maintaining a rigid, strict formation until his knife entered a halo of
red in the very center.

**[Upgrade concerning your Rusted Embalmer's Knife is now com-
mencing. Upgrades are dependent on your current level, orientations, and needs. Please dismiss this prompt if you do not wish the
upgrade to continue.]**

Riven ignored the spider's quip about eating Jalel again and merely stared,
not daring to dismiss this new prompt as the constellation of lights in the middle
of the room swirled and rapidly condensed. The sound of a chime rang out, soft
and long, and with another flash of light, a new item emerged from the system's
enchantment.

It was a beautiful weapon, made primarily of gray and deep-blue steel. Faint
trimmings of gold decorated various parts of the blade with intricate carvings,
with red metal of some sort thrown in through the center of the blade and along
the handle. Hesitantly, Riven reached out to grab the blade where it floated at
eye level.

Immediately he felt a chilling sensation run up his arm. He felt a sense of
dread enter him. He felt something beginning to bore and tear into his hand,
little tendrils of wriggling…things…and he quickly dropped the dagger to let it
clatter to the ground.

"Fuck!" he cursed and stepped away, with the other two doing the same.
From there, he was able to make out little fleshy tendrils snaking themselves back
into the red hilt of the blade and reforming around the shaft. "That's actual flesh
trying to worm itself into me!"

"So cool," Athela stated promptly with an even tone, and Jalel gave the dagger a look of disgust.

"Typical of your kind to get a system gift like this," Jalel muttered under his breath. "Warlocks… Ugh."

Riven shot him a glare but ignored the slight and approached the dagger again while getting back onto his knees. He was able to identify it and make out the details of the blade more thoroughly now, and he poked it with his finger once while going over the system-given details.

> [Sanguis Foedus (Totem, Sacrificial Dagger): 12 average damage on strike, high chance to apply Amplified Bleeding debuff on biological enemies when struck. Requires a 20% or higher Blood subpillar affinity to wield. This item has an abnormally high endurance and is hard to destroy.
> - **Totem Soul:** Low-grade primal, Incomplete Fragment, 6 Willpower requirement.
> - **Flesh Bond:** This totem binds to the wielder in a unique way, allowing you to manipulate it at a limited distance through a flesh bond. If the flesh bond is severed, it must be restored before undertaking further distal manipulation.
> - **Sacrifice:** Use this dagger to sacrifice an enemy and mentally activate this ritual ability to create a portal back to Negrada at any distance. Creating a portal will take up to twenty-four hours.]

It was a totem, of all things, with a pretty decent upgrade in damage. His embalming knife had only had an average damage of three…while this one was at twelve a strike? This was…pleasantly surprising. It wasn't anywhere near the damage that claymore wielded by the first ghoul he'd fought could dish out, but logically that was to be expected. The claymore had also required a massive Strength stat that Riven simply didn't have.

The big thing that was unique about this item was the sacrificial portal. He'd be able to travel back here whenever he left, and although he didn't necessarily want to stay now, he could see a lot of different reasons why he'd want to come back in the future. Be it an escape of sorts, a way to explore the multiverse, collecting loot, or grinding levels whenever he got stronger. It wouldn't be a bad thing, certainly.

Recalling what he'd learned of totems from his previous tutorial step one, and from the obvious reminder on Willpower requirements in the item description itself, he quickly realized he'd have to bind this thing to himself to use it properly. He reached out and touched the dagger again, this time not withdrawing his hand when fleshy tendrils started snaking off the hilt to meet his fingers. He winced slightly when they began digging into his skin, but soon the tendrils and his own body meshed together as one—and he felt the presence of the soul shard register when he accepted ownership of the item.

[Sanguis Foedus has been registered as your totem.]

A firm, tight cord of muscular flesh whipped the dagger up into the air—extending from his limb as the weapon snaked around his torso. Then it withdrew, slicing through the air in a cyclone of motion before smacking hilt first into Riven's outstretched palm.

Curiously, he came back with his arm and flung the dagger in a spinning arc through the air. Threads of flesh followed it all the way to the opposite side of the room, where it smacked against the stone wall. Riven's eyes dropped in disappointment when no lasting damage was seen in the thick stone, but what exactly had he been expecting, anyways?

"Huh. Well, at least it's an upgrade."

Riven blinked, finishing his admiration of the new weapon and sheathing it in his belt. He took a moment to apply more points toward his Intelligence, Willpower, and Sturdiness, too, with the level gains he'd achieved. Afterward, he turned to Jalel with an annoyed scowl while he placed the coin pouch in his backpack like nothing interesting had just happened. "Concerning what you said earlier, I have some questions for you, too."

Jalel frowned right back, settling into a more comfortable position against the wall with his arms over his knees and leaning his head back to stare at the mage and his minion. "Go ahead and ask them, Warlock."

Jalel tried to keep the disgust out of his voice as he said the word *warlock*, but he only partially succeeded. Riven could hear the underlying animosity.

"Why do you dislike warlocks so much?"

Jalel raised an incredulous eyebrow. "Excuse me?"

Riven tried to keep his cool and took in a long, drawn-out breath. Putting his hands on his temple to rub his forehead, he tried again. "Why is it that warlocks have a bad reputation? I'm assuming they do, based on your not-so-subtle hints."

Jalel's face lifted in surprise, and he put his arms around his knees with a curious glint to his eyes. "You…you're asking me why your kind is hated by the rest of civilization?"

"Is that how it is?"

"That's definitely how it is," Jalel confirmed. He lifted up a hand as if to pose a question, thought better of it, and asked something else. "Some countries or cities across the core worlds even outlaw warlocks entirely, though not all. I'm sure you'll eventually figure it out if you survive long enough. Is this your first time in hell?"

Riven laughed loudly, feeling Athela's weight shift as the spider's cold legs skittered off his back. Lifting up his arms to either side and motioning out the window, he gave Jalel a flat look. "Does it look like I'm a native to hell? I already told you that my world is being integrated. Use some context clues."

"I wouldn't know. Warlocks tend to do things like involve themselves with hell's inhabitants."

Riven face-palmed.

Jalel, on the other hand, kept going. "You're from the last wave of integration. You're going through the tutorials right now, that's what you said, isn't it? That means your world is integrating."

Riven gave the other man an incredulous stare and threw up his hands. Was this guy stupid? Or was Jalel doing this just to annoy him? "Yes. That is *literally* what I just said."

Jalel snorted, then nodded in confirmation of his own question. "Well, as I said earlier, I can't tell you too much about it, but there are some things that I can tell you. The integration is the merging of worlds from outside the multiverse. Every couple decades Elysium has a new integration of planets that join the systems of Elysium—a multitude of universes that it has underneath its own umbrella of control. It takes them from outer realms and stitches them into the realms of this multiverse, an ever-expanding and almost endless system of worlds. As to why you warlocks are hated…there's a very long history to that. Warlocks have been accountable for numerous atrocities throughout the millennia and care little for the people they harm in pursuit of greater power. The Unholy pillar in general is looked down upon by the other, more civilized sects of society."

The following silence was tangible, and only the sound of a far-off scream of panic broke the silence.

It caused Riven to turn and look out the balcony window onto the ruined city of flames and blood mists, but that scream could have been from anywhere… so it was only a minor distraction before Riven turned his attention back to the other man. "Tell me more of what you can, please. I'd really like to know as much as possible. Surely there is more you can say without angering the system."

CHAPTER 39

Riven's demand made Jalel chuckle. The silver-haired man shrugged indifferently, waving a hand about the room with a loud snort. "What is there to say? I cannot remember the specifics."

It was a blatant lie. Riven didn't know why this stranger would lie to them, but Jalel hadn't even attempted to hide it. He just didn't want to talk. Perhaps it was because he couldn't? Perhaps not, but the feeling he was getting from the snobbish smirk on Jalel's face made Riven consider him a liar.

Riven paused, immediately shifting his posture and considering the man for a moment. Whoever this guy was, Riven really didn't like him. "I see. Well, since you're rather useless to us and haven't wanted to share whatever is inside those bags after I saved your pathetic life, I'm done with you. You've insulted my minion numerous times and told me to leave her behind to die. We're parting and going our separate ways; I wish you luck in getting back to wherever the fuck it was you came from."

The abrasive, even somewhat aggressive stance Riven took caught Jalel off guard—and it was obvious in his face despite the defensive glower he shot Riven's way.

Jalel tapped his fingers along his shins, clearly not liking the idea of being left behind to fend for himself, then shrugged. "Fine. It won't hurt to tell you what I know—what isn't off-limits to tell you, anyways."

Riven shot him a disgusted look and turned, reaching down for his few belongings and beginning to pack up. "Get fucked."

Jalel's face grew even paler as he realized that Riven was serious. "Wait...this dungeon can't be traversed by just—"

"I said, get fucked. You're on your own, and I'm sure you'll do a fine job by yourself considering how I found you," Riven cut him off with another glare. Hoisting his wooden staff up and nodding to Athela as the demon chittered a long-winded laugh, he nodded toward the bolted door of the tower's top room. "Let's go, Athela."

"Wait!" Jalel started to get up but stumbled back and fell against the wall as Athela rushed him—stopping halfway between where he and Riven stood while she displayed her hostile fangs that began dripping cold, necrotic venom, leaving black droplets along the stone floor as she slowly crept ahead.

Jalel was terrified and began to scream, and Riven snapped his fingers with a command to get her back. "Athela, don't attack him. He's a jackass, but we're not murderers."

"But we *are* murderers!" she argued with a disappointed humph—not letting her gaze leave the potential meal. "We already killed all those people in the tutorial, and we killed that other warlock, too! This man is no different—let me eat him! Please?!"

Jalel's eyes went wide, and his knuckles turned white as he clenched his hands into fists. The outfit he'd put on after escaping, an outfit he'd drawn out of the bag, was made of leather and had a small knife in the side of a belt…and his fingers seemed to itch as they slowly went over to where it was sheathed.

Riven smirked, unintimidated by Jalel's action, and shook his head. "No, Athela."

"Please?!"

"I said no."

She gave him another humph, then backed up and went to rub against Riven's leg. "Okay."

The color came back to Jalel's face, and his hand dropped to his side. He just stared at Riven for a long moment before he cleared his throat and gestured to the bag. "What if I pay you to escort me out of here?"

Riven had been reaching for the door again, but that last statement gave him pause, and his frown deepened. The wind outside began to howl with a stark, brief blast of air before dying down again, and he turned to glance at the other man with suspicion.

"I thought you needed it to buy your way out?"

"I'll be the one to worry about that. I just need to leave."

There was another long pause. Eventually Riven lost that staring contest, faltered, and sighed. "What do you have to offer?"

Grudgingly, Jalel turned and stepped over to the large sack he'd taken with him. Opening it and rummaging around, he pulled out a smaller green sack that was tied with brown rope. He tossed it over to Riven, frowning. "Is that enough? You can use them at altars that will spawn in your world to buy items."

Riven gave him a flat stare, then opened the bag in his hands. The bag jingled lightly, and, peering down into its contents, Riven saw a good number of copper, silver, and gold coins—each of them with the same insignia he'd seen on the system's provided coins a minute before. There were likely a couple hundred in there, and Riven's eyes narrowed while he shifted his weight and placed the sack in his backpack. "Altars? Are they like shops?"

"Kind of. It's a little bit more complicated than that, but collecting these coins will allow you to exchange goods directly with the system, and it's common currency in the core realms. You get these coins by killing certain monsters, completing quests, or mining ore and enchanting it in a specific way."

"Really…" Riven glanced back down. Assuming he could use these to buy things in the outside world, money would be very important. "Athela, is this true?"

The arachnid nodded. "Yup! It looks like Jalel has fewer restrictions than I do when it comes to information exchange. Now that you know, though, I can confirm what he's telling you is right. Altars to the system can be used to buy goods from them as long as you have Elysium coins."

Riven evaluated the man for a time, then glanced over to the bag he still hadn't looked through. "I also get my choice of one item from that little treasure bag of yours."

"I can't do that! I need it to pay off my debts!"

"Then you're on your own. Assuming you even know the way out, it may be hard to leave."

Jalel hesitated, fidgeting slightly while looking out the window at the gloom of this nightmarish place. He opened his mouth to speak, closed it, and then clenched his fists in anger. "Fine. And yes, I know the way. Get me to the exit, and you'll have your choice of one item from the bag. Just one."

"Now we're talking. So, Jalel, knowing that you've been here and explored more than I have…I want you to lead us to the center of the city, where the statue of the bearded man with an axe is. Only after that can you show us the way out."

Jalel paused hesitantly to think and then slowly nodded. "Why do you want to go there?"

"Do you know where it is?" Athela asked while eagerly getting up on her hind legs to paw at the air. "We're supposed to finish a quest there!"

Jalel gave the demon a sour look, then bent down and picked up his bag to throw it over his shoulder. "Yes, I've seen it before. I'll take you to the statue, but I will not go near it. After you do whatever it is you need to do, I will lead you to the entrance as you escort me and kill anything that tries to attack us if we can't avoid it. I assume that if you leave the dungeon through my exit you'll be transported back into your integrating world, but I can't be sure. The system is picky with newly integrated civilizations and doesn't let you off world this early most of the time; your case being here in Negrada is pretty unique. Anyways, is that a deal?"

An odd request to not go near the statue, but Riven nodded and reached for the door. "What did you mean earlier by buying your way out of here? About paying your debts?"

Jalel frowned even more deeply and dusted off his shoulders as he adjusted his posture with a humph. "My family owes money… We borrowed too much from a loan shark. It's a long story I'd rather not talk about."

The last dead bolts on the door were unlocked, and the heavy wood swung open a second later as Jalel motioned toward the spiral staircase descending downward into the depths of the tower. Moisture was collecting from the ceiling, leaking through the old stones and dripping onto the stairway below. "Be careful not to slip. We're going all the way down to the ground level. Then we'll be heading to the statue, and from there we will make our way to the canal, where a boat is hidden on the river of blood and tethered underneath an outcropping of rock. After that, it'll be easier to traverse the city. The river of blood is safer than land."

"*KAJIT HAS WARES!*"

CRASH

Riven was so startled by the zombified ghost's appearance that he let loose a torrent of blood magic in the form of instantaneously summoned Bloody Razors. The magical projectiles blew through the image of the ghost and crashed into the opposite wall, not even fazing the decrepit woman as she laughed and giggled—pointing at him while his chest heaved up and down.

Jalel and Athela fared no better, with Athela now perched upside down on the ceiling—hissing at the ghost threateningly, while Jalel had fallen backward over the bag he'd dropped and smashed ass first into the ground.

"You again!" Riven spat while glaring up at the floating ghost with a mixture of irritation and curiosity. "Goddamn it, stop scaring people like that! It isn't funny!"

The ghost, however, thought it was quite funny, and black ichor dripped from her laughing, rotten mouth while her patchy hair drifted around her. Her semitranslucent state made her frail, bandaged body look even thinner than it'd been when he'd first stabbed the woman upon entering Negrada. "I very funny, you just no have humor. But that not why I come! I come for best price you find in hellscapes! How you like knife?"

Riven's brow furrowed and the other two remained quiet as his eyes tracked down to where the ghost was pointing at the newly acquired sacrificial dagger on his belt. "The knife? This one?"

He held up Sanguis Foedus in the dim red light of the room.

The ghost nodded with a smirk. "You like, yes? I take as special price, yes? I misplace other prize I sway you with, so I take this one instead!"

[Sanguis Foedus has been forcibly relinquished from your control.]

The ghost snapped her fingers, and instantly the dagger he'd just acquired was in her hands. The bond between Riven and the item also snapped, the disconnect causing his body to shudder slightly. Dumbfounded and confused, he grabbed at his waist and then quickly conjured a Wretched Snare that blasted out toward the spirit—but it merely fell right through her image as she laughed at his attempts.

Athela came next, spraying the ghost full-blast with red threads that didn't affect it, either. Jalel, meanwhile, just stared, confused and scared, huddling with his bag in the corner of the room near the door.

"Hey, bitch! I don't know who you are, but that dagger belongs to my master!" Athela waggled an angry arachnid limb at the cackling ghost, who sat clutching at her sides. "Give it back!"

More than anything, Riven was just confused. "Athela, doesn't magic usually work on spirits?"

"Of course it does!"

"Then why didn't mine work on her?"

Athela shot him a look, then glanced back at the amused ghost, who now was sitting cross-legged in the middle of the stone room. "I don't know."

Kajit, however, had an answer. She lazily rolled over onto her side and gave him a disgusting belch, then gestured at him with one of her gnarled hands. "I haunt you when you touch wooden ring, yes? Wooden ring powerful curse onetime-use item. You pick up, curse transfer to you. Strong death magic curse. You see: I now reside in soul structure like fly on hippopotamus bum. To get Kajit out, you must pay special price."

Riven gave the ghost an incredulous look, and then glanced worriedly toward Athela.

"YOU GOT HAUNTED?! When did *that* happen?!" Athela asked in a bewildered sputtering of words.

"Right after we got sent into the hellscape."

"AND WHY DIDN'T YOU TELL ME?!"

"She seemed harmless earlier and only appeared once after I killed her physical body."

"BEING HAUNTED IS A PRETTY BIG DEAL, RIVEN! And not many spirits can do that kind of thing! She's likely a gods-damned phantom!"

"Bleh!" The ghost held up her right hand after pretending to inspect the nails that weren't there. "I phantom, yes, but fear not, spider demon creature. I cannot eat soul even if try, even while haunted. Soul is too solid and likely eat me back, even before binding to great maw."

The spider blinked twice, then hopped down off the ceiling and stared curiously up at Riven from the floor. "Oh, really? What does she mean by *great maw*, Riven? It appears there are things you haven't told me yet since rescuing me yesterday."

It likely meant only one thing. Riven frowned, not wanting to discuss such things in front of Jalel if the man already had such a poor opinion of warlocks to begin with. Riven wanted to get out of this damnable place, and he wasn't sure someone like Jalel would lead him out willingly if they knew he had a piece of original sin in his soul structure.

He cleared his throat. "That's a story for another time."

"Yes, yes, now we talk about *special price*!" Kajit tossed the dagger over her shoulder, and it blipped out of existence, vanishing into thin air after a small portal of black swallowed it whole. "I take dagger now for my price, and then your price is next!"

Riven was beginning to get annoyed and crossed his arms, not so much threatened by the being in front of him but rather irritated by the way she'd just snagged the fancy dagger he'd been awarded. "So, to be clear, you're residing in my soul now?"

"Yes, yes."

"And you can't harm me?"

The ghost paused, then shook her head. "No, no. I can harm but can't eat soul. Complex death magic I explain another time if special price is paid. I even teach you like student. I once a great witch before I die and go to hell! Even if you stupid ape with noodle arms, I still teach!"

She beamed a brilliantly decrepit grin his way while wiggling her eyebrows. "Want to hear special price to take dagger back? I leave soul complex, and you learn death magic as Kajit's student?!"

He stared her down for a time, hands still clenched in frustration. Ugh. This was not going to be good, was it?

Riven slowly nodded. "Tell me what this price you keep talking about is."

Her smug look slowly turned upside down and into a frown. "You free Kajit's sister's soul from Tower of Fates before leaving hell."

[New Quest Obtained: The Tower of Fates—Kajit, a phantom whose decaying corpse you happily stabbed a couple times back in the day, now is asking for your help. The Tower of Fates, a spot in existence accessible from hell only by those with significant prophetic abilities, holds Kajit's sister captive. She wants you to get her sister out before you leave the dungeon. Failing this quest will no doubt result in the loss of your newly acquired dagger, an incredibly angry spirit, and the loss of knowledge otherwise obtained concerning death magic. As some free advice from the administrator, I would highly recommend you not decline trying, though...because otherwise you're probably not going to make it out of this room alive.]

CHAPTER 40

Riven sneered down at the prompt. Not going to make it out alive? What a fucking joke. As if he wasn't walking a knife's edge already. He'd been forced into scenario after scenario with little say in the matter, and he was goddamned tired of it. Anger and disgust surged through him, and his soul resonated with his will.

Fuck this phantom, fuck this hellscape, fuck Chalgathi, and fuck Elysium's administrator. He'd do what he fucking wanted to do.

A ripple ran out from where Riven stood in the middle of the room, ever so faint...but the phantom in front of him immediately lost her confidence.

"What are you doing?" Kajit asked warily, stiffly even, while moving slowly away to the other side of the room.

He focused on the shard of original sin in his soul complex, forcing it to wake up.

Another pulse radiated out from his body, and he gritted his teeth while clenching his fists in frustration. People or entities pushing him around would end now, right now, and after what Kajit had just said concerning not being able to devour his soul, it was only a matter of understanding. The pieces had clicked together, at least somewhat, because if the "great maw" was enough to deter a high-level phantom even while it wasn't finished constructing its core...

He searched for her. His magic might not damage the ghost because she was likely recognized as a part of him by the mana he controlled, but that didn't mean his Gluttony core wouldn't work. He searched inside himself, trying to scout out just where the phantom had lodged its own piece of being inside him, and it didn't take long to find it. There, on the outskirts of his complex, a faint teal bubble pulsed with unnatural light.

He flexed his will, and Gluttony came to life, howling inside his mind like an uncaged beast that tore through his spiritual grounds and rushed the phantom in a fury.

Kajit screamed, her body lighting up across the room with black and crimson flames as gash marks were torn through her ethereal form like invisible teeth biting off pieces of her body. She writhed about in the air, wailing and causing the room to reverberate with unrestrained power.

But she was unable to focus that power, and Riven's eyes pulsed a bright crimson before he forcefully restrained Kajit's presence with carnivorous jaws that clamped down threateningly.

Neither Jalel nor Athela knew what was going on, and both of them just gawked awkwardly while Riven slowly came to stand in front of the panting, badly wounded spirit in front of him on the floor. Part of her ethereal body was now phasing in between mist and solid form, and he placed his boot on her neck while she spluttered black ichor and neon-teal ghost fluids.

"How?!" she managed to sputter, denying what her eyes were telling her while scrambling to try and get his foot off her neck. It was a question that Athela and Jalel were also asking themselves.

He merely shook his head, beckoning at her with one open hand. "You were pretty ballsy to do what you did, but it was your own words that gave me the clue to finish you off if I so choose. Where does that leave us now?"

The jaws in his soulscape tightened on Kajit's soul, and she screamed again.

"However..." he muttered, letting up on the pressure he was putting on the phantom's neck. He took a step back, still frowning at her. "If you give the dagger back to me, we can discuss things on a more professional level. I'm not necessarily opposed to helping you, but I'm going to do it if I fucking want to and not because I was blackmailed or stolen from. Do you understand?"

"But..." the ghost spluttered an incoherent string of curses, then snarled from her position on the floor, "I cannot give you dagger. You must take dagger for yourself from Tower of Fates!"

"Wrong answer."

The jaws clenched, and Kajit started screaming again, invisible teeth ripping pieces of the phantom inside his soul bit by bit while startled onlookers watched. "I DO NOT HAVE DAGGER! DAGGER IN TOWER OF FATES! PLEASE!"

After a few seconds more, he let up. Crossing his arms and fuming angrily underneath his hood, Riven beckoned the phantom to continue. "Explain yourself, Kajit."

She took a moment to catch her breath, eyeing the warlock fearfully. "Sister and I have soul link, but I cannot travel without ensnaring myself in trap. I send dagger there through link to make sure you free her!"

The ghost spat, her body becoming more translucent again now that he'd let up on his shard of Gluttony. "I may steal dagger, yes. But if was Riven's sister, would you not do so, too?"

Riven mulled over the words slowly, keeping eyes locked on her own with a steady gaze. Eventually his clenched hands unfurled, and he let out a long, controlled sigh. His eyes softened, and he nodded. "Yes, I would. This is not over, Kajit—when Athela and I are done with our current quest to find the axe-wielding statue, you and I are going to have a long chat about what's happened."

He stared a little bit longer, battling internally about his feelings on the matter. But eventually he just shook his head and turned heel while glancing over to Athela and Jalel. Beckoning to them, he walked toward the spiral staircase leading down to the lower levels. "Let's go."

The statue the quest log spoke of was actually very close to the canal where Jalel's previous group had hidden their canoe, or so he claimed. He led Riven and Athela a little ways across the city using a skinny back street hidden by overgrown, wilting weeds as tall as they were, and they successfully managed to make it all the way to the statue's courtyard without any further incidents.

The trek took a little over an hour. The ground level of the city was far more intimidating than it'd been from above. Athela kept watch from up high—she was able to crawl up the sides of walls or over rooftops for better vantage points while they made their way to their destination. Flocks of crows flew overhead, and the sounds of distant battle echoed across stone monoliths, while bodies placed on spikes were left along the roadways for onlookers to silently evaluate. Ancient doorways promised hidden enemies at every turn, and movements in the mists foretold death as they swept across the ruined city.

They kept walking, keeping pace with Jalel and letting him lead by only ten feet until he came to a stop at the end of the corridor. The young hunter gripped his dagger more tightly, looking to his right and then his left, before pointing ahead into the thickening fog.

Riven gave Athela a signal to come down from her perch on a nearby tiled rooftop, not seeing anything but shrouds, but he inched forward and squinted for a better look. "This is it?"

Jalel nodded slowly, sweat beading on his forehead to intermix with the dew-drops accumulating there. "This is definitely it… The weather has been terrible lately—but it's here. This is a courtyard extending for many dozens of yards, and in the middle you'll see the statue."

Athela's light chittering alerted them to the spider's descent, as the dead-silent advance of her long spider legs was completely missed before she parked herself at Riven's side. There was nothing ahead of them that she could see except for ancient cobblestones, with weeds growing out from crevices or cracks in the ground. Immediately beside them, on either side, were tall stone buildings that faded away the farther up she looked—and behind them the long corridor loomed ominously as if to discourage them from turning back.

Athela moved ahead into the open space before them by about ten yards and gave Riven a backward glance. "I was able to make out part of the statue from atop that building, but I don't feel good about this. Let me go ahead. Now that I have been bound to you, I won't be able to die a permanent death any longer. It is better that I be the bait if there is any danger, rather than you."

Riven didn't feel good about it, either. It was way too open and exposed in terms of obstacles to hide himself behind, yet there was far less visibility than he'd like given the shrouds of black clouds and red mists drifting through the courtyard. Setting down his two remaining and half-completed totems, he activated them—each giving off minor flares of red light as he did on either side of the pathway—in preparation for anything that might be out there in the mists.

"Also, make sure Jalel doesn't stab you in the back. It is strange that he doesn't want to come into the courtyard with us and no doubt thinks this is a dangerous area," Athela stated a little less loudly, so that only Riven could hear. She gave the other man a hiss of discontent and then looked back to Riven. "I still think you should let me eat him. And that bitch of a ghost, too! I can't believe she took your pretty dagger and just flung it somewhere into the abyss like that! Especially because we have to play fetch now!"

Riven rolled his eyes and let out a low chuckle as Jalel continued to glance around nervously. "Just go on and scout the area. I'll stay within the range of my totems. Hey, Jalel, got any further information on why you're decided on staying back?"

It was obvious that Jalel didn't want to enter the courtyard. The way his breathing had picked up and the ever-firm grip on his dagger were testament to it. "I am sorry... I don't know why your quest took you here, but I have passed by here before. This is not a safe area of the city. Not that anywhere here is safe, but this statue is known to attract...certain creatures to it. Ones that fly, though I am not sure what they are, as I have never gotten close enough to find out."

He then turned around fully, gripping Riven firmly by the shoulder. "Are you sure you don't want to abandon this quest? Surely the gods will understand. Quests are not mandatory, and your lives are worth more than a simple reward."

Riven glanced at Athela, and he fidgeted thoughtfully with the demonic bauble in his pocket while he pulled up the quest he'd been given from his status page. It was an option he'd noticed first in Chalgathi's trials, and now was coming in rather handy to review information.

[New Quest (Updated): Find Your Spider Princess—You've rescued and bonded back to your minion, Athela, but you still need to bring her to the center of the city and touch the statue of the bearded,

axe-wielding man without dying to receive a reward. Dying would be less than ideal, for obvious and permanent reasons. But let's be real, you're probably going to die here, little warlock—so pucker up!]

Putting his quest log away, he returned to scanning the area. He thoughtfully tapped his fingers on his thigh a couple times, scowling hard at the ground as he went over the options. He could back out, run, and get to the canoe that Jalel had claimed was nearby. But then what? They'd just leave after coming so far already? Were these prizes important? How would he know if he was missing out when it could potentially be a boon to help him survive in this fucked-up new world of his?

He thought back to the choice of selflessness versus selfishness. Had other participants in Chalgathi's trials, the others of the fifty survivors, taken the one of selfishness? Had they been granted a similar option and been awarded with some legendary-tier outfits that he now didn't have? If so, he needed to make up for that here. Sure, he'd been awarded the piece of gluttony. Sure, he'd found a new spell here and a demonic bauble. Even the dagger had been nice. However, he no longer had the dagger and wasn't sure he was going to be able to get it back—and the bauble didn't respond to him. Whatever B-class demon was inside that thing hadn't responded to his summons yet. And if he had to guess, based on Chalgathi still interfering in his life and the Chalgathi cultist amulet hanging around his neck, those others of the fifty survivors would probably be involved with him again. In the past he'd been forced to fight one of them to the death—would he have to do so a second time? Just how overpowered had his peers become if his guess was correct? Whatever the case, Chalgathi obviously wasn't done with him and therefore wasn't likely done with the others. He could only anticipate the worst.

Back on Earth he'd been a nobody, a guy who barely got by. Jose, his best friend, had always been there for him. Allie, Riven's little sister, had always looked up to him for guidance that forced him to put on a strong front, but otherwise Riven had been utterly alone. And now he'd met Athela. He barely knew the sometimes annoying, yet rather cute arachnid, but he'd already connected to her on a level that he'd failed to reach with so many others of his own species.

Now that he was here on the cusp of a new life with Athela at his side, was he going to let things slide by him just because they were hard? He wanted to introduce her to his sister, and he knew Jose would like Athela—he was fascinated by spiders, and a talking, demonic version of one as a pseudo-pet would cause Jose to go green with envy. Riven had his entire life ahead of him, a new chance to become something and someone great. Would he balk now, just because the danger was unknown to him? It might not even be there at all.

He turned to Athela, bent down and lightly stroked her thorax with a smile of self-assurance. "If you don't want to do it, we can back out now."

Athela watched him for some time, unblinking and staring up at her warlock master while her eyes seemed to twinkle with delight. She slowly nodded, then opened her mandibles...a sly expression that Riven had come to know as an arachnid smile playing at the corners of her fangs. Carefully, she pushed one leg into his right pocket. "You're talking brave for being such a wuss! I think we should do it like we'd planned. But now that you're asking me, we have to proceed on one condition!"

Riven raised an eyebrow before sitting on the ground in front of her, a soft chuckle escaping his lips at the mischievousness of his minion. "What's that condition?"

She cocked her head and lightly tapped him on the nose with what could only be described as a giggle. Then she put two of her arachnid legs into his right pocket and pulled out the miracle stone they'd stolen from the Jabob demons. "You will address me as Princess from now on! And I get to wear this as a crown jewel until it accepts you!"

The spider did a silly dance with the glowing red orb placed on her head, held there by two of her twelve legs. She strutted around as well as a spider could, going back and forth while humming to herself and bobbing her thorax up and down to emphasize her importance.

Riven could only snort and laugh, covering his mouth as he tried to remain quiet despite her ridiculous behavior. "You can't be serious."

"I am serious!" Athela protested with a gnashing of her fangs. "I am a princess, and I deserve a crown. Humph!"

Riven almost failed to see the abrupt change in Jalel a second later.

Almost.

CHAPTER 41

Jalel's jaw had dropped when he saw what she held. It only took him a second before his face twisted in a strange mix of desperation and greed, rage, and hate, and their newfound acquaintance pulled out his dagger. He dropped his bag without even thinking while simultaneously lunging forward toward Athela and pulled out some sort of white potion.

Riven's eyes narrowed, and it was as if time stopped as she stood unaware of the impending attack.

"Athela, move!"

In an instant, Riven had rammed his foot into Jalel's chest—expelling the air from the man with an abrupt wheeze and sending the man off course. The potion that Jalel had been about to throw smashed against the ground, blinding everyone momentarily with a loud pop of sound like a flash-bang. Riven cursed and blindly slammed his staff into Jalel's chest, managing to hit him straight on. The man grunted, scrambling back across the ground, trying to get to the weapon that'd loudly clattered against the stone.

It took about ten seconds for everyone to recover. Riven blinked rapidly to clear his head, Athela screeched irritatedly while trying to rub her eyes, and the man on the ground groaned and coughed.

Athela was confused and disoriented by the blast, but she began to laugh at Riven's display of violence when the light cleared, and she slipped the stone back into Riven's pocket. "I would have been fine, Riven. This man is far too weak to kill me, and even if I died—I'd come back. Though I do appreciate the sentiment… you didn't address me by my *royal title*! Address me as *Princess*, you peasant slave!"

"I was worried about the stone!" Riven snarled and angrily kicked the downed man in the gut while he ignored the crazy arachnid demon nearby. He'd certainly felt that this guy was…off. Jalel had seemed desperate, untrustworthy, and all-around shady since the first conversation Riven had with him—but to see the miracle stone and go on the offensive to attain it…

Jalel had just sentenced himself to death. Why would he have been so utterly stupid? Was he truly that desperate to obtain something of value for his debts? Jalel knew he was weaker than Riven and Athela were, but he'd acted so brazenly Riven simply couldn't understand. Had he really expected to snatch it and run? Or had he been planning to stab Riven first on the way to the spider?

"That stone belongs to *me*!" Jalel half screamed and half gasped, short of breath after the kick and clutching at his stomach. He was half-mad with envy as he picked himself up and narrowly rolled to dodge a close-range flurry of spinning red blades that crashed into the wall behind him, eyes growing wide before howling his rage and swinging in an arc to take Riven's head.

Two thin tendrils of crimson from the leeching totems slammed into the man, catching him in the chest and neck and causing him to scream and miss his swing. The threads of red magic pulsed, drawing out his life force by the second as Jalel began to writhe about.

Though Riven himself was somewhat of a novice at fighting in hand-to-hand combat, the spider was not. In a blur of legs and fangs, the Blood Weaver slammed into Jalel with a screech as she sank her teeth into his arm wielding the dagger. Necrotic venom began to slide into his veins as Jalel gave a high-pitched wail, reeling back as Athela kicked off while simultaneously latching onto him with her blood webbing and spinning in an arc around the man's body to trip him.

The next moments were a blur of motion as Athela whipped back and forth, managing to wrap her webbing around Jalel numerous times before he was restrained enough that she could just roll him repeatedly with her legs as her spinnerets went nuts. Before long, only Jalel's strained face remained open to the air as his entire body was wrapped up in a red cocoon.

"You fucked up," Riven hissed at the horrified man with a malevolent sneer as Athela finally finished her wrapping job and hopped off proudly.

"May I eat him now, Master? May I?"

Jalel caught his breath with a panicked expression while still being pressed up against the bloodied wall, groaning in discomfort as Riven's arm shoved his face into the stone.

"I didn't mean anything by it... I swear by all the gods. I reacted on instinct—"

"Instinct?" Riven asked mockingly, picking up the knife Jalel had dropped and pressing the blade farther into the man's neck to draw a slight amount of blood. "Instinct to grab it from her without warning and attack us? Fucking liar."

Riven drew Jalel's head back and abruptly slammed it into the wall again with a violent thud—leaving a trail of Jalel's blood after releasing his pressing hold. "Now that I know I can't trust you, it's lights out, buddy. Any last words?"

"No!" Jalel interrupted after a quick yelp of pain with a desperate, wide-eyed shake of his head. "I do not want it! I was going to destroy it!"

Riven remained unimpressed, tightening his grip on the back of Jalel's hair, and he glanced up at Athela, who sat watching silently by. "You just said the stone was yours, but let's pretend you're telling me the truth. Why would you destroy it?"

"It is evil!" Jalel inhaled sharply as the freezing venom started climbing up his neck, glancing over at the glowing orb cupped between Athela's arachnid paws. "You have read the description, yes? Innocent souls have been sacrificed to wield its power! Demonic energy is a taint upon the land—you and your kind will all burn in the hells forever for your sacrilege! You will rot with them if you don't forsake the Unholy pillar!"

Jalel managed to spit at Riven with a look of contempt, his facade entirely gone now. Instead, a look of malice and hatred that Riven felt was rather misplaced overlapped every aspect of the other man's features.

A loud *thud* sounded from above them, and the wall shuddered slightly, bringing Riven's attention away from Jalel. Small rocks and pieces of debris began falling from above, and Riven took a couple steps back to get out of the way with Athela scrambling to the side. Then there was a loud and eerie screech from above them in the mist.

The three of them remained perfectly still, and Riven could feel his heart beating ever faster.

"Untie me!" Jalel hissed as he began to frantically struggle within his bindings. "Please! Please, I did not think before I acted; just let me go and I'll let you take everything I've collected while here!"

The strange cry came again, this time still up above—from the other side of the alley…with the soft flapping of wings accompanying it.

"SHRREEEEEEE!"

The scream was a mixture of both bird and man as a winged, semihumanoid creature dropped down from the sky to land in the path behind them. Taloned claws were present at the end of its stork-like feet, with wings where its arms should have been. Otherwise the torso, abdomen, and head were all more or less human. Thick plumes of brown feathers covered the head just above the eyes, spreading along its neck and along the rest of the body with a strange grace to it. Long, carnivorous teeth spread out in a grin as it eyed them hungrily from catlike yellow eyes, and its abdominal muscles contracted repeatedly while grunting in a crude and beast-like chuckle.

[Juvenile Harpy, Level 3]

Another one, similar to the first but displaying a prominent set of breasts to signify its gender as female, dropped down on the other side toward the statue. The tips of this one's feathers ended in silver edging, and as it spread its wings, it took a long step toward them with those insanely long legs. Talons grasped at the air hesitantly, as if it didn't know whether or not to strike yet, and it let off a cunning smile while thinking about its next meal.

[Juvenile Harpy, Level 4]

Then they moved into action.

"SHIT!" Riven swore loudly and backpedaled frantically, narrowly avoiding a swift jab from the male harpy as it struck out with its left foot. The talons came within an inch of his face like the strike of a mantis as it hissed at him.

He hit the wall, rolled onto his side, and fumbled for better footing before blocking another strike with his staff. "GET FUCKED, YOU OVERSIZED CHICKEN!"

A blast of black netting erupted in front of him and swallowed the creature, burying its Unholy needles into the harpy as it lurched back and screeched in panic while frantically flapping and tearing away from the magic. He activated the Blessing of the Crow, and his body reacted with a noticeable boost in speed as red sparks trickled along his skin—and he ducked a counterstrike before slamming his staff into the outstretched thigh of the harpy for a solid hit.

A multitude of crimson discs blasted into the harpy's chest a second later as he conjured Bloody Razors, and the creature screamed in fury to fall back and tend its gushing wounds while a third harpy charged in. It dived in fast from above, bowling Riven over and causing him to drop the staff as he stutter-stepped. He rolled over twice and gripped at the knife he'd picked up—starting to charge up a Blood Lance along his right side and slashing at the new harpy's wing when it blew up a dust cloud to blind him.

Coughing and removing himself from the debris, he briefly caught sight of Athela as she battled two more female harpies with silver coloring. The arachnid was fast...remarkably fast, and was dancing in between them or up the sides of the walls while spraying shards of sharpened bloody webbing akin to magically infused needles. She hissed and spun, dodging a taloned strike and wrapping the extended leg up with more webbing to yank and pull the harpy off balance before launching herself at the harpy's throat and digging into it with her fangs while the other harpy was knocked back with ribboning crimson lights as Riven's unfinished totems fired to latch onto new targets.

Another nearby screech brought him back to his own battle when his current combatant was joined by the harpy he'd injured earlier. Crimson razor discs still stuck out of his enemy's chest and acidic burn marks from where the snare had caught it showed easily. It charged him with bloodlust. Talons, wings, and sharpened teeth were used in conjunction as the harpy used its slightly larger size to try and bully him, and he was doing everything he could to dodge when its leg shot straight toward him like a snake's strike.

RIP

He cried out as the harpy's talons dug into his back. The monster's talons clawed at him three times with quick, consecutive motions that left deep bloody cuts through his robes and along his ribs.

"Riven!" Athela cried out, forcing herself to disengage from the two females to let them turn their attention on the totems, which were continually leeching life with little red threads as Jalel screamed, thrashed, and sobbed in his cocoon. He was being eviscerated by a fifth harpy that'd dropped from above to eat him alive. The creature was gorging itself on his innards, and he lay helpless within Athela's webbing, but the arachnid didn't even spare him a glance as she rushed past to help her master.

Riven landed on the ground and rolled, his enhanced speed allowing him to dodge a second strike and unleash his charged Blood Lance right into the second harpy that'd lunged his way. The right wing was completely torn off at the shoulder in a spray of bone, feathers, and muscle—sending the new harpy backward into a spinning crash against the far wall as debris from the structure tumbled onto it after the lance had made contact.

But even while Riven conjured another four Bloody Razors, his spell missed due to the frantic casting. The infuriated, injured male he'd originally hit tore into Riven's back again—only withdrawing with a hiss when Riven slammed his dagger desperately into the stork-like leg of the striking creature to leave a good-sized gash.

The harpy flapped its wings and raised into the air after that and prepared to dive when strings of red webbing latched themselves up onto its wings from below and yanked down hard—slamming the harpy into the stone ground with a squawk. Sharp fangs sank into its side to inject necrotic venom, the spider hissing ravenously while Athela clung to its body. Black areas of rot quickly began to spread, and the harpy screeched and clawed at Athela, panicking as the side of its chest began decaying until it managed to get ahold of one of Athela's legs with its teeth.

Chomping down hard and ripping the spider off its chest, the male harpy flung the spider into the females that were coming over from destroying Riven's totems and feeding on Jalel.

Riven's scream of rage caught their attention as two more snares flew toward the harpies, one capturing the damaged male to take it down and the other snare just falling short of the females after having miscalculated the distance. "DAMN IT!"

Athela spun in the air, locked onto the wall with another strand of webbing in a legendary display of agility and pulled herself just out of reach of the females' talons as they struck. Yanking herself up the webbing and onto the wall, Athela whirled. The arachnid then began firing more shards of condensed needles from her webbing, burying the projectiles into their flesh while scurrying across the side of the wall as the two infuriated females launched themselves airborne to give chase.

Riven scrambled for his staff, pain searing across his back with the effort while he slammed the gnarled end of the wood into the struggling harpy caught in his snare like a club. He struck again, and again, and again—sending blood splattering across the pavement as he huffed and heaved. When he finished it off and the harpy finally lay still, he looked up to see Jalel's dead eyes staring at him with mouth agape in horror. One of the harpies even continued to feed on the guts of the corpse. Another dead male, the one that Riven had hit with his Blood Lance, lay buried in rubble with one of its wings torn off and lying nearby. Athela was keeping the two female harpies occupied as she danced along the walls overhead and managed to catch one in a quickly constructed web while hopping across the short distance between walls of the alley, and Riven had decided to try his luck by taking out the monster feeding on Jalel's remnants by charging up another Blood Lance when he felt claws slam into his back again. The strike also seemed to draw mana from his body, almost like a leech would blood—and he felt physically depleted in an instant.

He screamed and was flung forward onto his face, feeling his muscles literally being torn out of his back as parts of him went numb while others lit up like they were on fire. He gasped and hit the ground, managing to turn and see a much larger harpy standing over him that'd flown in from above. This one, though still a juvenile male by the system's standards, was more muscular and a good two feet taller than the others with feathers dipped in orange at their ends.

[Juvenile Harpy, Level 7]

[You are experiencing Amplified Bleeding. This is a damage-over-time effect.]

The monster sneered down at him, drawing up the piece of his back it'd torn out with one taloned foot and chomping down to chew and swallow it seconds later. Then it let out a loud, screeching hiss. "SHHHHRRRRREEEEEEEE!"

Riven's head spun, his quivering hands tried to keep his grip on the staff so he could bring it around to protect himself, but he quickly realized he didn't have the mana to cast a snare. How was that possible? The earth beside him jolted when yet another silver female harpy landed beside Riven with a hiss, and his heart sank.

The hissing female came in closer, baring its teeth as it kicked the staff out of his hand to bounce against the ground a couple yards off. Riven's breathing was labored, but he spat blood at the creature in an act of defiance. "Fuck you, you bastard chickens!"

He was going to die here.

Riven closed his eyes and grunted in agony when he felt another chunk of his back get torn out by large, hooked talons—squinting them shut to mentally deny the pain and trying to hold back the tears that wanted to come. In some ways, death would be welcome…it'd stop the agony, at least. But it was still a hard pill to swallow, knowing that he'd wanted to do so much more and had spent so little time doing things he enjoyed in life.

"Sorry, Allie…"

His most treasured memories flashed before his eyes as he realized that these were probably the last moments of his life. The time when Riven had gone with his little sister to the mall and she'd bought him caramel apples with what little money she'd earned as a waitress that day. The time they'd gone to see the animals at the zoo, and how he'd let her feed the brightly colored fish after picking up some quarters they'd found by chance. Spending long nights walking through Chester's Grove when they were at their worst, a park in the city with a swing set he'd push her up high in.

Then the memory of when their mother vanished finally came…how Riven had spent days looking for her and how he'd filed numerous police reports only to come up empty-handed. His mother had been Riven's world, and suddenly that world had shattered. The final memory of visiting Chester's Grove to swing on that rusty swing set one more time before visiting the tree at their favorite spot with Allie… Their mother had always taken care of them since their father had disappeared. How was he expected to go on after losing both his parents? But he couldn't just give up; he had to get out of here and look after Allie. His sister needed him.

He hadn't believed in an afterlife, but he hoped he'd been wrong now with the system in place and the things he'd learned after integration. He wanted there to be a heaven, because if there was…maybe death wouldn't be that bad. Maybe he'd get to see his mom and dad again after all…because if that was true…then this would all have been worth it. He'd not been able to make the life for himself that he'd wanted, but at least he'd met Athela. It just turned out that this strange new world had unexpectedly decided to treat him unfairly…and he'd simply not been cut out for it. Not that it was any different from his old life.

Simply put, life just wasn't fair—and that was a pill he had finally decided to swallow.

A warm sensation in his pocket began to grow as he accepted the finality of it all, and he lifted his eyelids just enough to see the larger orange harpy raise his taloned leg overhead with a malicious grin unbefitting of a nonhuman creature. It just looked…wrong, out of place, and warped. Riven just barely had enough time and willpower to glance down at his pants, where the warmth was beginning to spread, and in that moment—the world went black.

CHAPTER 42

Jalel raised an eyebrow from where he pretended to be dead, cocooned on the hellscape floor in some rather pathetic bindings while a lowly harpy ate his entrails. They had made it through the poorly executed "bad guy" with only slight amounts of smirking whenever the inexperienced warlock wasn't looking. Even if Jalel did secretly hope for Riven's demise and actually kind of was the bad guy, so to speak. He'd faked death pretty well, even if it'd been someone his own level witnessing it, but the fun was now over. He'd give his report back to the queen as instructed, and he'd tag Riven's soul for when the barriers on the newly integrated world faltered in years to come, but the report wouldn't be anything worth mentioning. Not in Jalel's opinion. Riven's performance had been subpar.

And, of course, Jalel would completely leave out the part about Riven acquiring that shard of original sin. That was far too valuable a piece of information to give even to his matriarch, because Jalel wanted it for himself one day. How Riven had gone about acquiring it was something Jalel couldn't even begin to guess at.

True, Jalel had intervened and stopped the stone from binding to his cousin—forcing the demon in the miracle stone to remain there until Jalel was done assessing the youngster. True, Jalel had also stolen mana from Riven during the last fight in order to press him harder. He'd even stopped Riven's normal flesh regeneration so that the young man, many centuries younger than Jalel, couldn't repair his body at a normal rate. Part of this was to truly evaluate Riven, yes, but part of it had been in hopes that Riven would simply die so he could rip the sin out and acquire it. However, the system's warning curses had been stacking with each intervention, and the last one had been so severe that Jalel could only quiver at the thought of what would happen should he actually be responsible for Riven's death. Jalel had pushed the system's limits to the outer boundary, and now he was sure that any further intervention would definitely mean his own death. If he let Riven die here and the system considered it Jalel's fault, he was done for.

So disappointment was the only outcome. Sheer disappointment. As soon as the queen had sensed Riven's presence shift from the outer rim to a nearby hellscape realm, she'd sent Jalel to investigate in what was no doubt a system trial.

Regardless, Riven hadn't even detected the aura fluctuations that'd suppressed him, hadn't even had a hint. He literally had zero aura detection, which was baffling to Jalel. Based on what he'd witnessed when experimenting with blood magic early on in the venture through Negrada, he could say that Riven had a decent grasp of how to utilize blood magic but nothing overtly impressive. Riven wasn't nearly at the level at which he could be brought anywhere near the other counts lest they tear him limb from limb—and that wouldn't be acceptable, because after this tutorial was over, Jalel would be the one to strike the killing blow in some sort of freak accident or "situational mishap."

So he'd play the queen's game for now and report like a good little nephew. Riven had the gift; Jalel had literally watched it happen in front of his very eyes. Malignant Prophecy was something all of the royal bloodline had, and though he couldn't entirely make out Riven's vision, he could still tell he'd used it to save that worthless peasant girl. Yet Jalel could barely wrap his head around the fact that someone of their blood would be so…just so goddamn worthless. Ideologies, combat prowess, and fundamental decision-making in high-stress environments were all just way off.

Perhaps he was being too hard on Riven. Jalel had been trained by the best and brightest of their empire since birth and could have dealt with these opponents as a mere child, but Riven—to Jalel's knowledge—had only just been introduced to a violent life. He didn't even know what he was yet, which was actually quite funny to think about and caused Jalel to smirk.

Perhaps that's why he'd let the girl go, acquiring a malignancy point for something so lowly. To save the life of mere cattle with such a gift was unheard-of, yet to Riven, that girl had been one of his own. They were the same, in Riven's eyes. But in truth, they were an entirely different species from human.

Jalel sighed and shook his head, merely letting out a little bit of aura to shred the annoyingly loud harpy feeding on his guts. It evaporated in an instant—unnoticed by any of the other combatants, turning to a red mist with not even a screech to let its passing be known. His eyes glowed a bright crimson and he ended the suppression on Riven's body, immediately seeing Riven's flesh beginning to mend itself and the mana restore at a rapid pace. The stone in Riven's pocket reacted as well when Jalel's mana coils let up and allowed contact, then there was a flash of power when the demon finally reached out into Riven's soul.

Jalel rolled his eyes as the light in them dimmed to an unnatural brown color, and he went back to playing dead, letting his intestines lie out on the ground in splendid and fashionable designs like the artwork he used to paint with bodies of cattle back in his youth. He grimaced when he realized the curses applied to him by the system for interfering in the trial were still there, eating away at his stats and traits like rabid dogs, and it was likely he'd have to spend a fortune on spiritual fruits in order to get rid of them. Messing around in system-sponsored events without permission was a big no-no, and the residual curses would cost even a powerful prince of the empire such as himself an enormous sum of money that'd likely bankrupt him in the short term.

No doubt he'd have to check up on this little initiate again in the future, too, if Riven managed to survive the integration. Jalel's part to play in Riven's life was far from over. Perhaps Riven would die in that time and spare Jalel the effort, and perhaps then he'd be able to come collect his future prize a century or two later, but Jalel would not be caught again interfering with Riven's trials until the integration was done. He also needed to present himself as a dutiful, loyal servant to Her Majesty lest she suspect something was amiss—and he'd even do what needed to be done to help Riven along the way as much as the system allowed to avoid suspicion, at least until the system parameters were off-line and the defenses were down. Until the moment came, he would not be seen as the one who failed her. Oh, no, the queen would have his head for that, no doubt, as she already had big plans for this unexpected heir to appear so suddenly. It'd already thrown the nobility into a frenzy, and Jalel had no wish to draw pointed glances or daggers in the night should he do something as stupid as to harm one of the queen's pawns and other nephews before Riven's time played out to her satisfaction.

Well…at least he'd play the part until the time was right.

Riven was suddenly cast into a dark and endless void, devoid of any light, as he stood on solid ground. It was startling, going so suddenly from lying on the ground to being in an upright position—but he also quickly noticed that the pain was gone. He looked down but was still unable to see as his hands patted his bare body down. Again, he was wearing no clothes, and a chilling sensation rippled across his skin as his fingers made contact.

That's when a low and menacing growl echoed throughout the darkness.

The deep, guttural voice berated his senses like a typhoon. Not only did he hear it, but he could *feel* the power behind it, like it had been a physical object that'd slapped him upside the head. A familiar, warm sensation began to spread across his body very much like what he'd felt in his pocket just seconds before—but this time it was from all around him.

Riven whirled around, trying to figure out where the noise had come from—but still saw nothing. He wasn't scared, though…not nearly as scared as he should have been. He'd already mentally prepared and resigned himself to death just moments before this, and being taken from the harpy to wherever he was now was more of a relief than anything else.

Riven hesitantly called out into the shadows, "Hello?"

There was only silence, and Riven furrowed his brows to consider his situation. "Am I dead? Did I just die?"

The deep and guttural voice chuckled slightly, this time from his right—and a second later he felt a hot breath on his neck...only to turn his head just as it disappeared.

An image blinked into existence directly in front of him, and Riven was staring at his prone body, curled up in pain as the harpy's striking talons descended upon him in extremely slow motion. It was so slow, in fact, that he guessed he was watching somewhere around one one-thousandth of a second or even less.

Another low growl echoed out across the shadow, this time...a little closer.

Riven's eyes slowly went right in the direction of the sound, and using the light of the conjured image...he finally saw it. His eyes went wide, and he scanned the creature up and down in awe as his hands dropped to his side. Dear God... Was this the miracle stone's work in play? Was that why he'd felt that warm sensation from his pocket? If this creature was what the miracle stone contained, it certainly didn't look like an infant. The stone had called it an infant Hellscape Brutalisk, but this creature was a full-on brute. What in the seven hells would this thing look like when fully grown?!

"Uh... Why, hello there. What's your name?" He extended a hand hesitantly but put on a bright smile and nodded in confidence. "Mine is Riven."

Multiple rows of obsidian teeth glistened in the dim light as a hand many times the size of Riven's reached out and gently touched his hand with a single razor-tipped claw. The demon let out another deep, guttural echo and then withdrew the hand back into the darkness.

Riven kept his smile up, despite the lack of words on the demon's part, but he was definitely a little intimidated by the huge creature. He hadn't been attacked, though, and if he had to guess, this was almost definitely the demon bound to the miracle stone he was carrying...and there was only one reason he'd be here without this creature attacking if that was the case. He shook his head to clear it and clasped his hands behind his back with a brave and hopeful huff. "Let me guess... You're wanting a contract?"

The rows of teeth were exposed more as the demon's smile widened in the shadows—flames billowing in the back of its throat. Then the creature withdrew farther into the darkness, obscuring it completely while Riven waited patiently for it to explain.

Another pause, and then the demon uttered another deep growl as it raised a hand toward him. In an instant, a scroll of purple miasma exploded and unfurled in front of Riven—words being written out in red flames across the miasmic parchment at incredible speed.

[System Notification—Congratulations! Azmoth has chosen to offer you his services. You have received a demonic minion contract that you may choose to accept or decline:

Azmoth's Offers:
• Acquire Azmoth as a familiar.
• Acquire Hell's Armor as a spell. Unlike your minion, who uses Hell's Armor as a physical trait, your own Hell's Armor will require significant amounts of mana to use, as it is not inherent to your species. Your own Hell's Armor will therefore be registered as an Infernal-type spell instead of a trait. Hell's Armor bathes you in flames, regenerating health and damaging opponents while giving you a significant defense boost. This is a very high-mana-cost spell.

Azmoth's Demands:
• If the relationship between you two becomes less than amicable, the contract will become null and void.
• 20 Willpower requirement for initial contract.
• Freedom to come and go at will within reason; Azmoth may summon himself into the mortal realm on a whim as long as it does not directly violate your orders.
• Freedom to regularly hunt for prey.
• Freedom to apply his own stat points and choose his own evolutionary pathways.

• Do you accept this contract? Yes? No?

WARNING: If you choose to accept this contract, this will be your second demonic familiar. Your current class only allows two.]

Azmoth? That was his name? Well, the contract was very, very to the point. It didn't have anything Riven could pick out that rang any alarm bells. There wasn't any reason to say no. According to Athela, contracts with summoners were a way for demons to become more powerful without any actual danger to themselves, so perhaps that's all this really was—a win-win situation.

An irritated grunt from the darkness caused him to look back over his shoulder. He chuckled at the demon's obvious urgency as he went over its offer... but then took a serious and hard look at the harpy back in the image. His smile faded, and his fists clenched.

"I know why you're approaching me now, of all times—a little late, if you ask me. But why would I say anything but yes? You have yourself a deal, Azmoth. It's nice to make your acquaintance, and hopefully I'm not dead by the time you get there."

Riven hit the Yes for acceptance, and the purple miasma of the contract faded.

CHAPTER 43

[Your pact with Azmoth has been sealed under the watchful eye of the administrator. The demonic seal representing Azmoth has been etched into your flesh, and your body has been restored to perfect health. Congratulations on obtaining your new demonic minion.]

[Your Hell's Armor is an Infernal spell. Soul evolution is being expedited, and soul structure is now changing based upon parameters set by your contract with Azmoth. Infernal subpillar has been acquired.]

The next moment was a blur as Riven came back to the land of the living.

He gasped as a brief flash of a vision blipped across his thoughts, giving him a moment of pause as his soul acquired its third subpillar. A torrent of screaming souls, the image of a land bathed in hellfire, and the impression of eternal torment all burned into his insides in an excruciating moment of molten pain. Hot crimson lines were then etched into his sternum, right above the spider pentagram he'd gotten through Athela's contract—this one leaving the image of a grinning four-armed monstrosity within the pentagram burned into his skin right between and underneath his collarbones. He felt knowledge flood his mind in a whirlwind of thoughts and information as the system granted him the means of using his newfound gift. He felt his back wounds seal up, and the bleeding immediately stopped, along with the previous notification denoting the damage-over-time effect.

He was healing so fast…it was just like that time in the pool of blood. Why hadn't his body been healing earlier? Why now?

He still managed to watch in temporary slow motion as the harpy's talons shot down out for the killing blow to finish him off—just as one huge, clawed, armored hand shot forward in an explosion of flames as a dark portal erupted right on top of where Riven lay on that cobblestone ground.

The headache under the influx of information he received was killer, but even under the mind-numbing effects of his new achievements…Azmoth was quite a sight to behold. The demon stood over him protectively…eagerly… smashing the harpy's leg aside with an audible snap like a psychopathic child would a forsaken toy in anticipation of the violence to come. The Hellscape Brutalisk was an absolute tank of a creature—almost literally.

It had huge, thick, obsidian plates and jagged, bladelike protrusions of what looked like metal fused all over its body to the more fleshy, muscular parts seen in between the plates and underneath. It had four enormous arms, two enormous legs, and a humanoid form—more or less in the shape of a bodybuilder that ate steroids for breakfast with his Cheerios.

Azmoth's arms ended with hands that lacked fingernails but came to sharp points of black and hot-red metal, with the claws being created from the gauntlet-like obsidian or whatever the hell created those plates that were cast along the extensor surfaces. Rippling red and gray muscles lacking skin flexed at various points where the obsidian metal plates weren't present, giving him somewhat of a sickening yet simultaneously aesthetic appearance with the eight-pack abs he had.

The demon's face was covered from the upper lip upward in a helmetlike obsidian plating that fluidly formed a dorsal spine down the center, and it completely lacked any eyes. The armorlike plates then proceeded down the back of his neck and onto his chest, before intermittently being spaced along the rest of his back. He had two slits for nostrils right above a set of strong jaws with rows of gleaming, black razor-blade teeth. A feeling of dread accompanied the demon's presence—like a palpable presence, one that Riven hadn't felt in the void realm he'd just been in moments before. It was like a tidal wave of unease that physically shook not only him, but Athela and the nearby harpies as well. Even knowing that this creature was on his side, even having bound it to him with a contract, he could feel his hairs stand on end just being in Azmoth's presence.

But the catch to all this, and the most intimidating thing about Azmoth, was the flames that burst into life as the demon's roar echoed from the beyond. The afterimage of a dying forest in its pocket dimension behind the monstrosity began to fade away when the portal fizzled out, and in its place, the huge demon's entire body was quickly engulfed in blazing fire, rippling along its arms and searing the stunned harpy only a few feet away from the larger monster while maliciously grinning.

As the abruptly terrified harpy began to screech and frantically flap its wings—trying to get away in a hurried state of panic—Azmoth merely began to laugh. The deep, demonic laugh was filled with a mixture of joy, malice, and hunger. With a lunge and a violent yank, it pulled the larger orange harpy toward its opening jaws and snapped down shut—turning the hunter into the hunted as Azmoth's rows of teeth sank into the soft meat of the squealing harpy's neck.

Rearing back and yanking out the other monster's vocal cords with the sound of shredding flesh, Azmoth took time to savor the harpy's lifeblood as it trickled into his mouth. Then, with the roar of an apex predator, he took the dying harpy's body and swung it hard into the other, utterly shocked and newly arrived female harpy nearby—sending both of their bodies violently bouncing with a loud crunch across the cobblestone in trails of singed feathers and blood.

Riven had crawled back out from underneath his new demonic friend, watching with a mixture of amazement and relief as Azmoth utterly clobbered the two unfortunate monsters with a bloodlust that made him shudder. Bones broke, feathers burned, and flesh loudly tore all amid the laughter of his new demon and the squeals or gurgles of the terrified harpies as they were violently manhandled. It was like watching two human toddlers trying to fight a fully grown rhinoceros—utterly and completely one-sided.

He absent-mindedly let his finger slide down to his sternum, gently touching the second pentagram burned into his skin, before coming back to reality and reeling. He got up as fast as he could while picking up his staff, scrambling to find Athela and bolting over to where his minion was fighting a losing three-versus-one battle. Another harpy had joined the fray in attacking Athela, which had turned the tides in the harpies' favor.

But Riven could feel the power welling up within him, and confusingly enough, his mana felt like a faucet had just been turned on—pouring it in.

He sprinted forward and sprayed three consecutive attacks of five Bloody Razors apiece. The discs of sharpened, solidified blood erupted forward like a woodchipper come to life with killing intent, shredding the first of the harpies and catching it midair as it tried to dive down at Athela when she dropped to the ground.

Feathers, bone, and spraying bodily fluids shot ahead of him as the harpy essentially exploded from its many lacerations, falling to the floor dead and giving Athela an opening to dodge another attack before countering with a spray of sharp, solidified webbing.

The remaining two harpies shrieked and dived in together, both missing the agile spider as she jumped to the far wall and continued to spray—but this got their attention focused on Riven as he ran headlong into their path.

Aiming for his soft belly with its claws, the first of the harpies lunged forward, snarling. It already showed signs of battle—a missing eye, numerous needles made from webbing protruding from its body, and a wound with part of its thorax having rotted right off.

Riven took this moment to imbue himself with the new trait and ability Azmoth's bond had given him. Hellfire bloomed along his skin, intermixing with the red lightning of his speed-enhancing blessing. His staff also lit up, blazing to life with fire as he met the charge and slammed it into the harpy like a baseball bat.

He took no damage, but his Strength wasn't up to par with his defense, and the two basically collided and each fell over as the next harpy in line reeled backward to get away from the flames. Definitely not what he'd been wanting to accomplish, but it kinda worked. Riven shook his head from the jolt of the impact, but as he got up to attack his target again, he found that some of the feathers had lit up with flames that were spreading along the stunned creature.

The harpy struggled to get up, and Riven cackled like a maniac as he brought the staff back up, overhead, and struck down to begin ruthlessly beating the creature to death with the extra infernal damage and speed of the blessing empowering his strikes despite how physically weak he was compared to the monster.

The creature died flailing around on the ground, burning to death as it was repeatedly bludgeoned, and eventually let out a hiss of agony as its neck cracked and its lower body went limp.

Riven howled skyward in victory and turned to attack the final, fleeing enemy—but the flames immediately faltered and died when he deactivated the spell. It'd been chewing through mana at a rapid pace, and he didn't want to continue it needlessly.

His head swiveled as the fleeing harpy let out a screech when silky webbing shot out and entangled its wings. Athela was latched to the floor like glue, and despite the harpy's attempts to fly away, it was still being dragged down toward the cackling Blood Weaver as she gnashed her teeth hungrily and chittered at her entangled prey.

When the harpy got within jumping distance, Athela launched herself off the ground and slammed into the harpy—using all twelve legs to bring it down as she tore at it with her fangs—and they fell to the ground in a squirming mess of bodies.

Seconds later, Athela had gotten the upper hand, easily avoiding all the harpy's strikes with her rather impressive agility and leaving numerous bite marks that were spreading venom and necrosis along the quickly dying creature. Athela even jumped off and hissed at it, watching with greedy eyes as the harpy's efforts to move quickly devolved into nothing but twitches and sputtering breaths before she went in for the final kill.

There was a quick gush of blood, and then the harpy went completely limp. What followed...was rather surreal.

He'd actually lived.

Riven looked left and saw Azmoth feeding on the two harpies he'd killed and drawing out their entrails to rip and tear between chomps. Slightly closer down the alley was where Jalel's mutilated remains had once been—though, for whatever reason, the body had disappeared. Perhaps taken away by another of the monsters? There were also four bodies of the harpies and the various remnants of magic he'd used. To his right, Athela was sucking the harpy she'd killed dry—almost inhaling its blood as she danced a little victory dance with her twelve legs excitedly tapping the ground around her.

[You have gained one level. Congratulations! Be sure to visit your status page to apply points.]

Already knowing he'd slam most of those points into Intelligence, Riven opened up his status page and applied them. Then, waving down his minions, he told them to guard him as he got some rest. He was utterly exhausted, and he felt rather confident that all their enemies were dead. "Hey, Azmoth, Athela, see this crevice in the wall over here? I'm going to take a nap. Guard me while I do."

CHAPTER 44

[Riven Thane's Status Page:
- Level 11
- Pillar Orientations: Unholy Foundation, Blood, Infernal
- Core of Original Sin—Gluttony: (Under Construction) (???)
- Traits: Race: Human, Class: Novice Warlock, Adrenaline Junkie (Blood) (+15% to Agility)
- Abilities: Blessing of the Crow (Unholy), Wretched Snare (Unholy), Bloody Razors (Blood), Blood Lance (Blood) (Tier 2), Hell's Armor (Infernal)
- Stats: 8 Strength, 20 Sturdiness, 72 Intelligence, 10 Agility, 1 Luck, -4 Charisma, 3 Perception, 44 Willpower, 9 Faith
- Free Stat Points: 7
- Minions: Athela, Level 7 Blood Weaver [14 Willpower Requirement]. Azmoth, Level 2 Hellscape Brutalisk [20 Willpower Requirement].
- Equipped Items: Crude Cultist's Robes (1 def), Basic Casting Staff (4 dmg, 12% mana regen, +3 magic dmg), Chalgathi Cultist Amulet (???), Leather Boots (1 def), Backpack of Supplies, Witch's Ring of Grand Casting (+26 Intelligence)]

Riven slowly opened his eyes after the much-needed nap. The blue mana potion Athela had taken from Jalel's bag was being gently poured over his lips to slide down his throat. His head was propped up against that same bag, and she was watching him wide-eyed like a child on Christmas while remaining completely silent.

The headache quickly cleared as he accepted the rest of the potion, nodding to her in appreciation. "Thanks."

"Not a problem! Just glad you're okay!" The spider raised both of her front legs and chuckled with that usual chittering noise of hers, squinting and looking rather pleased with herself.

They were still in the alley, with mist dampening their bloodstained clothes and the body of a harpy not far off on the narrow path, though Athela had made sure to create an intricate pattern of webbing overhead to block any potential flyers from diving down. Riven was rather impressed by it. Not only for the protection, but for the shade it cast on them as well.

Jalel was gone, only a puddle of blood where he'd been before. Otherwise the damage wrought upon the surrounding area was evident by the torn-up stone alley and scattered dead harpies.

"I'm glad you're okay!" Athela whispered again, following up with another chittering laugh. Her legs trembled slightly, and she nodded to herself and pushed her head up against Riven in an action of affection that Riven would have thought to be very uncharacteristic of spiders. "We're okay now. It's all okay…"

Riven's body remained a little stiff, and his rib cage ached from where he'd met the harpy in a head-on collision, but he'd be fine.

The sounds of crunching, tearing, and chomping reached Riven's ears—causing him to furrow his brow and slowly turn his head to get a better look behind him. When he saw the huge flaming demon chowing down on pieces of harpy, he smirked and pushed himself into a sitting position. "Athela, have you met Azmoth yet?"

The arachnid proudly turned her head and chittered over her shoulder at the brute. "Yes! We talked while you were sleeping. He's a very nice young man!"

Riven had to suppress a laugh at that one and kept a straight face. "Nice young man? Really now… Wait, Azmoth talked to you?"

"Of course!"

"He doesn't talk to me. He just grunts."

"It's because he knows I'm royalty."

"Because you're a princess?"

"Mmm-hmm. Mortals like you are too beneath him to speak to."

Riven rolled his eyes, but the Hellscape Brutalisk overheard them and turned their way with a swivel of his head. Azmoth relinquished his flames; he currently had a mouth full of harpy guts, but the hunched-over demon gave a slight nod to Riven before resuming his feasting—clawed hands digging into the corpse of one of the harpies to rip out a bloody liver.

Riven didn't buy Athela's story one bit. "He really doesn't seem like much of a talker."

"He is, though!"

"Prove it."

"I can't!"

"Why not?"

"Because!"

Riven just shook his head, not wanting to bother with her shenanigans any longer, and gave her some pets before getting up. "Ready to finish the quest? Assuming that there aren't any more harpies around..."

Athela looked back into the mists and nodded. "There are definitely more...I've seen them flying around, but they're all juveniles and below level 5. None of them have been coming near us ever since I told them I'd cut them if they came."

"You told them you'd cut them?"

"I also threatened their mamas. THEY FEAR MEEE!" Athela wiggled her front legs around in exaggerated fashion.

"I see." Riven glanced over at Azmoth, raising an eyebrow, and hiked a thumb the demon's way. "Are you sure it isn't because he's here?"

The arachnid folded her front legs with an arrogant humph. "Nope. It was definitely me waving my legs around threateningly screaming into the mists that I'd cut them if they decided to try again."

"Uh-huh."

"Not all monsters are created equal, Riven!"

The arachnid swatted her large thorax and started another ridiculous dance, but the comment gave Riven pause. He studied Azmoth for a time, with his obvious assets for killing in the forms of fire, metallic plates, hulking muscles, and four clawed arms...and he slowly nodded. Her assessment was dead-on. He wasn't absolutely sure of how everything worked here in Elysium, but if numerous harpies were avoiding one level 2 demon despite outnumbering and outleveling him...this screamed to him that levels likely didn't mean everything.

Hell, Azmoth's stat percentage bonuses and stat rewards per level up alone were enough to testify to that. It made Riven wonder why a leveling system was even in place, because levels could be incredibly skewed across the board just on what he'd seen thus far. Was there a reason or rhyme to this?

He turned back to the dancing spider and pushed his hands into his pockets. "Athela, did you get to look at this bag at all?"

She stopped dancing and glared up at him. "You were using it as a pillow. I was only able to look at part of it without waking you up."

He nodded in acknowledgment. "All right. It's pretty large...but we can sort through it later, and I can take turns with Azmoth carrying it. Let's go finish this stupid quest and get out of here. I don't ever want to see this place again."

He picked up the large bag Jalel had insisted on bringing, grunting slightly at how heavy it was, and began to follow Athela out.

Athela skipped over to Azmoth and poked him on one of his plated, muscular legs. "Hey, Azmoth! Time to go!"

Azmoth finished ripping off a harpy thigh, tore into it with his jaws, and swallowed the fresh, messy meat before grinning back at them. Blood dripped down his face, and the rippling muscles of the demon bulged underneath the heavy obsidian plates of his body as Azmoth rose off the ground and burst into flames with a nod of his head and a guttural growl.

The deep, bestial noise the demon made put Riven on edge. The thing was huge, intimidating, and far beyond what he would have ever thought possible in terms of acquiring it so early in this new world. Or probably ever, actually.

With a command for Azmoth to take the lead, Athela and Riven followed behind at a short distance—warily glancing around the dimly lit area as shadows silently moved above them in the mist. Once more they even caught sight of a harpy's wing overhead through the red mist, accompanied by a high-pitched screech, but it never made a move on them.

Feeling relatively safer after having added a tank to their party, Riven was finally able to relax. "Athela, we need to get indoors somewhere and set up a temporary base… We don't know what's in this bag, and we need to figure out if any of it can be useful."

"Agreed, comrade Riven!" Athela replied enthusiastically with a skip in her step.

Riven snorted with amusement. "You're ridiculous."

A couple more steps into the mist over the smooth cobblestone blocks, and he saw the first signs of their destination. Riven's eyes widened at the size of the statue, and he really couldn't believe that he hadn't seen it before even with the thick mist in between.

First was the giant battle-axe. It was granite, was dozens of yards across, and was planted firmly in the ground—blades down, penetrating from a shadow above. As they progressed farther through the mist, the rest of the statue shortly appeared.

It was modeled after a confident-looking man with a neatly trimmed beard, pointed ears, and intricate, curved armor. His long hair was carved to look like it was majestically swaying out to his left as he looked out into the distance on his right. He held the shaft of his axe in both hands, resting his gauntleted hands on the weapon, and his armor had a symbol of a sun plastered across the breastplate. It was even what Riven would describe as awe-inspiring and was definitely out of place considering everything else around here had literally gone to hell.

It stood nearly five stories high, was well carved, and despite the moss was relatively well preserved compared to everything else in the city. But what caught Riven's attention most was the small altar at the bottom of the statue in between the warrior-elf's armored feet. The rectangular altar stood about three feet high and had two gleaming crystals hovering in the air, shimmering in and out of existence repetitively while the baseball-sized objects seemed to call out to him.

"Do you see those?!" Athela exclaimed excitedly while pointing—jabbing one foot toward the shimmering crystals ahead of them. "Are those the prizes?!"

Riven cocked an eyebrow and glanced at a harpy that'd perched far up, along the statue's outstretched arms between the body and the axe shaft, shrugging as he did. "I'd guess you're right... Let's get them so we can leave."

"Indeed!" Athela exclaimed, rapidly poking Riven in the shin and skipping forward to follow the other demonic familiar toward the elevated stone altar. "Can't wait!"

Riven chuckled at the humming noises Athela made and quickly pursued her, coming up beside her at the altar a minute later and observing the shimmering crystals in closer detail. Each of them was ethereal, with both of them being labeled as Quest Crystals.

[Congratulations! You have completed the final objective for your quest Find Your Spider Princess by meeting Athela at the base of the statue of the bearded, axe-wielding man. You and your minions have gained XP. You have received twenty-five Elysium coins and will now receive your tailored prizes!]

The crystals shattered upon deliverance of the notification, each of them dissolving into dust to reveal two new items. One was a cloak, and the other was a mask. There was also a new bag of twenty-five bronze coins, which he placed in his backpack before inspecting the other prizes.

[Cloak of the Tundra (Light Armor): 22 average defense, negates frost damage by an additional 56 average defense and significantly decreases effects from cold weather.]

[Breath of Valgeshia (Mask) (Vampiric) (Light Armor): 48 average defense, amplifies blood damage by an average of 13 base damage plus an additional +9% of mana input. Increases mana regeneration by 6%. If worn by a vampire, applied bonuses are tripled. Combat level 5 and Blood subpillar affiliation required to use.]

[Set Piece: one of five. This item is part of the Valgeshia set. Acquire three items of the Valgeshia set for additional bonuses. Acquire five items of the Valgeshia set for all bonuses.]

The cloak looked rather heavy; it was made from a thick brown cloth and was lined with fur along the outer rim. It had a hood that came up along the top, had two medium-length sleeves, and was otherwise rather plain. Grasping it from where it floated in the air and trying it on, Riven found the cloak was actually very comfortable and rather soft. The sleeves came down to his elbows and kept the cloak in place, while the hem reached his calves. He turned around, bowing as Athela started clapping like a fanatic.

"Stunning! Just stunning!" Athela cooed while her two front legs went crazy slapping at each other. "Bravo! Bravo!"

"Shucks," Riven said with a wink and a laugh while Azmoth looked from one to the other at a loss.

He turned back to the mask, which was obviously the better item of the set, given it had a percentage value to it, and took it from its floating position as well. It also had been titled as a vampiric item, and he had to admit to himself that he was a little disappointed that he couldn't utilize the entirety of the bonuses because he was a human…instead of a vampire…?

Or was that entirely accurate? Riven scratched his chin. That one was up for debate after the little incident where fangs exploded from his mouth in the blood pit. He'd tried not to think about it since then, but it had definitely been a little creepy, and he didn't know what to make of it. Regardless, it hadn't happened since, so he would cross that bridge later.

But it was also the first time he'd ever seen a set piece item… How was he supposed to go about finding other items in this set, exactly? There wasn't any instruction manual or guide, so he was at a complete loss as to how to even begin searching for the other pieces.

Unlike the cloak, this mask was somewhat impressive. Not amazing, as was indicated by the combat level requirement of 5, but definitely a good thing to add to his arsenal. Probably great for his level, but he'd definitely outgrow it. The mask was meant to cover just his chin, mouth, and nose—leaving his eyes open—and was black and red. The majority of the metal was thin, a sleek black with padding on the inside where it would be secured to his face, but crimson markings wove intricate runes of Unholy pentagrams, modified crucifixes, obscure sigils, and other designs into the surface that glowed faintly and had little holes for him to breathe through. It was polished, obviously enchanted with smooth surfaces that felt warm to the touch, and as his fingers grasped the mask, the dull glow of crimson runes began to smolder.

Bringing the mask up to his face, it sucked down against his skin when he was within a centimeter of his mouth and the padded inside quickly molded to the shape of his nose, mouth, and jaw. The back of it extended to his ears, where it abruptly stopped, and it had no problem staying there without any straps to keep it up. Breathing or talking through it caused tiny amounts of red mist to erupt from the mask, and it was rather sinister-looking as he looked down at his reflection in a pool of blood nearby.

On top of that, Athela definitely approved and came over to inspect it thoroughly by jumping up onto his chest and shoving her face within an inch of his own.

He'd really need to talk to her about personal bubbles, because it was apparent she didn't know about them at all.

He took the sack of coins and added it to his own backpack, giving the larger bag Jalel's old party had collected to Azmoth to carry and getting up to continue their trek. He had no idea where he was going, and neither did his minions...but it was getting dark, and he didn't want to be caught out here in the open when night fell.

CHAPTER 45

Riven and the two demons had found a small cellar, long abandoned, with a pair of dead bolts that still worked well enough after they closed the door behind them. It'd likely been someone else's lair a long, long time ago due to the way various odds and ends were strewn about and a worn-out bed was in the far corner—though it was all in a heavy state of disrepair and had a thin layer of dust.

"Trash." Athela threw one of the spare articles of clothing to the side, smacking Azmoth in the face while he grunted and sniffed at the pair of old underwear. "Also trash. This is trash, too."

She continued to dig through the bag Jalel had claimed to be "treasure," tossing it onto the growing pile atop Azmoth, and she let out a huff when she got to the end of it. "This is bullshit! All this crap was supposed to be more valuable than *me*?! How dare that insignificant little shit call you out like that!"

Athela was no doubt talking about when Jalel had been angry about Riven's choice to save his minion over the other bag of "treasure." Out of all the items Jalel had brought with him in that oversized sack of shit, not a single thing had been useful for Riven at all.

It was as if Jalel had intentionally been trying to deceive Riven concerning the bag's contents when he'd been overly hesitant to show the warlock or demon anything inside. Why that was, Riven would likely never know.

Yet Riven had bigger things to worry about, like how he was going to get out of here. He needed to find the exit; he'd been here far too long, and both Allie and Jose were counting on him.

"I need a way out," Riven stated flatly, staring down the phantom across the room while ignoring Azmoth's mindless, deep giggling or the enraged chittering of his spider. "I need to get out of the dungeon. If I help you, will you provide this for me?"

Kajit let out a frustrated growl. Her usual semitranslucent appearance of an old, bandaged, half-mummified woman was gone. Now, in its place was her "true form"—a rather insidious-looking, deep-blue spirit in the outline of a slender woman with long hair trailing past her bare back, long legs, and pitch-black orbs for eyes. She was still semitranslucent, but the energy creating her body was much more potent and had an aura of danger about it. "I already state, boy, I cannot show way out. Way out is blocked for spirits like me, to keep from escaping hell. If I find way out, I already leave centuries ago. Hellscapes turn my eyes blind to exits; it is the curse of death. It is like antimagnet. When I look—system shows me other path."

"Can't you just possess a body and see it that way?"

"Why I not do this if I could?"

Riven let out an exhausted sigh and shook his head, arms folded over his chest while he sat cross-legged on the ancient cellar floor. "Well, I honestly don't see a reason to help you, Kajit. I understand your plight, and I'd definitely love my dagger back, but I'm on a time limit here. I have no idea how my sister is doing or if she's in trouble—hell, I don't even know if she's even alive. But I won't find out until I leave this dungeon, and I have to keep looking for an exit. I'm sorry. You'll have to find someone else to help free your sister's spirit."

Kajit obviously didn't like that answer, and the room shuddered while black mana around her fluxed to respond to her rage. However, his piece of sin clamped down on her soul—the soul that resided within his own soulscape, the one she'd tried to inhabit him with—and her anger immediately simmered down to a more calm state of being. She'd essentially become his captive, one that he could use Gluttony to crush at any time due to her own stupidity and actions.

She took in a deep breath, then slowly exhaled as if she had a body to breathe with. Perhaps it was habit—he didn't know.

Her black eyes snapped open again, focusing on his own while she imitated his posturing while crossing her arms in front of her own chest. "My sister's soul is on time limit. It very hard to find entity inside dungeon who have prophecy; she likely die before I find another to visit tower."

Riven raised an eyebrow and leaned back on his hands. "What kind of time limit are we talking here?"

"Three hundred years, take or give."

"Seems like a long time to me."

Kajit sputtered a coughing laugh, and she looked at him incredulously. "Not long time to find another prophet here in hellscape dungeon Negrada, foolish boy!"

"I wouldn't know. Regardless, you have your priorities—and I have mine. I'm not risking my life to free a stranger from a prison they may or may not deserve."

Kajit's eyes narrowed. "I give my pledge I serve you if you save Kajit's sister."

"Serve me?" Riven shook his head slowly. "You're already bound to my will anyways, and I'm sure as shit not letting go. You'll probably kill me if I let you out of my soulscape. I can feel the power disparity after you entered to try and possess me. Why shouldn't I just make you my slave?"

"I will not do as you ask. You may kill me with sin, but I not do as you ask unless you help Kajit."

"No. Even if you don't 'obey' me, you're still not in a situation to make demands."

Kajit opened her mouth to speak, frowned, and then closed it again with a hateful glare cast in his direction. Then she opened her mouth again, with a bit of a waver to her voice and worry on her features. "Please."

"No."

Her features contorted back into rage, and with a shriek she ripped out of this existence and into another—vanishing from the room with an echo that nearly split Riven's eardrums. He could still feel her soul tethered to his own, though, the jaws of Gluttony holding her tightly in place, and he let on a slight frown. He understood where she was coming from, but he had his own goals. Sadly enough, now was just not the time to have a bleeding heart on display. One day, when he got stronger, he'd let Kajit go. Until that day came, though, he was keeping a firm grip on her to make sure she didn't cause him any trouble. God forbid she actually attacked him, because she'd likely be able to kill him the way he was now if her mana fluctuations during mood swings were any clue. Even now he could see her mana waves rippling back and forth across her own soul structure, and though she'd condensed hers to a smaller area, her potency was far greater than Riven's was.

Riven glanced over at where Athela was making a small nest out of the pile of clothes, odds and ends. "Do you think I made a bad choice?"

The spider demon stopped what she was doing, then cocked her head quizzically. "About Kajit? My advice on the matter is to do whatever you want to do. Don't let other people influence your decisions, rather, make your decisions based entirely on your own desires. You'll be a lot happier that way, not being burdened by thoughts of what others want or need or think of you. Just because Kajit has a bad situation going on doesn't mean you need to be the one that fixes it, and she was the one who tried blackmailing you first!"

Athela gave a quick head nod before going back to her pile, and Riven scratched his chin while pondering her words. He really did want that dagger back…and he felt slightly bad for Kajit. But in the end, those things weren't worth it when it compared to potentially leaving Jose or Allie high and dry in the outside world. Hell, he might even die in that so-called Tower of Fates, and he could never forgive himself if he abandoned those two to fend for themselves in this new world.

He had a duty to make it back fast, so that's what he'd focus on. Other things be damned, and the rest of the world could burn for all he cared. Family and friends first.

Allie stood amid the burning wreckage of a city block that had once belonged to the old world of Earth. Her red eyes narrowed on the man in a church-attire suit underneath her, sputtering pointless bullshit about how she was damned for all eternity while he bled out on the ground and tried to cast another holy spell to heal himself.

She didn't let him finish the incantation.

SHUNK

Her cursed, soul-woven wand snapped forward and unleashed a burst of black energy that ripped into the man's heart. He let out a screech and a low wheeze of an exhale, his body seizing up amid the shock of her mana strike. She could feel and almost even hear the soul trapped inside her weapon scream out while it began to soak in the life force of her newest victim.

"Keep your ramblings on faith, for I do not need them." Allie leaned over the man and sneered, "Save it for the sheep that follow your boss."

Her body hummed with energy, absorbing death mana from the dead and dying around her while she slowly walked through the wreckage of battle. When she felt two of her minions fall at the hands of the new-world "holy crusaders," she merely lifted her right hand. Teal and black mana flared along her forearm and fingertips before trailing off to give life to nearby bodies around her.

The corpses twitched, flesh began to melt, and slowly the two skeletons stood up with similarly teal-colored orbs lighting up the insides of their skulls in place of eyes.

With a thought, she sent them back into the battle taking place ahead of her, feeling an influx of XP with each death she brought to the ones foolish enough to challenge them.

POP—POP—POP

Three bullets ricocheted off her soul-woven gauntlets and pauldrons, cursed items created from bone just like the skull mask she wore and the bits stitched into her leather cuirass. One of the bullets did, however, manage to strike her in the thigh, where the armor had a gap. It was merely a flesh wound that would no doubt heal within minutes, but it still pissed her off.

She snarled and whipped around, locating the young man holding a pistol before he managed to get off another shot. She blurred left with inhuman speed and closed the distance, avoiding another blast from the gun and launching herself to slam her fist into her attacker's skull. The young man's head exploded, a normal human body no match for what she'd become in only weeks.

Another shot was fired from a rifle through an adjacent window amid screams and shrieks of the undead and the living alike—and she took aim with one hand to fire off a death ball. A globe of teal and black flames exploded out of her outstretched hands and ripped through the frail, damaged wall to violently eradicate the defender while three of her skeletons rushed over his body to continue their assault on the others.

She calmly walked ahead, entering through the burning hole she'd created, and looked down where a terrified man and a woman were being eaten alive while holding hands and frantically sobbing. Probably a couple, but honestly she didn't care. Not after what they'd done to Jose.

They all had this coming, and she was far from done with her work. They would pay for their sins in the blood of their family and friends, a sacrifice worthy of the ones who'd taken her own in the name of *purging the nonbelievers* in this new world where *God had made his presence known.*

Fucking fanatics.

She would bring them war, as they'd asked. She would bring them a crusade. She would see just who purged whom, and she would not stop until she stood upon a mountain of their corpses. She would find the one who called himself Prophet. She would hang his corpse from their church so all his holy-aligned nutjobs would see his body and despair, even if it was the last thing she ever did.

CHAPTER 46

Two weeks had passed since Jalel's death, with little gained other than a couple levels for each of them and no results in terms of a way out. Kajit had also been very quiet ever since Riven had denied her request, ever since he'd said he had more important things to do at the moment. She had yet to show up again at all, actually, which was a welcome thing in Riven's opinion.

They'd never found the boat Jalel had once spoken of, the one that was supposed to have been tethered to an outcropping of rock on the river of blood that traced itself through the city. Perhaps this was because Jalel hadn't specified *which* river of blood, as it was a far larger area than they'd anticipated, with many waterways branching off the main channel. They'd wandered aimlessly trying to find an exit, killing or running from undead and demon spawn alike when they weren't scavenging off the battles between different monsters.

The things he'd learned in that time were quite interesting.

First off, there was actually a way to see HP (health points), MP (mana points), or SP (stamina points) even though they were usually hidden. Athela was insistent that if they found someone that had attained an Identifier class title, these people would be able to join a party and allow visualization of such things. These identifiers at higher class tiers were also able to give a lot more detailed information concerning the durability of items, the tiers of said items, the estimated value of those items, and various other things that normal people with no class title or other class titles could not see. It was apparently commonplace for guilds, armies, or explorers to incorporate an Identifier into their journeys to get more accurate reads on their enemies.

Then Riven came across a lich one day in the process of resurrecting the dead. Not just raising it to become an undead itself, but actually resurrecting the creature. He hadn't realized that even possible until now, and he had gawked like a small child on Christmas when he'd learned that if he ever became powerful enough, he too would be able to perform feats such as that if given the right conditions. However, at the current moment that was way out of his league—the lich he'd seen do it was over level 200.

And finally, he was beginning to understand how magic worked at a deeper level than what he'd been able to glean in the past. Every day he practiced the ins and outs of the spells he already had, and he was now able to manipulate them far faster and with more efficiency than he'd been able to at the start of his journey. Athela had told him that he was *a magical genius and a born caster*, in her own words, and that he had an extreme talent for the Unholy arts. What would take people years to learn, Riven had learned in almost zero time, and the magic responded to him almost as if it was a separate limb he'd been able to use all his life. His spells were beginning to cost him less and less mana as time went on for the same amount of magical output, even disregarding level gains. Athela couldn't really piece together why this was happening, but she was always visibly excited about it whenever he found a way to improve or expand upon his magical output for less mana cost simply by changing the way he manipulated mana or visualized the spell.

This practice was what consumed Riven's time in the two weeks since Jalel's passing while they searched for a way out. Riven wanted to get back home to Earth, or to whatever Earth had become since this "multiverse" had incorporated it. He needed to get out of this hellscape dungeon. He still had yet to find a portal exit out of here, and he hadn't yet spotted any bosses or minibosses to attempt to kill for a ticket out.

But their efforts hadn't been entirely fruitless. While they'd been searching for a path out, they'd realized quite quickly that there were different tribes of creatures that lived here in Dungeon Negrada—and mapping out the city in small pieces at a time had doubtless saved them from stumbling into certain death on more than one occasion.

There were the red-skinned, three-eyed Jabob demons, like the cultists they'd encountered when Athela had been imprisoned. The Jabobs were brutal, barbaric little shits that often employed varieties of magic, making them rather dangerous at a distance, but they were physically weak up close. It made them easy targets for Azmoth, as he'd crush them one by one after barreling through their fire-based attacks head-on while having the time of his life. Meanwhile, Riven stayed in the back lines for suppressive fire, dealing heavy damage at a distance, and Athela would focus on keeping Riven safe or on assassinating the back lines of enemy casters, depending on the situation. The arachnid was particularly sneaky and was often able to subdue a target without ever being spotted prior to the all-out fight.

There were the harpies, too, which had nests scattered among the rooftops and higher places of these ruins. In particular, the juvenile harpies were far weaker and smaller than fully grown harpies. The adults were twice the size of the ones

Riven had first fought and far meaner. On one instance, Azmoth had nearly died fighting off three of them that'd tried to carry Athela away. Azmoth had the hardest time with the adults, as they were hard to catch and he had to rely on Riven or Athela to bring them down to ground level in order to tear them apart.

There were also the undead, with large packs of them each controlled by one or two minor liches. The liches in particular were incredibly powerful, and these were the enemies that worried Riven the most. They were often surrounded by monstrous flesh golems made from bunched-up corpses that smelled terrible or a small legion of ghouls and zombies, while being able to cast obliterating magics from the back lines, just like Riven preferred to do. Many of the undead also roamed the city without a pack, often unbound to any master and aimlessly wandering until they found food or were killed to be eaten themselves.

Then there were the lone solo monsters or less common species, ranging in size and variety. Aside from the liches, it was often these creatures that took the title of apex predators—often being some sort of demon or abomination that Riven had no intention of ever facing in battle lest he be immediately killed. They'd seen a huge yellow-eyed basilisk with shiny black scales, another muscular, axe-wielding minotaur twice the size of Azmoth, an elemental wolf created from fire and lightning, and even a gorgeous gorgon surrounded by statues and nesting atop a mountain of rotting bodies that they'd dared not approach. A couple of other tribal creatures also called this place home, but they were sparse in number and not a significant percentage of the dungeon's occupants.

Aside from the types of monsters, they'd also learned much about how the monsters came to be. The dungeon...this place that the system called Negrada... spawned monsters at random. Meanwhile, there were other certain species that were seen reproducing. The Jabob demons in particular had been seen carrying eggs, and one of these eggs had hatched into an infant while Athela watched from a distant window—as she'd been unfamiliar with this breed before now even though she was a demon herself. Meanwhile, Riven had actually seen a zombie ox being created out of thin air from nothing but mana. He'd even gotten a warning notification from the dungeon system saying he was in the spawn area of another creature.

That'd been the same day that Riven had learned the river of blood had healing properties. The first time he'd actually thought about utilizing it for this reason had been shortly after the encounter with the giant blood squid creature in the pit trap. Back then, right before Gluttony had ripped the monster apart, he'd been instinctively drawing on the blood pool to heal himself, and he was pretty damn sure it'd been the same type of blood as the stuff flowing through the rivers here. So after engaging in a battle nearby that'd been drawn out into the river, Riven had been made keenly aware that drinking it regenerated his body even faster than his already abnormal regeneration could produce.

They'd been quick to bottle it in the six glass vials taken from Jalel's bag—one of the few things that'd actually been worth anything in the supplies they'd dug through. The resultant pseudo-potions weren't really even potions at all, but rather had quite a different label to them entirely when inspecting them through system commands.

[Vial of Sinner's Blood. Restore an average of 70 health and mana simultaneously. May not be taken outside the realms of hell. Warning: Using Sinner's Blood frequently may have unwanted side effects over time.]

In turn, the description of this blood brought about two very serious questions. The first: Was he really willing to give up such valuable healing and mana-rejuvenating remedies just because of potential adverse side effects? Truly? The second: What kind of side effects was it talking about?

The first question had been answered immediately the day after the discovery, when he'd used two of them to not only heal a nearly fatal wound but also used the follow-up potion to regain mana midfight while helping Athela out of a bind. He couldn't afford to lose a minion to banishment after their defeat, not here in this horrible place, not when he likely couldn't afford the resurrection cost of a blood price (which, according to Athela, would be at least in the low thousands of Elysium coins that he'd have to pay the system in such a scenario), thus he would risk drinking the stuff time after time in order to make sure he didn't end up dead.

He'd also drunk tons of the stuff already without any serious problems, given that he'd regenerated his body numerous times in the pit trap by using it. So even if they knew that there were potentially unwanted side effects, there wasn't much they could do about it. They needed the Sinner's Blood; not only had it already saved his life, but it was also a means of sustenance. Jalel's sack unfortunately contained no food whatsoever. Riven had taken Athela and Azmoth hunting for more food in their spare time, and even though Athela laid her traps expertly—dropping webbing on her enemies or luring enemies into pits for her to wrap them up in—each encounter meant potential danger. After discovering that the blood would satiate their hunger to an extent, they would make regular trips to the river of blood to drink their fill despite how grotesque it'd seemed to Riven at first.

But it was certainly better than starving, and strangely enough, he was also beginning to like it. Logically he knew it was disgusting, but the taste…the taste resonated with him—and he couldn't help but remember the time fangs had sprouted from his mouth.

It was on one of these trips toward a nearby river, at the bottom floor of a ruined skyscraper within a thin stone hallway, that the three of them found themselves now.

The undead's shriveled hand raised high as it screeched, spewing saliva and a foul necrotic stench all over the dusty stone floors before it lunged. The downward stroke sank its copper blade into Riven's staff as he blocked, and he grunted with the effort before spartan kicking the creature in the chest and sending it backward a couple feet.

This gave him an opening, and a large crimson disc ripped through the air to embed itself within the ugly, half-decayed creature to force it stumbling back. Riven grinned, then looked over his shoulder at Azmoth and Athela just behind him in the hallway. "Watch this."

He snapped his fingers, and the Bloody Razor he'd already cast was infused with even more mana as it exploded in a spray of red shrapnel. The ghoul was shredded from the inside out, pieces of its body bathing the sides of the hallway, the ceiling, and the floor in gore. This was something Riven had recently perfected through trial and error, and it gave not only the initial strike damage but also the explosion damage as long as he remembered to infuse it again after impact.

He'd essentially created small bombs from the razors he could summon.

"Yay!" Athela rapidly clapped her front spider paws in excitement, and Azmoth gave a grunt of approval, watching what Athela did and mimicking her to clap all four of his clawed, armored hands together over and over again while smiling as if he'd learned a new trick, too.

They would often take turns like this. Though they'd experimented and figured out that they all shared a baseline XP even if they didn't participate in the kill, the more one participated in a fight, the more XP one got. Those who took the killing blows also acquired another boost of XP that the others in their party didn't get, and they were actually able to measure this through a feature Riven had not been aware of prior to Athela informing him of it.

With every kill, if he used "Visualize XP" as an out-loud system command, he would literally see the amount of XP he was getting with a glowing number over the heads of slain enemies before they passed away. He certainly didn't intend to use it a lot, but it was useful from time to time.

This particular ghoul had given him forty-four XP, as he'd done all the work, while his two minions each got a paltry six XP for what Athela called a "minion tax." It worked both ways, though, so in theory even if he commanded his minions to go do all the work, he'd still be able to sit back and level up—just at a slower pace than his contracted demons would until they hit the cap that limited them in growth, which was equivalent the summoner's own level. This cap was also the reason why summoners could not acquire demons far stronger than they were—as the demon contracted would need to be equal or lower level when the contract was signed.

So in the end, they decided to split it as evenly as possible—occasionally toggling the "Visualize XP" command on and off while trying to get Azmoth level with Athela and Riven. According to Athela, some events hosted by the system had absolute level requirements regardless of actual power—so they weren't just numbers for show. This also somewhat explained why levels were even a thing, because previously Riven had been questioning why they even existed if some creatures like Azmoth had such enormous stat gains in comparison to the average human, for example. A level 5 Hellscape Brutalisk would have gained about as many stat points as a level 15 to 20 human if they were both classless.

Then again, Athela had also told him that humans generally had a much more broad expanse of classes than demons did. Neither Athela nor Azmoth had classes yet, and they could only attain certain ones within a limited scope depending on their species. Humans enjoyed an incredibly large number of options, and classes could give stat points, too—so in the end, a high-level human with a really good class could still keep pace or even outpace Azmoth's stat point gains per level in certain circumstances.

Riven hummed to himself as he stepped over two more bodies of low-level ghouls he'd already killed, tossing the copper knife to Azmoth, who put it in their loot bag, and yawned as he turned a corner in the small hallway. With every breath he took, tiny puffs of blood mist would exit through small pores in the mask he wore…a rather cool visual effect for a vampiric item, and he was pretty damn sure the mask was also purifying the air around him, as every time he inhaled the air felt crisp and refreshing.

Looking down at his chipped, gnarled staff, he could only hope he'd get a new weapon soon, too. It was looking much worse than when he'd first gotten it, and although he kept it for the mana regeneration, he tried not to use it as a physical weapon anymore because he didn't want it to break.

He turned another corner and came to a stop as his eyes locked onto yet another undead, the last of the small pack that was inching its way toward them.

[Level 2 Ghoul, Undead]

The approaching ghoul, the straggler of the group, had finally seen him after turning the corner and nearly tripping over a small pile of rubble. With a roar and a phlegm-filled, barking cough, it began barreling down the narrow hallway with bloodlust in its eyes, either too stupid or too hungry to care about the peril it was in under the cold stare of the warlock.

Athela glanced Riven's way with a raised leg. "I believe it's still your turn?"

He nodded and wiped the sweat off his brow while stepping over a partially broken skeleton. "Mine."

Riven's fingers clenched into a tight fist as red ribbons of magic drew up the length of his arm to his right bicep, licking his skin and smoldering as the mana was condensed and prepared for a strike.

The blood magic immediately bristled, streaked through the veins of his forearm and into his fingertips—and his mind homed in on the intended target. It only took a few seconds, and the ghoul was still ten feet away from him as he let the magic soar through the air like a crimson torpedo. In an instant, the monster's body ripped apart in a blur—tearing into the shrieking, bloodthirsty creature with a clean hole the size of Riven's thigh carved out of its chest and left shoulder.

The blast ripped the undead creature backward, flipping it over and spraying black blood everywhere while it shrieked. It slammed into the ground with a wet splat, lying broken on the floor from the aftershock of the magic and only letting out low groans.

Riven snorted, then casually walked up to the monster—lifted his boot—and slammed it into the creature's head. He repeated this two more times until his heel went through the skull and into the groaning undead's brain.

[You have landed a critical hit. Max damage x 2.]
[You have grown one level. Congratulations!]

"Another critical?" Athela asked curiously with a paw to her mandibles as if in thought.

Riven chuckled and lowered his hand, accessing his character sheet to assign the stat points to Intelligence. "Yep. I mean, I did kick its skull in."

CHAPTER 47

She gave him a chittering nudge while walking by and began to stride ahead with Azmoth in tow. "Nicely done. As expected of my warlock slave!"

Riven snorted and downed another vial of Sinner's Blood, replenishing his mana to full and wiping the red liquid from his lips on his sleeve. "Warlock slave?! Hold on here…"

"Royal jester, warlock slave, servant to the princess… All acceptable titles for a plebian such as yourself," Athela stated with a dismissive wave of her spider paw while continuing down the hallway and bypassing larger chambers on her left that were illuminated with dull red light. "Whichever suits you best, little man. Just let me know and it shall be so!"

"Little man?! I'm three times your size, you little runt!"

"PLEBIAN! I'VE STOMPED BABIES STURDIER THAN YOU!"

Riven merely rolled his eyes. They continued their trek toward the river of blood for their daily meal, with Riven muttering to himself about how arachnids were stupid and Athela doing that strange thorax-bobbing swagger-walk she did whenever she won an argument or a battle.

The three of them had been doing very well in choosing their battles over the course of their time here. Low-level monsters were eagerly picked off in order to grind levels and increase their stats, while higher-level monsters or large groups of them were generally avoided. The exception was situations like this, where they were able to funnel larger groups of low-level monsters into a tight space with Azmoth as the front line if they needed him to be. It was incredibly likely Azmoth could have handled all these low-level ghouls by himself without much hassle if needed—or that Riven could kill multiple enemies with a single strike of his Blood Lance spell if they were lined up correctly.

At the very least, they were all improving at a steady rate. Quite a fast one at that, if Riven had to guess. According to Athela, they were all likely to get level-assigned abilities soon. Riven had been lucky enough to find ways to acquire

Blessing of the Crow and Blood Lance, but that'd been external and not an internal source of acquisition. It was all random as to when someone would get a new ability, yes, but the longer one went on without getting one, the more likely they were to get one the next time they leveled up.

Or, at the very least, they'd get a trait or upgrade or some sort. Athela had to correct herself and explain that one to Riven thoroughly, but long story short, a level up might actually give other types of bonuses instead of spells or abilities. Better classes and longer periods of time between skill gains or upgrades often presented better options, but it wasn't an absolute. Even then it was still random to a great extent.

On the way through the ruins, Riven picked up an old bronze coin he saw lying around and pocketed it with a smile, but otherwise he stepped over the corpses and chuckled at Azmoth when the four-armed demon dragged one of the corpses along to eat as he went. The crunching of bone, snapping of ligaments, and shredding of flesh that had once made Riven sick to hear…now it was welcome. It meant Azmoth was in a good mood, and he was really beginning to like the big guy.

"Hey, Azmoth—" Riven began with a genuine smile, skipping ahead to walk alongside Athela as they turned the corner and continued down their regular path through the dark, ruined building toward the river of blood. "I want to say thanks. Thanks for saving my life the day we met, and thanks for cooking all our meals. Roasted harpy isn't all that bad."

"A little like chicken!" Athela chimed in happily.

"You've never been out of the nether realms prior to becoming my minion. Have you ever eaten chicken before? For real, though."

"No…but I plan to!"

"Didn't think so."

Azmoth displayed his rows of glistening black teeth and smiled back Riven's way, letting out a deep and hissing laugh that'd become characteristic of the lumbering demon over the couple weeks they'd known him. "Tee hee hee. Harpies big chickens, yes. You like chickens. Right, Athela?"

Both Riven and Athela stopped in their tracks, looked at each other, and then gawked back at Azmoth.

"Did you just talk?" Riven stated, bewildered. "Or is this my mind playing tricks on me?"

"I think he just talked," Athela confirmed with a quick double nod. "Hurry, Azmoth, slap him to make sure he's not hallucinating!" Athela jumped up and aggressively smacked Riven across the face again to bring him back to reality. "HURRY, AZMOTH, HURRY!"

Riven scowled down at the arachnid and roughly kicked the spider into a wall with his foot. "Do *not* slap me, Azmoth. I'd likely die."

Athela bounced off the side of the hall, laughed, and glanced back over her shoulder as they passed by another window filtering crimson dungeon light into the narrow passage, and she gave Azmoth the widest, most genuine spider smile she could muster. "When we get out, I'll show you what *real* chickens are like!"

"Yes, yes," Azmoth stated, as if pondering the meaning of it. "Can you draw chicken for Azmoth? I want see."

Athela leaped at the opportunity. "Of course I can! When we get back, I'll draw you *all the chickens!*"

"Uh…" Riven shook his head and nudged Azmoth as they walked. "She doesn't know what a chicken looks like, either, mark my words. She'll draw you something more like a dinosaur."

"What's a dinosaur?" Azmoth asked in a deep rumbling voice.

Riven just grunted. "Never mind, but it's good to hear you talking. I didn't even know you could."

Azmoth just chortled again, flames flickering in the back of his throat through rows of sharp black teeth. "Tee hee hee."

Athela covered her mouth with her paw, hiding her arachnid smile as she scurried up along the side of the wall. "All righty, let's get a move on! We're almost to the river, and I want to be back before nightfall. All the scaries come out at night!"

Riven paused, shortening his step for a second as he thought about it with furrowed brows. "Actually, yeah. Most of the scariest creatures do come out at night."

An hour later they exited the series of closely knit buildings through a pseudo-tunnel to a spot they liked to frequent for visiting the river. Looming archways and the spires of a cathedral to their left stood ominously, casting shadows over a bend in the blood river that snaked into a recess between two mountains of rubble before exiting back into the inner city again. Across the river were ancient stone aqueducts spanning the length of many miles, and underneath these dried-up aqueducts were some of the only fields of plants that the group had encountered since getting here. Instead of grass or green foliage, though, these plants were black…and grew about a foot in length while occasionally flowering a bright white. There were also a couple scattered black trees, each with translucent leaves that gave off a strange, illuminating mist whenever night fell.

It was at this recess within the mountains of rubble that their tunnel exited next to a large bridge, and as usual Athela sighed with desire at the flowers across the river of blood while sporting a pouty frown. "I really wish we could go pick some."

"Uh-huh." Riven snorted and put his hands on his hips to stretch, obviously not willing to take that chance. He gave the spider a sidelong look. "Ask yourself this, Athela: Why is there an untouched field of flowers across that river? Why in all the dungeon we've explored thus far does this one area seem pristine and beautiful? Why are there no monsters over there, trampling the plants? Why have we not even one time seen a creature venture that way in the weeks we've been coming here?"

He gave her a knowing look with a raised eyebrow underneath the hood of his fur-lined brown cloak. "It's absolutely fishy, and I'm willing to bet that those plants are dangerous. What does a demonic spider want with flowers, anyways?"

She animatedly waved her front spider legs around in the air. "I'm a princess, Riven! I need pretty things!"

"Right."

Athela glared at him, and with a humph she trotted toward the river's edge to start filling up.

CHAPTER 48

Athela had already vaulted over the stone ledge encompassing their solitary refuge amid the rubble and was sliding down a large stone slab leading to the dirt below with a chittering cackle. Hitting the ground running, she lunged on all twelve legs toward the temple as fast as she could—which was pretty damn fast—with Riven and Azmoth scrambling to catch up.

His heart pounded, and his nerves were on edge. Those definitely sounded like human voices, but the screaming and pleas were quickly dying out and had altogether stopped by the time he'd made it halfway to the cathedral. Had some other group from Earth ended up here? Were there more people from the Elysium core worlds that'd decided to appear? He began summoning blood magic to charge up a lance along his right arm, keeping an eye out on his surroundings as he ran.

Thirty seconds later, his sprint slowed to a crawl, and he began sneaking heel to toe to avoid making noise, with Azmoth doing his best to make as little noise as possible, too, though the larger demon had a tough time of it given his bulk and the metal fused to his body.

The cathedral's towering entrance was ajar and always had been to the best of Riven's knowledge. Once these marble double doors had been neatly fixated into the front, but to move such massive pillars of stone to shut the entrance down would have taken a Herculean effort.

When he finally made it to the daunting, steepled passage at the front of the cathedral, his body pressed up against the marble and he began slinking ahead. Step-by-step, he cautiously moved forward, heart pounding ever harder as he got closer to what he knew to be a very dangerous lair even by standards of the ruins they lived in. He could hear crunching, ripping, and distant muffled shouts for mercy from deeper into the structure.

Coming to a stop at the edge of the ajar door and scowling down at Athela, who was already peering in, he gave his eyes time to adjust…and what he saw made him very confused.

The entrance led directly into a tall, domed area with a ruined set of two incomplete statues in the far back, worn away by time and obvious physical abuse. Pieces of the large statues littered the ground beneath, but judging by the remaining details he could tell that they had once been angels.

Around the room, hanging off the ceiling support struts, were at least two dozen torn tapestries. The colors of the tapestries had been worn away by age. A large spiral staircase was off to the right, a long dark hallway leading straight ahead and to the left, and then here in the main room of the spacious cathedral was a myriad of different items that really didn't belong. The most prominent of which was a yellow school bus.

It was an antique, and it even had letters written in English that said "Bakers ISD" along the side. The door had been ripped off, tossed to the side, and crumpled up next to the body of a human man wearing a flannel T-shirt that was being fed on by a creature that resembled the larger goat man they'd seen wandering the area in the past, though this satyr was much smaller and likely an adolescent. It also didn't have its insides partially exposed like the larger one did and had a full set of abdominal muscles instead.

[Fallen Satyr, Level 5]

There were two other fallen satyrs of similar levels searching the bus, each standing at around four feet tall, but otherwise the room was empty of living creatures. Piles of shit lay scattered across the dirty tiled floor, and trails of blood led from the bus all the way down the dark hallway to the left.

Athela's whispering voice from behind startled him. "Wow. That's a car, right? I've always wanted to see one since you told me stories about them! How did it get here? Ooh, and look at that dead guy...how tasty. Do you think there are more?"

Riven didn't bother looking down and kept his eyes focused on the nearest satyr, watching its sharp teeth chomp down on bits and pieces of the man as it carved off chunks of bloody flesh with a small, curved knife and popped them into its mouth. The dark fur along its lower half and head were caked in dirt, and Riven could smell the foul stench of the creatures from here.

"It is very likely there are more. I heard begging, and the voices were definitely female..."

He slowly inhaled and exhaled, building up the bravery needed for what he was about to do. He didn't know why a bus, of all things, had been brought to the dungeon, or why now and not earlier when they'd first been spawned here, but he didn't care. That wasn't important. What was important was finding whoever was down that hallway and helping them escape. "I didn't see the goat man. At least not the big one. We may have a chance to save them if there are people still alive and all that's left are these little guys..."

From behind them, a low, malevolent chuckle rose from Azmoth's chest as he knelt next to them and peered in—despite not having any eyes. "Can…can I eat satyr? I cook them and eat them, yes?"

Riven glanced back. Azmoth's toothy grin and giddiness really did remind Riven of a child, and he had to pause to really consider that Azmoth was indeed an infant.

"Yes…" Riven said slowly, placing a finger to his lips and keeping his voice low. "But in a little bit. We need to kill them quietly and then go deeper in to see if we can save the others…assuming there are more humans left."

Azmoth's armored, spiked head nodded avidly while imitating Riven with a finger up to his lips. "Yes, yes. We kill quietly and eat later. That's good."

Riven waited until the two fallen satyrs on the bus finally made their way off it, stepping down onto the stone of the dirty cathedral floor and carrying another mutilated body, that of a young woman, with them. It looked like her neck had been broken in two places, and a large gash was torn through her upper half…

What a grisly sight.

Despite this, Riven kept his cool and counted to three under his breath from where he sat with Athela. At the end of the count, he pushed a torrent of mana into his left arm and channeled five large discs of spinning red razors that thundered ahead at breakneck speed. They cleanly split the first of the fallen satyrs like it was made of paper, lopping off the head and cutting through its body at various points just as the second satyr was taken out by a lightning-fast strike of Riven's Blood Lance.

With a scream of surprise from the second satyr that made Riven scowl, he lunged forward to finish the job—only to see that it was already dead before it hit the floor.

The attack had been so fast that the third satyr was in a state of shock and confusion as Athela leaped onto it from behind and sank her fangs into the creature's throat. Rot quickly afflicted the remnants of its windpipe as the arachnid tore its jugular out, and she did a happy dance atop its corpse only a minute later while wiggling her front legs.

Despite the fight being a quick hit, the second creature's brief scream made Riven slightly nervous. He peered down the dark hallway to his left, watching carefully for any signs of movement as Azmoth and Athela crept up behind him.

Yet, despite Azmoth's best attempts to remain quiet, he did occasionally make noise with those big, armored feet of his.

"Azmoth, I'm going to unsummon you for now…but I'll resummon you at the first sign of a fight," Riven stated with a glance back at the large demon. "You're just a little loud. Not your fault! But we need to be sneaky."

Riven brought a finger up to his chest where Azmoth's red pentagram was burned into his skin between his clavicles, right above Athela's blue one, and concentrated on the command Unsummon.

With a nod of understanding, Azmoth vanished through a portal of fire into the abyssal forest he'd spawned from. Riven felt the dip in his mana immediately, frowning at the cost his unsummoning needed. Every time he summoned or unsummoned one of them, it was a pretty decent percentage of his total mana, so he had to be careful how often he did it.

Athela prodded him with a foot. "Anything on these guys?"

Riven shook his head with a frown while irreverently poking the wide-eyed goat man's face with his staff. "Other than lots of ugly? No, I don't see any loot. Let's keep moving; we can look for treasure later. Right now the priority is trying to find out whether or not there are still people alive."

The trail of blood led them a good forty meters down the hall as the light grew dimmer and dimmer. Both Riven and Athela did their best to keep their footsteps noiseless, with Athela having a much easier time of it as she scampered along the ceiling like a shadow.

Up until the end of the hall, it was pretty barren. There were two empty rooms on the right side with a lot of broken boxes, bones, and more goat excrement, but not much else. The stench was rather foul here, too, so they made their way as hastily as possible and came to a crossroads between hallways going left and right and a set of stone stairs that led underground.

Riven pointed to the trail of blood in the weak light of the ruin, and Athela rushed to scout ahead as he descended the steps.

The smell got worse when they hit the bottom, and the floor became thick with a viscous fluid that made it all the harder to remain quiet as they tried to sneak through. The low glow of a lantern hanging along the wall to Riven's left gave them a meager amount of sight, though, and he quickly found that the blood trail had been lost in the quarter-inch of dark fluid on the floor.

"Crap." Riven quickly looked around, seeing passages to his left, right, and front—none of which had obvious signs of recent passage. He was about to ask Athela her opinion on where to start when he heard another distant scream from his right.

They immediately started moving.

Ancient stonework riddled with splendid carvings of heroics, monsters, and cities lined the long, domed halls. Green moss, the first of this particular kind that they'd seen since turning up in this dungeon, was plastered along various corners and patches of ceiling. The viscous liquid Riven stood in, which they still didn't know the identity of, was everywhere...and about every other stretch of hallway had a dim lantern planted on a stone outcropping to light the way.

"We're already lost, aren't we?" Athela asked nonchalantly from her perch upside down on the ceiling.

"No. I'm memorizing the layout as we go."

Another scream and distant begging filtered through the underground maze, pushing them forward past many barred or empty rooms until eventually they came to a much bigger and cylindrical room spanning many dozens of yards across.

It was something between a prison and a sacrificial chamber.

The large room smelled like iron and viscera. Torches were placed at intervals along the walls, and a large pentagram with runic markings was etched into the ceiling high above. There were numerous cells holding captives along the entirety of the circumference, with the two exceptions being the entrance they now knelt in, keeping to the shadows, and the bloody stone altar on the opposite side of the room.

At the raised altar, two of the smaller satyrs, or goat men, stood at either side as they brutally carved daggers into a screaming woman's chest. Rope tied to stone circlets held the flailing woman down. There were also three more of the satyrs standing around and chanting as they waved their small glistening daggers around, with the firelight of the tomb's torches reflecting off the blades. One of them, obviously the leader of the pack, wore a hood.

The victim, who was likely in her forties, wore a ripped, bloodied mess of what had once been a shirt with a fast-food logo on it, and was begging for her life between screams and sobs. Those screams and sobs abruptly cut off, and she began to go into shock as one of the two goat men made a *baahhing* noise similar to that of a sheep and triumphantly lifted up the heart he'd carved out of the woman.

It was sickening to watch, and as Riven looked around he saw even more bodies.

There was only one other person left alive, a scrawny, shirtless man in his late teens or early twenties with a short blond mohawk in the cell closest to the altar on the left. Other than that, all the other cages were filled with monsters of various sorts. There were a couple undead, a harpy, and two Jabob demons—all of which were below level 3. All of which were screaming, growling, moaning, crying, or rattling the bars. A couple Jabob and ghoul corpses were already piled at the foot of the altar, covered in blood and missing pieces of their bodies at random that mixed with the human corpses.

[Fallen Satyr: Level 5 Demon]
[Fallen Satyr: Level 6 Demon]
[Fallen Satyr: Level 8 Demon]
[Fallen Satyr: Level 3 Demon]
[Fallen Satyr: Level 5 Demon]
[Fallen Satyr: Level 5 Demon]

CHAPTER 49

Riven's heart sank when he realized he'd been just barely too late to save the woman or the man out front, but there was still one person they could save.

His muscles flexed, his body stiffened, and he turned to Athela with a determined upward gesture of his hand. "Go."

She understood and immediately slunk into the room to start crawling up the wall while the satyrs were distracted. Riven took in a deep breath and exhaled; his warm breath blew out as a cloud of red mist from his mask. With a nod he activated the Blessing of the Crow, feeling his once-daily and hour-long speed boost activate. His heart raced, his muscles flexed, and electricity sparked across his body. He felt his stamina climb rapidly; it was as if he'd just simultaneously taken numerous energy drinks and snorted cocaine.

Now it was time to kill these sons of bitches, but his projectiles other than Blood Lance were too short in range to cast from here in such a large room. He could let off two of his Blood Lances first, but immediately after that he needed to get closer.

Wisps of blood energy radiated across either arm, and with curling motions to summon the magic, he felt his Blood subpillar radiate. He flexed his muscles again, shifted his weight, and launched both Blood Lances right before he lunged forward into the large room.

CRACK

ZIP

The Blood Lances blurred forward ahead of him and ripped through the skull of one and the leg of another before the satyrs even knew what'd happened. Numerous shards of spinning, razor-sharp blood projectiles followed him in and launched forward when he was close enough, tearing into his enemies in an arsenal of pain and surprised screeches. He saw a dismembered hand fly into the air and extended his staff forward to cast another volley—condensed blood accumulating around the weapon and then shooting forward to impale three of them for a second round. They exploded a second later, ripping the bodies apart even more with minor blasts of magical shrapnel after he infused more mana into the projectiles. Unfortunately two of the discs shattered against the bloodied stone altar, but the majority of his strikes rang true.

The yellow eyes of the hooded satyr went wide, and it animatedly flung its bloody dagger in a spinning arc at Riven's neck with a shriek, but he dodged left at high speed with his empowered agility and cackled when one of its comrades was yanked up toward the ceiling screaming as Athela's webbing bound it.

"Bitch!" Riven's hand produced two large snares on either side of him that expanded and shot forward to meet the charge of the three incoming cronies. Each of the satyrs made enraged bleating sounds as they waved their bloody daggers in the air and raced toward him, bloodlust in their eyes.

One of them managed to duck low and avoid the snares while the other two were caught in the one on Riven's right and tripped to the floor—screaming as needles along the black netting impaled them and began to sear away their flesh.

Green light erupted from the altar where the hooded figure was chanting, and a moment later an orb of sickly green power blasted forward toward Riven's position when the nearest of the satyrs—dagger in hand—also lunged for him.

But even as Athela leaped from above to try and take the hit herself, a portal of flame erupted in front of her, and Azmoth took the attack head-on in a rush.

The green magic impacted against the huge four-armed demon as Azmoth roared, pulsed with fire, and charged, shrugging off the magical blast like it was nothing and causing the satyr caster to start bleating with terrified wails. The last thing that small satyr ever saw was a rushing bulldozer of death in the form of a flaming clawed hand.

The next moment, the spell caster—along with the majority of the stone altar—exploded into a spray of body parts, flame, and stone. Azmoth's attack was utterly devastating given the brutalisk's impressive strength, and there was little left of the smaller demon after that.

Meanwhile, Riven had erupted into an inferno himself when he activated Hell's Armor and took the attack of the dagger-wielding satyr head-on—grunting as the demon slashed at him, but only taking minimal damage and countering with a flaming staff to the demon's face.

The demon screeched and fell back as one of its teeth was sent flying, only to be met with shards of red webbing that erupted from Athela's thorax—piercing it over numerous spots across its body and neck from where she was perched above.

The arachnid lunged ahead with Riven hot on her heels, the two of them beating and tearing at the downed, wailing demon together as Riven deactivated Hell's Armor to save mana before whirling around and firing another large disc of razor-sharp blood a few feet in width spinning ahead in an arc to catch one of the satyrs that'd escaped his bindings.

The demon was split in two, the blood magic exploding in a shower of shrapnel against the far wall after slicing through his target while Azmoth roared and smashed down on the last of them—tearing its head off and snapping down his jaws onto the skull of the decapitated creature to repeatedly crunch and swallow.

"Yes! That's what I'm fuckin' talking about!" Riven screamed as he whooped and high-fived Athela—then gave Azmoth a thumbs-up. "Good shit!"

WHAM

Riven was sent reeling onto his back as pain shot along his staff-bearing arm. He felt teeth and claws digging through his sleeve into his skin, the sensation lighting up his nerves like they'd been hit by lightning.

Despite the immense pain, Riven's abrupt fall was due to surprise rather than damage. There were more of them? He hadn't even seen the little goat bastard come for him, but it must have come through the entrance they'd taken.

Gritting his teeth and making eye contact with the crazed, bloodthirsty, bulging eyeball of the creature that was trying to tear away his left bicep, Riven pulled his head back and slammed it into the demon's face.

His skull rattled and he immediately got woozy, but the effect was shared by the satyr. The small demon released its grip and rolled off him just in time to be met with a heavy, clawed hand.

Azmoth's flames burned into the creature while it squealed and writhed. The brutalisk's deep hiss was one of animosity and amusement, and with one hand, it kept the satyr midair and began to squeeze the creature's neck. "Tee hee hee."

The bleating, kicking, and struggling became fierce as the satyr's last attempts to escape were met with a deep chuckle, then the sound of a spine snapping met their ears and the quickly charring goat man went limp in Azmoth's grip.

"Puny satyr." Azmoth chuckled once more and irreverently tossed the smoldering, broken body over his shoulder and onto the corpse of a caster near the broken stone altar nearby. "Like taking baby."

Riven's grunt of pain was quickly cut off with a raised eyebrow of confusion as Azmoth stopped producing flames from his body and lent a hand to pull Riven up, but Athela just began to laugh.

"It's 'like taking candy from a baby.' Or 'I'm gonna stomp that baby,' Not 'taking baby.' Big difference." Athela patted Azmoth on the back when his flames died away, then gave Riven a sideways glance. "I think Azmoth is trying to learn a couple of my catchphrases from your world."

Azmoth nodded, his knives of wicked black teeth growing into a grin of his own.

Oh, God. Athela's bad habits were rubbing off on Azmoth.

Riven grimaced and began tending to his injured arm. The teeth had gone deep, letting blood flow freely out of his body, and he let out a groan of satisfaction when his body began its abnormal regeneration to seal the wounds. To restore his mana, he also took a vial of Sinner's Blood, downing it while simultaneously feeling his soul's Blood subpillar quiver ravenously at the taste. He felt invigorated, alive, and, standing up straighter, he flexed his arm again to inspect it and made sure nothing was still injured.

"Health and mana are back up, good as new." Riven gave Athela a fist bump. Then he did the same to Azmoth. "Good shit on that attack where you crushed the altar. You really put that caster into an early grave."

"Tee hee hee."

He rubbed his temple with his fingers and did a once-over around the room, glazing over the rows of monsters that were causing a rather loud ruckus just as they'd been doing so when he'd first entered. With a menacing glare of distaste, Riven reached over to his staff and got to his feet. "Let's get started, then, shall we?"

Ten minutes later, all the caged monsters were dead with shards and discs of crimson embedded in their corpses.

[You have gained one level. Congratulations!]

Nice.

After finishing off the last of the ghouls within the cells with another Bloody Razor, Riven stepped over the mangled corpse of a nearby satyr and grabbed the gleaming set of ringed keys from the creature's robes.

He shook his head and kept going. His attention was quickly turned over to the guy with the mohawk, who was sitting in his cell silently watching them with folded arms over his knees and his back to the wall.

Riven held up a finger and cleared his throat to get the man's attention. "You're from Earth, right? Hold on just a moment, I need to assign my stat points just in case something comes up."

The man gave him a bewildered and simultaneously confused look, and Riven's snort came out as another cloud of red mist while he got to work. When he put his points back into his usuals, his status page was coming along nicely. He'd really come a long way.

[Riven Thane's Status Page:
- **Level 16**
- **Pillar Orientations: Unholy Foundation, Blood, Infernal**
- **Core of Original Sin—Gluttony: (Under Construction) (???)**
- **Traits: Race: Human, Class: Novice Warlock, Adrenaline Junkie (Blood) (+15% to Agility)**
- **Abilities: Blessing of the Crow (Unholy), Wretched Snare (Unholy), Bloody Razors (Blood), Blood Lance (Blood) (Tier 2),**

Hell's Armor (Infernal)
- Stats: 8 Strength, 24 Sturdiness, 112 Intelligence, 10 Agility, 1 Luck, -4 Charisma, 3 Perception, 57 Willpower, 9 Faith
- Free Stat Points: 0
- Minions: Athela, Level 13 Blood Weaver [14 Willpower Requirement]. Azmoth, Level 9 Hellscape Brutalisk [20 Willpower Requirement].
- Equipped Items: Basic Casting Staff (4 dmg, 12% mana regen, +3 magic dmg), Chalgathi Cultist Amulet (???), Leather Boots (1 def), Backpack of Supplies, Witch's Ring of Grand Casting (+26 Intelligence), Cloak of the Tundra (22 def, +56 bonus def vs. frost), Breath of Valgeshia (48 def, +13 dmg & +9% mana output dmg for blood dmg, 6% mana regen)]

He nodded in affirmation of his stats and closed the window. He'd been pushing most of his points into Intelligence and Willpower, and he'd also sunk a few into Sturdiness to keep himself alive. The result was that he could tell a very stark difference in the power of his magical casting when compared to the spells he'd started with in the beginning, back in Chalgathi's trials. The snares and razors were the same type of spells, but now they had a hell of a punch and could manifest bigger and better for less mana.

CHAPTER 50

He was going to complain about the pain still radiating across his recently injured arm to Athela when he paused in what he was about to say…and a lump in his throat began to form. Farther back in the darker recess of the cell, past the blond man, there was a pile of four small bodies. All of them human, all of them children, and all of them dead with dark marks of bruising around their necks… Riven had a good idea where they'd come from, considering there was a school bus out there in the front room of the temple.

Riven went rigid and immediately turned away, but he refocused his attention as the other man got up and placed his head against the thick cell bars. In the torchlight, it was evident that the guy was a natural athlete. "So as I was saying, you're from Earth?"

He looked to have the body of a long-distance runner, was just slightly shorter than Riven by half an inch, and wore a pair of sweatpants with a tight black shirt. The man looked up at him, and their eyes met, and he sluggishly drawled out a reply. "Yes. These creatures killed any who resisted and dragged them away, and after I saw what they did to my friend Shawn, I pretended to be unconscious as they dragged me here. What is this place? We were trying to outrun some monsters, and all of a sudden we drove through a fiery door that appeared out of nowhere and ended up here…"

His voice carried with it a very slight, almost unnoticeable Irish accent. Worry was etched into the man's features, and his grip against the bars of his cell tightened, but he remained composed. "First the world goes crazy and invading monsters roam the streets, killing everyone, and then we're transported to some woodlands where the trees came alive to attack us. Now this… I end up here, I watched my friend get killed before I'm saved by magic-wielding humans. At least you're human, though. My name is Ben."

Ben extended a hand through the cell bars, and Riven grasped it to shake firmly. It was nice, after all these weeks, finally seeing another person. Talking to another person…though Riven could tell Ben didn't feel the same way about the situation.

"My name is Riven. This is Athela, and this is Azmoth. Apparently we're in hell, in a dungeon called Negrada. I have a lot of questions for you, too, but that can wait for later. As can our explanations for what we know individually. Here."

He began fidgeting with the keys and trying them out, one by one, on the cell. The keys were a little different than the ones he was used to—they were larger, thicker, and had different protrusions at all angles along the circumference of the circular rod that formed the base of the key. However, he was able to get the lock open soon enough, and Ben stepped out.

Ben warily glanced Azmoth and Athela over. "They seem friendly enough… How did you get two of them on your side?"

"Long story," Riven stated sourly underneath his hood as he glared at the pile of small bodies. "I don't feel like talking the entire thing through right now."

Surprisingly, Ben wasn't in much of a state of shock. Nor did he seem overly grateful about being saved. Rather, he seemed sad. He glanced around the room, quickly accepting it for what it was, and let out a slow sigh. "This is terrible."

Riven watched him as he slowly strode up to where the corpse of the woman he'd known was lying. Her heart was carved out, and what was left of her after Azmoth's shattering attack to kill the caster was still tied down to chunks of the broken stone altar.

"Negrada…" Ben said slowly after a moment of pondering. He walked over to let his fingers lightly touch the remnants of the stone altar. He turned around and faced Riven, doing his best to ignore Azmoth, who was staring him down a few feet away. "You said we're in hell? That's what this notification I just got says, too. How weird."

Riven nodded just once, then thought a bit and slowly came to a realization. Stepping over another corpse and coming to stand directly in front of Ben, Riven picked up a dagger from one of the fallen satyrs and handed it over to the other man. "You'll be needing this. Honestly, I'm surprised you're showing up now. I'd assumed everybody was making the transition over at the same time and the same way… Did you ever go through the tutorial?"

Ben nervously took the blade, awkwardly palming it before shaking his head no. "What's the tutorial? I never went through any tutorial. I was on Earth until I arrived here, but the planet…it looked like it was being rearranged. It was really weird—pieces of land mass were shifted and teleported or replaced by other things. Some areas we drove by looked like they were going through a time warp with trees aging at incredible rates, and other areas looked like they were staying the same. I didn't know what to make of it…"

Riven frowned, remembering his own experience back in Dallas when he, Jose, and Allie had managed to escape into the pillar of light right before he was told he was being separated from his childhood friend and sister. There were too many questions and too few answers for his liking, but it did give him some sick measure of comfort knowing that he wasn't alone on this ride of insanity. "You mentioned monsters back on Earth. What were yours like? I was originally attacked by monsters back in Dallas before escaping into the pillars."

Ben looked surprised. "It was all over the news, mate. Before the TV stations went down. Monsters started appearing and killing anyone who was left, with a timer lighting up in vision along the top right-hand side... It was horrible."

"I only saw snippets of the news. My phone was low on battery when it all happened and it died on the way out."

"Oh. Half of Earth's population was pretty much annihilated all at once, or that's what people were guessing right before shit really started hitting the fan."

Riven stared at the younger man for some time in silent thought.

Half?

But knowing news stations back on Earth, that number could have been blown way out of proportion. There was no real way to tell just how many people had died. Nevertheless, it was likely in the many millions at the very least, since it'd been a worldwide event.

Ben gave a long, exasperated sigh and uncomfortably folded his arms over his chest. "I was an elementary school teacher... The school seemed to be an area where everyone had remained behind, and none of my students were abducted, so I piled them in the school bus and tried to make a run for it when the school got attacked by what I now think are werewolves. Some of the other teachers came with me. You saw how that all ended... I think I'm in a state of shock. It doesn't feel real to me. Anyways, I was pulled into an abyss when we drove through the fiery door... It was almost like a portal. Probably was one, in hindsight. These strange symbols started appearing everywhere, ones I didn't recognize, and now I'm here. Where is everyone else? Have you seen anyone else other than us?"

Riven frowned even more deeply and nodded slowly. This guy hadn't seen the pillars of light? He'd been taken through a portal? And why had it been so much later than when Riven had gotten here?

Something didn't add up.

"There was one other person I've personally met here in the dungeon who claimed to be from another planet...but he's dead now. Saw another girl, but she ran off. Before that there were people in my tutorial, too, and they were all from Earth as well. Then there was my friend and my sister, and the system prompt I originally got before starting this whole mess said if I survived the tutorial I would get to reunite with them. So that's the current goal. I'm not sure about all the pieces to the puzzle just yet, but from what I can gather, this is some kind of event that's merging Earth with another world, or worlds in the plural, and into a multiverse of some sort. I can't get answers from my minions because of some kind of rules set up by the system…and I'm on a unique starting path when compared to most of the other people from Earth. Again, this is a hellscape dungeon, instead of the tutorial dungeon most people go through, and I had to choose between taking the hard road myself or sacrificing the people I'd made acquaintances with for an easy way out. Obviously I'm here, so I took the hard road."

There was a very long pause.

"I see…" Ben replied flatly, eyes boring into the stone floor beneath his feet. They both stared silently at the floor, and then Ben spoke up again. "Well, I'm too deep into this shit to question your sanity. So… What's with your demons?"

Riven gave a slight smile and motioned over to his minions—outlined in the firelight of the torches along the walls. "I started a path that appears to be molding me into a warlock, even got a class title for it. You get race and class points to add to your stat page with every level up, but if you don't know what I'm talking about, then you're farther behind than I'd hoped for."

"Yes, I know about the leveling system. One of my friends leveled up by running over one of the monsters in our way. Any chance you know of a way out of here?"

Riven shook his head sourly. "Not yet, but I'm working on it. Surprisingly enough, I think this dungeon is an extension of the core system worlds—which are worlds outside the realm of Earth, from what I've been told."

"To Elysium?"

"Yes, if I'm understanding things correctly. Elysium is apparently a bunch of interconnected worlds. Like I mentioned earlier, it's a multiverse of some sort, like the ones you read about in comics as a kid…but I'm not entirely sure how it works."

Riven took the next ten minutes explaining the various things he'd learned since getting there. He explained how quests worked, system notifications, skills, attribute pillars, how he'd gotten his own class title, and how there were various ways to orient to a given pillar if Ben found the means through happenstance or study. He explained stats, the hidden health/mana/stamina that everyone apparently had, and he explained in detail what he'd been doing there in the dungeon for a couple weeks while trying to find a way out. Lastly he told Ben about the "Dao" that was currently not available until the tutorial was over, whatever the hell Dao was, but it'd been mentioned enough times to likely be important. Then again: Weren't his pillars Dao-related? Ugh. He really needed to get his head on straight; maybe when he got out of here he'd figure things out.

Ben took it in stride and at face value, taking in another deep breath and shaking his head in wonder as Riven finished his condensed version of the story. "We're really fucked, then, aren't we? And no, I don't know what Dao is, either."

CHAPTER 51

Riven glanced around at the bodies of the satyrs, then smirked and shrugged. "I figured you wouldn't know...which sucks, but that was expected. Either way, I seem to be doing okay so far. I'm more worried about Allie and Jose—the two I'm gunning to meet with after this. The real problem here is that *you* don't have any abilities or oriented pillars."

Riven refrained from letting Ben know he had two ability scrolls in his bag. He didn't know the man yet, and he was hesitant to just hand such valuable stuff out. Especially when he might be able to give them to Allie. And the likelihood of Ben also having affinities for that particular type of pillar just by happenstance wasn't high anyways.

"Fuck."

"I know."

Athela raised a front spider paw and waved it at them shortly thereafter. "I can help you orient toward the Unholy pillar without scrolls! If that's what you want."

Ben nearly jumped out of his skin as the spider spoke and swore, clutching at his rising chest as he stared dumbly at the arachnid. "Did she just talk?"

"Of course I talk, you insulting little shit!" Athela squealed back up at him, hissing and chittering angrily before settling down. "I'm a *princess*! Address me appropriately, you unworthy ape!"

Riven sighed, rolled his eyes, and motioned to the spider with his right hand. "All right, Athela, go ahead and explain it to him in detail, then."

"Ahem." Athela got up on her back legs and animatedly started waving her front four around while explaining to them just what to do. "First, you'll need an affinity to bind to a pillar, and acquiring affinities can either be impossible or doable depending on the person—but raising an affinity percentage is very hard to do past a baseline point. There are a couple of ways to do it, but Riven here got an easy way out if you don't include the life-and-death struggles he had to endure. Some events, like the ones Riven had, will give them to you.

Others specifically from your world will get them in the tutorial. However, the vast majority of people in Elysium and most of the people from Earth will get their abilities by hard work, training, studying, and repeated activities. Once presented with an ability related to your efforts, it will orient you toward the chosen pillar. Each of the main pillars has its own subpillars, those subpillars have specialty pillars, and the Unholy Foundational Pillar is the one demons are oriented toward from birth. The Unholy pillar has the major subpillars of Blood, Shadow, Death, Infernal, Depravity, and Chaos—each with their own innumerable unique pillars depending on how you evolve them. You'll need to attain the Unholy pillar before you ever get any of the subpillars, and to attain the Unholy pillar you'll have to do something that the system considers evil. Like murdering someone, or repeatedly stealing from the needy, or manipulating your way through life for your own gain and at the cost of others. Or you can be born into it, like a sentient undead or a demon like me."

Ben gave the spider a horrified look, and then gave Riven a similar stare as well as he began to back up. "Wait…"

Riven quickly held up a hand of dispute. "I got mine from an event."

"But that still doesn't explain why you were able to acquire the foundational pillar in the first place, because you'd still have to qualify," Athela stated in an upbeat tone. "There must have been *something* that you did to qualify you. Unless you had some sort of bloodline that imbued you with the Unholy pillar. Do you have any bloodlines that you haven't made me aware of, Riven?"

Riven slowly opened his mouth, closed it, and glanced back down to his status page. She was obviously teasing him and knew about the shard of original sin and how he'd acquired it through his bloodline, though she had said little about it in the past two weeks. Her eyes had gone wide when he'd mentioned it, but like most other things she'd been unable to tell him what exactly it meant.

Riven gave her the side-eye in the firelight of the sacrificial chamber amid the piled-up bodies all around them. "You caught me, Athela."

Ben gave Athela another uncomfortable glance and took another step back. "And if I choose the Unholy pillar, can I switch to another pillar later?"

"Nope! The foundational pillars are permanent."

"I think I'll pass on the Unholy pillar, then…thank you for the offer, though."

"No problem!" Athela took a couple steps to the left and sat along a firm outcropping of what had once been the end of the stone altar. She hunched down and rocked forward slightly, tapping her fangs on the stone. "I hate this place. It's very ugly."

Riven shrugged. "Me, too. But you've gotta realize that life is all about per-spective. I had a friend who had sex two or three times a day, exercised twice a day, read a couple books a week… You'd think it was a good life, right? Yet every day he complained about how much he hated prison."

Athela and Azmoth each just gave Riven a confused stare, but Ben actually had to suppress a laugh. It was the first time Ben hadn't looked utterly depressed.

An echoing thud from the hallway Riven had just come through alerted all of them to the approach of something or someone else. Riven slowly turned his head… The sound was like something had been dropped from a great height. Subsequent sounds further escalated the situation as another two bangs sounded against the stone of the hall around the corner.

The sounds continued to get louder, closer, and were soon intermixed with heavy breathing as a shadowy figure finally emerged from around the corner to stare at them with black-and-yellow eyes.

Oh, fuck. There he was…the big kahuna himself.

It was *the* goat man, the monster that they'd been avoiding for weeks due to the sheer size of the prey it brought back with it to feed on. And with nowhere to run, they were trapped in this circular sacrificial room like cattle in a pen. The description of the monster burned with a fiery bright-gold lettering, and this monster had a new word at the end of the hologram identification box that likely signified why.

[Fallen Satyr Warlord, Level 21. DUNGEON MINIBOSS. ELITE.]

Unlike the other fallen satyrs they'd faced thus far, this creature was an absolute beast. Even more so than what they'd originally thought, now that they were up close and in person. Huge, rippling muscles with veins outlined along its chest and arms flexed in anticipation as it held that giant spiked club they always saw it carrying around. It was a very crude weapon, about the size of Riven's entire body, and had jutting pieces of metal sticking out of the wood.

Two curling ram horns were set on either side of its skull above the bulging eyes, and saliva dripped from an open mouth of sharp, bloodied teeth. Hot breath and vapor visibly expelled from the creature every couple of seconds as it panted in a rabid-like state—reminding Riven of himself after he'd gotten his mask—and fleshy strands of musculature partially covering up its hollow abdominal cavity became tense as its exposed spine flexed forward in anticipation of a charge. A purple light from within its chest illuminated the innards of the strange creature, and a moment later the satyr erupted with a purple miasma of energy that floated into the air about it like smoke.

It slammed its left hoof into the ground, grunted, and roared as its muscles all tensed with veins protruding along the entirety of its body. "RRRAAAAHHHH!"

Then time froze, and a series of pop-ups appeared in Riven's vision.

WARNING
WARNING
WARNING
DUNGEON MINIBOSS FIGHT FALLEN SATYR WARLORD
HAS BEEN INITIATED.
DUNGEON NEGRADA HAS SEALED OFF YOUR POINT OF
EXIT UNTIL THE BATTLE IS COMPLETE.
SPECIAL EVENT: DUNGEON NEGRADA HAS BET 400,000
ELYSIUM COINS IN FAVOR OF FALLEN SATYR WARLORD.
CHALGATHI HAS ACCEPTED THIS BET IN FAVOR OF
RIVEN THANE.
BEGINNING BATTLE IN
5...
4...
3...
2...
1...

The pentagram on the ceiling burned bright crimson as a thick wall of white mana erupted from the ground to seal the hallway leading out, and time immediately resumed a normal pace.

In an instant, the room was chaos. Riven immediately began charging his Blood Lance, and his two minions launched into action.

"Come on, then!" Riven roared, barely activating Hell's Armor in time as the huge satyr barreled past Azmoth and flashed forward in a split second. Riven was immediately flung right like a comet of flames when the goat man used his momentum to collide with the warlock in a brutal shoulder charge, but the creature slipped on one of the bodies, and the impact wasn't as drastic as it would have been otherwise.

Riven slammed into the remnants of the broken stone altar and cursed while pain radiated through his back. His flickering body, covered in protective hellfire, had significantly decreased the damage, but not wanting to spend all his mana on the ability, he disabled it a second later. Meanwhile, Ben screamed in horror and managed to make it back into his cell, slamming the cage door behind him.

Athela rapidly tried to tie the satyr warlord down with strings of webbing, and Azmoth simply charged back with sheer weight and power behind him, roaring while he slashed at the satyr with his two right sets of claws.

CRASH

CHAPTER 52

The two behemoths collided, and the room reverberated underneath the weight of their strikes. Azmoth's flaming fingers tore chunks out of the other large demon in huge gashes, but the sturdiness and regeneration of the satyr were obvious immediately afterward. The purple miasma surrounding the satyr quickly healed the slashes and burns Azmoth was dealing, and the enormous miniboss stood to its full height a second later—tearing through the strands of webbing encasing its right arm and swinging its club backward at full force and crushing one of Azmoth's arms with a thunderous boom. Azmoth roared and counterattacked by leaping at it and bringing it back down to the ground to tear and bite at it, ripping out large pieces of flesh as the two titans went crazy trying to kill one another. Athela managed to get in there as well with multiple hit-and-run bites that sank venom into the satyr for applications of necrosis.

Watching the fight unfold was like watching a brutal episode of *National Geographic* where male lions fight—but this was the hellscape version.

Riven's Blessing of the Crow was still in effect, and he whipped around the platform at high speed while pushing more mana into the ability. He was sure-footed, sprinting at a rate easily twice as fast as anything he could have ever accomplished back on Earth. Riven was likely going somewhere beyond thirty miles per hour with the combination of both movement buffs, and it wasn't tiring him, either.

Coming around and getting a good positioning for his attack, he launched the Blood Lance he'd been channeling into his arm. The flickering crimson power shot out like a comet through the dusty air and made impact with the back of the warlord's head, narrowly missing Azmoth as they flailed on the ground to claw and bite at one another, but instead of impaling the satyr, the magic just exploded and created a large but superficial wound to momentarily stun the creature.

That was more than enough time for his minions to take advantage of it.

Azmoth howled and sank his many rows of teeth into the creature's shoulder and began ripping out its deltoid muscle while Athela shot ahead and rapidly began digging into the creature's left eye with her fangs.

The eye burst, and the echoing scream of rage made the room tremble as it slammed a fist down into the spot where Athela had been just a moment before the arachnid had launched herself backward with amazing speed.

Azmoth, however, was not as lucky, and the half-blinded warlord's anger simmered to full effect as the purple miasma around it exploded outward from the gem hovering in its chest and sent Azmoth shooting up into the ceiling far above like a rocket launcher. The room shuddered under the impact, the purple miasma that'd been rejuvenating the satyr disappeared, and the Hellscape Brutalisk went flailing back down many dozens of feet only to meet the satyr's spiked club. Azmoth was hit like a baseball and smashed through one of the sets of bars of a cage and slammed into the far wall—debris billowing out like a cloud as the satyr roared in fury and violently shook its head back and forth while blinking rapidly.

Riven's volley of razor-sharp discs slammed into the creature's back a second later, and each had a secondary explosion of shrapnel as he infused his blood-magic projectiles with more mana after impact, tearing into its flesh just as it stomped down and sent a shock wave of mana across the room.

It was like being hit with a brick wall. Riven's footing was thrown off when the wave hit, and he grunted with the impact, expelling all the air in his lungs. He and Athela were flung in opposite directions from the ability's power, and each toppled head over heels until they too came to abrupt and violent halts against the bars along the perimeter of the room.

Riven screamed, feeling his right leg shatter under the impact, and he cursed while the satyr snarled his way.

The monster turned, dripping saliva and wiping viscous fluid from the ruined eyeball Athela had ripped open. It bellowed once, twice, and then charged—making it halfway to Riven's position and completely tearing through a Wretched Snare that latched onto its legs to finish him off when Azmoth leaped onto its back to bring it down with a predatory roar.

Azmoth's face was caved in on the left side with half of his long, obsidian teeth missing. Two of his arms were mangled and broken, and one of his knees looked rather useless as it hung at his side, but he was ravenously biting and clawing at the satyr anyways. Completely ignoring his pain, he continued to rip away at the larger demon like a tiger that had nearly overdosed on stimulants.

With the miasma gone, the wounds on the satyr were there to stay and obviously had taken a toll on the struggling monster. Modified blood webbing bombarded it as a plethora of small needles erupted from Athela's curled thorax, and Riven continued to launch volleys of discs at the creature's back whenever Azmoth wasn't in the way.

The satyr bellowed, got up and nearly fell over immediately after that as it grunted amid the barrage and readjusted its posture. It clamped its own razor teeth into Azmoth's burning neck, but the obsidian plating covering the brutalisk's body kept it from effectively doing any damage. Snarling, the satyr flexed its muscles, began to glow a deep purple, and, with a burst of power, ripped Azmoth off it and bodily slammed the large demon into the ground.

Stone sprayed up from the ground as Azmoth's body made contact, and as Azmoth tried to scramble back up with another roar, the satyr warlord lifted up its gigantic club and brought it down upon Azmoth's head.

Riven was now getting low mana after the last volley of discs embedded in the satyr's oozing back, and his leg was healing but at a much slower pace than normal. Faint traces of purple miasma coated his wounds; it was somehow inhibiting his natural healing abilities, but despite this Riven tried to save the infant brutalisk with everything he had. Drawing out a small knife, he brought his arm back and flung it forward as hard as he possibly could.

He watched the dagger fly through the air. The brutal beating that the satyr warlord was giving Azmoth was hard to watch…the spiked tips of the club were tearing out large pieces of the demon's body and face despite Azmoth's metal plating, and one arm was being utterly crushed as the flaming demon tried to get back up. The look of crazed glee from the drooling, wide-eyed satyr was interwoven with bleating cackles…

Until the dagger zipped through the air and embedded itself into the satyr's remaining good eye with a wet thud.

"RRRRRRRAAAAAAAAAAHHHHHHHHHHHHHHH!"

The warlord reeled, dropping its spiked club, and clutched at its newly ruined eyeball with shaky hands before yanking the dagger out and flinging it to the ground. It continued to bellow and almost doubled over while covering up its injury, only to whirl and snarl Riven's way.

It could still smell and hear, but the satyr warlord was now completely blinded.

Riven snarled right back. Without a second thought and with anger rising up in his chest, Riven pulled a vial of Sinner's Blood from his bag. Downing the contents, he felt his mana quickly replenish, and his leg began to mend itself more rapidly. "Come on, you cocksucking *goat*!"

The remnants of the monster's ruined eyes narrowed, and hot vapor trailed out of its mouth while it panted. It wiped its bloodied lips on one arm, hoisted its club above its head, and with a roar threw the club as hard as it could in Riven's direction.

The enormous weapon spun through the air in an arc as the monster used the opportunity to ram its foot into the ground—creating a shock wave that was supposed to knock him down so the throw would hit true. For a moment it looked like it'd work.

Thus, Athela screeched in disbelief and awe as Riven jumped up and to the left to avoid the waist-high shock wave and conjured not one, not two, but eight simultaneous Wretched Snares that he molded together into one large net. He held on to the net with a reinforced mana connection from a location just above his hands and willed the black magic to expand, opening up to catch the spinning meteor of a club before he was nearly taken off his feet as the projectile's force pulled him backward.

But Riven continued to infuse the conjured and reinforced net with mana as he quickly slid across the floor, silently screaming at his magic to do his bidding while he was dragged backward to a likely death at high speed. Over and over again, he pictured what he wanted and willed the mana to act, pouring his heart and soul into the internal motion while using the Unholy and Blood subpillars attached to his soul like a sieve to purify the raw mana into blood magic. The pillars responded, embracing him, and it promptly came blazing to life under his extreme mental state.

"Do as you're told!"

The words left Riven's mouth as he gave vision and meaning to what he wanted the blood magic to do, and to Athela's continued amazement, the corpses around Riven were drained and erupted around him. The blood of the bodies all whirled in a vortex to come to his call, and for the first time since the blood pit, he willed his environmental resources to do his bidding just like the textbooks had talked about. The result was a massively reduced mana cost and a vastly increased power output.

POP—BOOM

[The Blood subpillar recognizes your authority, and the system has labeled your Blood subpillar as your specialty pillar. You may now evolve your Blood subpillar, and you are now restricted from obtaining any other specialty pillars.]

[Your bloodline begins to stir. You have created the blood spell Crimson Ice.]

[Crimson Ice (Blood): Summon ice created from blood to cover an area around or on you. You may utilize this crystallized blood to form objects or walls, cause your opponents to slip, and create temporary body modifications with variable utility. Mana cost is situational and can vary from extremely high to extremely low. Dependent on both Intelligence (40%) and Willpower (60%) stats. No cooldown.]

CHAPTER 53

Riven hadn't realized that only one specialty pillar could be obtained beyond normal subpillars, but he didn't dwell on that for more than a half second.

The exploding corpses nearly blew Riven's eardrums out and tore into the satyr with intense ferocity that covered the surrounding walls in layers of red. Simultaneously, streams of blood from all around the room began icing over and flowing across the floor at insane speed to race up Riven's legs. The thick red ice crept up all the way past his knees only momentarily to act as a pair of brakes, stopping him right before he hit the opposite side of the room, and he grinned. The crystallized ice fluidly followed him as he rotated his body, using his projected mana to hold the Wretched Snares intact, and spun around with the momentum of the club in a way that most magic casters at his level would have never even dreamed of doing before now.

Usually, catching a club that size would require a Herculean amount of strength. But when he was using mana to do the heavy lifting for him, he only needed to reinforce his spells.

With a grunt from Riven, the caught club rotated with his pivot and circled around his body before being launched from the snares back at the demon like a stone from a slingshot.

WHOOSH

CRASH

The badly wounded warlord's right arm was taken off as the club smashed through it like a high-velocity hammer into a sponge. Cries of disbelief erupted from the shocked onlookers. The blinded demon staggered backward, looking down at its missing stump of an arm despite not being able to see.

But the demon was not done, and in fact it became even more enraged.

"PUNY HUMANNN!"

The satyr initially slipped upon the sheet of blood ice covering the floor but rammed a foot into the ground, which shattered the magic Riven had imbued.

Flecks and shards were sent skyward, and Riven was thrown back along with Athela just as she'd tried to ambush the creature. With another scream of rage after that, the satyr didn't let up, blindly barreling toward him at breakneck speed that far outmatched Riven's own.

Riven had anticipated this and rolled to his feet.

He summoned another sheet of red ice along the floor and felt it surge up his legs again; he could literally feel the blood surrounding him and mold it to his will with the spell he'd created through sheer willpower. With narrowed eyes and a snarl, he felt the Blessing of the Crow kick into high gear along with his newer ability as they both shot him forward. The blood ice molded to his skin and pumped his legs harder, giving them more power as he vaulted ahead to slide underneath the oncoming satyr's body between its cloven feet. Simultaneously and with a victorious scream of hate, Riven sent razor-sharp discs firing into the creature's crotch as the monster tore through the air over him.

The satyr stumbled for only a moment. It looked down—trying to pinpoint his location—then turned to Riven again and brought an injured hoof up with a bleating noise to slam the foot down into the stone floor yet again.

Riven's knees buckled as the room shook again amid a brief shock wave of unnatural kinetic energy, and he scrambled to pick himself up from where he'd been thrown before the satyr closed the gap in a sprint of its own.

Athela screeched and launched herself at its back, sinking her venom into its neck and creating a quickly spreading area of necrosis before weaving in and out of its strikes as she continued to crawl all over the creature at breakneck speed—interrupting its charge as it slipped on the ice again and slammed onto the ground. The satyr continued to roll, flail, bleat, and swing its weapon in an attempt to crush the spider—but missed each time and roared when another Blood Lance pierced its chest in a blur of red magic.

Riven downed another vial of Sinner's Blood to speed up the healing process of his body. His previously shattered leg was still killing him due to the purple miasma digging into his injury, and it was hard to move despite Crimson Ice supporting his body. Red lightning still coursed over his body, and his breath was creating bloody vapor clouds as he panted, his cloak whirling around him in the winds of the aftershock, and he snarled at his enemy before casting the vial aside with a clattering sound.

Riven began channeling another Blood Lance into his arm and rushed backward over the ice to put distance between them when the satyr's strike blurred downward during its attempts to find Athela. Riven's eyes went wide in shock as he heard the screech of pain end abruptly, and Athela's body was crushed against the ground in a spray of green ichor.

[Your minion Athela has died. She will be returned to you twenty-four hours after you pay the blood price for your minion. To resurrect your level 13 Blood Weaver demon, you will be required to pay Elysium directly with a sum of thirteen thousand Elysium coins. Simply will this transaction to happen and make sure you have the required payment to further this agenda.]

Azmoth was not in a much better situation. Though alive, the demon was struggling to get back up as he dripped blood and his flames died away into nothing. Apparently even Hell's Armor had its limits, despite it being an intrinsic property of the demon.

Having realized it'd killed one of its opponents, the satyr stood up to its full height, put its mouth to the ceiling where the glowing crimson pentagram remained, and roared with a hungering delight. Numerous injuries, patches of necrosis, protruding shards of solidified webbing, open wounds, and burned streaks from where the Wretched Snares had riddled the creature's body were obvious. It was missing both of its eyes and one of its arms, but it was still standing.

It was now winning.

Riven silently cursed and launched his Blood Lance at the creature's head, hitting it full-on along the jaw and causing it to stumble back as sharp teeth shattered. It bellowed and fell on the ice Riven had summoned while smacking its face into the ground, and Riven immediately capitalized on that bought time with another flurry of razor discs that crashed into the monster's body. Despite this, the beast picked itself up after receiving the barrage like an unkillable behemoth and snarled his way. Turning to the general direction it'd been hit from, the creature lifted up a foot yet again to slam it down into the ground.

The resultant shock wave tore through the ice covering the floor once more as a nearly perfect counter to Riven's new spell—simultaneously sending Riven head over heels and causing him to drop his staff when his head hit the ground. He blinked rapidly, trying to get ahold of his surroundings after he'd nearly been knocked unconscious. Dropping his weapon was also a serious loss in the moment, because that staff had been the source of increased mana regeneration for him through this fight.

He groaned, his vision blurry and his head aching like crazy, and his groan turned to a scream when the satyr's spiked club came down on the location it thought him to be in. It hadn't outright killed him because the aim was off, but the bones in his arm shattered in an instant.

Pain radiated up his useless, mangled limb as he screamed profanities, only to be silenced by another backward swipe from the spiked club. He felt a rusty metal spike pierce his lung before the wood of the club's bulk made contact, flinging him against the stone altar with a crunch and thud.

Riven's head pounded, and he could vaguely hear Ben screaming at him to get up—but his body was hardly moving. It was too damaged, too broken to respond to his commands. His ribs were broken. His arms were both useless— his right was bent backward at an awkward angle. He had a punctured lung, purple miasma was still spreading across his injuries to inhibit his healing, and he'd had back-to-back concussions.

In the haze that'd become his vision over the past ten seconds, he saw Azmoth, who was also severely injured, take two clawed hands and tear into the back of the satyr's spine. He roared, arms flaming again and straining with all his might as he tried to rip and tear at the exposed bone along the satyr's midsection.

The two titans violently clashed again, both on death's doorstep and struggling to overpower one another with biting, clawing, and the swinging of their limbs.

Riven was fading in and out of consciousness, losing blood rapidly and feeling his body going cold. But anger and a refusal to quit throbbed inside his chest, and he managed to stand shakily despite his broken body. The shouts and sounds of combat grew dimmer as he stumbled and leaned against the nearby wall, shaking his head to clear his vision.

His hand quivered as he forced the broken bones and torn muscles to move forward, reaching back into the bag where he still had four remaining vials of Sinner's Blood left. Like an uncoordinated toddler using unfamiliar fingers, he limply selected two vials.

He coughed and spat blood, then glared up at the monster across the room. "Fuck this goat."

His shaking fingers lost their grip, dropping both vials next to him to clatter along the ground. He felt drunk.

"Shit."

Riven grimaced in pain and bent over to pick the vial up while Azmoth held the monster off. He tried to pull off the cork of the closest bottle, doing so by touch just as much as by sight at this point due to his vision coming in and out.

[Your minion Azmoth has died. He will be returned to you twenty-four hours after you pay the blood price for your minion. To resurrect your level 9 infant Hellscape Brutalisk demon, you will be required to pay Elysium directly with a sum of nine thousand Elysium coins. Simply will this transaction to happen and make sure you have the required payment to further this agenda.]

With a massive surge of willpower, Riven popped the cork and brought one vial of Sinner's Blood to his lips. Simultaneously he flipped the gigantic satyr off when it sniffed and turned his way—despite knowing the gesture was lost on the blinded demon.

[Vial of Sinner's Blood, restore an average of 70 health and mana simultaneously, may not be taken outside the realms of hell. Warning: Using frequent amounts of Sinner's Blood may have unwanted side effects over time. Unique Tier.]

The tainted red liquid trickled down his throat, and within seconds he felt himself begin to heal. Frankly, he should be dead by any normal human standards after his lungs had been gouged, though he still managed to hold on while his Blood subpillar radiated upon the warm touch of Sinner's Blood. His primary pillar seemed to pulse, generously feeding off the cursed liquid and causing him to feel whole again—despite the ominous message the system gave off concerning regularly using the river's liquid.

But even though it was taking effect, the miasma was spreading, and the potion was still far too slow for the battle at hand. His eyesight began to stabilize again, as did his other senses, and he got a better look at what'd just happened to his second contracted demon.

Azmoth was on the ground, broken and still. The familiar's natural plate armor had been crushed and a leg had been torn off, and his long, bony teeth were broken off on the left side of his face where the jaw was unhinged and torn at a gruesome angle. Ben was sprinting across the room while holding an obviously broken hand where the bones had been crushed; his dagger was embedded in the satyr's right flank, and he was in a state of absolute panic. Then there was Athela, who remained as a splattering of green and white ichor with various spider body parts along the stone floor—intermixing with the corpses of the other, smaller satyrs.

The blinded, one-armed satyr was lumbering forward in a slow chase to catch Ben; ravaged by deep claw marks and other wounds, patches of necrotic flesh were falling off in chunks and burned fur was scattered across its body, with numerous needlelike shards of modified webbing lodged in its chest and back. The monster was an absolute mess, missing one eye completely from when Athela had ripped it open, while the other eye was deflated from where Riven's dagger had punctured it—but the bloodlust was evident in the creature's slow, ominous walk toward Ben's screams.

"Riven! Riven, help me!"

Riven, help me? Seriously, man? Did it look like Riven could help yet?! What a fucking idiot—did this guy not realize he was drawing the demon his way? Toward both of them?

CHAPTER 54

Riven began to push himself off the wall when he felt the bones in his arms snap back into place. The pain was immense, and he could barely breathe as he began violently coughing up fluid that his lungs had accumulated—but he managed to get to his knees.

He needed to speed up his recovery.

That's when he saw the second vial of Sinner's Blood he'd accidentally dropped on the floor. He reached for it, fumbling with the cork.

The second vial was drained in an instant, and just as the monster bellowed to charge Ben up against the wall with its horned head down, Riven knew that Ben was about to die. There was no way the slender man could take the many-ton monster crushing him against a stone backdrop...and in that instant, Riven's heart twisted with hate. Visions of the school bus, of the dead children, of his sister's wish that they find the courage to make a better life for themselves that last night they'd spent together scrounging for scraps of food... They all flashed through his mind.

He had failed to save the others, but he wasn't going to let the satyr get its way.

Riven's vision began to turn red, his muscles began to pulse, and a hunger for the satyr's blood boiled over to envelop his very soul. Everything he'd been imbued with, from the way his magic worked at a base level, to the hate boiling up in his gut, to how the power felt when summoned and unleashed, was brought to bear. The way his muscles tensed and his mind warped with each casting came to light, and he applied all of it here and now.

Then something finally clicked, something primal that had been there ever since he'd been born but had never surfaced until now, and his entire life abruptly changed in that instant.

[Sinner's Blood has caused the remnant biological locks on your body to finally degrade. You have regained your dormant heritage:

[Pureblooded Vampire, Malignancy Heritage (Blood/Shadow/ Death)—Your heritage as a pureblooded vampire has finally come to fruition and is no longer repressed. As a person holding one of the original vampiric lineages and as a greater undead, you are a favored descendant of the Blood god. Your heritage empowers you with many bonuses, but it also comes at a steep price. Please review the following changes.

Negatives:

- You suffer 400% additional damage from any silver-based weapons.
- You suffer 300% additional damage from any Light and Sun subpillar abilities.
- You may not be healed or have active buffs applied to you by any Light or Sun subpillar abilities.
- Your mana and stamina slowly drain while your skin is exposed to direct sunlight. If exposed to sunlight when they start to run low, your health will also deteriorate.
- You are required to feed on the blood of mortals on a regular basis. You will lose your sanity and go into a rage if underfed.
- Your heritage bestows a baseline -300 Charisma. -2 Charisma per level.

Positives:

- 100% affinity to the Blood subpillar, 96% affinity to the Shadow subpillar, and 95% affinity to the Death subpillar. These pillars now take less resource consumption to use abilities with, control is increased, and potency is increased.
- Your heritage also bestows upon you a baseline +40 Strength, + 70 Sturdiness, +70 Intelligence, +150 Perception, and + 80 Agility.
- Perception has been upgraded to Vampiric Perception and has extra emphasis per stat point applied for heartbeats, dark vision, and smell.
- Your race change to Pureblooded Vampire upgrades the number of stat points per level to +1 Strength, +2 Sturdiness, + 1 Intelligence, +4 Agility, +1 Perception, and +5 free stat points per level.
- You gain extreme regeneration while in dark places.
- You are immune to most diseases.
- You will not die of old age.
- You may currently create new vampires at a thirty-day cooldown period without risk to yourself; how much they inherit from your gift is partially dependent on them and partially randomized.

- Ancient Vampiric Lineage—Malignancy Heritage: Allows you to acquire a shard of original sin through Breath of Malignancy. Allows you to utilize Malignant Prophecy.]

[Your bloodline has directly affected your current minions. Athela has three possible upgrades available to her, undisclosed until her blood price has been paid and resurrection commences. Azmoth has one possible upgrade available to him, undisclosed until his blood price has been paid and resurrection commences.]

[You have been granted four class upgrade options to choose from, undisclosed until your current battle is over.]

[You are severely underfed and require the blood of mortals to satiate your hunger. Insanity takes hold of your mind until you feed.]

Riven's mind blew a fuse, and the internal scream of hunger and hatred that overwhelmed him escaped his lips as a bone-chilling roar. Fangs ripped out of his mouth underneath his mask, and his eyes turned from their normal green to a bright crimson. His muscles tensed and ripped through skin as they toned and gained mass, only for his body to quickly regenerate the superficial wounds within seconds. His body's skin tone became pale white, and it felt like a boulder had taken residence in his stomach as hunger clawed at his insides.

Just before insanity fully engulfed him and he lost his mind, Riven was able to scream out a single phrase toward his opponent: "Eat shit!"

He took a single step forward and lunged, streams of blood ripping from the walls, floors, and corpses around the room to fly in ribbons through the air toward him, condensing into blades of red ice along his outstretched hands and forearms in the instant it took for him to cross the room and collide with the demon who'd killed his minions. The strike, empowered by his blood mana, was devastating.

BOOM

The satyr roared in conjunction with Riven's bloodthirsty screech of madness, and the two of them blew by Ben like a tidal wave of violence, ripping through the bars of a nearby cage and sending rubble into the air as the back wall partially gave way.

Riven's mind was devoid of everything except the need to kill this creature and the extreme hunger building up inside him. Like a viper, he struck at the downed demon in the pile of stone over and over again, ripping out pieces of muscle and bone as the satyr—already on death's doorstep—wailed and tried to break out of its confinement.

"RAAAAAHHHHHH!"

The familiar sound of a feral beast reached Riven's ears, but he was too far gone to realize that it wasn't the satyr making that noise—rather, it was him this time.

CRUNCH—SNAP—BAM

Riven's head jerked back and snapped forward, headbutting the satyr's mutilated face, which sent the huge demon jerking backward with a newly broken nose.

WRENCH—THUD—RIP

Riven's hands, turned into clawed crimson gauntlets of ice with protruding blades coming out of his arms on either side, tore into the creature like a Gatling gun. His now-enhanced limbs shot forward like lightning strikes and deflected the desperate attempts of the monster to get back up, and before he knew it he was standing over the remnants of what had once been a powerful demon.

His heart pounded, his chest heaved, and his ears rang from the noise of the battle as he started to cough. Dust filled the room from where the warlord had been launched through bent and torn metal bars after Riven had collided with it in a rage. The satyr, or what remained of it, had been reduced to a shredded mess of bones and viscera within a crater in the stone ahead of him. Blood was splattered on the walls alongside scorch marks, and the remaining corpse was plastered into the indentation like glue on paper.

CONGRATULATIONS
CONGRATULATIONS
CONGRATULATIONS
YOU HAVE DEFEATED THE MINIBOSS FALLEN SATYR
WARLORD. DUNGEON NEGRADA HAS LOST ITS BET.
FOUR HUNDRED THOUSAND ELYSIUM COINS HAVE
BEEN DISPENSED, WITH HALF GOING TO CHALGATHI
AND HALF GOING TO RIVEN THANE.

[Instead of the normal prize for beating a dungeon miniboss, you have received half the betting pool, two hundred thousand Elysium coins, as the key player in Chalgathi's won bet.]

[You have gained two levels. Congratulations!]

[Your minions, though temporarily dead and banished to the nether realms, have received their XP and level ups as well. Congratulations!]

[You are now able to exit your tutorial dungeon and proceed to the starter area, where you will pick your starting destination and be

provided details of what Elysium has in store for you. In order to do so, please focus on the command *Exit Dungeon* to summon a stair portal to your location.]

Riven remained there: panting, hunched over, and in a good amount of pain as two enormous wooden chests of platinum, gold, silver, and bronze coins bloomed into being in front of him—setting themselves down one after the other as the lids flipped up to reveal their contents. His body was covered in viscera, body parts, and blood, and gingerly he picked his mask up off the floor; it had fallen off at an undisclosed time in the conflict. His insides burned and recoiled with every movement he made, but the hunger...the hunger still persisted.

It was an extreme, compulsive feeling. Something that he couldn't shake no matter how hard he tried. It clawed painfully at his gut and his mind, forcing his will to submit to it as it became an all-encompassing need.

He wanted to feed.

He needed to feed.

He needed blood.

Desperately, he got down on his knees and began licking up the satyr's blood, but he quickly spat it out and let a primal hiss of disgust escape his lips. It made him want to gag, and the compulsion became even greater as he let out a scream of rage that it wasn't what his body needed to satiate the painful, ruthless craving he was experiencing.

"Riven?"

Ben's hesitant voice called out to him from behind, and Riven stiffened.

Fangs extended, Riven whirled with a manic look in his eyes—hungrily staring Ben down.

The other man shrieked in terror upon seeing the obvious change, and he didn't take more than another second to start running, but he was far too slow. The last thing that Ben ever saw was Riven's bloody, clawed hand reaching out for him—and then everything went black.

CHAPTER 55

[You are now well-fed. Your insanity fades.]

Riven regained his sanity an hour later, with the fuzzy details beginning to outline themselves now that he was in a right state of mind. He rapidly blinked and furrowed his brows, finding himself wrist-deep in Ben's intestines. Once he realized what he was doing, he began to backpedal and scream. It was a scream not filled with the primal rage or hunger he'd experienced before, but now it was that of horror at what he'd done—a scream of disgust and revulsion. He began to hyperventilate and stumbled backward away from the corpse, not knowing how or why he'd come to do this until memories of his primal hunger flooded back into his mind as one memory after the other.

The pleading, crying last moments of the man Riven had known for less than half an hour came pouring in.

Riven gagged and vomited profusely, feeling sick with himself and incredibly confused. The notifications he'd received when his vampiric bloodline had been awakened had come so fast and the change had been so sudden that he'd had no time to really comprehend what it'd all meant up until now. He managed to calm down after that and remained staring at the floor between his knees in a hunched-over position amid a mountain of body parts while he took time to reflect upon the day's events.

[You are now able to exit your tutorial dungeon and proceed to the starter area, where you will pick your starting destination and be provided details of what Elysium has in store for you. In order to do so, please focus on the command *Exit Dungeon* to summon a stair portal to your location.]

The two chests of Elysium coins were still there. Five of the torches had been blown out or extinguished during the fight, so the lighting in the room was far darker than it'd been when he'd first gotten there, but he could still see perfectly into the darkest crevices of the chamber. The sacrificial room was completely devoid of life, and there were even two more satyr corpses near the doorway that hadn't been there before his change—ones he must have killed while in his crazed state of mind. The doorway was also devoid of any magical barrier that'd sealed him inside in the first place, so he was free to go whenever he pleased.

He felt a small amount of pride after having passed the tutorial dungeon and finding a way out now, but that feeling was utterly dwarfed by what he'd done to Ben. Riven had truly become a monster in every sense of the word.

He'd been right with his earlier suspicions after his encounter with the giant blood squid. Even in the beginning, the notifications he'd received talked to him about how his affinity for blood magic was incredibly high. Now Chalgathi was making bets on his behalf like one would gamble on a prized racing horse.

The thought of it made Riven go from sullen and guilty to incredibly angry in the course of a couple seconds. He gritted his teeth, spat, and hopped up to his feet with clenched fists. However, he went a little bit too fast and found himself jumping instead of just clambering up. He landed without much issue, though, and quickly realized just how thoroughly his body had changed after all—even its outward appearance. He had slightly thicker, broader shoulders and was toned all over. In the poor reflection of a pool of bodily fluids, he was barely able to see that his eyes had changed to a glowing crimson color and his facial features looked far more symmetrical than they had been in the past—though he was slightly paler, too.

Extending his right hand, he flexed his muscles and felt power there that'd never been present before. He felt good…though one glance down at the dead man at his feet made him cringe inwardly and outwardly.

No, this wasn't his fault. He hadn't known any of this would happen, and he hadn't been in his right mind when he'd murdered Ben. Even as disgusting of an act as it was, Riven was not at fault here.

Or at least that's what he was going to tell himself in order to allow himself to sleep at night for the foreseeable future.

He gritted his teeth, shook his head, and turned from the grisly sight while pushing the subject out of mind. He'd talk to Athela and Azmoth about this later and get their opinion on what to do, but in the meantime he first had to summon them back.

Gratefully eyeing the chests of money, he walked over and placed his hand on one of them. Then he resummoned the notifications concerning the deaths of his minions from his status page to reexamine just how much he'd have to pay for their returns.

[Your minion Athela has died. She will be returned to you twenty-four hours after you pay the blood price for your minion. To

resurrect your level 15 Blood Weaver demon, you will be required to pay Elysium directly with a sum of fifteen thousand Elysium coins. Simply will this transaction to happen and make sure you have the required payment to further this agenda.]

[Your minion Azmoth has died. He will be returned to you twenty-four hours after you pay the blood price for your minion. To resurrect your level 11 infant Hellscape Brutalisk demon, you will be required to pay Elysium directly with a sum of eleven thousand Elysium coins. Simply will this transaction to happen and make sure you have the required payment to further this agenda.]

Riven took a moment to go ahead with the transactions, noting how the original levels of his minions had shot up, and saw thousands of the coins from the two chests evaporate. However, he thankfully had a good amount left after that, and Riven was suddenly very worried about how he was even going to get this money to a safe place. There was no way he could carry it. Even one of those chests looked like it weighed a literal ton.

[You have paid the blood price of twenty-six thousand Elysium coins to resummon your contracted minions from the nether realms after their untimely demise. Athela and Azmoth will both be returned to you within twenty-four hours.]

Riven shook his head and rubbed his eyes, and looking around again, he noticed a stark difference in the darker areas of the room and cells. The black recesses that'd once been hidden in the backs of the cells out of the torchlight were still dark in various shades of gray, but their details were outlined for him to make out anyway, with highlighted black or gray etchings that'd never been there before.

Well, at least it wasn't entirely bad. He had survived, after all.

"Greetings."

The voice was unfamiliar, alien, and raspy. It echoed through the room as light and heat bloomed from behind Riven's back.

It was a smaller version of the flaming eye that illuminated the dungeon's sky, though it was still four feet in circumference. Made of orange, yellow, and red flames, the lidless eye gazed at him as it hovered midair. Unblinking and staring directly at him, the visage curiously evaluated the vampire. "I must say…I'm rather impressed. An ascension into a pureblooded vampire was not expected… Perhaps knowing you were on the verge of an ascension is why the creature that calls itself Chalgathi accepted the bet in the first place. Such is the way of things, I suppose. I am Dungeon Negrada and am pleased to make your acquaintance."

There was Chalgathi's name again, and it was beginning to grate on Riven's nerves. It appeared this Chalgathi character had a very keen interest in his life.

Riven's scowl deepened, and he took a step forward to get a better look at what was apparently the representation of the dungeon itself. "I didn't realize dungeons were living things."

The entity chuckled, flames writhing along its conjured body as it focused solely on him. "Well, I'm pleased to inform you that we dungeons are indeed alive, though I'm a little less pleased that I lost my bet. That was a good number of Elysium coins to lose, and along with your gained levels and class upgrades, it appears this encounter has been quite the boon for you. Tell me...as the one who dealt the killing blow and received half of the fruits of my failed bet, would you be interested in a deal? Chalgathi seems uninterested in trading those coins back to me, and I cannot break the laws of Elysium and cheat you of your winnings without incurring the wrath of the system—at least not for a little while. But you... I think you may see things my way as a path to mutual benefit."

Class upgrades? That caught Riven's attention.

But this situation was getting weirder and weirder. Riven glanced over at the entrance to the room, which had just recently resealed itself with another wall of white mana, and then looked back to the floating eye.

It was very interesting to him that dungeons were actually living entities. Could dungeons use these coins, too? What would dungeons even use them for? Riven knew that they'd be valuable eventually, but he didn't really know how to use them other than the brief description he'd gotten earlier about **"system altars"** that were like stores you could buy supplies from.

He also didn't know why he'd acquired even half the coins instead of Chalgathi getting them all—as he was the one who'd made the bet, but he assumed this Chalgathi entity found them useful as well. Chalgathi had retained the other half of the prize money and was apparently refusing to trade them back to this dungeon, which was slightly amusing if not baffling to Riven.

But this dungeon, Negrada, was correct in its assumption that Riven was more than willing to strike a deal with this dungeon entity before he left this literal hellhole. Riven had no way to transport this massive amount of money. With the coins he'd accumulated throughout the time spent here in the dungeon, the two hundred thousand he'd just gotten, and then the twenty-six thousand he'd spent on reviving his minions, he had just over 174,000 left over. It was all just sitting there in front of him or in the bag he'd thrown to the wayside during his fight, and with no way to move it, why *shouldn't* he trade with the dungeon?

No doubt Dungeon Negrada knew this. How could Riven carry two enormous, heavy chests of coins? Perhaps it'd be different if Azmoth was here, but he wasn't.

The monetary system here was very straightforward, from what Athela had told him in her brief lecture of Elysium economics, and the system had done a good job of integrating the currency and making system altars the basis of most prices—sometimes even being on the higher end of things if people wanted to be competitive. It often was able to stabilize inflation this way. Of course, rarer items often didn't appear in the Elysium altar shops, and one had to look elsewhere for them. Often the system altars were completely random or sometimes even had unique selections based on the specific altar, refreshing every month with a new set of inventory. He'd also gathered that one copper piece was worth slightly less than one US dollar when comparing altar prices on foodstuffs to those at a local grocery store back home... Ten copper pieces equaled a silver piece, ten silver pieces equaled a gold piece, and ten gold pieces equaled a platinum piece, meaning that one platinum coin was worth about nine hundred to one thousand US dollars in comparison to old-world money, and then there were a few other types of coins above that, which Riven likely wouldn't see for a very, very long time, if ever.

But Riven wasn't quite sure this was still the case, as Athela hadn't gone into much detail during her brief overview, and he quickly decided that he was going to play dumb here and act like he simply didn't know. He'd press the dungeon for information and see what he could find out.

So Riven nodded. "Sure. What's your deal? Let's hear it."

CHAPTER 56

The more he thought about it, the better an idea doing a deal here and now became. He wasn't about to just hand the money over, but there was a good chance he'd be killed and robbed for this amount of wealth if people realized how much he had—even if he *did* find some way to move it all out of here when he summoned the portal to exit. And even if he *did* find an Elysium altar after that to buy from. So he was going to use as much of it as he could as long as the deals were reasonable, because he didn't want to leave it behind in this wretched place.

Then again, how would he know what was reasonable? He literally had zilch to go off. That was going to pose a problem.

The eye evaluated Riven for some time, then let out a wheezing noise as its pupil expanded. "I have a variety of different items you may be interested in trading for. I obviously want those Elysium coins back… Instead of buying from the local Elysium altars, perhaps you can trade them back to me instead? The coins you already carry with you in those sacks can be traded to me as well…if you wish… There's one item in particular that I could offer you a rather good deal on…and I think you won't be disappointed."

Riven nodded, wiping sweat from his brow. It was becoming hotter in here…or maybe he was just feeling off because of the recent fight and damage to his body. "Sounds fair…and I think I'll be able to trade some of them back to you. Under some conditions."

There was a long pause.

"What conditions?"

He slowly exhaled. "I want information. I'm going to ask you some questions, and you're going to answer them."

A deep, rich laugh echoed throughout the enclosed room in response to his request. The laugh grew louder as the eye thrummed with mana, unnerving Riven just slightly, but eventually it settled down. "Very well! I can provide you with what I know as long as the system permits it…free of charge…though I am surprised by your request. I was under the impression that you were more acquainted with the system than the average newly integrated person, given how easily you managed to survive here. How hilarious. Though this is only the first level of my dungeon...your request explains much of the bumbling about that I have seen."

The eye circled Riven curiously, slowly moving with a wisp of flame trailing out behind it as it studied him. Stopping in front of him once more, the pupil dilated yet again. "What information do you seek, little vampire?"

Riven didn't hesitate. "Chalgathi. Who or what the hell is Chalgathi? Why did I get half the money from its bet?"

The flaming eye pulsed, narrowed, and stared at him for some time. "You don't know?"

Riven shook his head.

There was another long pause before the dungeon answered. "I am not quite sure myself. It offered to take up my bet when Elysium decided to decline it. All I know is that I was able to sense an Unholy aura from its presence as it watched. If I had to guess, it is likely an archdemon or a minor god that isn't well-known...or perhaps some kind of greater lich. But those are only guesses. I had assumed that you knew or that you were affiliated with it somehow. If this is not the case, it vexes me greatly...because it could have taken the money for itself. Usually bets at such high stakes between greater entities are clean-cut and done behind the scenes, with only the system acting as a mediator. How very odd..."

The dungeon's voice trailed off, leaving Riven even more confused than he'd been a minute before. So Chalgathi had decided to just give half of the money away as a token of goodwill? Well, Riven had earned Chalgathi that money in the first place—but it appeared that Chalgathi didn't need to have done what he'd done at all. Riven could still be broke and without reward, by that logic, and he'd not only have been unable to pay the blood price for regaining his minions after their deaths, but he'd never have been able to utilize that money here and now.

Riven pushed the information acquisition to the back burner as he pondered these new details, deciding to go ahead and spend the money while he thought on things. "I see... Let's take a look at your offers?"

"Certainly. Though you must remember...many of these items will be very hard to come by if you leave here without making a deal. Each of them is also an item customized to your...situation. Instead of a straight price, we will use the barter system with one another, and if you have questions, feel free to ask. None of the creatures within my body will bother you while you decide."

A series of three screens abruptly displayed in front of Riven, and he soon found himself looking at a three rather pricey, but very high-quality, items.

[Negrada's List of Items for the Little Bastard Riven Thane:

[Amulet of Many Faces (Relic): Once a day you may change your facial features and identify information for a maximum of three hours at a near-perfect level that cannot be detected by the vast majority of counterspells, identifier abilities, or miracles. Increases all Stealth capabilities by a bonus of 20%.]

[Black Redemption (Tier 1 Awakened Staff): 74 average shadow damage on strike, with each hit drawing a small amount of mana from you to apply a knock-back effect with a minor explosion of shadow magic. All cost of Shadow spells is decreased by 7%; mana regeneration is increased by 68%. Shadow magics all have damage modifiers applied by +27% while channeling through this staff.

[Black Lightning: This staff can passively build up charges of black lightning. Power of black lightning depends on the amount of charge emitted.]

[Sleeper (Vampiric) (Tier 1 Awakened Claymore): 118 average damage on strike, 1%-62% bonus chance to stun on strike. 3% leech life applied on biological enemies when struck. Requires vampiric heritage to wield.

[Crescent Strike: Sweep your blade in an arc and imbue it with mana to send out a wave of blood magic to cut down your enemies.]

The amulet was definitely good, no doubt about it. He could pose as someone else and people wouldn't be any wiser. It was almost like a superpower from the comic books he'd read as a kid.

But Riven stopped right there after seeing the word *Awakened*. The Black Redemption staff was exactly the kind of weapon he'd been looking for this entire time, even having hit effects with shadow explosions and black lightning discharges as a special. Looking at the staff's physical attacks alone, it was comparable to the other claymore he'd seen early on in the dungeon that the crazed ghoul had nearly smashed him with right after he'd acquired Blood Lance. More than anything else, though, it gave a passive mana regeneration boost of 68 percent— which was absolutely huge. It was almost six times more of a regeneration boost than he got from his current staff. That would be invaluable in fights, allowing him to push more mana into more spells for more damage. Spell-damage output was in large part based on mana consumption in creating the spell, so mana regeneration was in essence almost a bonus to continued damage output for any mage that entered an elongated battle.

[Damaged Orchalium Claymore, 58 average damage, two-handed for full effect, 89 Strength requirement.]

And if he remembered right, these awakened weapons didn't have souls, but rather were alive in their own right. They were supposed to have conscious thoughts of their own.

He clarified just to make sure. "So…what does 'awakened' mean, exactly?"

The floating eyeball made of flames chuckled slightly. "It means that they are able to grow with you. Though they grow in leaps and bounds, through tiers, instead of leveling up like you would. These particular awakened items would be a good starting point for someone such as yourself… They aren't grand now, but they could become so. I would sell you something better, but you wouldn't be able to afford them."

"I see. How would I get them to grow, then?"

"Through experience and finding the right materials for their required upgrades. Every awakened item is unique in what they want or need to evolve, and their experiences will guide their evolutionary pathways depending on use by the wielder. However, some awakened items won't bind to you because your personalities, fighting styles, or wills do not match up."

"Gotcha." Riven rubbed his chin thoughtfully. "Well, I'll be out of here in a bit, according to the system notifications, so I won't be bothering you much anymore. Thus I assume you'd have no problem giving me some advice on what to pick if you were me?"

The eyeball gave him a thoughtful stare, then had another amused laughing fit that lasted a little longer than his mere chuckles from before. "You're asking me for advice after killing my miniboss and taking my coins? The audacity. I love it… To answer your question, I believe any of these three items would be useful to you. As I said, I custom made this list for you based on what you'd need most from the wares in my dungeon. Or at least the ones you could afford with the money you have… There are others in my wares that would benefit you, but they are far too valuable to part with for what you have to offer."

Riven blinked, then pulled up his status page to examine his stats before he went on with the conversation.

[Riven Thane's Status Page:
- **Level 18**
- **Pillar Orientations: Unholy Foundation, Blood Specialty, Infernal**
- **Core of Original Sin—Gluttony: (Under Construction) (???)**

- Traits: Race: Pureblooded Vampire (Extreme Darkness Regeneration) (Sunlight Decay) (Extreme Weakness to silver weapons, Sun subpillar, and Light subpillar attacks), Class: Novice Warlock, Adrenaline Junkie (Blood) (+15% to Agility)
- Abilities: Blessing of the Crow (Unholy), Wretched Snare (Unholy), Bloody Razors (Blood), Crimson Ice (Blood), Blood Lance (Blood) (Tier 2), Hell's Armor (Infernal)
- Stats: 50 Strength, 98 Sturdiness, 188 Intelligence, 98 Agility, 1 Luck, -308 Charisma, 155 Vampiric Perception, 59 Willpower, 9 Faith
- Free Stat Points: 14
- Minions: Athela, Level 15 Blood Weaver [14 Willpower Requirement]. Azmoth, Level 11 Hellscape Brutalisk [20 Willpower Requirement].
- Equipped Items: Crude Cultist's Robes (1 def), Basic Casting Staff (4 dmg, 12% mana regen, +3 magic dmg), Chalgathi Cultist Amulet (???), Leather Boots (1 def), Backpack of Supplies, Witch's Ring of Grand Casting (+26 Intelligence), Cloak of the Tundra (22 def, +56 bonus def vs. frost), Breath of Valgeshia (48 def, +13 dmg and +9% mana output dmg for blood dmg, 6% mana regen)
- Notices: Class Upgrades Available]

"Well, my minion Athela told me that I shouldn't be trying to specialize in more than one route to power. She said to stick with my magic because I was good at it, and that generally it's hard to level up combination classes that utilize martial arts and magic. If you're offering me the claymore right now, I'm assuming you think I'd utilize it. Why would you think that after I only used magic in that last fight?"

The eyeball scoffed audibly, then shook itself from side to side as the fires lighting it danced along the walls to illuminate the stone room. "That advice was certainly given to you before your evolution into a vampire, and you haven't even bothered to look at your class option choices yet. I can see them for what they are—it is within my ability to do so—and it would be foolish not to capitalize upon a combination class now that your race empowers you in physical aspects more so than magical ones. Perhaps specializing in magic could be your primary, but having a secondary focus because of your physical stats would be quite wise. Not only that, but you utilized your spells Blessing of the Crow and Crimson Ice to modify your body so that you could better engage in physical contact with my satyr in the end of the fight. You were in close quarters for about a third of the fight despite claiming to be a mage. I believe it would be in your best interest to reevaluate your classes soon, and if you're thinking about taking one of the spirit weapons, they would be a good foundation for you to proceed with. However, these items are very expensive and would cost everything you have just for one of them."

"Everything?!"

"Everything. Even then, I'd be losing a slight amount of what they're really worth."

"Huh. That's not going to fly." Riven shook his head promptly, and a low growl escaped the depths of the floating eyeball. "Sorry. I have nothing to go off, so unless you have some way to prove to me that these items are worth that much, you can fuck right off into the sunset. Or…"

There was a pause for dramatic effect.

"Or what?" Negrada eventually asked, obviously irritated.

"Or you could make it very much worth my while." Riven tapped a finger to his forehead a couple times. "I have a decent idea of what a general price range is for food, but I have no idea what magical items would go for. I don't know how rare they are, or how hard you're trying to swindle me. But there's gotta be something you have that would obviously be worth it for me to part ways with the cash, yet it holds little value to you. I need it to be obvious if you want it all back, otherwise it's a no go."

There was a long, deep sigh—making Riven wonder just what Negrada was thinking. Then the dungeon bobbed up and down once. "Very well, vampire. I have instructed a team of my treasurers to report back to me within the next few minutes after they search my wares, and I'll get back to you soon."

"Fine. In the meantime, I'll look at my class upgrade options."

"Take your time, little vampire."

CHAPTER 57

Riven gave Negrada a skeptical look and then pulled up the options for his new class choices. To his surprise, they were indeed combination classes for two of the three options, just like Negrada had talked about—so apparently the system thought Riven was a good match. Athela had told Riven that the system only handed out class options for those who earned them, and apparently the last fight he'd had with the satyr warlord in conjunction with his race evolution was more than enough to get him a spot with these three.

[Class Upgrade Options:

Warlock Adept: The Warlock Adept is a direct upgrade from the class Novice Warlock and emphasizes demonic minions with a high damage output through magical attacks. You gain additional negative charisma. You will have a percentage upgrade to all Unholy pillar and related subpillar spells through this class, you will acquire an additional demonic contract slot when you hit level 35, you will acquire more stat points per level than you did as a novice, and you will experience visions from the system concerning Unholy pillar abilities more often by taking this class. Bonus structure for Staves, Cloth Armor, Willpower, and Intelligence included. (Comes with the knowledge of the Shadow subpillar and the Shadow spell Riftwalk.)

Reaper Initiate: The Reaper Initiate is the first in line for a class style that primarily focuses on physical attributes, encompassing Unholy, Blood, Death, and Shadow abilities. This class employs Stealth bonuses for those who would be assassins, spies, or thieves. This class has bonus structures for Scythes, Crossbows, Small

Blades, Axes, Cloth Armor, and Light Armor, as well as Agility and Strength, but also applies smaller bonuses to Intelligence. (Comes with the knowledge of the Blood martial art Flurry.)

Blood Paladin: As a Blood subpillar specialist primarily focusing on physical attributes with martial arts, the Blood Paladin will also gain bonuses to magical and miracle-based abilities to a lesser degree. This class gives very good bonuses to heavy armor, shields, mental defense, and large weapons, as well as good Sturdiness and Strength stat increases per level. It also has a very high bonus structure for the Blood subpillar abilities but has no bonus structure concerning any other pillars. (Comes with the Blood miracle Crimson Wings.)]

He immediately noticed a couple things here. The first was that each of these class upgrades came with a new ability…which was pretty sweet, considering his first class hadn't had that. He'd had to learn his abilities in the Chalgathi trials when he'd been given the Novice Warlock class.

The Warlock Adept had a huge bonus that Riven really wanted—the third demonic minion. Having two demonic minions was already a huge boon, and having a third? That just seemed downright unfair. But the big seller on this one was the spell Riftwalk, which he could only assume was some kind of teleport or movement ability. If that was the case, he very much wanted that martial art. Being a mobile caster was something that Athela said wasn't done often, and not being mobile was often the downfall of many once-successful casters or mages in the end.

The Reaper Initiate class was apparently the type of fighting style that Negrada said Riven had, and although it sounded neat, Riven was a little bit hesitant to choose it based on how it described the class being a "primarily physical" class. He liked magic a lot, and he didn't see his fighting style changing all that much. Sure, he'd used a hatchet to kill a bunch of thugs prior to the dungeon, and yeah, he'd killed the satyr warlord with his bare hands after enchanting himself with Crimson Ice, but he'd primarily been using magic all along to get to where he was now. To switch it up after investing most of his points into Intelligence thus far would seem a little off to him. He also didn't know what Flurry was or how it could be used, but it was a martial art, and if he had to guess from the name, it likely involved quick successive strikes against an enemy.

Then lastly there was Blood Paladin, with the strength and defensive bonuses. It would definitely be a good fit for the claymore. The idea of walking around in a cool set of heavy armor, wielding large intimidating weapons, and being hard to kill definitely appealed to him for obvious reasons, as did Crimson Wings if it meant flying. Flying would be even cooler than a teleport, but Riven really didn't like the idea of utilizing only the Blood subpillar. What if he wanted variety? He was way too early into this new world to be focusing down like that. Not only that, but this class also utilized primarily physical attributes according to the description, and he was dead set on utilizing magic as his primary function—even if he was possibly going to switch it up a bit with martial arts in the future given his new racial evolution.

He thought long and hard about the decision for quite some time, with Negrada waiting patiently.

His thought process was this: he definitely would have liked to become some kind of magical assassin or paladin, but he had no real training in close combat using medieval weapons. He had no real training using a sword, no real training in daggers or assassinating people. Those were relatively high skill-cap classes, and the only reason he'd done as well as he had so far was because he could control mana at a freakish level. He was gifted in magic, according to Athela, which was a rarity in itself but didn't require the type of training for Riven that it might for other people. It didn't require the type of training he'd need to be a successful assassin or close-combat fighter. So maybe, one day, if he ever got the training realistically needed to do that kind of close-combat fighting, he'd consider it. Until then he'd stick with what he knew.

He also just couldn't pass up a teleport—it was too tempting to leave behind. In the end, though, Riven selected Warlock Adept. The draw of another demonic familiar, a teleport spell, and a bonus to all spells under the Unholy umbrella was just too tempting despite what the dungeon had advised. He was staying on the straight and narrow magic route, at least for now, and if he changed his mind, he could always try for a different type of class later.

[You have chosen Warlock Adept as your class upgrade. Congratulations! You now are able to contract a third demonic servant when you reach level 35. Your comparisons between Novice Warlock and Warlock Adept are shown below:

> Old Class: Novice Warlock (+1 Willpower, +2 Intelligence, +2 free stat points per level, -5 base Charisma, allows otherworldly contact, allows two demonic contracts)
> New Class: Warlock Adept (+2 Willpower, +3 Intelligence, +2 free stat points per level, -5 base Charisma, -1 Charisma per level. Allows otherworldly contact, allows three demonic contracts, with the third contract being available starting at level 35. +5% stat bonus for Staves and Cloth Armor.)

You are now being imbued with knowledge of the Shadow subpillar

and the spell Riftwalk. Failing to recognize the vision for what it is will result in you failing to obtain the spell Riftwalk. Good luck.]

The following experience was a lot more pleasant than his previous ones. There was no headache, no failure to understand what was happening, and the visions were incredibly straightforward. Or perhaps this is just what Athela had meant on one of their recent scouting trips around the city when she said that Riven was "a magical prodigy" and that he learned things quickly. Perhaps it had to do with his incredibly high affinity for Blood, Death, and Shadow pillars that led him to acquiring these things with such ease—but he was thankful for it regardless. He could only wonder what higher-tiered spells would be like in terms of learning, as he'd understood Tier 3 spells to be significantly worse in terms of failure rates for people obtaining them.

As the process started, his mind went black, and he found himself internally evaluating his soul again. The images and lights representing his memories all passed him by until the core soul structure, a sphere of bright white light, radiated in the center of his vision. The fiery pillar representing the Infernal path was now attached to it as well—a torch of raging inferno alongside the pure, smooth, and bright-crimson Blood subpillar. The Unholy foundational pillar was a multicolored green, black, and red coloring, with Blood being a brighter and purer crimson. They stuck out from the sides of his spherical, radiating soul and acted as converters for his power channels, enabling him to utilize certain abilities as long as the pillars were attached. Then there was the rotating black orb of his forming Gluttony core, which still phased in and out between solid and translucent states. And out of the abyss from beyond the scattered lights representing his thoughts and memories came yet another.

This one was different, though. Instead of radiating light like the rest did, it absorbed light. It was a black mark, in stark contrast to the light of his soul or any of the other pillars, and it gingerly edged its way past the blazing Infernal subpillar to settle down beside it. As it attached itself to Riven's soul, he felt a cold rush flow through his body. It was a welcome feeling, though, and it felt…right. Just like the Blood subpillar, the Shadow subpillar seemed to welcome him home as if it'd always intended to find him. Unholy and Infernal certainly vibed with his soul well, but in comparison to Blood and Shadow, neither of them could quite compare in how they felt or the synchronizing feeling they had whenever their mana channels reached out.

As the Shadow subpillar solidified and finished fusing to the edge of his soul, Riven then felt and saw another vision.

It was that of the birth of a sun after the passing wave from a supernova. The vision condensed time and space, comparing the stark contrast of the black void to the light given off by the sun—and then it showed the death of the star and the continuity of the void even in its absence. From what he gathered and the feelings he was receiving, the Shadow subpillar was essentially showing him that Shadow was always there and would always remain there even in the absolute absence of light. In the eventual death of the universe, light would cease to exist—yet Shadow would forever remain.

The vision switched again, this time showing a series of holes in time and space, ones that he could travel through by forcing a rift in space—holding that rift open with his mana channels. Where there was absence of light, Riven could find passage and sanctuary. The wormholes continued on and on, forever reaching out into the expanse and onto solid earth until they came upon places where the shadows could not reach.

Channeling mana through the Shadow subpillar, understanding the vision for what it was, and applying meaning to it were the three fundamental pieces to any Tier 1 spell. Channeling mana was a given and easy enough to do. Understanding what he needed and wanted by the ability was also easy enough. Applying meaning and understanding to the vision was the hard part, but unbeknownst to him, even that was child's play for Riven when compared to the average caster. Pondering the vision of the wormholes led him to a single and obvious conclusion: there was a path to sanctuary in the absence of light that he could tread upon. In fact, he might even be able to establish links between spots by pushing light away even in its presence, expanding the wormholes, tying the loops together like so, and—

[You have successfully acquired the Shadow subpillar. You have successfully interpreted and learned the spell Riftwalk. Congratulations!]

[Riftwalk (Shadow): Channel mana into your Shadow subpillar and focus on the place you wish to travel to. Then rip open a portal in space and pass through it, allowing you and other people or objects nearby to pass through until you close the rift. Mana cost is dependent upon length of space traveled and time maintaining rift.]

Huh. That was all it took? Honestly, it seemed rather simple to him, and it made him question whether or not the system was just screwing with him and trying to make him feel good about himself. Was it belittling him? He'd thought that solution was a rather obvious one.

"I see you have made your choice," Negrada commented patiently, narrowing its pupil slightly as Riven turned to him. "You acquired your pillar rather... fast...no doubt due to your affinities being so absurdly high. Have you made up your mind on what you want to trade for?"

CHAPTER 58

Riven took in what the dungeon avatar had said concerning his affinities and rubbed his forehead. "Have you found something obviously worth the full amount yet?"

"My treasurers are still looking."

The only thing he could truly compare to with Athela gone was the basic system of one copper equals one dollar, give or take. Trying to gauge just how much each of these were worth without a baseline was guesswork, so he put out some feelers and tried a shot in the dark—calling Negrada out on potential bluff. The dungeon had said one item was worth all the money Riven had, but there's no way he'd part with everything over one item. Not when the dungeon seemed so eager to get the money back.

"Well, if you don't find anything that is of obvious value beyond these items, I want both the staff and the amulet. I think that'd be a fair trade for both."

Negrada scoffed. "Absolutely not. The Amulet of Many Faces or the staff, not both."

"The staff and the claymore, then."

"No."

"The staff is what I primarily want here, but I feel like it might not be worth all the money I have. Sure, it's good, but it's not that good, and I'd be foolish to trust you outright."

"What makes you think that, little vampire?"

"Because I found a low-quality claymore in the dungeon that dealt just slightly more damage than the staff and just a little bit less than the claymore you're offering me."

"That claymore had a Strength requirement and wasn't a spirit weapon, thus it could never better itself, eventually have sentience, or evolve. It also didn't have any abilities associated with it or a mana-regeneration perk."

Riven thought about it, then nodded in agreement. "Fair point. However, I'm at a distinct disadvantage here, not knowing what these items are really worth, so if you don't bend here, I'll just take the money, conjure a portal, and leave. Again, I frankly don't trust you." Riven stared the flaming eyeball down in challenge, and when there was no reply, he continued. "Final offer. The staff and something else thrown in for...let's say one hundred and fifty thousand. I keep twenty-four thousand of the coins for you being a pain in the ass. Is it a deal or not? You're giving me bad vibes, so I'm not backing down from this. At the very least, I'll know it's a fair deal if I find an altar to the system beyond this dungeon. Plus, what do you have to lose? I'm sure you don't get many buyers here."

The eyeball narrowed its pupil slightly and grumbled something in a language Riven didn't understand but eventually nodded. "Very well. You have yourself a deal, fledgling undead."

"Well, you've still gotta add something to the pot."

"Patience. I'm working on finding something I have no use for. In the meantime, here is your staff. The deal is not struck yet; you will have your coins returned if you do not find the additional item worthy."

In a burst of light, Riven saw a single item appear in front of him as the coins in the chests quickly began to vanish—though he did see his backpack fill up as Negrada deposited a few thousand different types of coins into the bag along with the ones he already had in there.

It was a staff far superior to the shoddy, chipped one he'd been carrying around since the Chalgathi trials. It may have been basic, according to Negrada, but to Riven, who was newly oriented in this universe, it was great. This gnarled staff was a beauty despite its plain design, carved from black-stained oak that was polished to glint in the dim light. It came up to a knobby, twisted end where the tree branch had been left somewhat intact, and upon touching it he could feel a mana influx that was far superior to his normal rejuvenation potential.

[**Black Redemption (Tier 1 Awakened Staff):** 74 average shadow damage on strike, with each hit drawing a small amount of mana from you to apply a knock-back effect with a minor explosion of shadow magic. All cost of Shadow spells is decreased by 7%, mana regeneration is increased by 68%. Shadow magics all have damage modifiers applied by +27% while channeling through this staff. **Black Lightning:** This staff can passively build up charges of black lightning. Power of black lightning depends on the amount of charge emitted.]

The gnarled staff was cool to the touch and just a little shorter than he was when placed on the ground, making it rather large. He also didn't have any offensive Shadow abilities, with only Riftwalk being available as a movement ability. Despite this, though, the 68 percent buff to mana regeneration alone was reason enough to carry it, and he was sure he'd be getting some more Shadow abilities over time. Plus the black lightning attack seemed pretty nifty, and upon trying to push mana into the staff, he felt the weapon in his hands begin to slowly charge up—storing the mana within the wooden shaft, which began to lightly flare with shadows when he pressed on the power mentally.

"Neat."

He slid his hands along the polished black wood of the staff for another few moments until a jolt of surprise ran through him, and he felt a consciousness touch his mind.

It wasn't an overwhelming presence, but he could still feel the consciousness of the staff in his hand as it evaluated him just like he was evaluating it. Curiously staring at the weapon for some time, Riven eventually got a prompt:

[Black Redemption accepts you as a suitable wielder for surface-level bonding. Do you wish to bond with this spirit weapon?]

Surface level? He could only assume that meant there were deeper levels of connection that he could attain. Riven nodded thoughtfully with a small grin, and the prompt went away to be replaced by a new one.

[Black Redemption is now bonded to you on a surface level, allowing it the opportunity to grow based on shared experiences with you. Congratulations.]

Riven gave a thoughtful humph and rested the end of his new staff onto the ground. He put his runic mask back on and picked up his sturdy bag and hoisted it over his shoulder to strap it onto his back. He would have once thought the bag heavy, but now he could carry it pretty easily with one hand.

"I have found something suitable," Negrada stated after a few more moments of Riven admiring the staff. "However, there is a catch."

A vision was conjured, and then another, and another. It was a series of pictures showing off a rather luxurious-looking stone mansion, three stories high, resembling Victorian architecture with a rectangular build and a wide tower climbing up over the front entrance. Stone gargoyles lined the balconies, and a wide metal gate encircled a courtyard out front with gardens in the back.

"A house?" Riven asked doubtfully.

"Not just a house, a guild hall. One that I took off a foolhardy group of adventurers a few years ago."

The pictures changed, this time showing the interior. Red carpets lined the hallways, with picture frames hanging empty on the walls. An indoor pool with a skylight, a large dining room and kitchen, dozens of rooms or storage areas, a large library at the top of the tower, and a huge meeting area for social gatherings in the front were all present. There was even a small dungeon and an armory in the lower levels, displayed last before the images winked out.

"It looks fancy, " Riven stated with a shrug and sideways glance. "Though in terms of end-of-the-world stuff, I can't say I'd find it useful. How am I supposed to move a house, anyways?"

Negrada gave off an amused hum. "Guild halls are only called such by the system when they have three basic conveniences that other buildings do not. The first would be a recall option, allowing you and anyone in your guild to recall back to the guild hall after channeling for a given time based on distance away from the guild hall. This can be done from anywhere in the cosmos, though you can't teleport back once you arrive home again. The second would be the binding of servants, creatures, or guardians. Guild halls can bind these to their cores and maintain permanence within a radius, meaning that bound beings cannot venture outside a certain perimeter from the hall's core based on how advanced your guild hall is, lest it teleport them back, but it also keeps them from dying permanently as long as the core remains intact. Then, third and last, would be the ability for guild halls to transition between locations. Per system rules, it takes an entire year of channeling the core to transition between guild hall locations. There are also a lot of restrictions to prevent interplanetary guild hall invasions, sometimes requiring a system administrator request ticket, but otherwise the location will be able to move. Everything and everyone bound to it can transition."

"Oh." Riven blinked a couple times and folded his arms. "Now, that actually is interesting. A teleporting home that keeps bound workers and guards alive as long as it isn't destroyed? Very neat."

"Elysium emphasizes guild activities quite often, so guild halls are a commodity many would consider valuable. Being a dungeon, I do not find it so. However, you would probably make better use of it. Take this orb, plant it where you want this guild hall to appear, and it shall materialize. Remember, after your initial use it will need to be channeled for an entire year before it can change locations. So be wary about where you plant it."

"And by servants, creatures, or guardians…would I be able to hire on additional demonic familiars?"

"Ones that you could not summon to you, yes. They'd need to stay within the guild hall's perimeter. This particular hall allows them to travel out a few miles from the hall's core, but then it forcefully relocates them back when they go beyond the boundary. You'll also be limited based on how advanced your core is. This one, though the building itself looks pristine, is a low-quality guild core and only allows for fifteen hiree spots. Each spot also requires you to pay Elysium's administrator a tax to keep your attendants on board… Here, I'll just pass over the information and you can take a look at it yourself."

[Guild Hall: Stone Manor
*Plant this at a chosen location to create your premade guild hall.
This is a packaged, onetime-use item*
Homeward Teleportation: Very long channel time
Fifteen attendant spots available; six hundred Elysium coins per
month per active attendant are taxed by the system administrator.
Three-mile exploration radius for attendants before forced retrieval
back to guild hall.
Core Sturdiness: Moderate
Defensive wards: None
Other features: Library, kitchen, dungeon, cellar, armory]

"So if I hire attendants as guards, servants, etc., if they die—will they respawn later or what?"

"Their souls are bound to the guild hall. As long as the core remains intact, they will live. If they are bound to the hall when the core is shattered, they will then lose their permanence. It's very much like the contracts you already have, except that they're bound to a specific physical area and cost upkeep paid directly to the system administrator. I hear many mortals like to hire cooks, smiths, and other craftsmen, too. Others aside from just soldiers to guard your home, but ultimately it is up to you."

"I see. How often will they be able to bind and unbind?"

"I'm not sure. I've never used one of these things before, but I do know there are limits. So how is that for making it obvious? Is the deal struck?"

Riven could only nod slowly. The price to keep attendants was a little rough for him now, but it likely wouldn't be in the future, and it provided a nice home base of sorts. "Yeah. Keep the hundred and fifty thousand."

"No. I'll be taking all of it if you want the guild hall, too, including the money you managed to scrounge up while here before the satyr fight."

Riven opened his mouth to protest, but then closed it again. The guild hall alone was probably worth a hell of a lot more than two hundred grand, so he nodded again. "Fine, take all the money I have and be done with it."

"Nice doing business with you."

His backpack suddenly felt lighter, and all the coins in those two splendid chests evaporated in a wink of light. A portal appeared a second later, and out of it materialized a globe of sparkling lights. It was the size of a golf ball but weighed significantly more as he took it out of the air and embraced it between his fingers.

"Feels warm."

He placed the bauble inside his backpack. Dusting himself off, he gave another sidelong look at the corpse of Ben and felt a little sick to his stomach, but he brushed the feeling off with a shake of his head. He still had to pick up the supplies that he'd taken off Jalel a while back, but then he'd get the hell out of here and onto the next stage of his life. Hopefully it'd be a more pleasant experience than this one had been.

"Well, I'm off to see the wizard. Thanks for the transaction, Negrada, it's been a pleasure."

The flaming eye did a literal eye roll and gave a snorting sound in return. "Truly. But before you go, I have some words of advice for you, vampire. Advice, and yet another deal."

Riven raised an eyebrow. "Advice?"

"Yes, advice. I realize you are new to the transition, so I thought I should tell you. It is the least I could do considering you were willing to barter with me and trade some of the coins back to me, even if you are somewhat of a thief about it." Negrada's avatar paused, and it examined Riven a little bit more thoroughly this time. "When you exit this dungeon and finish your tutorial, you must try to find a destination that holds a coven if you wish to survive. That, or you will need to create your own."

Riven frowned from underneath the black mask that glowed with red sigils and turned fully to face the eyeball, holding his rickety old staff in one hand and his new staff in the other as he curiously cocked his head to the side. "Why?"

A deep chuckle was elicited from the dungeon's avatar. "Your kind are considered monsters by the rest of the multiverse. Just like I am plundered for being what I am, just like so many invaders try to find my core to destroy me for being a native to the hells, so, too, will you be hunted down simply because you are a vampire. For every level you gain, you will likely go deeper and deeper into the negative with your Charisma, and that alone will cause humans and other mortal races to both fear and hate you. They will be repulsed by negative emotions upon first meeting you, and making good impressions with those who are not of your kind or do not also have negative Charisma will be a hard thing indeed. If you do not join your own kind, you will find it all the more difficult to survive... and believe me when I say that the early years of integration for any new world are not easy ones. You may falsely assume acquiring your newfound power as a vampire will benefit you, and in some cases it will, but in the grand scheme of things, you have just doomed yourself to a very hard life."

Riven didn't know what to think of that. He just stared blankly back at the floating fiery eyeball, trying to find what words to say. Eventually he let out a sigh and pursued the other topic the dungeon had mentioned. "What's this other deal you're talking about, then?"

Negrada chuckled. "Well...that phantom you've got locked down in your soul? I want her."

Immediately there was a flare of power, and Kajit was floating there, wide-eyed and panicked. She whipped around to lay eyes on Riven, brought up a hand to begin casting a spell with a flare of neon-teal light, and for a brief moment he thought the attack was going to discharge.

Immediately he clamped down on her soul with Gluttony, and she let out a shriek.

The attempted attack had been so sudden he hadn't had time to comprehend anything but a knee-jerk reaction, and the phantom began writhing around on the floor screaming while Gluttony's jaws ripped at her soul structure from within his own.

"You see...she is untrustworthy," Negrada coolly stated with a billow of flames. "Let me take her off your hands... She just tried to kill you and escape, after all. I've been trying to catch this one for a very long time, and she's been rather pesky. She and her sister..."

"Riven, please!" Kajit shrieked between gasps, but after what he'd just seen her try to do, he wasn't even going to try and hear her out.

Riven blinked, and his heart rate began to settle down.

Wait. Wasn't he undead now? Why did he still have a heartbeat?

He scratched his head and looked at the floating eyeball. "What do I get?"

"What she stole from you," Negrada stated simply. "The dagger the system provided, the one that allows you to gain access back to my dungeon."

Riven glanced back over to the writhing, deep-blue spirit on the floor—and nodded. He certainly had no love for the phantom. "She tried to blackmail me and stole my stuff. Then she tried to kill me. So go right ahead—it'll be good to get her out of my soul space."

Kajit's eyes went wide, and teal power surged out of them just before a pool of flames tore out of the floor underneath her. Arms of souls damned to the hells reached for her and began to drag her down, screaming and writhing, while she cursed both Negrada and Riven.

"THIS WILL NOT BE THE LAST TIME YOU SEE ME, RIVEN THANE! I WILL REMEMBER THIS! KAJIT TAKE REVENGE!" The phantom swore, screaming in rage just before she was sucked under and the pool of fire died away.

Riven promptly felt her soul's presence leave his own soul structure.

"No need to worry about that one," Negrada stated rather happily, or as happily as a floating fiery eyeball could. "Now, let me fetch your dagger. It's located in an older acquaintance of mine, another dungeon holding that one's sister, but shouldn't be too hard to get ahold of. In the meantime, as you complete your stay here in my very humble first level, I'd like to wish you luck when you get back to your world. Thanks for doing business with me."

ABOUT THE AUTHOR

Ranyhin1 is the pen name of Trent Boehm, author of Elysium's Multiverse, an apocalypse LitRPG he originally released on Royal Road. A lifelong lover of fantasy, Boehm is also a science nerd, Dallas Cowboys fan, and wannabe gym rat. He hopes one day to pursue writing full-time.

Printed in the USA
CPSIA information can be obtained
at www.ICGtesting.com
JSHW022208140824
68134JS00018B/932